HERBS AND APPLES

HELEN HOOVEN SANTMYER

ST. MARTIN'S PRESS/NEW YORK

Grateful acknowledgment is made for permission to reprint the profile of Helen Hooven Santmyer, which appeared in somewhat different form as "Helen Santmyer and Her Ladies of the Club" in *The Magazine*, Dayton *Daily News*, July 1, 1984. Copyright © 1984 by Roz Young.

HERBS AND APPLES

Published by arrangement with Harper & Row, Publishers, Inc.

Library of Congress Catalog Card Number: 85-42885

ISBN: 0-312-90601-3   Can. ISBN: 0-312-90602-1

Printed in the United States of America

First St. Martin's Press mass market edition/April 1987

10 9 8 7 6 5 4 3 2 1

Contents

Introduction to the
1985 Edition

WHEN I WAS STILL A CHILD and first read *Little Women*, I made up my mind that I, like Louisa May Alcott, would like to write books for children.

At the time this is being written I am eighty-eight and a half years old, and during the long span of my life I have written only four books (none for children) which I was willing to submit for publication over my name. Of these four books, three have been novels and one a collection of essays about the town of Xenia, in which I have spent most of my lifetime.

I was born in Cincinnati, on November 25, 1895, but the family moved to Xenia when I was still young enough to enter the first grade there. And so all my grade school and high school years were spent in Xenia, as have been all of the years from 1931 to 1935 and from 1937 or so until 1953 or '54. During the span in the early thirties, my father accepted a position as manager of a rope factory located in Orange County, California, and moved my mother, my brother, and myself there with him. He retired after some five or so years and my mother and I returned with him to live in Xenia. By then I was convinced that I would never earn enough from my writing to provide the funds to take care of myself and to help take care of my father and mother.

And so at that point I accepted an appointment as head of the English Department and dean of women at a small Presbyterian college located just eight miles from Xenia. I rented an apartment in Cedarville and the three of us lived there all during the approximately seventeen years of my teaching at the college.

At the end of that time my mother, my father, and I moved back to Xenia and lived in the old house on West Third Street which had belonged to some members of my family and been lived in by them ever since 1868.

My last position was as a reference assistant on the staff of the public library of Dayton and Montgomery County. During those years I commuted back and forth to Dayton, but I was a resident of Xenia, the town that I have always loved so much.

The first novel I wrote, *Herbs and Apples*, was a trial balloon to see whether I could tell a pleasant story of young people, living in New York and working at professions they were happy in, well enough to get it published by a reputable New York concern. As is true with so many young authors, my book was in large part autobiographical. After one or two rejections by other firms, Houghton Mifflin agreed to publish it. They required quite a bit of revision before being completely satisfied with it, but it was finally printed in 1925, with a fair number of satisfactory reviews, and a small number of readers took the trouble to tell me that they liked the story I had told.

At that point I was confident that I could write a book that I was not ashamed of, and so I had jumped the first hurdle. The second hurdle was whether or not I could create believable characters out of thin air. In *The Fierce Dispute* I located my story for the first time in Xenia. There, at the northernmost edge of the town, stood a large house surrounded by some acres of meadow and marshland, and with a small stream which flowed into a little pond. Within the house, Xenians knew, there lived three females: a grandmother, her daughter, and her child. One Negro houseman took care of the house and its residents and was the only connecting link between the townspeople and the residents of the Roberts Villa. When the book was finished and I was fairly satisfied with it, I sent it off to Houghton Mifflin and again they agreed to print it. Once again the critics were reasonably kind to my book and once again it sold to quite a few people, but not enough to make me feel that I was ever going to be able to live upon the results of my writing.

It was at that point I thought I had better turn to my second love, teaching. Had my health been less of a problem, I might have been able to combine my two loves, but unfortunately such was not the case, and it was not until after I resigned from the faculty at Cedarville that I began work on my collection of essays. (True, during my years in California I had written some of the essays that are included in *Ohio Town*, but the largest number were written between the mid '50s and the early '60s, when the book was accepted by the Ohio State University Press and appeared in 1962.)

There has been much discussion about how long it took me to write my last book, ". . . *And Ladies of the Club.*" Actually, for as long as I can remember I was collecting scraps of information and putting away bits that I had heard discussed around the dining table in my home, and making notes from books about the Civil War and the long span of years from then until the early 1930s, when our country took the turn toward socialism. And so, in a way, to say that it took me fifty years to write it is not entirely untrue. But if one measures how long I was in completing it from the time I put pencil to paper and began to tell the story I wanted people to read, I can only say that as nearly as I can remember, I began it in the mid '60s, and took it to the publishers for their decision about publishing it in 1975.

Herbs and Apples and *The Fierce Dispute* were my first two books, written long ago, and not looked into for many years.

They could not be revised or rewritten: they are what they are—the first one autobiographical, more or less, the other inspired by the setting, but pure invention as to characters and events. I hardly dare hope that they can stand unsupported after so long a passage of time.

Helen Hooven Santmyer

Xenia, Ohio

For Herbs and Apples

I.

"Cold is the gleaming hair
    Crowning your brow
As if you had been running with the wind in
    your face.
How can it be when there
    Is no wind now?
When there stirs not a breath?"
"I lost my way, blown far down the emptiness
    of space
By the cold wind of death."

"Cold is the ivory breast
    Against my heart
As if you had been swimming in a bitter sea.
But the shore and where we rest
    Are far apart,
As far as the earth is wide."
"And should I know until its foam flew over
    me
The strength of Lethe's tide?"

"Remote are the shadowed eyes
    Once full of light
As if you had been searching where night and
    choas are

Tell me what dark wing flies
    The visioned night?
What is the thing you see?"
"Ah, far enough I flew to learn, beyond the
    last star
Lies but infinity!"

II.

The old warden Life awaits at the door
    The hour that sends me away.
Why should he solemnly finger his beard
    And bid me kneel and pray?

For I am not a craven and
    Of prayers I have but one.
I shall not fear, remembering
    The wind and sky and sun.

I only pray thee, Life, release me
    While in the green-gold sky
About the cold black chimney at twilight
    The fleet-winged swallows fly:

The birds who came with whir of wings
    Beneath the elm-tree boughs
To nest above me while I dwelt
    Shut in this empty house;

Whose beautiful wings awakened in me
    Memories of wind and sky,
Sun on the hills and windy plain when
    But one were wind and I.

Fair would I see those wings again as
    I go out to the sky and sun:
Then should I have no dread at all of
    Our being eternally one.

III.

Winds flow south on August nights,
    In September, north,
August nights are myriad-voiced
    When the winds go forth.

August nights are sweet with scent
    Of mown clover-hay,
Noisy with the locusts and
    The light leaves at play.

From the south, September winds
    Blow but listlessly;
Nothing speaks, September nights,
    Save a whispering tree.

August nights are nights to sleep:
    The north winds are cool;
Warm September nights (the moon
    Is very gold when full)

Are nights for lovers to remark
    Shadows of blown leaves,
Moonlight on the bannered corn
    Grain in silver sheaves.

But night winds warm and silent,
    Moons that wane and low,
What are they to you who sleep
    Where no winds blow?

August nights are myriad-voiced
    September nights are still,
All are one to you who sleep
    So sound upon your hill.

Wellesley, 1924

Foreword

THE SUNDAY MORNING ACCOMMODATION train puffed slowly up the river valley. It was very hot and very dirty; dust blew in at the open windows and hung visible in the aisles. I turned my back on the almost empty car and through the flying smoke watched the countryside: the green, wooded hills, the squalid hamlets tucked at their feet on the riverbank. It was strange to me, a city child, as if I had belonged at the other end of the continent instead of at the opposite corner of the State; it was rather wild and dreadful . . . it seemed to me quite uncivilized, despite the fact that all the hills were under cultivation. At least, they were under cultivation where there were no trees, no thick lines of bushes, no underbrush . . . it was as if here a man must struggle, not to make his crops grow, but to keep the rank native vegetation from growing too fast, from choking his corn, encroaching on his pastures. Even the tumbledown farmhouses were threatened by the thick, heavy vines that had clambered over them.

"It's a pity," said my father, peering out of the window across my lap, "that Dick Thornton had to bury himself in a little country town. He might have been as great a surgeon as any in the country."

We were to stop in Tecumseh for the day as we returned to Cleveland from a doctors' convention in Cincinnati. My father and Dr. Thornton had gone to medical school together, but had seen each other only semi-occasionally since.

1

I did not look forward to the visit with pleasure: I supposed that Tecumseh would be like the little river towns we had passed, and the thought of a whole day spent in one of them, in the cruel heat, the choking dust, made my head ache, my eyes burn. . . .

Before we reached our station, the train left the river, the country flattened out, and became a wide panorama of undulating, gentle hills . . . but the heat increased rather than diminished, and there was still the threat of the crowding vegetation: weeds higher than a man's head along the railroad track, and trees everywhere: in wide, shady groves cleared of underbrush, in brief stretches of untouched forest, dense and impenetrable, and even in the fields, singly or in groups. The fields were larger here than they had been a few miles farther south: there were long stretches of open country, and the eye could see for unimaginable distances across the succession of low hills, but on no horizon did earth and air meet in a clear, unbroken line: always, between, there was a dark mass of trees, whether so close that the sky could be seen in brief flashes between their trunks, or so distant that they were a blue gray in the August haze of heat and dust.

As the train stopped in the dingy Tecumseh station, my father took my hand and drew me down the aisle.

"I think the oldest of the Thorntons is just your age. You must be nice to her."

Somehow, he gave me the impression that the "buried" doctor and his family could be little more than half-civilized, dwellers in a remote and half-civilized country.

On that hot Sunday morning, Tecumseh was a town of deserted squares, shuttered windows, and empty streets. These wide, brick streets had been taken from limitless countryside, in the faith that the little settlement would one day be a metropolis; now, not a human being stirred in all their length and breadth. A merciless sun blazed upon them, waves of heat rose shimmering from unshaded cement sidewalks. The light and glare centered on the court-house, and on the bony sycamores and dust-laden elms that lined the curb around it. From this square one passed with relief to a neighborhood where the houses were so surrounded with lawns and shaded by low-branching maple trees that they hardly seemed to be touched by the sun.

The Thornton house was not far from the center of town; it stood on a corner, and directly at the pavement's edge, so that all the yard lay at one side and behind it. In its plan it was like the old farmhouses we had passed in the river valley: long, high, and narrow, with two wings, and between them square-pillared porches, upstairs and down; it was built of yellowish-gray brick, and hung with vines—a tangle of honeysuckle, trumpet-vines, and clematis. The end of the house faced the main street, and white stone steps, with a curved iron railing, led from the sidewalk to the front door. Even this railing was covered with clematis. To the right of the steps a gate in the iron fence gave entrance to the side yard; once beyond the hedge and shrubbery that lined the fence, you could see, beneath the high branches of great black-boughed tulip-trees, a wide stretch of lawn, ending in a green lattice, and, beyond the lattice, the tops of fruit trees; you could see the side of the house that looked out on the cool shadows and into the boughs of trees, the set-in porch, with the vine-covered railing upstairs and the slim, white pillars, and the small, fan-shaped terrace that extended from the edge of the porch into the lawn. Around this terrace there was a retaining wall of brick, and on that a low iron fence; both wall and fence were smothered in honeysuckle. A path descended from the terrace by three shallow brick steps and crossed to the opposite side of the lawn, where, beneath the trees, stood a mouldy fountain: a moss-grown faun playing in the silvery water. A fountain, where the birds splashed and the shadows of leaves quivered on the pool, and the sun made rainbows. . . . I was enchanted, and forgot all that I had thought about this wild back country. To my knowledge, fountains existed only in

3

parks and fairy tales. Yet my father felt sorry for a man who had one in his own side yard!

Derrick Thornton sat on the terrace step, chin on her fists, elbows on her knees, and looked at me speculatively out of her imperturbable, heavy-lidded eyes.

"What would you like to do now? Mother says I must entertain you nicely." She smiled a little, deprecatingly, as though to say that she would not intentionally deceive me: she was polite of necessity, and not from choice. I felt lumpish and stupid . . . and my father had told me to be nice to her!

"Let's not do anything," I said sullenly. "It's too hot. Let's just talk."

"All right. Talk." She leaned back and smiled at me again, mockingly.

"I'd rather you'd talk," I stammered. I wanted to ask about the fountain, but I did not dare—at least, not at once. "Tell me about your house. Why did they build the houses 'round here like that—with the porches in-between instead of sticking out?"

She stared at me, and her brilliant hazel eyes darkened a little. She leaned forward.

"Indians!" she assured me solemnly. "You see—on a porch like that they couldn't take you by surprise. Couldn't sneak up on you, from behind." I gaped at her, but she stared me down. "I can tell you all about the Indians, if that's what you want to talk about."

Before I could stop her, she drew a long breath and plunged headlong into a vivid, if highly impossible, narrative . . . and I, listening, forgot the house and shadowed lawn, and even the fountain.

From the court-house square the main street of Tecumseh drops slowly down a dusty hill; trees lined the walks at one time, but were cut down long ago to give the town a more business-like appearance. At the foot of the hill, the railroad crosses the street, and the tracks stretch away between the weeds around "Nigger Curve." Beyond the crossing, the street climbs uphill again between the shaded curbstones, where, on that first Sunday when I walked there, stone carriage steps stood before every iron gate; it comes to an end abruptly before a high hedge and a brick house on the crest of the hill. There is no gate, but a break in the hedge leads from the dust in the street to the dusty path across the lawn.

The air that day was saturated with dust; a film of it hung in the street and settled on the trees; the sun was reflected through it by the railroad tracks; the waste ground alongside them was a jungle of dust-colored goldenrod. In the heat and dust, the silence and torpor of Sunday afternoon, my father and I walked with all the Thorntons in solemn procession down this street and toward the square old brick house on the hill. Derrick and I were together; she was as silent now as she had been loquacious before dinner. I listened to the doctor and my father behind us; they were the only ones in the group who made any attempt at conversation—the former was explaining the necessity of this Sunday afternoon visit to his grandmother, who lived with her daughters Sophia and Ursula in the old house.

"The Old Place" was, according to tradition, a duplicate of the house of the Fergusons in Ulster, built of bricks made in a kiln set up for the purpose in a clearing in the forest. The first Dr. Ferguson had come to America early in the century and had lived to be an old, old man, dying not until after the close of the Civil War. The only son had been killed in the war, and the house had gone to his widow and daughters. One of the latter had married, but had died after a few years, and her children, Dr. Thornton and his sisters, had been sent back to the old home to grow up there; they, in their turn, had married and departed, but on Sunday afternoons still assembled with their families to have supper with the three old women who were left. Dr. Thornton explained all this, then added that he would have spared his

5

children the rigors of the Scotch Sabbath, as it was still observed by his grandmother, had he not owed her too much to neglect paying her this one slight attention.

While I listened to this, I watched Mrs. Thornton, who walked in front of us with the boys, Billy and Hunter: to apply my father's adjective "buried" to her was an impossibility. I had supposed that all mothers were like my own and the mothers of my friends: comfortable and invaluable as mothers, but imposing and dignified women of affairs, who took their world of committees seriously, and who seemed as old as the hills and as unchangeable. Mrs. Thornton was young and slight and graceful; she moved swiftly and lightly, on winged feet; her hair was black and lustrous, and her eyes were black and brimming with mirth and love of life. She wore a wide flower-wreathed hat and one of the ruffled dimity dresses of that era with a long, flowing skirt that continually tripped up the eager small boys who clung one to each hand and looked up into her face as they talked.

Derrick, beside me, pushed the go-cart in which her sister Margaret rode. She was the least "buried" member of the family. I was ill at ease in her company, yet fascinated. She confessed, long afterward, that she had not liked me that day either, because our coming had made her mother unhappy. . . . "She asked Father if he was sorry he had stayed in Tecumseh—if he had gone to the city he might have been Great, too"—Derrick had always an exaggerated idea of my father's greatness; "but she had insisted on staying in Tecumseh when they were married, because a small town is the place to bring up children." . . . On that afternoon, I watched her from the corner of my eye as we walked. She was a quaint-looking child: her dress was a straight, box-plaited white piqué, with a scarlet belt and a round collar; her nondescript-colored hair hung in a braid down her back and was tied with scarlet ribbons, and there was a thin "bang" cut straight across her forehead. Bangs were not being worn that summer . . . I asked her why she had had it cut that way.

"I did it myself. It got in my eyes. Father thinks it looks funny." Her direct gaze defied me to think, too, that it was funny. Then the corner of her mouth lifted in an aloof, humorous little smile. "But Mother says it will never show on a galloping horse."

Her next remark may have been prompted by a desire to make up in my eyes for her father's lack of greatness.

"What are you going to be when you grow up?"

"Married, I suppose."

"I'm not. I'm going to write books."

I said nothing: I was too surprised, and at any rate we had reached the one gap in the untrimmed hedge of osage-orange that led to the Ferguson house. It was grim, austere, unmellowed, unadorned except by small, square, austere porches, one on each side. . . .

I stared down the length of the vast, dusky drawing-room where the great-grandmother received her family, and was filled with awe. At the end of the room beside the carved white marble mantelpiece, Mrs. Ferguson sat in a high-backed rocking-chair, her heavily veined hands, splotched with the pale-brown marks of old age, folded in her lap. She wore a stiff black silk dress with a lace shawl and a bit of white lace on her head. In the midst of her family she sat apart, and seemingly as little attended to as the furniture, yet occasionally she caught up a word from the conversation and developed from it an anecdote, to which the family listened with grave politeness, however inapropos it might be.

When we entered, she sat gazing into the mighty fire-place, while the great-aunts gossiped with the relatives scattered about the room. We were presented with due formality; the children kissed the white cheek of their great-grandmother, and told her the Golden Text of the Sunday-school lesson before she could ask for it. The boys then joined a tiptoe game of hide-the-thimble with their cousins in the rooms across the hall, and Derrick drew me to a window halfway between the groups of grown-ups, where the thick wall of the house made a sill a foot or so wide; we could sit there unseen when we had pulled the heavy, musty-smelling curtains around us.

At first we sat in silence: I would not speak, because I could see that I amused Derrick; and she stared intently out across the cornfields. Finally she turned around.

"Do you like the country? I don't in winter, much, but when things are growing in the fields I do. Especially now, when the corn is high, and looks as if the trees were wading in it, knee-deep."

If her remark was a test of my mind, I was measured and found wanting, for I could only look at her blankly. In a moment she began again abruptly on a different subject.

"Aren't you going to be great when you grow up?"

"Great?"

"I mean, don't you want to be great?"

"I don't know. Do you?"

"Yes—write books."

"Oh—can you?"

"I'm going to."

"But how do you know you can?"

She looked at me as if she wondered whether or not I could understand if told, then—"I don't know," she said, and turned to the window again. I looked, too, across the lawn to the hedge, through the hedge to the cornfield, and listened to the gossip of those in the room behind us.

"Nell looks thin, Sophie. She's had her children almost too fast, hasn't she?"

"She was always thin. There's several years between 'em all."

"Really? Well—they say a doctor has to have a big family as an advertisement. Derrick must be small for her age—"

"Well, yes—but her mother was always a skinny little thing."

"And harum-scarum, too. Into everything. But Derrick hasn't that something-or-other that made you like Nell even when she was such a little demon . . ."

8

"Remember the stories they used to tell about Nell when she went to Art School? Such goings-on . . ."

"Sophie, did you know that your grandmother was a drunkard?" Mrs. Ferguson's thin, high voice silenced them all. "Yes, she was. A tea-drunkard. My father-in-law was the only doctor for miles around in those days—doctor and surgeon he was—took him eight years to get both, at the University of Edinburgh. And he used to ride all over the country on horseback, when there was nothing but a clearing here and there in the woods, and whatever hour of the night he came in, Mother Ferguson had a cup of tea ready for him—and for herself, too—so that's what she was—a tea-drunkard."

The voice wavered, cracked, and then went on again.

"He was a little bit of a man, bow-legged, a fiery abolitionist, and for years before the war he rode with loaded pistols in his holster. When he went into a tavern, he took the pistols and laid 'em on the table in front of him, then, if there were arguments, folks had to agree with him . . . yes —don't breed men like him nowadays. When first I knew him, you couldn't hardly tell him for Irish—Ulster, he came from—but the older he got, the thicker was his brogue, so that, when he died, there couldn't any of us hardly understand him."

Mrs. Ferguson sighed and lapsed again into silence. Derrick turned to me again.

"Didn't you ever write poetry?"

I shook my head. "Did you?"

"Yes. The other day I said to Father that writing poetry seemed to me an easy way to earn a living, and he said, 'Humph! I'll give you a dollar for every poem you write'; so I said, 'Humph! I'll write one.' "

"Did you?"

"Yes."

Silence.

"I just happen to have it with me."

"Have you?"

Silence.

"Well—do you want to see it?"

I did, but assumed indifference; she had, of course, brought it with the sole purpose of showing it to me, but now she pretended to be reluctant. It was several minutes before we arrived at an understanding, and I was given it to read. I was stricken dumb with admiration.

"Like it?"

"M-hm." I shoved the precious paper back to her across the window-sill with properly reverent fingers.

"Then," she said, with the easy gesture of a queen bestowing duchies, "you can have it to keep."

I folded it and tucked it in the low neck of my dress; it dropped to the waistband, where it rested and tickled me mercilessly the rest of the day. I have it still: a soiled page torn from a five-cent "composition" book:

"There is rain sweeping over the swamp land:
          It is gray, it is heavy and harsh,
And winter-browned reeds that have stood there
          Lie flattened and wet in the marsh.
But the rain is the rain of the springtime,
          And the smell of it drifts on the wind,
While the swaying wet blades of the swamp grass
          With the old weeds are entwined.

"There is rain sweeping over the swamp land,
          And it splashes and drips from the trees,
But the marsh lies all hushed in the dampness,
          And the brook only sighs in the breeze,
Like the wrath of the dread Lord of Hosts.
          When he knows that repentance is nigh,
Is the rain on the tangle of cat-tails
          Breathing 'Spring' as the wind hurries by."

"Did your father like it?" I asked.

"He gave me the dollar."

"Did your mother?"

She smiled again, that humorous, cool smile. "She laughed, an' said she guessed it was all right. But the next one I write will be one she'll like."

In the pause that followed we caught another sentence of the talk behind us.

"Derrick is almost as bad as her mother used to be. Mose —you know—nigger Mose, who digs my garden—calls her an 'orn'ry brat.'"

"I know. Nell is too easy on her, I think."

Derrick nudged me.

"Are you a tom-boy?"

I admitted that I was not. There is little opportunity to be a tom-boy in a city back yard.

"I am; and ain't it lucky?—because, you know, I think that people that turn out to be great always were tom-boys. It's lucky that I was, anyway, before I decided about writing books, and now I can be, more than ever. Of course, Father an' no one will like it, but some day they won't mind."

Derrick was the subject of one more bit of the conversation. Her Great-Aunt Ursula assured Dr. Thornton solemnly that the child was thin and languid.

("She thinks it's unladylike to be healthy," Derrick whispered in my ear; "an' look at 'er—round as a balloon!")

"Aren't you giving her cod-liver oil or something, Dick?"

"I don't think she's sick, Aunt Sue," Mrs. Thornton laughed. "It's just a phase. She's just beginning to realize the existence of the universe and to be afraid of it. She read in some paper that a comet was going to hit us, and worried herself sick until the day was past."

"It wasn't the comet," Derrick muttered. "It was what I kept dreaming about the end of the world. Do you know that dream? You are trying to run to school, because you are tardy, but, however you try, you can't budge an inch—then suddenly the clock strikes, and you know that the world is coming to an end. The sun begins to rush toward the earth, and you can't run away, but have to stand and watch it. It

11

moves nearer and nearer, until you see that it isn't the sun, after all, but the face of God, very angry. Then just at the instant when It would happen, you wake up. It's a horrible dream."

A moment later all conversation was interrupted by the entrance of the Ferguson cook, who stood bobbing curtsies in the door, wiping her hands on her checked gingham apron.

"Y'all kin come along now. All whut we's gwine hab is on de table."

The doctor helped his grandmother from her chair and walked behind her to the dining-room, a hand at each elbow, while the mothers called their children from across the hall and hastily examined their hands for possible grime. Derrick and I followed from behind the curtain.

When we left the house, after supper, the sun had almost reached the horizon behind the pasture hill; it floated like a fiery balloon in the dust-dimmed air. The shadows of the walnut trees beside the house stretched across the lawn and over the hedge to the street. The Sabbath silence weighted the air, but to leave the house brought us all a sense of relief. The two boys raced over the grass, kicking through yellow poplar leaves that already had fallen. Their mother sighed as she watched them.

"Here it is, only August, and it looks like fall already. And school in a couple of weeks . . ."

She took the baby-carriage, and Derrick and I walked one on each side of her, back again up Main Street, which stretched ahead of us, still deserted, wide, desolate, and empty. But the Thornton house, around the corner, and the two streets that met where it stood, were dim and cool beneath the maple trees.

That evening we spent on the porch that faces out across the terrace to the fountain. I was overwhelmed by the beauty so strange to a city child: the moonlight on a giant tulip-tree, the pungent scent of the clematis on the pillars, the shrill insistence of the katydids, and the never-ceasing sound of running water, which rose into the moonlight, and fell, and rose again. . . . Also, I was desperately weary, exhausted in part by the great number of strangers I had met, and in part by my bewilderment at Derrick She was contemptuous, derisive, mocking . . . and yet . . . I remembered the Indians, and wished desperately that she lived next door to me. . . . Throughout the evening she sat on the edge of the porch against one of the pillars and said nothing. I pretended not to notice her, but was never for an instant unaware of her presence. When we departed to catch the night train home, the Thorntons assembled in the front door to watch us drive away with the doctor in his buggy. Only Derrick did not wave, but drooped languidly across the railing of the front steps.

When, long afterward, Derrick told stories of herself and of her childhood, I looked back to that day, and I came, in time, to know the strange child with the straight bangs and the brilliant hazel eyes better than I knew the fat little girl that had been myself. Derrick's spoken narrative was more vivid and more effective than that of any one else I have known. In a perfectly cool and detached fashion she recounted an experience of her own with such immediacy that it became for her hearers forever a thing of the present, as timeless as though printed in enduring ink. It might be an encounter she had had an hour before, or a place she had seen the previous year, or an emotion known five or ten or twenty years ago: whatever it was, she had forgotten not the slightest detail, and you saw it as she saw it, and felt what she had felt; there was a power in the quiet voice, the quick phrase, capable of stirring you so that you were glad to be listening in the dark, with your face decently hidden. You learned of her exultations and agonies when they had slipped so far into the past that she could laugh at them, yet even as you laughed with her, you ached for the passionate child, and rejoiced that she had grown so aloof and indifferent. Then, if you had ever seen her as a child, you remembered that even at that time she had seemed contemptuous and cold, so that you had hated her . . . she had built her defenses early . . . while she told you of tempests long past, you realized that there were no doubt present storms that you might hear of some ten years hence. Inscrutable, imperturbable . . . I found her so the first time we were together, and so she remained; not once, but many times, I was bewildered.

At any rate, there is proof enough of her power in the fact that more clear in my mind than the recollection of all that happened afterward, in the years when I knew Derrick and was with her, are the stories of her childhood that she told us. I have only to string them together, with the aid of a little imagination . . . and, as I write, I think of her, not as she was when I listened to her anecdotes, but as she was on that moonlit August night, when she leaned against the pillar beside me and stared indifferently at the fountain and the tree-tops.

Part One

Morning

Wishes

ANY STORY that would chronicle genius must begin with the revelation of that attribute to its unhappy possessor.

Derrick sat alone on the terrace steps and stared with unseeing eyes across the dusky lawn at trees and fountain. Her heart thumped in her breast, in her ears, and she breathed heavily; the world rocked beneath her. A revelation had come to her from the last pages of the book she had been reading: "The Life, Letters, and Journals of Louisa May Alcott." The veil had been lifted, she had Known. She would be a Great Writer when she grew up.

The evening had begun as one of the most ordinary in that summer of ordinary evenings. She had left the dinner-table before her family had finished the gossip that accompanies dessert and coffee, and had gone through the dining-room door to the porch, where she had dropped her book reluctantly at Cassie's summons. She picked it up, noted how few pages she had to read, and, loath to have it finished and done with, she tucked it under her arm, sauntered to the front gate, and leaned on it, dreaming . . .

She liked Duane Street: the deep, green shadows, the intense quiet—there was no sound except the harsh chatter of the blackbirds in the tops of the elms around the courthouse a block away. Next to the Thorntons lived Tecumseh's leading manufacturer, Mr. Devlin, in an ugly house of white frame with porches, towers, and bay windows—a house which achieved pleasantness somehow: helped to it, perhaps, by the dolls and toys on the porch, and the rope swing which hung crookedly from the largest maple tree. Beyond the Devlins' was a white cottage, hidden by the trees, and next to it the "Opera House," an unbelievably hideous structure of brick, of the late-General-Grant style of architecture, which housed on its ground floor the police station and the town jail. On the corner opposite was a square brick building with an ornate cornice, half of which was a drug-store, and the other half, according to the sign, the "Hotel Venice." Above were the offices of dentists and physicians, Dr. Thornton's among them. As to the street itself, it was, if one could pretend that it ended before the Opera House and the Hotel Venice, a wide handsome street of square brick houses set back behind low iron fences, its curb lined with trees—lined, as Derrick put it to herself, "with maples and elms, with here and there one of the buckeyes that gave the State its name—"

From her revery she was awakened by the approach of a rattling, ramshackle wagon and bony horse, driven by a big Negro with a brigandish black mustache . . . Ben, come after Cassie, to take her home. He hitched his horse and crossed the path, a shining fish in one hand, a bucket in the other.

"Hi, Ben."

"H'ah yuh?" he responded jovially. "H'yah's the fish yo' mothah o'duhed, an' some minnies fo' the boys."

"Minnies?" Derrick peered into the bucket. "They're eatin' supper yet. Cassie's in the kitchen."

"Yas'm. Ah'll jes' tek these back, an' clean the fish whalst ah wait."

He turned down the side street toward the kitchen door. Derrick stood whistling tunelessly a moment or two, then returned to the terrace step and opened her book. She read in the growing dusk, swiftly and with a devouring eagerness. When she had finished, she was drunk with emotion, and sat staring blindly into the twilight. There was no doubt in her, no question. She Knew . . .

The exultation waned. She looked for a star to wish on . . . by twenty at least she would be famous . . . what fun to show old Tecumseh! With the book closed in her lap, she gave herself over to blissful contemplation.

She was eleven—that gave her nine more years—ages and ages and ages of time. When she was famous, some one would want to write her "Life"; she hoped that it could be done before she died. She would like to read it—they could write about her death in an appendix afterward.

Unfortunately, there was nothing in her life so far to write about. An ordinary life in an ordinary town in Ohio. Her family: mother, father, two brothers, and a sister. No material there, except that her mother was beautiful and her father unusually handsome. Her mother could win a race against any of them—that seemed, somehow, to prove her youth and beauty. She always knew what you were thinking. It was only occasionally that she revealed this clairvoyant power, but then you knew that at all other times she must have it, and it made you careful what you thought in her presence. Her name had been Reneltje Derrick—most awfully Dutch; but people called her Nell, which wasn't so bad. Derrick supposed there was nothing to be ashamed of in having been Dutch originally, some three hundred years ago, but she would hate to see it said of her mother in a book. It made you think of fat people, and of women rocking with their hands in their laps. Her mother was not like that at all: there was hardly a minute in the day when she found time to sit still and rock. Once, she had intended to be an artist, and she had even now a table with clay on it under the skylight in the attic. Once she had modeled the children there: Derrick on her stomach at full length, with a book, Billy on his hobby-horse, Hunter with his feet apart and his hands in his pockets, scowling. . . . But the clay had not been touched for a long while: she had never done the baby, and Margaret would be three in the fall.

Her father was impressive-looking, with a distinguished nose, and every one thought him very dignified, and didn't

know how he shouted in the morning when they were getting up, the song about the monkey.

> "Oh, I went to the animal fair,
> And the birds and the beasts were there."

He wouldn't let Mother say that any book in his library
was too old for you—he had a sublime faith in the coming-
out-rightness of things—so you read books you knew he
never suspected would prove of interest, or he would have
agreed with Mother. He was particular about table manners and ways of speaking, and he talked about "preserving
the subjunctive" when you hadn't the slightest idea what a
subjunctive was, but classed it with all the old-fashioned
graces of life. He worried, sometimes, about education,
and talked about sending you away, but nothing ever came
of it. . . .

There were Cassie, the cook and the maid-of-all-work,
and Annie, the washwoman. Annie came only two days in
the week, but Cassie was ever-present. You were always
welcome in her kitchen, because she loved an audience, but
it was the youngest who received her serious attention, so
that it was now Margaret who was beguiled by tales of
'possums and rabbits as she rode about on Cassie's hip, held
there astraddle with one hand, while the cooking was done
with the other. And there was also Ben, who tended the
furnace and hitched and fed the horse, and kept the sidewalks shoveled in winter. He was not exactly related to
Cassie, but they were one family, so to speak: his last wife
had refused to divorce him, so he and Cassie just lived
together. He brought the boys rabbits and guinea-pigs, and
advised her what to feed her crawdads and tadpoles in the
spring when she collected them.

Any family in town would make as interesting reading,
any one's life would be as exciting as hers. She searched her
memory fruitlessly . . . sighed at the barrenness of the past,
then opened the book in her lap at the first chapter to see

if the life therein described was more eventful. The twilight deepened as she huddled over the pages.

Her father came to the door.

"Good Heavens, Derrick—reading in this light?"

She closed the book guiltily.

"I thought we might wander down-street. Want to go?"

"No, I don't think so . . . I'm going out in the hammock until bedtime."

The hammock hung in the back yard between the grape arbor and an apple tree; she stretched herself in it, spread her short skirt tight beneath her, and picked up the loose end of a rope fastened to a tree some distance away. She folded her hands across her stomach, so that by quick jerks of her wrist she could pull the rope and swing the hammock.

At once she resumed her meditations. The past might be empty of interest, but the future was full of glory. One triumph after another was conceived, enlarged upon, gone over again from first to last for the perfection of detail. Eventually her attention was diverted by the stars that shone between the branches of the apple tree—different stars, here, here, and here—as she pulled the rope that swung the hammock. The long fringe swished sleepily across the grass beneath her. Suddenly there came, cutting through the silence of the night, a long-drawn-out, far-off whistle of a train —once—twice. Derrick drew a long breath, thrilled by it, somehow, in a rather frightened way. When it came a third time, eerie and thin, as though from the edge of the world, she shivered—she would rather finish thinking about the things she had been thinking about, in bed. She stopped the hammock and stumbled sleepily into the house.

Long afterward, when Derrick gave us her account of that night, she concluded: "Which all goes to show how futile life is: there's never a child who does not fancy himself the subject of a biography, and nine hundred and ninety-nine out of a thousand achieve nothing but a line on a tombstone. Biographies are inadequate for the few who are worth it, anyway, for no one can possibly know what are the important things—the *internals* of one's life."

But, after speaking of the inadequacy of biographies, she went on to explain what she meant.

"The only thing that I didn't think of that night as biographical material was the one thing that might have done—either because it was unusual, or because it happens to every child, and no one writes about it. That was the ability to sort of—well, sort of get out of myself—out of the body, I mean, and hover around and look at it from some place in the air. And I always hung on to my recollection of that feeling afterward as being perhaps a proof that body and soul *were* two divisible things. What about it, Fran?"

Frances, the one philosopher among us, jeered at her. "It's one of the commonest experiences in the world, and proves absolutely nothing. The psychologists have some name for it, I forget what. I remember the first time I ever felt it."

" 'Let's talk of graves and worms and epitaphs,' " Alice flung into the circle. "I'll tell you about the first time it ever happened to me."

We exchanged experiences then, but it is only Derrick's that are important here. They belong with her decision that she would grow up to write books, I think, because, even although it may be true, as she said, that all children expect to grow up famous, this feeling, and her undimmed recollection of it, would be a proof of her difference from ordinary children.

It came upon her for the first time in the fall when she was nearly five, when her Great-Aunt Rhoda died.

Derrick's Aunt Rhoda was the sister of Aunt Ursula and Aunt Sophia; she had lain helpless for five years, paralyzed, unable to move even so much as a finger. Every fall, when her two sisters went away for a rest, the Thorntons went down to take care of her, and the fall when Derrick was five was the fall of her death.

It had happened with appalling suddenness—at five one takes it for granted that things will go on endlessly as they are, and Derrick supposed that Aunt Rhoda, motionless and speechless in the big bed in the front room, would lie there forever. But one morning the door to the room was closed, and the whole house was full of the sound of hoarse breathing. Derrick crawled halfway down the staircase and crouched there in the dark and stopped her ears. Her mother found her and sent her outdoors, but even there she could not get far enough away from the sound. She ran across to the high fence between the yard and a field of corn, climbed the gate, and from its top looked across the cornfield to the horizon; she sat and looked at it, and the horror slipped from her. The field sloped away before her, and in the valley was a clump of willow trees, like a green island in a golden sea; far beyond them the field rose again and stretched away as far as the eye could see. The child forgot everything, hypnotized; there was nothing in the world but the sky—a very blue sky with a few very white clouds near the horizon—and that limitless sea of golden-tasseled corn.

After a long time, her nurse Leila came across the yard to find her.

"Come along in now, honey. Yo' po' Aunt Rhody is gone."

"Gone?"

"Daid, honey."

Derrick looked at her in silence a moment, then burst into terrified sobs.

"Why, honey lamb!" Leila lifted her from the gate and hid the wet face on her bosom. "Hush, now—hush! Yo' don' know whut yo' cryin fo'."

And Derrick had stopped crying at once. Not that Leila was right, who thought she cried for Aunt Rhoda. That wasn't it at all: she cried because she had been so suddenly torn away from earth and sky and clouds, and thrust back into a world where there was the penetrating horror of that sound which they called "dying."

23

The summer of the comet (the same summer, Derrick reminded me, that my father and I had spent the day in Tecumseh) brought her the same feeling. She had read that with the comet would come the end of the world; she had dreamed about it one night, and then, when she was wide awake, she had felt what the end of the world would mean.

The children of the neighborhood were playing hide-and-seek, and some chance of the game had left her alone, crossing the back yard. A sudden hush had seemed to fall, and halted her in her flight. The tree-tops had never seemed so far away, nor the distance of the thin silver clouds above them so illimitable, nor the vast sweep of the heavens and the numberless hosts of the stars so infinite nor so dread. A falling star dropped in a flaming arc from behind the veil of cloud, and vanished into nothingness. She caught her breath and dropped on her knees in the grass, waiting—nothing happened; . . . after a long while she opened her eyes and looked about—and found a once familiar world changed and eerie and strange—tall trees and deep shadows and great, looming houses dark and mysterious. It was not the world she had known as Derrick Thornton—there was no such person as that, really—but if any one should call "Derrick," she would find herself broken away from sky and stars, back in that body kneeling on the grass, and she would have to answer to the name until she died. . . . She wished that the comet had come; that every one would have died together, holding on to each other. It would be worse, dying alone. She looked curiously at her hands, that lay motionless on her knees, thin and grayish in the starlight. *Those very hands* would drop into dust in the earth. She moved them as if experimenting. She, Derrick Thornton, must die. In a terror of infinite darkness, in an everlasting void through which she seemed to drop, she bowed her head and prayed. Her feeling she could not put into words: she could only ask to be so good that dying wouldn't matter, and that her mother would love her, forever and ever amen. She had arisen then, had explained her withdrawal from the game by saying that she didn't "feel very good," and had gone to seek Mrs. Thornton over on the Devlins' porch.

That one moment of unearthliness left a shadow which clung to her the rest of the summer, and she would not be separated long, nor for any distance, from her mother, where alone she felt safe. She thought of It, always, when alone, and suffered many times the fear of death, with the succeeding sense of rising from herself to be, not so much a part of earth and sky and air—for a part may be separated from the whole—as one with them, indivisible . . . then, finally, the disbelief in the existence of Derrick Thornton, and the strange rebellion at having to return to act the part. As the summer passed, the experience recurred less frequently, until she began to invite it—she almost forgot it between times, and wondered—and she found then that it would come at her will. She had only to watch a swallow wheeling high overhead, or the wind across a wheatfield, or the glimmering light on a silver poplar tree when the wind turned its leaves. Or, lying on her face across her bed, she would spend a summer afternoon listening to the breeze in her window curtains, the voices of the children in the yard, and the sound of a horse in the street; she would meditate on death and would win through to the other feeling, itself not unmixed with terror, of being air in the air, wind in the wind . . . and the world a dream, queer, like all dreams, full of hard bright things with sharp corners, like the dining-room with its silver and old pewter . . . and then, finally, of having to go back to be Derrick, when some one called her . . . and grow old as Derrick, and have things happen to her that she didn't want to happen . . . until, returned to sanity, she would remember all that she meant to do before she died, and would go over in her mind her plans for a glorious future and her dreams of fame.

∽∽∽∽∽∽∽∽ II ∽∽∽∽∽∽∽∽

DERRICK HAD FASHIONED her purpose in life, and she entered at once upon her education as an artist. The first lesson had to do with her recognition of the need for biographical material, with the consequent innovations in her way of living, and her pose as a person of temperament, a wayward and whimsical spirit. . . .

Audience she had at hand in the persons of her friends. There had always been Jack Devlin, next door: they had learned to walk together, and had been accustomed from earliest infancy to try once any misdeed that occurred to either of them as a possibility. By the time they were eleven, there were also Mary Graham and Esther Greeley and Andrew MacLauchlan.

Mary's grandfather, a portly and somewhat pompous old gentleman, was an eminent figure in the town: a retired business man who continued to increase his comfortable fortune through his interest in the waterworks and the ice company. He had accepted Mary in his household willingly enough when his son suggested that she might be better off in a town, where she could go to school, than on his ranch, but he was forced to remain more or less oblivious of her in order to retain his dignity. Mary was large for her age, moved more slowly than Derrick, but with an irresistible force. Her yellow hair she wore in a smooth mane about her shoulders, and nothing disturbed it: she could skin-the-cat on a hitching bar, and once right side up again, her hair hung close about her neck with a soft sheen as though newly brushed. It made Derrick catch her breath, sometimes, when the sun shone on it . . . and it gave Mary an appearance of innocence highly desirable . . . she looked like the pictures of "Sunshine" on the billboards when "Tempest and Sunshine" came to the Opera House.

Esther had not been welcomed by the parents of the neighborhood when her mother bought the cottage beyond the Devlins'. Mrs. Thornton had condemned them as "hillbillies" and "briar-hoppers" after the first time she had seen Esther at the gate with Derrick.

"They're not briar-hoppers! They come from Summerville."

"Yes—Summerville—it's on the river, isn't it? You ask her, and if they didn't come from Kentucky, I miss my guess. Poor white!"

"Nell!"

"Dick, you know they are. One's own kind of people are never that dingy yellow color."

Esther was yellow: she had a flat, thin face, with heavy blue eyes, and hair skinned tight away from her forehead. Her hands were yellow, too, and the nails bitten. But Mrs. Thornton had to surrender her opposition to her, lest the town should whisper "jealousy," for Esther's mother (there was no Mr. Greeley) was a "healer." She cured any disease or deformity by rubbing, by thumping, by hypnotism; the little white cottage became a sort of hospital, and in the parlor gathered the sick and the crippled. It was a room to make you shudder in passing through: there was the man who had always struggled to get about on two crutches, and could manage with one now, but who still glared at you wildly, and muttered to himself. There were farmers' wives with goiters who tried to be kind to the shrinking children. There was the little girl (Esther and Derrick hid behind the stuffy-smelling curtain in the doorway between the hospital part of the house and the part in which the Greeleys lived, while Esther pointed her out and recounted her sufferings

in dramatic whispers) whose leg had been cut off: there had
been an infection, and the leg had swelled as big as a tea-
kettle, the little girl's mother had said, and because she
couldn't afford to have it treated, she had had "them" cut
it off. But the child had not recovered, and her mother had
to bring her to Mrs. Greeley for treatments, after all. Derrick wrote in her diary that "she had a sweet, patient, flower-
like face which showed how she endured her suffering
nobly." It seemed the thing to say, but it wasn't true. Only
rarely could you see her face, she was so wrapped about with
blankets and shawls, but when you could, there was no
character in its whiteness: she looked utterly sick, that was
all. She finally left Mrs. Greeley's, and later died, the children heard. Mrs. Thornton refused to believe any of the
story, but the doctor paced the floor in a fury because it was
none of his business what happened two doors down the
street. "As though Mrs. Greeley," Derrick said, "would ever
have cut her leg off, in the first place!"

The Greeley parlor continued to hold for Derrick the
fascination of horror; it was not for that, however, that she
accepted Esther: it was because she, like Jack, was always
there, to be had for the whistling.

Then there was Andrew. They had found him at the last
band concert of the preceding summer, when they were
engaged in a game of hide-and-seek in the crowd on the
court-house lawn, with the fountain on Main Street as
"home." As Derrick and Esther slipped like snakes in and
out of the throng in their attempt to win their way to the
fountain, they found their path stopped by a group of street
gamins teasing some one in their midst. They elbowed their
way to the center and saw there a distressed and grimacing
boy, of their own age, dressed most amazingly. His hat was
a funny little plaid thing with streamers, tipped over one ear;
he wore plaid socks and his knees were bare, and he had on
a short plaid skirt.

"I know—they call 'em kilts," Derrick whispered. "Father told us about him to-night. They're Scotch, 'n' just

come over—his father's the new super'ntendent at Devlin's mill, 'n' their name's MacLauchlan. Father said 'e cried because they hadn't bought 'im any American clothes yet."

She kicked the nearest young ruffian on the shin to attract his attention.

"Look here, you Bill Sheehan! Leave 'im alone, hear?"

Bill turned and wriggled his fingers at her, vulgarly. She stuck out her tongue.

"He's Scotch, an' has a right to dress Scotch if he wants to. That's nothing to be ashamed of, bein' Scotch. Half this ol' town's Scotch. Had a Scotch ancestor myself, once."

"Aw, criminy! Listen t' whut's talkin'. You're dago, 's whut you are."

Derrick shook with rage. "That's a lie, and you know it. . . . Anyway, you leave 'im alone—he's going to play with us now." And Andrew had become one of them.

Derrick had hardly needed to remember that her life must in some way show her early flowering of genius; the days the five of them spent out-of-doors required little change to make them worthy the most unhampered of spirits. But she did remember. . . . For a long while, however, the demands of everyday life obtruded themselves upon her to what seemed an unwarranted degree: there was no time for dramatic activity, and the only moments she could spend thinking were those of the early morning and late evening. She kept a mottled-covered blank-book and a chewed pencil under her mattress . . . this book would someday be a cherished possession of her biographer, or her great-great-grandchild would find the yellowed paper in the attic, and would reveal to an eager world the early writings of the famous and beloved Derrick Thornton. . . Even on the most active days, however, there ran through her mind a steady undercurrent of imaginary narrative: chapters of her life not yet lived composed for her biographer, or that same biographer's probable rendering of the passing moment. When she said good-bye to her friends at the gate, then

"Our young heroine stepped gracefully up the walk, and having gently closed the front door, lest the baby be asleep, called to her mother to see if there were any errands she could do."

Some of this imagined nobility was translated into real life. One could not be Great before one attained maturity, but one could not begin too young to be Noble. Sunday-school became bearable when you attended it upheld by the thought that one day the world would know and applaud. Heretofore, her attendance at church had depended on the weather: on rainy Sundays she followed her mother and father down the aisle, but on days when the sun shone and the musty church seemed unendurable, she went home from Sunday-school by a back way, to avoid her parents. Now, rain or shine, she waited and allowed herself to be ushered down to their pew by fat, important Mr. Chandler, Tecumseh's leading dry-goods merchant. Once resigned to this course, she found a certain pleasure in it. The unheeded harangue of the minister offered a wonderful opportunity for Thought. Derrick's only fear, as she grew more and more devout, was that God would call her to be a missionary. A Christian must, she was well aware, respond eagerly to such a Call, so, by refusing to think of Heathen or Foreign Field, she, metaphorically speaking, stuffed her ears with cotton. She had decided on Authorship and did not desire the interference of a God who demanded missionaries.

Her piety went hand in hand with a calculated recklessness of behavior. She devised escapades that brought down upon her the parental wrath, and, after she had been sent to bed in the evenings, wrote repentant paragraphs in her diary; she said, always in her best youthful-diarist manner, that she was sorry for the misdemeanor in question—these were insincere paragraphs written for the always-to-be-considered public eye. It is to be feared that she did not genuinely regret even those misdeeds which were the result of chance, and not of choice. There was, for instance, the Glass-Throwing Episode.

Of all the people whom Derrick knew, there were none whom she hated as she hated Bill Sheehan. Once upon a time, with the other boys, he had offered her licorice shoe-strings and all-day suckers, but even in the first grade she had snubbed him unrelentingly, had pushed his gifts from the desk to the floor, had thrown his Maybaskets into the street, had torn up his valentines. This hatred was not due to the fact that Bill's father was a saloon-keeper, as Derrick replied firmly to her mother's "He can't help what his father does —it's nothing against him." It was largely the result of his appearance, prosperously dressed though he was. "Just sumpin' about him," Derrick had said at eight or nine. He had puffy little green eyes, a thin hook nose, greasy red hair, and walked with a tough swagger. This year, Bill returned Derrick's scorn with more bitter scorn, which he expressed in words she did not know; he jeered and mocked and flouted with less readiness of wit, but with greater volume of sound.

Forced to sit near him in school, she devoted as much time as possible to tormenting him; one day, driven beyond endurance, he told on her, and she was "kep' in" for interminable minutes. When Derrick finally walked down the deserted steps of the schoolhouse, she found Bill wheeling slowly up and down the quiet street on his bicycle. Oblivious to his presence, she surveyed with interest the flagpole and the chain, which clanked against it sharply as it swayed a little, and the flag which snapped in the breeze.

"Derrick!" Bill stopped his wheel with one foot on the curb. "I wouldn't 'a' tol' if I'd 'a' knowed she'd 'a' kep' you."

She didn't turn until he had repeated himself, once— twice; finally she surveyed him coldly, her inner fury hidden behind a shell of ice.

"That's a lie, an' you know it."

She turned her attention to the sidewalk, avoiding the cracks meticulously. He rode slowly along the gutter, and, when she reached the corner, she found him before her, his wheel against the curb, his foot on the sidewalk.

31

"Can't go past till y' take it back. Can't nobody call me a liar, 'n' git away with it, hear? Take it back."

"You make me!"

"Y'—y' ol'—"

"It's the truth, an' you know it."

"If y' was a boy, I'd make y' eat them words, awright."

"Try it."

"I would awright—'n' by cracky, I'll show y' some day, y' ol'—"

"Think I'll be a boy some day?"

"Think yer smart, doncha! Smarty—smarty—by criminy, I'll marry y' some day, 'n' then I'll show yuh!"

Derrick had with difficulty kept from her lips the taunt her mother had forbidden—"Ol' s'loon-keeper—s'loon-keeper!" At his crowning insult she caught her breath, dizzy with rage. In the gutter lay a three-cornered fragment of green bottle glass. She snatched it from the dust and threw it before he could dodge.

In the next instant she flew for the alley, while Bill, in a daze, stood with his hand clapped to his cheek, where the blood trickled down in a thin stream toward his grimy shirt-collar.

He shouted after her a string of curses, and the threat to go and tell the police. Her feet winged with terror, Derrick raced down the alley that lay behind Duane Street and her own back yard; with a tremendous leap she hung to the top of their back fence, flung one leg over, and dropped in a heap on the other side. She entered the house through the kitchen, called to her mother that she was home, and, without waiting to explain her tardiness, proceeded to the front door. She peeked with some trepidation toward the police station. There was no visible commotion: the chief sat on the pavement smoking serenely, his hat pulled over his eyes, his chair tipped back against the awning pole, his feet in the air.

Still frightened, and thinking over and over—*what* if she had hit him in the eye!—she stole down the steps to the front gate. Beyond the dozing policeman stood Jack and Bill, in heated argument. The latter was still wiping his face and looking for blood on his fingers; Jack, usually so pacific, was making belligerent gestures with his clenched fist. Bill finally mounted his wheel and rode away.

Derrick swung violently back and forth on the clanging gate, as she awaited her deliverer.

"Some shot, Derrick."

" 'D he tell you? Gee whiz, Jack—it was luck it didn't hit 'im in the eye. What'd he say?"

"Wanted to tell the p'lice. I wouldn't let 'im, the ol' son-of-a-gun. I told him he prob'bly started it."

"Sure he did. 'D he tell you what he said? Ol' s'loon-keeper."

"Ye-eh. Said he would marry you some day, 'n' you could see how you would like livin' over the s'loon. He guessed you wouldn't be so high an' mighty then."

"What'd you say?"

"I said fat chance he'd have to marry you—that I was gonna do it myself."

"Jack! Did you really? I'm gonna tell Lucy!"

"Aw, Derrick—listen! I just said it so's he'd leave you alone. I didn't mean it."

"Oh, you didn't, didn't you?" Derrick had long ago decided that her friendship with Jack was identical with that of Jo and Laurie, so that, although she intended to refuse him firmly, she objected to his bolting in this way. "Well, I guess I'd never marry you, anyway, Jack Devlin. We're too much alike. We'd never get along. We'd fight all the time."

"Why, Derrick!" Jack's honest blue eyes showed his bewilderment. "We never fight!"

"We're fighting now. You said you didn't mean it, that you intended to marry me."

"Aw, say! How d' I know now who I want to marry? Don't be mad!"

But Derrick felt that he should have known. She turned on her heel and marched into the house.

Bill wore, for many more days than he needed them, two dirty strips of adhesive plaster crossed on his cheek, but he never told how he got the cut. After her first fright, Derrick was rather disappointed that no one heard of the incident; she must take care to be spectacular before a larger public, even although it meant, as she knew it must, increasing conflict with her parents.

Table Manners and Parlor Behavior had always been subjects of discussion in the Thornton house; they were time-worn and threadbare; now there came to be added to these a Lady's Deportment in Public. Until this year, Derrick had been accounted rather shy, and her adventures had been confined to back yards—theirs and others'—to barns and back streets, or woods and fields; in the mad roller-skate races around the court-house square, in the pursuit of farm wagons down Main Street of a hitch, she had been inconspicuously one of many. Now she seemed to have forgotten her bashfulness—except when sent back to the butcher's for the right change, or to the dry-goods store with an article to be returned—and her mother and father were amazed and troubled. They could not even hold the influence of Mary responsible, because so often Derrick figured alone. They had no way of knowing that she did not particularly enjoy the conspicuous things she did, that she was armed against her shyness by a defiant faith in her future vindication. She expected them to be disagreeable, now—was not genius always misunderstood in its youth? . . . At home, dissertations on Manners in Public grew to be her chief annoyance; they were given more and more frequently, until they included the threat of a year in a convent school, a threat that came first from her father one night at the dinner-table after he had witnessed a mountebank performance in the square.

Derrick had been sent by her mother to the meat-store; she had worn her skates, and moved with that rush and thunder that so terrified old ladies. She dashed into the store, spoiling the broom-laid pattern of the sawdust on the floor; she twirled her coins impatiently on the marble counter until the chops were handed to her, when she dashed out again. Outside she met Cassie, who shuffled in her unhurried tranquility from the "South End" to the Thorntons' every afternoon; Derrick hailed her, shoved the meat under her arm, and hastened across the street after some friends who had appeared in the distance. The establishment of Mr. Garnett the grocer stood on the opposite corner. As Derrick approached, the delivery horse, left standing by the curb, snorted a little, tossed his head, and started hesitantly down the street. A simple "Whoa" would have stopped him—he looked as if he expected it. The word trembled on her tongue, but she saw it as a Test, an Opportunity. None of the grocer's men were in sight. She caught hold of the end of the wagon, pulled herself up, and with her skates still on, lurched perilously toward the seat. The horse started off at a trot; Derrick snapped the reins across his back, and began what seemed a mad flight down the street. By the time he had reached the square, he was going with some enthusiasm. Derrick felt very silly, but pretended that she saw herself as Ben-Hur, the street a Roman arena, and she urged him to a greater speed. She stood crouched, her arms bent like a chariot-driver's, the wind in her hair: her footing, on skates, was uncertain, and every jerk of the wagon threw her against the dashboard. People in the street paused in pleased amazement to look after her.

Dr. Thornton, as she was to learn that evening, had seen her from the window of the bank.

Derrick drove the horse around the square and back to the store, and pulled him up at the curb with a flourish. She was inwardly terrified, but outwardly at ease. The grocers were still inside, fortunately; only the delivery boy was in sight, and his black face shone with relief as she alighted.

"I brought your horse back. He was running away."

"Y'all sho is a limb o' th' ol Nick!" But he let her go with no more than that. She had caught Cassie feeding him pie in the kitchen one day, and hadn't told.

As she skated away, Derrick considered the incident closed, but her father introduced the subject at the dinner-table.

"Did Derrick tell you what she did this afternoon?" He unfolded his napkin with a snap.

"No—what? Hunter, be careful, dear—you'll upset the baby's high chair. What, Derrick?"

But she was dumb under the accusing eyes. The doctor answered for her.

"As near as I can make it out, she ran away with Garnett's horse and wagon."

He related the story.

"I'm sure I don't know what's gotten into the child. Just yesterday she refused to tell Mr. Garnett he had given us bad eggs . . . you know, I never buy grocer's eggs, but we were out and had to have them . . . and she wouldn't tell him because she was afraid of him. And to-day she walks off with his delivery wagon . . . Derrick?"

But she couldn't explain it. She hadn't wanted to complain about the rotten eggs to kind old Mr. Garnett, who gave her candy or an apple whenever she went into the store: funny old Mr. Garnett, who wore his eye-glasses hanging on his ear out of his way, instead of on his nose where they belonged. To-day she had had to take the horse, to prove to herself, as well as to the town, that she was that sort of person. It was like getting into a tub full of scalding water without flinching, to prove to yourself that you could have been a martyr burned in oil without denying your faith.

"Answer me, my dear!"

Derrick felt that her mother was going to be cross in a minute, and she slumped miserably in her chair.

"Don't you know that a lady never does anything to make herself conspicuous in a public place?"

"I think we'll have to send her to a convent school, Nell. There are good ones in Cincinnati. There she'll have to learn the things she should. Manners, and penmanship—"

Derrick was aghast. She knew a girl—Agnes Patterson—

who had been sent to a convent school, and she had to wear her hair shingled like a boy's and dress in black. But her mother came to her rescue.

"They're generally only wilder when released from such restraint. Besides, the nuns would try to convert her: they say the Patterson girl wants to turn Catholic. She would think you and I were headed straight for Hell, and that would make us awfully uncomfortable. And besides—what would your grandmother say?"

"I don't raise my children to suit my grandmother." But he smiled ruefully as he thought of her. "Lord, wouldn't she stew! Remember when we got the organ in the church and she left the services the first time it was played, because it was 'Popish'? . . . But mark my words, Derrick: one more performance like that and off you go."

For a long time after that she walked circumspectly in public places, her mind torn between dread of disapproval at home and her ever-present convictions. One Saturday afternoon she again fell victim to the latter, and on this occasion her mother was her witness.

She and "the others" were skating around the court-house square. The Saturday afternoon crowd of farmers, market-men, and mill hands made their races even more exhilarating than usual, and they dodged in and out recklessly, hair flying, shoestrings flapping, their faces flushed in the wind of the bleak November day. Mrs. Thornton had come out to buy provisions for Sunday, and, with her market-basket over her arm, had loitered along before the fish and poultry wagons drawn up to the curb, and had finally paused at the corner. Here, beneath the maple trees, stood a load of round golden pumpkins, piled so high that the top of the pyramid was brushed by the tips of the branches; the pale sun fell slanting upon them through the almost leafless boughs and found warmth and color concentrated in them. When she heard the roar of the skates, Mrs. Thornton turned from her critical inspection of the pumpkins to watch the opposite corner, where the rag-rug woman spread her wares on the

37

court-house lawn for exhibition. Once Derrick had turned the corner too sharply and had run over a pale blue rug with her mucky skates; she had bought the rug to save herself from the wrath of the country woman, and had charged it to her mother.

To-day, they swung around the corner in a wide curve only to fall over in a heap when the foremost of them stopped abruptly. A mangy yellow cat, pursued by Topsy, the woolly black dog that belonged to the chief of police, had dashed across the sidewalk. The children scrambled apart and chased away the dog, but the cat had climbed into a tree and sat there spitting, heedless of their pleas. Derrick stood aside, studying the tree, the telephone-pole not six feet from it, and a farm wagon beneath them in the gutter. When she stooped to fling off her skates, Mrs. Thornton divined her purpose, but was too far away to stop her.

From the side of the wagon she could reach with the tip of her toe the lowest spike on the pole; she pulled herself up and climbed until she came to a heavy bough of the tree that scraped against it—down this she walked, without one hesitating step, or one glance into the street below, and then clambered up the tree after the cat. Mrs. Thornton suspected that she urged it on, chased it higher and higher. At any rate, they had risen to slender branches that swayed perilously before she seized the struggling animal and tucked it under her arm. She paused a moment, as though to acknowledge due applause, and began the descent. She was the most conspicuous figure for blocks, high against the black boughs of the tree, outlined against the sky, her scarlet tam-o'-shanter over one ear; market-men and their customers paused in their bargaining to watch, and even the Negroes and tobacco-spitting "poor whites" congregated on the court-house steps were quickened to attention. From the lowest bough of the tree she tossed the cat to the ground, and lowered herself for the drop.

Her mother was there to help her to her feet. Derrick noted her grim expression, but, with a pretense of unconcern, examined her scratches and wiped away the blood with a grimy handkerchief.

"Come on home, Derrick. If you won't behave properly in public, you simply mustn't appear in public, that's all."

Derrick picked up her skates.

"What's the matter with that, I'd like to know? Poor ol' cat!"

"You little hypocrite!"

"Why, Mother!"

They crossed the street and passed the police station in silence. Derrick kicked at Topsy furtively. If she were scolded now, it was her fault.

"I think I must give in about the convent school, Derrick. I'll tell your father so to-night." She hid a lurking smile at the same moment that Derrick began to look really dismayed.

"I'll be good, Mother, honest."

She held her tongue then until they reached their own gate, which sagged a little on its hinges because they had swung on it so often. Billy and Hunter rushed out and clung to their mother. Derrick glared at them. She would not be snatched from the sweet comfortableness of home, and leave her mother to the boys' possession. She made another attempt to conciliate her.

"If I'm not good for you, you don't think I'd be good for any ol' nuns, do you?"

"What, Derrick?" Mrs. Thornton, in the dusky front hall, exchanged with Cassie the full market-basket for a warm, sleepy baby.

"They wouldn't teach me the things you want me to know. How do they know what you want me to be? Teaching girls to flop on their knees to pictures an' things, an' if you wear their ol' beads nothing can happen to you. Faith, I suppose you call it. But," said Derrick in her oily Sunday-school voice, "Faith without works is dead. An' I guess I'll ask Grandmother Ferguson what she thinks . . ."

"You'll do nothing of the kind—you just dare!" Mrs.

Thornton laughed at last. "Get along with you, and show me some works. Prove the worth of a Presbyterian education by some Presbyterian activity."

"I was, Mother. Savin' the poor ol' cat."

With the air of one who had been victorious in an argument, she took from the table the book she was reading. But her mother, who had brought in the evening paper, gazed at her speculatively over the crisp white edges.

"I think you're a Whited Sepulcher, Derrick. I'm afraid that I've been so busy with the children that I've neglected your moral and spiritual development. I can't tell whether you're simple-minded or whether you're trying to be funny, repeating that stuff like a parrot. You must have some thoughts of your own. What do you think of things?"

"Things?" She looked up at her mother from where she squatted, cross-legged on the floor in front of the glowing coal-grate.

"Yes: Sunday-school—church—"

"God, you mean?" Derrick was embarrassed by her own abrupt utterance of the word.

"Yes. Don't you think at all about the things you gulp down?"

"I thought I was supposed to believe it all . . ." Believing things said in church was the easiest way: to think of things like that brought always that dread sensation of being, not Derrick Thornton, but Something . . . she put the thought from her and answered her mother with the Catechism. " 'God is a Spirit, infinite, eternal, and unchangeable, in His Being, wisdom, power, holiness, justice, goodness, and truth.' And our Sunday-school teacher says there aren't many that know that as well . . ."

"But that's one of the things you've gulped—"

"I know, but I think it's what I think. I mean—the rest of it—the Ark, and Moses and the burning bush, an' all—sounds funny, but you believe it like you believe a fairy tale, because you might see a fairy—an' if it was true, and you didn't believe it, God might be mad. But that Catechism is better to hold on to, because if it's true, nothing else matters. I mean, if none of the other things are true, if God's like that, then what is true must be nicer even than the things we think may be true."

She stopped in confusion, playing nervously with the fringe of the rug. She had not discussed religion with her mother since the day she had first asked about God, and had been told that God was everywhere, everything, always—which conflicted with her idea of God on a remote throne, dreadfully bearded and lightning-eyed. She hadn't liked God to be everywhere, especially when left in the room alone with Him . . . there had been a constant fear that a great booming voice would break the silence. But that, of course, had been when she was very small.

Now . . . she sighed, then straightened suddenly. She knew one way in which to circumvent any plan to send her to a convent school.

"Mother—I think I'll join the church."

"Derrick! You're too young!"

"I'm not! And what does youngness have to do with it?"

"Ten years from now, you might wish you'd never joined."

"D'you wish you'd never joined?"

"Oh, no!" quickly.

"Well, then—"

"Here's your father. Ask him." Mrs. Thornton flapped the newspaper feebly.

"Ask me what?" The doctor tossed his gloves on the table on top of the mêlée of newspapers, magazines, caps, and toys, and picked Margaret up from the floor where the boys had been playing with her.

"Don't you think it's time for me to be joining the church?"

"Oh, Sister! Wait until you're old enough to know your own mind."

"Father!"

"Until you're fifteen, at least."

"But I may not want to when I'm fifteen. I may never want to again. It's like telling me to go to the Devil."

"Derrick, what language! The church wouldn't hurt you—"

Her father murmured something about the church having to get them young, or not at all, when her mother interrupted, suddenly on her side.

"You'll have to let her, Dick. You couldn't *refuse* to let any one join the church."

On the next Communion Sunday she was called to the front of the church with a group of farmers' children; she shone resplendent among them in a new dress with scarlet ribbons; she wore a new turquoise ring given her by one of her aunts to commemorate the occasion, and carried a new Bible which her great-grandmother had bought. She was given courage to support the brief ceremony by the reflection that if her father and mother lacked enthusiasm, at least her more remote relatives were glad to have her safe in the fold; and by the imagined sentence in her obituary: "Since the age of twelve an earnest and loyal member of the Presbyterian Church of Tecumseh, Ohio."

"At any rate," she said to her father as they walked home, "all they asked me was whether I believe in God or not, and I'll still believe in Him ten years from now. So what was there to fuss about?"

Derrick saw no reason why Nobility and Notoriety-Seeking should not go hand in hand: joining the church was intended, not as a final stop to her career of crime, but as an antidote to it. It was not from the Presbyterian Church that she learned her lesson, but from her friends. In one moment she was made to realize, not only that she was a fool to think that they would not see through her pose, but that any one must be a fool who thought that people in general do not see through a pose. Derrick did not like fools.

One afternoon, after some particularly lurid behavior at

school had caused her to be kept for an hour, and then sent home with the request that she bring a note from her father to say that she would never do it again, in shame she took the alley route home, and stopped in the haymow to compose her feelings before going in to her mother.

She had been there only a few minutes when she heard voices in the alley below the window! Jack and Mary. She lifted her head to answer if they should whistle.

"Wonder if Derrick's got away yet?" Jack said.

"Don't let's stop for her, anyway. The way she's been actin' is sickening."

"Sickening? Why?"

"Thinks she's so smart. Never wants to do anything with us any more—only by herself. Always showin' off. Let 'er stay in all night after school, 's all I got to say—"

"But, Mary—" Jack moved to her defense, a little weakly. "She's diff'rent from us, she says. Sumpthing inside of 'er makes 'er feel wild—"

"Diff'rent!" Mary snorted. "Diff'rent! An' who couldn't be diff'rent, I'd like to know, if they wanted to stay in an hour after school—"

Derrick swung the haymow window open and glared down at them.

"You crazy galoots! What's eatin' you?"

"Who's a crazy galoot?" Jack pretended not to be taken aback as he leaned against the fence across the alley and watched her lower herself from the window and drop.

"You are, that's who." She picked herself up and dusted her hands on her skirt. "I never said I thought I was diff' rent!"

"You did so!"

"I never! An' whatever you think you're going to do now, I'm going with you, so there!"

And here ended, abruptly, the first lesson. Family opposition would never have accomplished it: families are not supposed to be pleased with the ways of genius—but life would have been a poor thing, indeed, without Jack and

Mary. Derrick had learned what many artists never learn at all: that to one's intimates Temperament is not Temperament, but a Pose . . . and after all, one's intimates count for more than the world at large.

ᴐᴎᴎᴎᴎ **III** ᴐᴎᴎᴎᴎ

AN ARTIST must know his country and its people; it is an education that has no beginning and no end, except with life itself. . . .

Derrick had felt no conscious love of the country, nor pride in it, before the first summer when the MacLauchlans had lived in Tecumseh, when she and Jack had taken it upon themselves to educate Andrew in its ways. It was not until the winter when she joined the church that a chance word revealed to her the possibilities of the town as literary material. Thereafter she studied it with a keen eye, and forgot nothing that she saw.

They had not seen that Andrew must be taught to admit the superiority of Ohio and Tecumseh until one October day when they had taken him nutting with them. . . . They had followed the banks of the creek from the bridge by the Devlin mill, where the water was full of oil and filth, back through the outskirts of town towards its source in the country. The way led first across an open pasture, a purple level of wild asters. Beyond rose a short, abrupt hill with deep gullies washed in its slope from its crest to the creek. They pointed to it proudly as their winter coasting-place. Andrew scorned it.

" 'N' you call thot a hill? . . . If I could show you our hills!" When he boasted of Scotland, he spoke with a thick accent that put them on their mettle.

Farther along, the creek ran between limestone cliffs;

45

they followed the ascending path, and walked single file in the narrow trail between the trees that grew close on either side. They walked silently, on tiptoe. They had played Indian so many times in going over that path that the feeling of it was in their blood; they could not walk beneath those ancient walnuts and tulip-trees without thinking of all the years whose passing they had witnessed.

"Do you know what?" Derrick said, suddenly, to Andrew.

"No—what?"

"We're on an ol' Indian trail! These very trees—"

Mary and Esther and Jack turned to listen and support.

" 'Twas lang ago the Indians was here. The history says so."

"Oh, a hundred years, maybe. But these trees are more'n a hundred years old." Derrick surveyed them judiciously: oaks turned a glowing bronze by the frost, walnuts, and tulip-trees, of a brilliant yellow, with a thick underbrush of young locusts and ailanthus and scarlet sumach. There was one giant silver poplar, its greenish-white trunk glimmering among the other trees, a hundred little silver poplars clustered at its base.

"Pooh—I don't believe nane o't. There niver wor Indians here."

They gasped at this heresy.

"We c'n prove it . . . we c'n prove. Hurry along, 'n' we'll show you."

They came presently to an open space, perhaps twenty feet across, on the edge of the cliff. The yellow locust brush surrounded it, and a wealth of goldenrod, but the edge of the cliff was clear. Fifty feet below ran the water, with little silvery noises against the limestone wall. The opposite bank was low, and beyond lay a cornfield in the bottomland, the corn cut and shocked; wigwam beyond wigwam, row beyond row, stretched far into the hazy, amethystine distance, where a line of trees on the horizon merged land and sky.

"Look, Andrew—the last Indian chief's buried here." Jack swung his arm to indicate the cleared spot before them.

"Really? Who said so?"

Jack and Derrick stared at each other. . . . Some one must have told them!

"Aw, shoot!" said Jack. "Don't anybody need to say so. Everybody knows it. He was the last chief of the tribe. They cut down the trees here an' buried him where he could look out acrost the ground that used to be theirs. 'N' what was left o' them went off an' joined another tribe."

"An' if you don't believe it, I'll find you an Indian arrowhead."

"Derrick!" This seemed to Jack a rash promise.

"Ye niver found an arrowhead."

"I have so. I've got a collection: arrowheads an' a stone hammer. But I didn't find the hammer myself."

"Let's look, then, right awa'." Andrew's gray eyes kindled, and he was excited in spite of himself.

"Derrick, you'll never find one, looking for it," Jack pleaded. "Besides, we want to find a place where nobody's beat us to the walnuts . . ."

"Betcha all the nuts we get to-day that we find one."

Jack hesitated, and wisely shook his head. She led Andrew to a place where a break in the cliff gave foothold to the stream.

"Come on—the crick's the place to look."

Derrick had an arrowhead on a string around her neck—"for luck." She bit the string hurriedly as she followed Andrew down the cliff, and when he stepped out on to the stones in the creek bed, she dropped it at the edge where the water curled against the gray stone.

"Look—this is the way." Derrick stopped, scraped up a handful of pebbles, and let the water drain out between her fingers. They looked in vain through half a dozen handfuls of stones.

"Come over to the edge, Andrew," Jack called. "They wouldn't have fallen in the middle of the crick."

Derrick looked up at them suspiciously, but they would never tell, if they had seen. Andrew returned to the spot

47

beneath them; with the third handful he got it—and would have thrown it away had not Derrick shrieked at him.

"Oh, you dummy! You've got one!"

He looked stupidly into his hands as Derrick picked out the triangular bit of flint.

"Thot's an arrowhead? How d'ye know?"

"How else d'you think those pieces got chipped out of it?" She showed the nicks at the base, and touched the irregular dents in it with a wet forefinger. "How else would it be that shape?"

When late in the afternoon they struggled to the road with their full burlap sacks, and waited astride the fence to catch a "hitch" back into town, they were still boasting to Andrew of the Indians. "This was the road where Simon Kenton ran the gantlet . . ."

Thereafter, when they wandered over the countryside, they remembered that he must be "shown." When they came on an old apple tree in the midst of a remaining bit of forest, with the rotting fruit smelling like wine in the grass at its roots, they told him the story of Ol' Johnny Appleseed, who had wandered through the territory unmolested of Indian or backwoodsman, with his sack of fruit seeds over his shoulder, planting them here, there, and everywhere against the day when pioneers should make their homes in the wilderness and find ready for them the friendly fruit trees.

When they came upon the old canal, stagnant, with green slime across the top of it, and tumbledown shacks among the weeds on its banks, they told the stories they had heard: how the canals were built before the railroads, and were the chief thoroughfare across the State, and how in the region south of Tecumseh, the Dutch from New Jersey had built their towns along the canal-banks, all the houses facing the water, their gardens full of bright tulips, their gates opening on to the tow-path. They told how a ride on a canal-boat was like a ride down a street, and how, on the decks of the packet-boats traveled the ladies and gentlemen of the pioneers: the

men with high, bell-shaped beaver hats, the women with
hoopskirts and bonnets and tiny fringed parasols.

They learned many new things about the country, in
order to have more stories to tell Andrew. Derrick sometimes drove with her father on his daily rounds in the country; as the fat horse plodded along the empty roads he
showed her the old landmarks, pointing with his whip into
the woods or across a river valley to a narrow lane between
the hills, or to some distant spot on a dust-veiled horizon
. . . the quiet pool in the river where the Indian maiden was
drowned, and where she still came, weeping, on moonlit
nights . . . the old Covenanter burying-ground . . . the
disreputable brick building in a godforsaken hamlet that had
been a famous tavern on the post road to Detroit. North of
town, wide sunbaked roads ran between level fields, where
late in the summer the corn was a flood that buried hedges,
fences, and lanes like a sea overflowing its dykes. This had
been section land once, and now arrow-straight roads criss-
crossed at right angles between the fields and pastures and
immaculate oak groves. To the south lay a wilder and more
beautiful country . . . Virginia military land . . . Derrick
loved the whole country with a passionate patriotism, but
most particularly that part of it which was south of town.
Here there were roads that lay on top of the world, or
climbed along the side of a hill, where on one hand were
century-old farmhouses, and on the other deep wooded ra-
vines . . . you looked sometimes through high branches and
sometimes over the thick tops of trees, across a fertile bottomland and the strips of virgin forest that marked the
river-bed, to a parallel line of hills. . . . And there were river
roads, hot and breathless, with weeds alongside higher than
the buggy-top, and beyond them, on one side, narrow cornfields and then the hills; on the other, the woods, dark,
gloomy, impenetrable, with their dank, pungent, not unpleasant smell. Occasionally there were glimpses, between
the weeds, between the trees, hung as they were with wild
grapevines, of the slow-moving, deep-shaded, tranquil

49

stream, where the branches of willows were washed in its muddy water. Here and there on these wild, grass-grown roads were vast, empty, weather-beaten mills, full of owls' nests, and log cabins whose roofs had fallen and whose doors were gone. Derrick could easily believe that but a day had passed since the Indian wars, since St. Clair and Harrison. . . .

Still other stories they heard from Jennie, Great-Grandmother Ferguson's cook. Every Sunday, Derrick took home from the Fergusons' the library books they had read that week; on Monday she exchanged them at the library and went down to the end of Main Street with the new lot. It was a thankless task, for they never liked the books, even when they had written the titles on little slips of paper to be handed to the librarian, but after the coming of Andrew, these trips were made pleasurable and exciting by Jennie's tales of the past. Derrick took her friends with her, sent them around to the kitchen door, while she entered the front hall, delivered the books, and passed on through to the back porch. Jennie sat above them in a big rocker and talked to a rapt audience crowded on kitchen steps. She had come up from Kentucky as a child—how old she had no idea—with her mother, in pre-war days, by the underground railroad. At the "last station" before Dr. Ferguson's, they had been hidden in a load of hay, and thus concealed had been sent on to him; somehow their pursuers had got hold of the message to Dr. Ferguson about "the load of hay overdue from Brown's," and had come to the house to search for them. The doctor had wanted to resist, but Jennie's mother, weeping and wringing her hands, had persuaded him to try to save only her baby. He had taken Jennie from her mother, and had hidden her in a tiny closet under the eaves in the attic.

" 'N' right hyah in dis kitchen, mah honies, Ah seed meh po' ol' mammy fo' de las' time on dis hyah e'th."

Jennie had told other stories, too: of feeding other fugitive slaves in the doctor's kitchen in the middle of the night

. . . of war-times, of the grief when the news came of the death of Derrick's great-grandfather, of Morgan's raid, and the "squirrel-hunters" who pursued him, and how they had buried the silver in the garden.

Once Mrs. Ferguson came upon them on the kitchen steps. She sent Jennie about her work, and shepherded the children into the front parlor while she hunted in the secretary for a daguerreotype of her husband in his uniform. Her account of the war was less emotional than Jennie's, but somehow—to Derrick, at least—it was more impressive.

"It was the judgment of God upon us, for we had sinned beyond forgiveness." Withered, shrunken, trembling as she was, the furious fires of righteousness yet burned in Mrs. Ferguson's eyes. "The crime of slavery was the crime of the North as well as of the South . . . we could have stopped it in the beginning . . . and for such sin, only blood could atone: the blood of the North as well as the blood of the South . . . the righteous judgment of the Lord. . . ."

The Past had become of absorbing interest to Derrick; in the following year her thoughts of it were linked to her dreams of the Future: she would tell others than Andrew of it. But for the Present she had no thought, until she overheard a casual conversation at a Ladies' Aid Society meeting.

This was in January, at the Thorntons'; Derrick had to be there to take care of Margaret when the ladies finished talking to her, and to help Cassie and her mother pass the refreshments. Until they needed her, she sat on the floor beside the library window, with a book, while near her the murmur of voices rose and fell: her mother and Mrs. Devlin and crackly-voiced old Miss McFarland, with her towering black bonnet, were gossiping together in the corner. Miss McFarland whispered her name, which attracted her attention, and she heard her mother's reply that Derrick never noticed anything if she had a book . . . the skies could fall . . . so then, of course, she listened while Miss McFarland repeated a bit of unsavory scandal. Derrick's cheeks burned, and she did not look up from her book, but she thought that

51

"the old vulture" oughtn't to mind being heard if she would talk about things like that.

She was relieved when the conversation turned to Professor Walker and his wife: he had taught in a Female Seminary in Tecumseh once, and was still "Professor." He looked like the picture of Carlyle in their game of Authors: wide-brimmed hat, wrinkled frock-coat, white beard, and sunken cheeks. Derrick saw the resemblance, but was too young to realize that it was probably not accidental. The story was that he had returned recently from a two years' absence in Europe, on a Wednesday night, and found his house locked and a note from his wife on the door. She had gone to prayer meeting, and had left the dining-room window open so that he could climb in. Her mother and Mrs. Devlin laughed until their voices were husky, but Miss McFarland said, her words cracking, shrill, "He might have known better than to come home on a Wednesday night. She hasn't missed prayer meeting for thirty years."

Mrs. Devlin agreed, then added, "It was funny of her, you know. But Tecumseh is full of people like that. I often think what a circus Dickens might have had in this town."

Derrick looked up, startled—at Mrs. Devlin, and then across at the brown leather backs of the fat volumes of Dickens. . . . Her father read Dickens aloud, on Sunday nights, and the children listened or not, as they chose. It was not long ago that she had first begun really to enjoy the reading, and even now her mother and father chuckled over bits of "Pickwick Papers" that she thought decidedly dull. But Dickens—in Tecumseh! Perhaps now that Dickens was dead, and knew about Tecumseh, he envied her her opportunity. She had wasted a lot of time: the last story she had started was laid in Boston, because all noteworthy people lived there, and she had given it up after a page or two, because she knew nothing of Boston except what was in the geography; and there were innumerable occasions when she had written for her composition class descriptions of the autumn leaves, or the clouds in a moonlit sky, or the departure of the birds for the South. Hereafter, she would search the town over for the queer people whom Dickens would have liked, and would make them the subject of her "Observations."

She had need at that time for a new quest. Life had been rather empty after she had definitely surrendered her determination to prove her genius by her behavior. She had found it ridiculously easy to win back her friends, and home and school and after-school adventuring with Jack and Mary, strenuous as it might have seemed to grown-ups, was not enough to occupy the mind. But now—if she were to be, not, perhaps, a new Dickens, but at least a new Alcott—she saw that she must look about her at the people in the town with the eye of the author, of the student of human nature. . . .

There was the woman who lived behind the livery-stable on a downtown corner: one never saw her except at the window that looked on the side street. Derrick was forbidden to play with her little boy, a wistful, grubby child who had the paper route on Duane Street. The restriction seemed silly to her: the boys all played with him, and her mother always gave him cookies or an apple when he came to collect for the paper on Saturday mornings. What difference did it make in him, the fact that his mother was queer, and spent all day and all evening at the window with the curtain lifted up, watching for some one who never came— or whose coming Derrick never witnessed? One morning early in March, when the first spring rain was falling, Derrick passed the livery-stable at the moment when the woman brought her flower-pots and stood them in a row in the narrow bit of grass between the house and the pavement: hyacinths and narcissi, and primroses . . . the hyacinths were rather pitiful, but the rain brought out their fragrance, and the narcissi were full of bloom. As Derrick passed, she saw the woman stoop to pick dead leaves from the primroses; she suddenly felt sorrier for her than she had ever felt for any one: no one could be so very queer who cared so much for flowers.

In the Roman Catholic end of town there was a hill favored as a place for roller-skate coasting. In one of the shabby little houses halfway down the hill lived a cripple whose legs were cut off above the knees, and who moved by means of roller skates fastened somehow to the ends of his legs. His arms were very long and strong; he pushed himself with his hands, and swung up and down the curbs with amazing agility. In spite of his crippled condition, he was much feared by the children: he had never been seen to smile, and his countenance was brutal, dark, and threatening, so that, if he was in the yard when the children coasted on his street, they crossed to the other side rather than pass before his leering eye. One day, when they bore down toward his gate like a whirlwind, he swept from his doorstep to the sidewalk just at the moment to make a collision unavoidable. The force of the clash sent him downhill before them, and, after futile attempts to catch the pickets of the fences as he passed, he fell at the foot of the hill and rolled over against a fire hydrant with such force that he was left gasping. The children, in terror, darted past him, at the next corner crossed the street, and struggled uphill again as swiftly as they could— all except Derrick, who removed her skates so that she could flee with no handicap and returned to his side.

"Are you hurt much? I'm awf'lly sorry."

He struggled to get up, and glared at her with such fury that she withdrew beyond his reach.

"We didn't go to do it," she said, "honestly—"

He swung himself upright, twisted his face hideously, and poured forth a torrent of curses. Derrick fled, aghast, her heart pounding. . . . From that moment the cripple became for her the embodiment of villainy; she never exchanged another word with him, and to her knowledge he never did anything worse than frighten children, but he appeared to her in nightmares, she pictured Bill Sikes with that dark, twisted face, and she never created a villain in her imagination that she did not hear again his violent black oaths.

There were other individuals whom Derrick stalked up one block and down another, with the stealth of a red Indian, and there were certain collections of people worthy the attention of a fictionist's eye: the congregation of the Presbyterian Church, for instance, and audiences of all kinds, and particularly the Saturday night throng that congested the streets of Tecumseh. She believed that people came to town on Saturday nights who never at any other time left their homes. There were Negroes who crowded in rapt attention around the patent-medicine hawkers whose wagons stood at the curbs by the court-house; and sallow Kentuckians from the mountains—"hillions," or "briar-hoppers," who slouched about the streets, hands in their overalls pockets, or leaned against the mail-boxes and telegraphpoles, always silent, always chewing; there were farmers from remote districts, their trousers tucked in heavy boots, whose daughters and wives wore shiny cotton-backed silks of blatant colors, vivid blues and pinks, draped generally with cheap lace of a large pattern; there were hard-faced factory girls, hair frizzed, cheeks too bright, voices shrill—and those who had been factory girls a few years before, but were now prematurely aged, surrounded by bow-legged children, their backs bowed from constant service at washtub and ironing board. And everywhere in the shifting crowd, so numerous that you stumbled against them as you walked, farmers' children, overdressed, queerly combed and hatted, staring round-eyed, or whimpering with weariness. Endless variety, but always the same, week after week—to Derrick a spectacle of never-ceasing fascination.

Her constant practice in the observation of humanity made Derrick, long afterward, the one of all friends most to be desired as a companion on any excursion: in Boston, which is inhabited by a greater proportion of grotesques than any other city in the country, she was constantly on the alert, and even in New York, where it is hard to see individuals in the hordes of people, she was forever plucking at your elbow.

There, together, in our spare moments, we watched the people, from the Lower East Side, where we prowled through one overflowing street after another, our particular delight the swarms of children who shrieked in the gutters, who pursued ice-cream-cone vendors, and the traveling merry-go-round; who bought their roasted chestnuts from the man whose stove sizzled and steamed on the corner, their bananas from those whose carts lined the curbs—up to the Metropolitan Museum, where there were artists and society women at the special exhibits, and immigrants and schoolchildren and tourists.

One time, when we were together, she spoke of Dickens. "It infuriates me to have people damn his books because his people are caricatures. Ninety of every hundred of the human race are caricatures of the ten who approximate normal."

We were walking up Fifth Avenue behind an old woman bowed under a burlap sack of papers and sticks of wood— a shapeless bundle of an old woman, wrapped about with skirts and shawls, who shuffled along close to the houses on the thick pads of carpet that she wore instead of shoes.

"There's a woman like that in Tecumseh," Derrick continued. "When one dress gets so soiled that even she can't stand it, she puts another one on top, until she's wearing four or five, and the under ones are always longer and darker, so that you can see all the layers as she walks. And if it weren't for Dickens, we shouldn't be able to imagine backgrounds for people like that. . . ."

But because she watched them for so long, Derrick could imagine for herself the backgrounds and behavior,

the thoughts and desires, the hidden, secret workings of
the minds, not only of Dickensian beggars, but of all the
stray odds and ends of the human race that came before
her eyes.

THE LESSON to which the next few years of Derrick's life were devoted belongs not only to the education of an artist, but to that of the most ordinary human; it is a lesson which is always a part of growing-up, one of the most uncomfortable accompaniments of which is the awakening consciousness of the fact that happiness is not to be taken for granted nor to be depended on.

Derrick would probably never have thought of Happiness —a capitalized Happiness—if it had not been one of the subjects for a composition assigned by the eighth-grade teacher not long after school had begun. Derrick stared at the list of subjects on the blackboard in amazed contempt and glowered at the woman who smiled so benignly upon them from behind her desk. For almost fifteen minutes she glowered, determined to write nothing . . . then she realized that only fifteen minutes of the period were left, and took up her pencil grimly, resolved to say anything about happiness but what Miss Black would expect her to say. To begin with, she would indicate that she didn't believe what she had been taught to believe.

"Most people say that you are happy if you are good, and unhappy if you are not good, because then you will be punished. This doesn't seem to me very sensible, because if you are not good, then you expect to be punished, and if you expect to be punished, you can be prepared for it, and anything you are prepared for won't make you unhappy, and it doesn't last long, and afterward you can remember what fun you had doing the thing you wanted to do, and forget the punishment. Unless what you did made some one else unhappy, the punishment for that is finding out how unhappy you made them, and that makes you unhappy. But you ought to know enough in the first place not to do anything that will make somebody else unhappy."

She thus dismissed what she credited with being the universal theory of happiness, and advanced to the statement of her own ideas.

"It seems to me the most important way to get happiness is by being so nice that the people you like can't help liking you. You must be generous and unselfish and good-tempered, and you must keep promises and never be a tattletale. And the next to the most important way is by doing something to be proud of—something that will make your family glad that you belong to them. Of course, it would be nice if everybody could be famous, but if everybody can't, at least they can do something that will be worth leaving behind them."

She tried to think of a sounding quotation with which to end . . . but discarded "something accomplished, something done," because there was no particular credit in quoting what she had had to learn in school. The only quotation that she knew about happiness had to do with wisdom, and not with fame. To make it fit, she added a sentence and then scribbled at the end the passage from Proverbs which had come to her by way of the Presbyterian Sunday-school:

"The third thing necessary for happiness is education. The more you know about everything in the world, the happier you are. As Solomon said, 'Happy is the man that findeth wisdom, and the man that getteth understanding . . . Her ways are ways of pleasantness, and all her paths are peace. She is a tree of life to them that lay hold upon her, and happy is every one that retaineth her.'"

When Miss Black gave back the papers, a few days later, Derrick glanced at hers to see if there were any marks on it, then folded it into a two-inch square and put it in her geography, where there was an accumulation of arithmetic and spelling papers and grimy notes. And after that, for many months, she gave no thought to Happiness.

No one would have thought of Derrick, that winter, that she was growing up, or was about to begin to grow up; she still devoted odd moments to pursuits as childish as possible. When the cold weather came, she joined with the boys in an enthusiasm for a new sport: trapping muskrats. It was not an amusement which her family regarded with favor, but there was no ground on which it could be prohibited. At first she borrowed traps from the boys, but Billy, perhaps with an eye to the future, insisted upon giving her one for Christmas. There were things about trapping that she disliked: the dead muskrats, toward which she affected a Spartan unconcern, telling herself that the farmers would rejoice to have them killed; and the necessity of putting her hands in icy water when she had nothing but a handkerchief with which to dry them, so that they were raw and cracked and bleeding as high as the wrist-bones, and her mother exclaimed over them in horror and compassion when she tied them up in mutton tallow at night. But there was pleasure in it, too: a sense of freedom and adventure that came with the wandering in the fields on bleak winter afternoons. The very aspect of those fields—dull, brown, barren, beneath a leaden sky— made her feel that she was engaged in an uncomfortable and even hazardous enterprise.

The traps required constant attention, for the colored boys from the South End were on the alert for every opportunity to steal both trap and trapped. Derrick went out to the creek with Jack and Pete McInnis and Andrew in the afternoons after school, and, if her trap produced a victim, one of the boys loosened it and carried it home for her. Ben skinned it, then cured the skin by nailing it on the woodshed door, in payment for which service he kept the carcass, unaccountably prized as meat by Cassie and himself. It happened that on the same week that Jack had offered to substitute for a friend on a paper route, and while Andrew had the mumps, Mr. McInnis's assistant in the meat-store deserted without a warning, and an unwilling Pete was thrust behind the counter to slice "bologny" and weigh chops on a pair of scales that he could hardly reach. The two distressed boys interviewed Derrick on the corner when school was dismissed on Monday afternoon.

"You'll haf to watch them traps fer all of us, 't's all there is to it," Pete said firmly, teetering on one foot as he prepared to dash for the store.

"Can't we just let 'em go till your father gets some one to help?"

"No, we can't. It'll only be to-day. Mom said she'd help to-morrow if he don't get anybody."

"Well, I'll watch the traps till you come, but I won't empty 'em. You just come along's quick as you can."

They argued with her in vain; they could only persuade her to patrol the creek-bank until Pete could get there, which would be sometime after five. . . . She ran home to tell her mother where she was going, but not that she was going alone—and departed for their hunting-ground. She rejoiced in the chance to take the walk by herself, her meditations uninterrupted by conversation; she had just finished "Jane Eyre," and it was very much on her mind. She half expected, so fitting were the season and the hour, to meet Jane in the wagon trail that crossed the empty field, her cloak blown around her huddling figure by the bitter wind, her background the gray, interminable, swift-moving clouds, and the brown slope of the meadow where the wind whistled through the dead grass. Over the bare spots of earth lay a thin sprinkling of snowflakes; a few sped past now and then, in the wind, and there was a white line of them around the base of the twisted black-thorn tree. The tree looked as if it might spring into life at any moment in the shape of an evil, humpbacked witch. Derrick shivered and plunged into a stretch of cat-tails that rattled in the wind, through which

61

one could take a short cut to the creek, in winter, when the swampy ground was frozen into hummocks of grass and roots scattered through black patches of ice.

The creek itself was too swift to freeze easily; it was with some surprise that Derrick found in the shallows ice so thick that she could not break it. Promptly she took to the stream as thoroughfare, and approached the bend where their traps lay. It was very quiet—oppressively quiet; nowhere, as far as she could see through the frozen swamp, was there any living thing in sight. She had just decided that there was no need for her to stand guard, when she heard voices, and stopped still to listen. They came from a distance, carried on the wind, and with them was mingled a noise as of chains clinking, and of horses that dragged something. She started up the bank to investigate . . . it was no one ploughing, of course, nor hunting rabbits, with that noise . . . but, when she reached the top, she laughed at her mystification: they were cutting ice . . . who would have thought that it was cold enough to freeze the pond? And it was not strange that the sound should come so dim and queer, as if thinned by distance: they were not on the pond near the foot of the slope where she stood, but on the second one, farther away. They were cutting ice from the wrong pond. . . .

There were two ponds, connected by a creek which flowed away across the fields. It was on the nearer one that the icehouse stood, but on the more remote that men and horses clustered, ready to leave their work for the day. Derrick was surprised and troubled. There was some reason why they should not cut ice from that second pond. She wrinkled her brow. Her father had explained it over the telephone to Mr. Graham, Mary's grandfather, who owned the ice company. Something about sewage—that was it: the plant to dispose of it lay in a field beyond the first pond, and if anything drained out of it—it wasn't supposed to, but if it did—it would drain into the second pond. Not into the first, because nothing could drain uphill, but into the second— therefore, they were not supposed to cut ice from it. It was as clear as the sum of two and two. Of course, there never was much ice in a winter, and they thought they wouldn't have enough if they didn't take it all—but they knew they weren't supposed to.

Derrick left the hilltop, where the wind was particularly keen and shrill, and, while she tramped up and down the frozen creek, she planned a dramatic announcement of her discovery to her father. When Pete finally appeared out of the growing darkness, she ran to meet him with her news. He was not impressed.

"Who'd ever 'a' thought it was cold enough to cut ice! Ain't there no muskrats in the traps?"

"I didn't look."

"Well, you are the limit! How we gonna see, now it's so dark?"

"I was thinking of something else."

"You must 'a' been! Wha' d'you think you come for?"

"Well, nobody took the traps, anyhow, because nobody came anyways near!"

Fortunately for Pete's peace of mind, there were muskrats, one in his trap, and one in Derrick's. She justified her presence by holding matches for him while he opened the traps and reset them. The walk back to town they made in as short time as possible, and with no conversation until they came to the meat-store, where Pete left his muskrat in the charge of his father while he carried Derrick's home for her. She stopped long enough to tell Mr. McInnis how she had seen them cut ice from the wrong pond, but he would not take it seriously.

"These here microbes ain't carried in runnin' water, are they? I thought runnin' water was good as ever seventeen or eighteen feet beyond where it run over a dead hog . . . something like that . . ."

Even at home, Derrick's carefully rehearsed announcement of startling news could not be made, for nowhere in the house, upstairs or down, could she find either her father or mother. She stuck her head around the swinging door between back hall and kitchen.

"Cassie, where's Mother?"

"Yo' mom an' yo' pop hes gone to yo' Aunt Anne's for dinneh. Yo' an' the chilluns a' to hev yo' dinneh hyah an' go to bed e'ly, 'thout waitin' up fo'm."

"It smells like fried mush." Derrick went into the kitchen, and let the door swing shut behind her. "Cassie, is it fried mush?"

Cassie stopped beside the open oven door, while Margaret took up the rolling-pin from the kitchen table.

"It a' fried mush, an' maple molasses, an' yo' kin git right out o' mah kitchen fo' yo' smells the desse't. It a' intended fo' a su'prise."

"Oh, Cassie! Hot gingerbread and whipped cream! How can I help guessing, when Margaret's smeared all over with dough? Gee, aren't you nice!" And she went back into the living-room to tell the boys.

In the morning Derrick was so late that she had no time for breakfast, but picked up a piece of toast and fled. By evening she had forgotten what she had seen the day before, and was only on the lookout for opportunities to enter the conversation with tales of that day's adventures. After that, it was only once in a long while that she remembered about the ice, and then never when her father and mother were around.

It was not long before the muskrat season was over, and after that it was no time until spring, and in the spring you were conscious of little but the succession of days, each of which marked an advance in delight over the day before. There was, first of all, the moment in February when the last snow melted, when you could smell spring, or feel it, in some sixth sense, when the wheat in the fields was green as emeralds, although it was long before time for the grass to be warmed back to life. Then there were the soft rains when March began that covered the sidewalks with fishing-worms —they brought sprouts of hyacinths and narcissi, and tiny, almost invisible buds on violets and marsh-marigolds. Flocks of robins came back, their breasts as vivid in color as though newly dyed. Then crocuses in bloom, and marsh-marigolds; then—miraculous day!—the first violet, followed by dozens of violets, and handfuls . . . then roadsides blue with them, thickets floored with them, the creek-bank a wall of them . . . violets so myriad in number that one hardly bothered with them, but exulted in rarer delights.

When the planting of seeds began, they followed Cassie's calendar of superstition, beginning with the sweet-pea seeds on Saint Patrick's day. Before the violets were gone, the lilies-of-the-valley blossomed in the garden, and the lilacs, and the red flowers of the maple trees were thick on the sidewalks, to be crushed beneath your heel with every step. Spring games were played in swift succession: jump-the-rope and hopscotch, and, when stone steps were dry and warm enough to sit on, jackstones; and when the maple flowers were swept from the sidewalks, before the rains had washed away the black stains they left, roller skates were out, and after that you rarely walked until summer had come and it was too hot to skate. . . .

In the woods there were spring mushrooms and trilliums and may-apples, and, later, the pink and lavender and blue carpet of the wild phlox, knee deep, and faintly sweet. The woods themselves were a transcendent glory of white dogwood and the exotic color of the redbud trees. All the birds were back, the fruit trees blossomed, and there were flowering branches of apple trees for May-baskets. It generally seemed, provokingly enough, that spring rested for a breathing space, just at May Day . . . the earlier flowers were gone, the later ones not in bloom . . . but when that particular need was past, there was a sudden outburst of them: all the shrubs, from bridal wreath and syringa to the snowball bushes; all the trees, from the horse-chestnut flowers like spires, held upright on the tips of branches, to the locust trees so full of creamy blossoms that the air was sweet with them on warm spring evenings, and, finally, the yellow cups of the tulip-trees, splashed with red—those cups so easily shattered by the wind and blown untidily across the lawn and into the pool where the water from the fountain flowed. Always, by Decoration Day, it was summer, and there were roses and peonies in such profusion that one ceased to keep tally with spring's offerings.

That year, spring came with a rush, as though eager to have the whole pageant over and done with in a hurry. By the middle of May it was very hot, and the children in school were languidly rebellious and indifferent, and had no interest whatsoever in anything within four walls.

Derrick arrived at such a state of weariness and lassitude that she wondered at herself, and decided that she must be bilious; she even went so far as to admit it, not at home, to be sure, where there was a certainty of being dosed, but to Mary and Esther one afternoon when they had gone to Grahams' after school. They had dropped on the steps of the back porch, exhausted by the innumerable exasperations of a hot, sticky day at school; it was natural that they should eye with some eagerness the vast refrigerator, the most conspicuous object on the porch.

"Any ice in it?" Esther asked.

"Sure. Want a piece? Or—no—wait a minute—if I can find the lemons we'll make lemonade."

Mary held the screen door open for them, and they, not at all backward, helped her prowl in the pantry until they found what they wanted. Derrick, in an access of strong will, announced that she was really ill and suffering and would take her lemon plain.

"Lemons plain," she explained, "will cure biliousness, but not lemons mixed with sugar 'n' ice." And she cut the tip off so that she could suck it. Mary and Esther made their lemonade. After they had squirted lemon juice over the zinc-topped table in blackening spots, and had chipped ice so vigorously that chunks of it were scattered over the porch floor, and melted there in little pools, they withdrew to the steps again and sipped from their glasses slowly and exultantly while Derrick made faces over her lemon, and rubbed the edges of her teeth together, experimenting.

The hot days were followed by rain, and, when it turned cooler, Derrick at once recovered her health and spirits. Had it not been so, she would have decided against biliousness and in favor of typhoid fever, for just at that time half a dozen cases developed in the town.

Before the board of health had discovered the source of the infection, Mary was stricken, if "stricken" could be applied to the spirit in which she succumbed to the disease. The doctor assured the family that she did have typhoid, but it seemed to bother her very little: not half so much as it bothered her grandmother, who was responsible for keeping her in bed.

A few nights after Mary's illness was diagnosed as the fever, Dr. Thornton dropped into his chair at the dinner-table, worn out with the care of his increasing number of patients, and said that the germs must be in the ice, that they had been unable to find them anywhere else, and that it was a relic of barbarism, anyway, to use ice taken from the top of a pond.

Sudden recollection smote Derrick. She sat frozen in horror, knife and fork suspended above her plate.

"Father! I knew the ice was dirty, and I forgot to tell you!"

She wished immediately that she had not spoken, but it was too late. Her father did not, perhaps, take her seriously, but nevertheless insisted on hearing the whole story. When she had finished, he looked at her in dismay and disbelief, a grim expression on his weary face.

"How old are you, Derrick?"

"Thirteen."

"You knew they weren't supposed to cut ice from the lower pond?"

"Yes, I knew it."

"Didn't you know that you ought to report it?"

"Yes."

"Why didn't you?"

"Forgot it."

"Forgot it! And what has happened because you forgot?"

That was all. The meal was finished speedily and in silence. Derrick tried to persuade herself that it was a dream; for the first time in her life she knew the sick desire to go back and do differently what had been done erringly before. . . . After she had gone to bed, she was struck by another horrible thought. If Mary had typhoid, Esther would have it, too, for they had drunk iced lemonade together. Her two best friends! She fell asleep with her head under the pillow, trying to shut out the voice of her conscience—strange conscience, that had been so silent since the day she had seen the ice cut, and that spoke so violently now!

It hardly occurred to Dr. Thornton afterward that Derrick might have taken upon her shoulders responsibility for the epidemic; he was too much wearied by the care of his own patients to waste energy on the question of who was to blame. As he told his wife, they could not fix the responsibility for it, nor make it public. Scores of people must have seen the ice cut, but no one had reported it. But Derrick woke every morning with a sense of dread and regret only too easily accounted for; she dragged herself to school reluctantly, afraid of what she might hear, yet unable to hold herself away from any group that seemed to whisper of awful things. She was not surprised to find, in a day or two, that her worst fears were justified. Esther was not at school, and the inevitable conclusion was that she must have the fever. Derrick stopped at the Greeley house in the afternoon and found Esther on the couch in the tiny living-room that she and her mother used for themselves. She seated herself cross-legged on the floor beside her, and eyed her dubiously. Esther looked sleepy; she was flushed and swollen-eyed.

"What's the matter?"

"Nothin'. Felt kind-a funny this morning, 's all. Mom wanted me to go to school, but my back ached, so I made her lea' me stay at home. But I'll be back to-morrow."

"It's not typhoid, then?"

"Shoot, no! Mom ga' me a treatment this morning, an' said I wasn't gonna have nothin'."

Derrick, somewhat eased in her mind, said nothing to her family about Esther, but after two or three days had passed, and still she "felt kind-a funny," and didn't get back to school, she screwed up her courage, and again brought up the dread subject at the dinner-table.

"Father, d'you know Esther's sick?"

"No, is she? What's the matter? Her mother can take care of her, can't she?"

"But her mother *isn't.* Nothing but giving her those ol' treatments. And they wouldn't do any good for typhoid, would they?"

"I should hardly think so. But it can't be typhoid, can it? Any woman who knew *anything* would have better sense—"

"Well, if you ask me, I think she's got it. She's sicker'n Mary, by a good deal. What I want to know is, if I make her come down here, will you look at her an' see?"

"Good Heavens! Isn't she in bed?"

"No, she isn't. Her mother keeps tellin' her there's nothin' really the matter, an' she won't even lie on the couch when her mother's around. An' she eats just any old thing. Aren't you supposed to be careful what you eat when you've got typhoid?"

"But she can't have typhoid, Derrick. Don't be silly."

"Will you just look at her if I bring her over?"

But the doctor negatived this proposal firmly; professional ethics forbade that he should steal a glance at some one else's patient. He persisted in his refusal, even although Mrs. Thornton, too, begged him to have a look at the child.

The next afternoon, Derrick returned weeping from her visit with Esther, and fled to her mother for aid and comfort.

"She's so sick she can't even talk good sense. She didn't care anything at all about seeing me. I don't even think she

69

knew it *was* me. Oh, Mother," wringing her hands, "won't Father go?"

"He's busy with his own patients, dear. And, besides, he told you last night, it wouldn't be right for him to go."

"Well, it wouldn't be right for him just to let her die, would it?"

"Oh, honey—she isn't that sick. You're frightened because you're not used to seeing sick people."

"Then, Mother, you go see."

"I!" She recoiled. "But what could I do? It would just make Mrs. Greeley furious—"

"It wouldn't. You could take her something to eat, an' Mrs. Greeley'd never know the difference. An' you could tell me if she's as sick as I think she is."

Mrs. Thornton consented, finally, and departed with a bowl of the chocolate pudding Cassie had made for dessert, while Derrick sat on the front steps to watch. But the visit was fruitless. Mrs. Thornton could do no more than bid Mrs. Greeley call on them if she needed anything. Although she understood Derrick's state of mind, and would not let her see, therefore, how desperately ill she thought Esther was, there was little that she could say to cheer her.

On the next afternoon, Derrick was not admitted at the Greeley's; in the instant that she stood at the door, she suffered in a flash of feeling the certainty that the worst of her fears had come to pass. She struggled against this as she looked back at the inscrutable, portentous windows of the cottage, and succeeded in reasoning herself into what was almost worse—a frantic state of suspense. There was nothing she could do at home but flee to her own room, bolt the door, and throw herself on the bed.

But, secure in that haven, she could not order her thoughts nor bring them to any conclusion; she forgot everything, and listened to her brain, which said over and over, "Esther—Esther—poor Esther! She did not deserve to be sick—Esther, that every one, even Mother, thought was so homely and queer, that she didn't matter very much—it would not have been so bad if it were Mary who was so awfully sick—Mary always came out of things all right. But Esther, who couldn't do anything for herself, and who hadn't any one to do things for her." Derrick clenched her hands, torn by the desire to do something herself; then suddenly her brain stopped saying those things, and into the deathly stillness that followed swept the recollection: it was only because of what she had done last winter that Esther had the fever!

She tried to pray. She had forgotten to tell about the ice cut from that pond. But she had not meant—surely God knew that she had not meant—that anything should happen to any one. That was the burden of her prayer. Would not God, assured of her remorse and sense of guilt, even although she had intended no guilt—would not God relent and remove his heavy hand?

She went to dinner reluctantly, and ate so little that her father asked her for the fiftieth time if she were sure she had not had ice in anything, anywhere. After dinner she moved restlessly about the living-room, she picked up books and tossed them down again, she quarreled noisily and violently with the boys, burst into tears when she was rebuked, and immediately went upstairs again. If Mrs. Thornton knew that it was on Esther's account that she was miserable, she had not regarded seriously enough her confession about the ice to realize that the worst of her suffering was remorse or she might have tried to comfort her; the doctor was too preoccupied even to remember that Derrick was worried about Esther.

As she fumbled with the buttons on her clothes, Derrick tried in agony of mind to determine how long it would be before she could know just how sick Esther was—she must be very sick for her mother not to let her have company—or perhaps she didn't want company?—or how long it would be before she could know whether Esther would get well or not—it might be days before any one knew anything about it—Mrs. Greeley might just shut up that cottage and not let any one in or out who could tell—Derrick was in no state of mind to be reasonable. Time seemed to stretch before her infinitely; even the night, usually nothing, loomed before her like an eternity to be lived through.

She went to sleep, finally—what she would call finally, although her mother and father had not yet come upstairs. In the middle of the night she was awakened by the ringing of the doorbell. Startled so that she trembled all over, she climbed out of bed to listen at her door; when her father had gone downstairs, she crept to the banisters to watch. He switched on the light in the hall, so that she could see that it was Mrs. Greeley who entered. Then, indeed she turned sick and weak. Mrs. Greeley had come for her father—in the middle of the night—

As the doctor turned back to dress, Derrick retreated to her own room—her heart beat so that it shook her from head to foot—it seemed even to shake the bed—so silly of it—it kept her from listening, and from thinking; she spoke to it as though it were outside herself—a dog or a cat—told it to be quiet, and not to be silly—to hush, and stop bothering her. The treatment proved effective, eventually, and she could withdraw her attention from it enough to hear her father go downstairs and close the door behind him.

She felt faint and shaken when her heart stopped knocking against the bones in her chest. She had heard nothing of the colloquy in the hall; they had spoken in undertones; but she knew how ill Esther must be to frighten Mrs. Greeley to such an extent.

As soon as Derrick thought her mother must have fallen asleep again, she rose, took a blanket from her bed, and went into the hall, determined to sit at the head of the stairs until her father should return, there to waylay him. She wrapped the blanket around her and wadded up one corner of it to tuck between her head and the banisters. She was not in the least sleepy, but felt queer inside, and had to keep swallowing; she had to listen constantly for the return of her father, and, after every time she swallowed, she listened with redoubled intentness, afraid that in the instant something might have escaped her ears. She could not listen so well with her eyes closed as with them open, and she could not hold them open without staring into the darkness of the lower hall. At first she was glad to be able to turn her thoughts to her immediate surroundings—her courage oozed from her drop by drop and second by second, as she sat there, but she deliberately invited terror to come upon her and bring forgetfulness of her worse dread.

It was thick black dark below where she sat the staircase twisted down into an abysmal pit which echoed now and then to strange noises: creakings and tickings the darkness was accentuated by thin rays from the street light that shone through a narrow line of glass on each side of the front door. That light came through the parlor window, too, and a patch of it, full of the moving shadow of leaves, fell on the staircase wall a little below where she sat. This did not cease to startle her, nor did the noises decrease in terror as she grew accustomed to the darkness and could see a little into the pit. She could distinguish the parlor door and the library door: nothing could come unseen into the hall from right or left, but from where she sat she could not watch the sitting-room door, under the staircase, nor did she have any assurance that there was not already some one there. . . . She crept down the stairs, step by step—she wondered why her mother didn't hear her, and why, since she didn't, it would not be possible for a burglar to come any night and prowl through the house unheard—she looked under the staircase, closed the sitting-room door, and returned, convinced that now she would be quite safe on the top step, for no one, surely, could open the door so silently as to come upon her unexpectedly. But when the game of terror she had played with herself no longer served to occupy her mind, there swept over her again the thought of Esther. What was it like to be so sick that you might die? What was it like to die of typhoid? Did Esther lie quietly, as though asleep, just able to hold on, breath by breath? Did she breathe harshly, so

that the sound of it could be heard in every room of the
house—or was it noisier than that, and wilder?

Derrick shifted her position, put her head down on her
knees, and, in desperation, gabbled over to herself the States
and their capitals—the Ten Commandments—the twelve
apostles; still there was nothing but silence outside, and
creaking within. Once she thought she heard some one at
the door she had closed; she held her breath, but it was
nothing, after all. She counted a thousand, and then went
over the States again, rocking back and forth as she chanted
in a whisper, "Maine, Augusta, New Hampshire, Con-
cord—" When she finished, she sat up and listened. Her
father had been gone an endless while—she had not expected him much before this—but now, surely! . . . There
was nothing. She tried to name the Presidents and the Kings
of England, but she didn't really know them, and when she
stopped to think who came next, her thoughts leaped away
again to Esther. She returned to the Ten Commandments,
but into the midst of "Remember the Sabbath Day" broke
the sound of voices outside. She could not decide from
which direction they approached, but that they did approach was certain. Fear and horror clutched at her throat,
and her heart raced again in that violent way. . . . The
footsteps passed, with inexplicably strengthened and diminished and strengthened waves of sound. From the sick sense
of relief that swept over her, she saw that she could not, after
all, wait there for her father. She could not hear about
Esther in the night, in the darkness. . . . In an insane haste
she rose, stumbling and tripping over her blanket, and flew
into her own room again. Once in bed, she pulled the pillow
over her ears, so that she could not know when he came in.

She must have fallen asleep, for she heard nothing more
until she awoke, startled, in the early morning. The dim gray
of dawn filled the room—she wondered what had awakened
her, then heard her father's voice from the bedroom down
the hall, and realized that he must have come in at that
moment. She did not call to him, but half rose in an impulse

to creep to the door and listen. The very thought of what he might have to say made her feel weak and sick, and she cowered again beneath the covers. The sound of voices ceased, after a while, and she listened for the court-house clock to strike, and watched the light increase and fill the room. She heard the milkman's wagon at the gate, the clinking of his bottles, his departure. At half-past six the whistles blew, and then there came the sounds of Cassie getting breakfast. Derrick from that moment listened for her mother—if when she rose, she came toward her room, it would mean that the doctor had not got there in time, because her mother would tell her if anything had happened. But if she went downstairs just as she always did, without coming in, it would be a sign that nothing had happened.

So, when finally she heard her mother approach her door, she knew. She felt herself drop as from a breathless height into a bottomless pit of despair. She pretended to be asleep, not to make it harder for her mother, but instinctively, to save herself as long as possible. Then her mother's voice, from a remote distance, reached her in the depths through which she had fallen.

"She had a hemorrhage, and her mother came down after your father. She had hemorrhage after hemorrhage, and he couldn't stop them. He held her in his arms all night, wrapped in wet blanket, but it was too late. . ."

Days followed that were to Derrick the most impossible of nightmares: the time that she had spent on the stairs that night seemed in her memory the length of a week, or a month, or a year . . . but those days afterward had the swiftness and unreality of a dream. There remained in her mind pictures of hushed children from whom she held herself apart; of the cold, glaring church full of flowers and children, stiff, in rows . . of their church, which seemed like a strange place, with the hard light and the flower scent and the rows of white-faced children.

75

After the funeral followed the still worse nightmare of whispered threats against Mrs. Greeley . . . kind-hearted Mrs. Greeley. As though it were her fault! Esther had done all she could to hide her illness from her! Derrick imagined dramatic scenes in which she shouted to a multitude that she was to blame, and not Mrs. Greeley . . . but not the most agonizing of imagined penances could make up to her for having to listen to the unsparing comment in the town. She dodged every one, and skulked around corners, close to fences and buildings, but could not escape, first, the news that Mrs. Greeley had lost all her patients, and then that she had moved out in the night and gone to the city. . . .

Esther's death came at a most unfortunate time for Derrick, for vacation began almost at once; Jack went with his family to Michigan for the summer, and as soon as Mary had recovered she was sent West to her father. Andrew worked that summer as errand boy in one of the grocery-stores, and Pete went into his father's meat-store. Derrick did not seek companionship; all that she asked was to be let alone . . . but if Jack or Andrew had been there to whistle at the front gate for her, she would have responded, and little time would have been left for morbid contemplation of her sins.

Her only defense against her thoughts and against her desolate loneliness she found in books. She went through her father's library systematically, and tried at least a page or two of everything she had not read before. Some of them proved to be tales that she would be ashamed to be found reading, so she took to crawling under the couch in the library. She lay flat on her stomach, only her shoulders and elbows and head projecting from the end of the couch above the book. It was not a very comfortable position, but one that enabled her to withdraw, like a turtle, into complete obscurity when she heard the approach of any one. But from entire forgetfulness of the world she would be swept suddenly by a flood of despair when she caught herself listening for Esther's whistle, or wondering what kept her so long. . . . Once, when, because of the tears that dropped on her page, she had had to give up all pretense of reading, and lay sobbing with her head on her arms, she remembered the composition she had written about Happiness. That had been only last September . . . not a year ago . . . but it seemed like another life and another world and another person. She could not remember what she had said, but the very thought of having written about Happiness with such assurance seemed fantastic.

Although Mrs. Thornton rightly attributed Derrick's languor and indifference to the shock of Esther's death, she was not conscious for a while of the unnatural state of Derrick's mind, nor of the unhappy and unhealthy way in which she spent her time. When, finally, she awakened to the fact that Derrick had hardly been out-of-doors all summer, she was puzzled to find some way in which to rouse her; she could not order her to go out and play: there was no one for her to play with. In the end she decided to accompany the doctor every day on his country calls, and to leave Derrick to "keep an eye on the children." Derrick, although of course ignorant of why she was left with them, rebelled anew each day, and begged and scolded, but her mother was obdurate.

"Keeping an eye on the children" was too strenuous for one who had for some time led the life of a melancholy ascetic—for one, who had suddenly—in a night, it seemed —outgrown the time when she could endure more than half an hour of screeching and scuffling and tumbling up and down the terrace wall and about the yard. For several days, Mrs. Thornton returned to find Derrick sullenly withdrawn from the tumult, the boys irritable and disheveled, and Margaret in tears. She appealed to Derrick's vanity then, by asking her if she could not manage them better than that —and Derrick, realizing that from a certain point of view Billy and Hunter and Margaret could be looked upon as characters, became interested at once.

Billy, she found, could be argued with: if he could be made to see reason, he acted upon it. If you could prove to him that, if he didn't come and wash at once, he wouldn't be washed when dinner was ready, he responded promptly. Once in a while he refused to be convinced, and then all the king's horses and men could not move him. Hunter could be appealed to only through his affections: if he would not come in and clean up because you and your mother and father would be ashamed of him if he didn't, then nothing would serve but physical force. Derrick knew that it was stupid of her to have to resort to violence so often, and she marveled at her mother's ability to avoid coming to an issue with him. Derrick's method was to wrestle and bang away at him until she had him pushed into a fence corner, where she held him with her hands on his chest, her eyes battling his. Ten minutes after complete physical collapse, he would come to her with some cherished treasure as a propitiatory gift. Once, when she held him in a corner of the living-room, he glared at her with such insane fury in his black eyes that she was terrified . . . her taunts died on her lips, she let him go, and dropped into a chair trembling. They looked at each other, first in amazement, then with the dawn of a new understanding. A little later he brought her his favorite engine as a gift; after that she had less trouble with him.

Her interest in her brothers as problems to be solved soon became a whole-hearted liking for them both, particularly for Hunter, whose expressions of affection made almost welcome the outbursts which preceded them. Not that she had disliked them before, but rather that they had entered her consideration very little, except at Christmas and birthdays, which hardly count as the gauge of one's everyday feelings.

When the summer came to an end, Derrick was almost fortified in spirit, and ready to meet Jack and Mary when they returned quite as though nothing had happened. To their tales of the summer's adventures, she listened with no more than the usual amount of envy, and with no fear in regard to their attitude toward her; as if they could have known, anyway, she told herself, that she had been responsible for Esther's death!

If they continued to miss Esther, they said little of it; but the experience left Derrick with a feeling of uncertainty as to the future. At any moment punishment might descend upon her for some long-forgotten sin. The only guard—and what a feeble one, if a sin were not recognized as such when it was committed!—was to walk carefully in the strait and narrow path, and to make a mental note of all the little sins as you went along, in order to be prepared. But that would make life awfully complicated: you could not do the simplest thing without stopping to ask whether or not it would come back like a boomerang and knock you down . . . . Life, she decided, was not a road at all, but a swamp, and whatever direction you took, there were sure to be holes to fall into, more or less deep. And there were no signs posted for the deepest ones, to warn you. . . . But she did not wonder then whether it were your own fault if you fell into them. It was not quite so simple as she had thought once: you could not always decide beforehand whether you would sin or not, and, sinning, be ready for your punishment; but it had not yet been complicated still further by a doubt as to whether unhappiness was a punishment, and a deserved one. That question she met the next year. . . .

ᕫᕫᕫᕫᕫᕫᕫ V ᕫᕫᕫᕫᕫᕫᕫ

WHEN THE DELIGHTS of the autumn offered themselves in
the same old way, to be had for the asking, all the children
—Mary and Derrick and Andrew and Jack—tried to pretend that they would, of course, go on as they always had
done: racing through the streets of Tecumseh and rambling
over the countryside. But Derrick was always conscious of
effort, not only on her own part, but on the part of the
others: she thought that, if she did not hold them firmly to
the old ways, they would break from them. She could not
explain the cause: it was not the loss of Esther, for she had
been a follower and not a leader; it was not that their
numbers were less, for Agnes Patterson, who had been taken
out of the convent school and sent to school in Tecumseh,
had been accepted as one of them without question. Derrick
rebelled at the idea of any change, unconscious that the
change was in herself as much as in the others. She would
have denied it indignantly. She refused to see that there
could be any life but the old life, and refused so stalwartly
that there was no slightest hint from the others that there
was anything they would change. But they were not adept
at self-deception.

Derrick found that they did not always join her in things
they had previously done together. There was the "Uncle
Tom's Cabin" parade . . . they had stood on the corner after
school, while they waited, surrounded by other children,
black and white . . . it had not occurred to Derrick to spend

the afternoon in any other way; she was no less interested than she had always been. At the passing of little Eva in her pony-cart, Derrick was brushed into the gutter by the press of children behind her; she did not look around to see if her friends were there, too, but followed after the pony-cart. It was the orthodox thing to do, following little Eva up one street and down another, and this year, as a student of character, she looked upon her with more interest than before: looked less adoringly and more speculatively. She saw that the velvet dress was worn and the lace coarse; that the long golden curls were unnatural, the cheeks beneath the rouge pathetically thin, the smile a mere stamp. This was not disillusion, but an invitation to the imagination to revel freely: Derrick wondered how Eva lived, when she slept, when she went to school . . . perhaps she was starved, perhaps she was beaten when she didn't act well. . . . She stared at the thin face intently, and was pleased when, as she thought, the child really smiled at her. She turned to call Mary's attention to the smile, and saw at once that neither Mary nor Jack, nor any one she knew, was anywhere to be seen. She was alone in the throng of bareheaded, barefooted little colored children, whose white teeth gleamed with delight at the unparalleled beauty of Eva and the antics of Topsy; the only white children, so far as she could see, were little ragamuffins from the "Bottoms." She withdrew in chagrin.

Billy pointed the finger of scorn at her that night at the dinner-table. Billy at twelve was the perfect picture of a future leading citizen.

"Mother, what do you think I saw this afternoon? Derrick, following the parade, along with all the little niggers from the South End!"

"Derrick!"

"Well, if I did—it's none of his business!"

She was furious with Billy and with her friends who had betrayed her, but on that one point she could bring herself to agree with the world. She admitted that perhaps when you were in High School you were too old to follow parades.

Soon afterward there occurred at school an incident which might have shown Derrick that on one subject at least she could never feel with her friends, but her whole being was so flooded with sick disgust and loathing that she failed to realize that the rest of them were amused. . . . She hardly noticed them; she could think of nothing but that she was glad she had always hated Bill Sheehan. .

One morning he had come to school shaken and pallid . . . "sick," the boys had said, grinning uncomfortably. Bill trembled when he rose, and had to hold on to the desk, and his face was a startling pasty color. When one of the teachers spoke to him suddenly, he turned green and fled from the room, a grimy hand across his mouth and terror in his eyes. Later, their English class was interrupted by a rap at the door; Miss Herbert opened it, and they saw on the threshold the Catholic priest with the High-School Principal. Bill was called from the room—he staggered as he got to his feet and lurched against the blackboard as he walked out. The door closed behind him, and he did not reappear. Derrick could see that practically every one in the class except herself knew why Father Reilly had come for Bill. They kept glancing at the closed door with a furtive, knowing curiosity.

After school, Derrick wormed the story out of Mary. Agnes had told her. Derrick did not ask who had told Agnes, nor why, if Agnes had been willing to repeat it to Mary, she had not told her, too. . . . Maggie Seddon, who lived in the "Bottoms" behind the railroad station, had had a baby the night before, and every one knew the baby was Bill's. The priest had come for him to make him marry Maggie; he would have to stop school, now, and get a job. . . . Mary's cheeks were flushed, yet even she could laugh a little, shame-facedly. Derrick tried to laugh, but could not.

Still, Derrick held Mary and Jack and Andrew to their old customs, in which they dared not admit they found little pleasure. There came a Saturday in October, however, so exactly like all the other glorious October Saturdays—and had they not known October immemorially?—that it would have been impossible to believe that they could be different in any way. When above them there were the same crystalline sky, the same piling white clouds, the same old vivid reds in maple and oak trees—when at their feet they found again tawny grasses and piles of poplar leaves blowing—could they think that they themselves had changed?

They had planned beforehand to spend the day gathering chestnuts, and they had asked Dr. Thornton to have Ben hitch the carriage in the morning instead of the buggy, so that when he went into the country on his calls, he could take them as far as the lane that led back to the woods. . . . Here they raced down the grass-grown way between a row of young locust trees whose yellow leaves blew in gusts from the branches; they scrambled over the gray snake fence whose corners were full of goldenrod and plunged headlong into the woods. Certainly, here, all was as it had always been: the same deep hush, the same golden light that fell through thinning branches, the same silent water flowing over the brown leaves of the summer just gone, dark where the banks were high, translucent in the shallows where the sun fell on it. They shouted their exultation, they swung on every grapevine that would hold them, and played tag back and forth across the creek. Beyond sight of the lane they came upon an old wagon trail where fresh-cut timber was piled in cords, and where the acrid scent of the raw wood filled the air. There was no sound: whoever had cut the wood was gone. The trail led them to a small clearing where stood what might once have been called a van; now its wheels were so buried in grass and weeds, its general air was one of such decay, as to preclude any idea of its being moved.

They stopped short and gazed at it. From the crazy iron stovepipe, wired to the roof, came a thin wisp of smoke. Three dubious steps led to a door in the rear, which was closed; there were torn and soiled lace curtains in the tiny unglazed windows.

"Gypsies," said Derrick.

"Woodcutter," said Jack. "Didn't you see the wood layin' back there?"

"What do you bet? Woodcutters live in huts, and, besides, whoever heard of a woodcutter outside of fairy tales?"

"I betcha whatcha dare. How y' gonna prove it? I dare you go an' ask."

"I'll ask 'em. I'll ask 'em for a drink, an' then I'll say, 'Are you a woodcutter?' An' if it's gypsies . . . if it's gypsies. . . ."

"If it's gypsies," said Jack gallantly, "we'll yell bloody-murder."

She left the others where they stood, and advanced with caution. When she was half a dozen paces from the door, it was opened and a man came heavily down one step, and stopped there. Derrick stopped, too, terror clutching at her heart. He was a tall, clumsy man in shapeless overalls and a corduroy coat . . . he was unshaven and unkempt, his bloodshot eyes stared at her without curiosity. She realized that he did not intend to speak, and so she stammered a request for a drink.

"Drink? If the's water, hit's in th' bucket hangin' on the nail here."

Driven by some instinct of hospitality, he came stumbling down the steps to show her where the bucket and the cup hung on the side of the wagon. As he did so, some one within moaned and called out hoarsely. Derrick backed away, her hand over her mouth to suppress her startled exclamation, but she did not go so far that she could not look through the door he had left open. On one side, within, was a battered rusty stove and a box covered with a piece of carpet, evidently used as a chair. On the other side was a cot heaped with a confusion of soiled bedding in the midst of which lay some one tossing ceaselessly from side to side. It was a woman: Derrick could see her matted hair as she turned her head on the mattress, first one way, and then the other.

The man brought the cup of water, and Derrick moved forward to take it. From where she stood there she could see within more plainly. The woman gripped, as if her life depended on it, the end of a lace curtain tied to the wooden bar across the foot of the cot. Her face was a deadly whitish yellow, and the flesh so sunken that it looked as if her cheekbones might cut through it. And she moaned continually . . . dreadful moans, with nothing human in them, but guttural and loud and uncontrolled, like an animal.

"Is there," said Derrick choking, "some one sick?"

"She's havin' a kid." The man's hand shook so that he could hardly hold the teacup out to her . . . and she could not take it. She was sick and dizzy, as though some one had hit her a terrific blow just below the end of her breastbone.

"Why don't you get a doctor?"

"They ain't no doctor inside o five mile, an' I hain't no way to git one."

"My father's a doctor, an' he's just down the road apiece. I could get him in fifteen minutes if I ran."

"Then, fer Gawd's sake, kid, run!" He poured what was left of the water out on the grass, and, dangling the cup from his finger, staggered back to the wagon. "Mame—there's a kid here says she'll fetch a doctor!"

Derrick did not wait to hear if the moaning had stopped, but turned and ran. The others had been beyond earshot, but when she plunged toward them, white as a sheet, they took to their heels and raced noisily through the woods, tripping, tearing their clothes on briars, and whipping their faces with twigs. They did not stop until they were safely in the lane.

"Was it gypsies?" Agnes asked, as Derrick emerged from the woods.

She stopped astride the rails to catch her breath and brush the hair out of her eyes.

"Scared-y cats! Nothin' but a woman sick, an' I said I'd get a doctor. Andrew, you're a better runner'n I am. You run, too—Father had to stop at Jackson's just down the hill

85

from the end of the lane—if he's gone from there, telephone McFarland's for him. Th' rest of you needn't hurry—there's no one after you." She leaped from the fence, drew a long breath, and flung back her head. "Ol' cowardy-calves!" And she darted away down the lane.

Andrew was ahead of her from the start, but she felt that she must go as fast as she could: it was her obligation, not his. She could have gone faster, she thought, if she hadn't seen the woman. She couldn't help thinking about her, and it made her choke and stumble. This October day had turned out differently from other October days, after all. It wasn't, perhaps, that things were different, but just that she was finding out that they had never been like what she thought. What she thought the world was like was just an outside shell over the horror underneath. Perhaps your own happiness depended not at all on what you did or didn't do, and had to be punished for, but on how well you avoided breaking through that pleasant shell to look upon the reality underneath . . . you might forget that it was there if you didn't see it often. . . .

This that passed through her mind as she ran, breathless and agonized, was a confused jumble with other more reasonable thoughts—that she had no idea the lane was so long; that it was hard to run where the long grass hid the ruts and you tripped in them; that no wonder Bill Sheehan had looked sick, if he knew that *that* was what it was like; that she must wait for a minute to get her breath and stop the pain in her side; that Andrew was so far ahead of her that it didn't matter, now, whether she ran or not.

When, after a lifetime of racing and staggering, recovering her breath and losing it, after a lifetime of looking at clumps of grass as she approached them and as they disappeared under her feet she finally came to the end of the lane, she saw her father's carriage at the foot of the hill. Andrew had reached him already. She dropped onto the trunk of a willow at the edge of the road, a willow that had been cut down, but whose branches had already taken root in the ditch by the culvert. Strange the things you notice! She waved to her father as he passed, then waited for Andrew to come from down the road, and the others from the lane.

They didn't wait for the doctor, but walked in, without any chestnuts. They could get nothing from Derrick beyond the fact that the man's wife was sick, and he had asked her to bring a doctor. Nor did Derrick ask her father about the woman afterward, her reticence due to her desire to forget it all. She did not want any one, ever, to say anything that would remind her of it.

The occurrence was not so completely forgotten that Derrick did not, now and then, congratulate herself because she had not thought of it for a long while, but, as a matter of fact, most of her attention was successfully diverted, in the following weeks, by affairs at school and on games indoors and out. It grew colder, darkness came earlier, and evenings out-of-doors were given up for everings in the house, with books around the library table, or with some game-board by the fireplace. Derrick forgot her feeling that her friends were not all that they had been. She became the unquestioned authority on doubtful points of Latin or algebra, and Mary and Jack were glad enough to accept her "Come around to-night, and we'll study together." Their evening's business was sometimes interspersed with gossip about those lordly creatures, the Juniors and Seniors, some of whom, the football-players particularly, were extravagantly admired, and with delightful plans, which never quite met the approval of their stern and Puritanic parents, for one of those evening affairs which you attended in prearranged couples. . . . But the even tenor of their way was spoiled for Derrick by a quarrel with Jack.

She met him one afternoon, with Billy, starting off with their muskrat traps. Jack refused flatly and stubbornly—growing more stubborn and more frank in the face of her amazement—to let her go with them.

"The fellas don't want a lot o' girls taggin' along."

"But I don't tag!" she said furiously, "and I'm not 'a lot o' girls.'"

"If you went, the others'd want to."

"But they never did want to—"

"Well, I can't help what the fellas say, can I? Y' can't go, an' that's all there is to it."

Derrick said no more. Pride supported her—pride that would not let her reveal before Billy the depth of her hurt. But for Jack to scorn her! Strange and inconsistent world that reversed in one short year, simply because of their difference in sex, the positions of Billy and her as accepted equal, now rejected "tagger"! But no one should know that Jack did not want her, and he would not soon be put in a position where he could scorn her again.

Her opportunity for revenge came sooner even than she had hoped. Their class, which now for the first time, being in High School, counted in its membership a number of children from the country, was invited to end a Friday night hayride with supper at the Wheelers'. This was the Wheeler who had a flour-mill down the river near the ruins of the old stone mill of the pioneers. It was their first party of the kind, and, though outwardly they were blasé, it was recognized as an occasion.

Jack, anxious to remove from himself the blight of Derrick's cool indifference, accosted her after school one afternoon.

"Derrick—wait a minute, can't you?"

She waited, with the abstracted air of one who can snatch but a moment from some weighty affair.

"Got a bid for Friday night?"

"What's that to you?"

"Aw, Derrick, listen!" Jack reddened. "What I want to know is, will you go with me?"

"How's it come you want me to go to a party with you, but not trapping?"

Jack's flush faded, and his eyes glittered.

"It's different. Girls are all right at parties."

"It isn't different at all. If you don't want my company once, you don't get it the next time."

"All right. I'll ask somebody else."

He walked on, and left Derrick with a blank, empty feeling. She had expected to be softened and won over by his pleading. It took quite a little reasoning to convince her that only this severe measure would really avenge her wrongs— reasoning that was shattered when she learned that Jack had promptly asked Agnes to go with him, and that she had as promptly accepted. Derrick was not in the least unaware of Agnes's superior attractions. . . .

Her severity with Jack left her a problem of her own. She was sure that Pete McInnis intended to ask her, and while Pete was all right to go trapping with, she was not sure that she wanted to go to a party with him. But suppose it were a choice of Pete or no party at all? One could not go without an escort, Andrew had already asked Mary to go with him, and Bill Stewart—a gray-eyed, dark-haired, and handsome country boy, with whom she had grown friendly in study periods—was too uncertain a possibility: she was afraid that, if Bill couldn't take Agnes, he wouldn't take any one. It was very complicated. She finally asked her mother's advice.

"Has he asked you yet?" Mrs. Thornton wanted to know.

"No . . ."

"Aren't you crossing a bridge—?"

"He's going to. I dodged him all day to-day, but I could see it in his eye. And it's either him or nobody," she added gloomily.

"Are you sure? Won't Jack—?"

"Jack did, but I'm mad at him."

"So that's it! I thought he hadn't been around much lately. Well, I tell you, Derrick: at a class party, in a small town like this, where you know every one, and there's no real reason why you shouldn't go with a person, it would be mean and contemptible to refuse him unless you really had a previous engagement."

Accordingly, Derrick went to the party with Pete. The hayride she liked—down the river road in the shadow of the hills, beneath the great bare black trees: it didn't matter then with whom you were coupled, although she suspected, with disgust, that some pairs were holding hands under the blankets. She kept her muff outside, to avoid suspicion. The party proper she found almost wholly unpleasant . . . they played post-office, while she watched, in rage and chagrin; she so obviously disapproved that she was left severely alone, and spent most of the evening on the couch with two lumpish country girls. Derrick couldn't decide whether they really disapproved of the game, or only pretended to because no one asked for them . . . it gave her a comfortable feeling of superiority, because there would have been "letters" enough for her if she had wanted them. At any rate, she couldn't have had such a miserable time as they because she enjoyed the evening as a spectacle. To dispose of her classmates, she thought of their discomfiture when they should find themselves in her printed pages, their behavior portrayed in its disgustingness . . . she then turned her attention to the setting: a cramped, airtight little farmhouse filled to the bursting point with commotion. She consciously memorized its details: false mantelpiece, with a looped drapery, littered ornaments, and bright-colored glass vases; walls hung with fantastic oil paintings, enlarged portraits and framed family groups; an upright piano, draped like the mantelpiece; a set of horsehair furniture, and, in one corner, a massive chair elevated on a framework that groaned protestingly beneath the rockers. The room was lighted by a coal-oil lamp hung on chains from the ceiling . . . later in the evening, when they danced the Virginia reel so violently that the house shook, one of the taller boys leaped against the lamp, and some of the oil spilled out on him and the carpet; Mrs. Wheeler came hastily and unfastened the chains and hitched the lamp higher.

Only two parts of the evening were really pleasant: the Virginia reel, which they danced because most of them

were Presbyterians or Methodists who were not allowed to
dance anything else, and the supper, which they spread on
a long table that completely filled the dining-room. . . .
But Derrick's indignation over the kissing games was
somewhat mollified by Mary and Agnes. When she went
upstairs for her coat, she found them in the corner of the
low-ceilinged room, where they were attempting, both at
once, to regard themselves in a little square mirror framed
in a wide expanse of carved walnut. They whispered excitedly as they adjusted their woolly tams. Mary turned as
Derrick came in.

"Don't bite our heads off! What's the matter with you
to-night, anyway?"

"You know well enough what's the matter. I think you're
both perfectly sickening and disgusting."

Mary laughed, but Agnes cocked her head on one side
with a troubled air.

"We weren't disgusting, were we, Mary? We weren't
really soft at all. You don't have to be. All you have to do
is dodge around 'em and let 'em think the next time you will.
. . . Anyway, you've got to pretend to do what the rest do."

"Well, if you ask me, I think it's perfectly disgusting, and
I'm not coming to another single party this old class gives."

"Oh, Derrick! Don't get mad at us—"

"I'm not, but I might be if I came to another one."

She did not mean it, of course, and they knew that she
did not, but before the next party her mind was so absorbed
by other things that it caused her only the slightest pang to
discover that evidently no one of the boys cared to escort her
to it.

Derrick lingered in the dining-room one evening to tease
Margaret, after her father and the boys had gone. Her
mother had stopped to give Cassie some directions for the
morning. As they turned to go, Derrick pulled Margaret's
chair back from the table and help her to slide without
disaster from the dictionary on which she sat.

"It will seem funny, won't it, not to have a baby in the family when she goes to school next year." Derrick laughed as chubby Margaret dashed into the living-room after the boys. Her mother answered her remark so casually that at first she hardly bothered to listen.

"By next September when Margaret goes to school . . . there'll be another one in the family."

Derrick turned, startled.

"When?"

"March."

Derrick was embarrassed . . . but most of all she was frightened . . . and she could have bitten her tongue out for having given her mother the opportunity to tell her something she would have preferred not to know.

She realized at once that she had not in the least forgotten the glimpse of the sick woman in the van in the woods. Asleep and awake, thereafter, she had before her eyes the tumbled bed, the hands twisting the rag they clung to, the matted hair on the dirty mattress.

And, asleep and awake, there sounded in her ears the hoarse animal groans. She did not believe that anything in the world could be so awful as to make her mother groan like that . . . as though it were easier to groan than to keep from groaning. Derrick went out to the haymow, and, buried beyond earshot in the hay, practiced it, to see: at first, it took a lot of effort to do it at all, but finally, she let herself go enough to moan a little with every breath. But they were mild gentle moans . . . she could not drive her imagination to the point where she could make the noises that woman had made. . . . She wondered if the woman had recovered afterward. They didn't sometimes, of course . . . she knew enough to know that. Her mind, which never stopped short of the ultimate possibility, dwelt upon that contingency and recoiled. . . . She lay in the hay for a long while fighting that thought.

She would not let herself think of that again. Sometime in March, her mother had said; she must, then, shut off all her thoughts of the future this side of March, as though a wall were built, or a curtain let down, at the end of February. As the days passed, she became absorbed in her dread. Before this her refuge from any unpleasant thought had been her dreams of the distant future; now she recalled her mind sharply from any such flight. She was forced to live in the immediate present. In a swift alternation of moods, she was driven from Mary and Agnes to a constant attendance on her mother, and then was driven back to them to escape seeing her convulsed with agony as the woman in the van had been convulsed. She said not a word to anyone; her mother, somewhat preoccupied herself, took no note of Derrick's apprehension, but accepted with pleasure her willingness, which she attributed to the breach with Jack, to stay in the house and keep her company or to run on errands for her.

Derrick concentrated her thought on the holidays with a passion she had never felt before . . . but because Christmas was so perfect it seemed to her almost like an omen. Afterward, there was nothing before her but suspense . . . nothing to anticipate in January and February . . . nothing to which she could give her thoughts, as she had pinned them to Christmas throughout December. Whenever she had done her best to forget that the year would go beyond the first of March, something inevitably came up to remind her of it. The simplest conversation was fraught with peril, full of references to spring or summer, and hence likely to twist her mind away from the present and throw it, recoiling, into the future.

There was Washington's Birthday, for instance: a holiday celebrated, according to family tradition, by serving cherry pie for dinner. But this year there were no cherries left on the pantry shelves when February came, and Derrick was in the kitchen when her mother scolded Cassie for her improvidence.

"This summer we'll have to put up more cherries, though

how you could have used all those jars I cannot see. Remind me of it when the cherries are ripe, and, if I'm too busy with the baby to bother, I'll get some one to help you."

Derrick said, in a matter-of-fact tone, that she guessed she could seed cherries for Cassie, but she shivered apprehensively.

Worse than that casual reference was Cassie's remark to the doctor at the dinner-table one night. He had refused dessert because he had to hurry off to the South End for a visit to Liz Tyler. Liz was a neighbor of Cassie's and not regarded by her with any great amount of respect. She stopped behind his chair with the rejected plate of apple dumpling.

"Lawdy, suh! Y'ain't gwine widout yo' desse't jes' 'cause Liz done had anudde' baby? Dat gal jes' lak a rabbit—she heb one eb'ry time de moon change!"

To Derrick's horror, her father laughed . . . and even her mother, she suspected, in spite of the fact that she spoke sharply to Cassie, for she retired behind her napkin, shaking. . . . Poor miserable self-conscious Derrick sat stonily as if she had not heard.

One snowy afternoon in February, she went up into her room after school and found her mother there in the midst of a pile of last summer's gingham dresses, which she had taken out of the bureau drawers.

"Why, Mother! What on earth are you doing with those things to-day?"

"Well—I just thought—it may turn warm suddenly—it always does—and then you will want these to put right on, and it may be just when I'm too busy or not able to let them down. I thought I'd get them out and do it while I can. If you will, you can help me—carry these to the sewing room, and rip out the hems."

Derrick kissed her mother as she stooped over for an armful of the outgrown dresses, and turned away quickly, so that she would not be asked what was the matter with her, anyway. . . .

The weeks dragged on slowly, and Derrick's fears shadowed her night and day; when she dressed in the morning, when she went from classroom to classroom, when she lay in bed at night, unable to sleep. She was so unhappy that she thought again about Happiness.

"After all," she decided, "unhappiness must come whether you deserve it as a punishment or not. Lots of people that deserve to be punished are happy. . ." She rose one night and got her Bible: it was the only authority on punishments and rewards that she knew. She turned at once to "All the ways of a man are clean in his own eyes, but the Lord weigheth the spirits." It was conceivable, of course, that while you held yourself blameless, the Lord might not —and, as for the wicked, it might be true that they would be punished after death. . . Her eye ran on down the page and came to "A man's heart deviseth his way: but the Lord directeth his steps." How then could a man be responsible for what he did? She had always known that he couldn't help doing things—had she not had to learn the Catechism that said so? Then why must he be punished? The Bible was a poor comfort . . . she slapped it shut and stared at it rebelliously. How did anyone find any consolation in it when it said one thing on one page and another on the next? She thought of her great-grandmother, sitting day after day with the Bible open on her knee. She might ask her, sometime, what she thought—she was too little interested in Derrick to regard it as anything but a theological question—she would not wonder why she was troubling her head about things like that.

When she next took her great-aunts their library books, she found old Mrs. Ferguson in her bedroom, beside the hearth, her slippered feet on the fender, her black silk dress turned back over her knees, the tiny hunched figure dwarfed by the old canopied feather bed behind her.

Derrick delivered the messages from her family, and then wandered restlessly around the room, while she tried to think of an opening remark. She stopped beside the window to look at the circle of rosebushes in the yard below, wrapped in straw and burlap to save them from freezing.

"Don't stand there in the cold, Anne." Her great-grandmother never attached the right name to the right person, now. "Come sit by the fire and stop fidgeting. What is there to see?"

"The rosebushes. They look like crooked old witches playing ring-around-the-rosy."

But the old lady said only, "Eh? What's that you say?" in her quavering, bewildered voice. Derrick came to the fire, pulled up a stool, and sat there playing with the fire tongs.

"I have to write a composition about 'Happiness.'" Her recollection that she had had to write one once suggested a beginning that sounded plausible. "I thought maybe you could help me."

"Happiness? I disremember that I ever wrote anything about that. There was one about 'Spring,' I think, and 'Death' and 'The Life Eternal' and 'The Last Farewell.' My exercise book that I wrote in when I was a girl in school is in the box with all my letters under the bed."

"Oh, no, Grandma—that isn't what I mean. What I mean is, do you ever think about happiness now?"

"What? Why should I think about happiness?"

"Well—you've lived so long—you've got as good a chance to know about it as any one. What I want to ask is —do you think everybody deserves the unhappiness they get?"

"Why, what a question! What has come over the child!"

"Well, it's for the composition."

"It's not for us to question Providence. The Lord Almighty sends us what unhappiness is needed to rebuke our spirits and turn our minds to Him—"

"But what if our spirits haven't done anything to be rebuked for?"

The old lady shook her head. "We are all sinners, Nell,

my dear. 'In Adam's fall, we sinned all.' Because of that we endure misery on earth for all our length of days—and if our sins had not been redeemed, the punishment would have been an eternal one. As it is, we may hope for salvation."

"But the Bible says the Lord makes us do the things we do—"

"Yes—because of the original sin, all mankind is foreordained to sin."

"But it isn't fair to punish us for things we can't help. Weren't you ever unhappy because of something you couldn't help doing?"

Mrs. Ferguson looked at her for a moment vaguely, as from a great distance, then leaned over suddenly and patted Derrick's shoulder.

"Honey, all of us, lots of times, are unhappy because we worry about things we don't need to worry about. But even that is a punishment we deserve, for not having more faith in the Lord Almighty." Derrick shrank back, aghast at the thought that, after all, her great-grandmother might realize that she was unhappy about something. The quavering voice continued, "No, I can't think now that I was ever more unhappy than I deserved—"

"But, Grandma! You never sinned so very much, and so many dreadful things happened—"

"You don't know anything about the sins, and the punishment was never more than what I could bear."

"But, Grandma—"

"The worst was when I set too much store by some one in the family—thought more of them than of the Lord Himself—then, when they were taken, I thought I couldn't stand it—but now for thirty, thirty-five years I have remembered that 'man's chief end is to glorify God'—and I have my reward—"

"Do you mean that the last thirty years of your life have been the happiest?" Derrick demanded inexorably.

The old lady looked at her startled. "I haven't been *unhappy*, to amount to anything, in thirty years—" But she sighed, and stared at the fire vacantly. From a rather awe-inspiring seer, she changed once more to a feeble, garrulous old lady. Derrick sighed, too, and wondered—she couldn't see that everything her great-grandmother had said was entirely reasonable, but it was plain that no argument could shake the theory that you got what you deserved, no more and no less—

After a moment of silence, she rose to leave.

"Going now, are you? Well—as you go out, I wish you would tell Ursula to send more coal for my grate. And you might ask your father to bring me some more of that medicine for my indigestion when he comes down for Sabbath-day supper."

Before Derrick had decided whether the whole Thornton family deserved to be punished for loving her mother more than God, the day that she had dreaded came and went, and amounted to very little, after all. Early one Saturday morning she heard her father talking to Aunt Anne on the telephone, and when she went in to breakfast he told her that she and Billy had been invited to go down to Cincinnati with Aunt Anne and her children to spend the day shopping. They were overjoyed, of course—they went to the city too seldom not to be excited by the trip; it was not until they were on the train coming home that Derrick's conscience reproached her for having left her mother. She was stunned to learn on their arrival that the day was the long dreaded day of horror, but that no disaster had occurred, and the house still stood on its foundations.

With a passionate revulsion of feeling, Derrick loved the new baby. There could have been nothing so perfect as the cloudy-eyed, downy-haired mite. He spent his waking moments in her arms before the fireplace in her mother's room, where she rocked him and patted him and toasted his feet at the blaze. She fought bitterly the name "Henry" chosen by her parents, and insisted upon calling him "Henshi," which she saw in her mind's eye spelled "Hänsje."

It was easy to see, now, that her great-grandmother had been right about happiness and unhappiness. She had worried unnecessarily about what had been in the hands of God, and her unhappiness of those months had been due to her lack of faith . . . that question she dismissed as settled. There remained in her mind, however, a shadow of misgiving. She remembered the shell on the surface of things that must not be broken through . . . what you had to learn, evidently, was how to live so that you would not break through it. What was that quotation about "Happy is the man that findeth wisdom"? But wisdom and knowledge were different things, of course: that had been made quite clear in Sunday-school on that long-past day when she had learned the quotation. It was knowledge that you gained by breaking through the shell and looking upon reality. Wisdom . . . what was the greatest wisdom? If refraining from doing things kept you from being unhappy, surely doing things—the right things —brought you greater happiness. But what were the right things? At that time it seemed to her that she must choose either to live with people and run the risk of being brought face to face with horror, or to hold herself aloof and refuse to give things a chance to happen.

She was fortified in her prompt choice of the latter course by a favorable circumstance. At the end of April, her father had bought an automobile, in order that he might more easily and more speedily make his country calls. There were not many automobiles in Tecumseh then, and you could justify your possession of one only by proving that it was essential to the success of your business. When the doctor was not using his for that purpose, he took his family out with him; at other times, Derrick rode in the country behind her father's old horse Tom. The doctor would not sell him, but the horse could not spend his life in the stable, therefore Derrick was given permission to take him out whenever and wherever she chose, provided she herself hitched and unhitched him. Ben was too busy now with the new automobile to wait on Derrick and her friends. It was practically the same thing, as she told Mary and Agnes when she invited them to go with her, as having a horse of your own; and the pride of ownership was strong in her when she slapped the reins across the back of fat old Tom.

VI

BUT RENUNCIATION was not enough. Derrick learned, finally, the last chapter of the lesson on happiness: that you might fight for it in vain; that often it was only a choice of the less unhappy course; but it took her two years to discover what unhappiness she could accept in the struggle for that happiness which she would not surrender.

It was not difficult to persuade Agnes and Mary to ride with her: any new amusement was entered upon with enthusiasm. Every pleasant afternoon they spent crowded in the narrow seat of the buggy, where, one on each side of Derrick, they disputed with her as to what direction they should take. That their conversation, once they had started, turned upon recent and more or less entertaining encounters with the opposite sex did not bother Derrick: she was too absorbed in the responsibility of driving Tom to heed them much, and too engrossed in her own thoughts. That the road chosen led almost always to a farmhouse where dwelt one or another of the boys in their class was the most natural thing in the world: there was hardly a road from town that would not do that, and it was to Derrick as to the others an hilarious moment when they passed a field where Bill Stewart was ploughing, or when they met him on a lonely road on the seat of a rattling farmwagon, clad in overalls, boots, and corduroys, and laughed to see him pull his straw hat down over his face and, thus sheltered, pretend not to see them.

The advent of summer, Derrick found, was a new and different thing, watched day by day from some road that wound up and down across the countryside. Before, spring had meant a succession of beauties, but small beauties that you stumbled upon in the woods or the garden; this year she saw the picture as a whole: a never-ending procession of slow little hills, separated from each other at wide distances by a line of hedge, or by a rail fence that twisted itself awkwardly to the top of a hill and down again, or by a stream that wound in and out and away into the distance, lined on both sides by willow trees that changed day by day from pale yellow to vivid green, and by gaunt sycamores, still naked white when there were leaves on all the other trees. Some of the fields, where grain had been planted in the fall, were emerald when the last of the snow had melted, and grew more brilliant with every day's sunlight; some changed slowly their winter browns and russets to spring green, and in these groups of cattle fed lazily, or lay, all with their heads in one direction; or there were flocks of sheep beneath the ancient trees, gray against the grass. Always, here and there, a road climbed into sight and fell away, and there were farmhouses, the dwelling itself concealed in trees, but the barn unprotected in the open spaces, the orchards at one side, flowering against a background of young catalpa trees, the whole group insignificant in the wide landscape.

Then, when they turned toward home, there was the town stretched out before them on the horizon: a few roofs above the trees, church steeples, and high above all others, the court-house tower, with the great clock visible so far in the clear air.

In the evenings, Derrick turned with the delight of a discoverer to poems that she had had to memorize in school, or to those that her father had recommended and that she had read indifferently before. Echoes of them rang in her head all day; for the first time in her life, she saw the reason for poetry: men had seen these things: the "ploughman near at hand," who drove his horse along a rise of ground not far from the road, man and beast black against the sky; "hedge-row elms and hillocks green" . . . "shallow brooks and rivers wide" . . . at least, moderately wide; rivers bank-full in the spring, mud-colored, but reflecting, nevertheless, sky and cloud and overhanging trees . . . then, when they faced homeward, "towers and battlements bosomed high in tufted trees" . . . or, haunting her more persistently though less applicably, "What little town . . . is emptied of its fold this quiet morn?"

There was something about the endless sweep of the countryside—its deep peace and tranquillity—that made her think even more frequently of the Psalms than of the poems. This she would have been even less willing to say to the girls than she would have been to quote poetry: once she was betrayed into an allusion to the Bible, and made all three of them uncomfortable for a moment. All afternoon the clouds had hung motionless in the still air, although they towered so high that it looked as if a puff of wind would tumble them over; one, particularly, stood above the south-ern horizon like a burst of white smoke that had risen in a column and then had been frozen there, immobile. As the sun dropped from sight, the cloud turned the color of flame. They all exclaimed with delight, and Derrick said, "It was the pillar of cloud by day, and now it is the pillar of fire. I always wondered how it was done, really!"

But there was something about the land that was different from the poets' country, and from the Psalms: it was so limitless, and the ploughman was so tiny against the sky. It impressed Derrick as a living thing, greater and more endur-ing than mankind, and she tried to write, herself, a poem about it: something about the mighty land . . . the mighty land that lies sleeping while men strive and plough and reap and die, and all that they have done is lost . . . barns fall in, and orchards are blown and broken, and other men come and strive and plough and reap, and their grandsons plough and reap and die, and what they have done is destroyed, and the fields return again to what they were, and the forests creep back and grow tall and dark and impenetrable, and still the time is only a moment in the duration of the sleep that the land is sleeping. But Derrick couldn't write it, and she tore her paper into little bits and burned them, because she wanted to remember the idea as she had thought it in the first place, and not as it had turned out in black and white.

When school closed, Agnes and Mary left town for the vacation; Jack was at home that summer, but he was busy with his own amusements: the boys had a camp on the river where they went to fish and swim. Derrick saw him only once in a long while, when he came into town to spend a night and get some clean clothes. But she hardly thought of them. When she was at home, she played with the baby, or read, or lay in the hammock weaving intricate plots for stories that she intended to write—sometime. But usually she was not at home: she spent her days on the country roads, alone, or with a brother or a sister beside her in the buggy.

It was almost harvest-time, and the wheat, that had been green and but a hand's breadth high so short a while ago, was now above your shoulder, and turning from greenish yellow to gold . . . a gold that seemed even warmer and brighter where it alternated with the soft gray green of a field of oats. When July came, they cut the grain, and piled it in long lines across the fields; then, in a little while, they threshed. Every boy who could boast a friend in the country spent these days, from dawn until dark, on the farm. Billy disappeared every morning immediately after breakfast, and did not return until evening, when he came in exhausted and went at once to bed, shaking the chaff from his shoes and clothes onto the floor of the room that he and Hunter shared. Derrick regarded him with envy; she knew when she drove past Bill Stewart's that she would not be asked in, but hoped, always.

Every day she stopped the buggy at the entrance to the Stewart lane, and watched . . . the threshing-machine was hidden by the barns; you could see only the smoke and cloud of chaff blown across the fields, but you could hear the engine and the voices of the men, and the shrill whistle blown when they were ready for another load of grain. At the summons, one of the wagons in a distant field—so distant that the men and horses seemed like magic toys in the sunlight—would stop just long enough for one more sheaf to be pitchforked onto the load, then would come in a leisurely way through the field to the gate, across another field to a barely marked road at the edge of the pasture, and thence to the barnyard. If several wagons were full at the same time, they followed each other through the fields, a distant, slow procession.

When the harvest season ended, and one crop after another had been cut, and it seemed as if nothing could compensate for the lost beauty of the windblown grain, then the corn grew higher and higher, until its tossing green banners filled the lowlands, and you forgot the emptiness where the wheat had been and where now the tall weeds blossomed. When it was so high as to shut out all the landscape on both sides of the road, and the narrow lanes were like long green alleys, Derrick had not yet tired of exploring the country behind old Tom.

When September came, Derrick could no longer deny that they had changed, all of them, even from what they had been last year. The boys had put on long trousers during the summer, so that by the time school opened they were wearing them with an accustomed air. Derrick hated it . . . there never was anything so ridiculous, she told her mother, as those spidery-legged creatures. Then Agnes returned from the lake resort where they spent their summers, with her hair up and her skirts down; Derrick's first glimpse of her filled her with foreboding. Mary promptly had her skirts let down to her shoetops: that was to be expected; but Derrick fought when she turned her hair up like Agnes's, and rolled it in a knot under a bow at her neck; Mary's hair was too lovely to be hidden that way: the year before she had let it fall loose halfway down her back, where a ribbon had caught it together. But Mary laughed at her, and she gave up and followed suit, with a sort of bitter resignation; she could not deny, when Mary accused her of it, that she was fifteen. . . .

The three of them resumed their rides together, but even that was less pleasant than it had been. Agnes had brought back from her vacation an endless number of anecdotes of flirtations, and Mary, after a dull summer on the ranch, listened to them hungrily. Derrick wondered how Mary, who looked so angelic, and so—well, so untouchable, could care about that sort of thing. It didn't matter to her, really, what Agnes was like, but she preferred to think, until it should be proved otherwise, that Mary was untouchable.

Early in December, the farmers in the Stewart neighborhood planned a great fox drive and barbecue, in which every one in the county was invited to join. Bill insisted that his friends should make up a crowd, dress like tramps, and take part. The "crowd" proved to be Agnes and Mary, Andrew and Jack, and Derrick. The arrangement was that Derrick should take one of them—and she chose Jack to be that one —in the Thornton buggy, and Bill should come in with their carriage for the other; then Derrick could unhitch Tom at the Stewarts', and leave him in their barn for the day.

Although a fox drive is not a sport in which recognized members of society usually participate, Mary and Agnes looked forward to it with great eagerness—they were "dying," they said, to see what a fox drive was like. Derrick wondered at them: they did not like to walk; you would not think, now, that either of them had ever done anything so unladylike as to climb a fence, and they were not in the least curious, as Derrick was, to see what sort of people attended fox drives. . . . But it was only when she and Jack drove into the Stewart barnyard, where the others waited for them, that she discovered their perfidy. She had worn last winter's short skirt and Billy's old mackinaw and sweater and cap; but Agnes and Mary were arrayed to captivate. She would not have minded so much if the boys had been annoyed, as they would have been, once, to have on their hands two girls with long skirts and thin shoes and new cloaks, but to-day they looked upon them with admiration; for not only were they glorious in their apparel, but the wind had made their cheeks and eyes bright and had tossed Agnes's hair in curls on her forehead, while the sun, in Mary's was like spun gold. Derrick surveyed them in gloom; she pulled the peak of Billy's cap down over one eye, thrust her hands into the pockets of his mackinaw, and scowled. . . .

Once they had started, however, she forgot her displeasure in her excitement. She and Jack were alone on a hilltop, with Andrew and Mary in a field on one side, and Bill and Agnes on the other. The methods to be employed were primitive ones: a circle of men surrounded the country in a radius of five or six miles from the schoolhouse where the drive was to end; at first, when the circle was at its largest, there was only one man to a field. The foxes, and what other animals happened to respond, were roused by a clamor of horns and shouts and beaten tin pans, then, as the circle closed in about them, they were driven to the center, where they were clubbed to death. Any fox that ran in the wrong direction must be met and turned back, the other animals —rabbits, mostly, and skunks, were allowed to escape, unless they stupidly chose to run to the center, where they, too, were slaughtered. Your own responsibility, once your prey started in the right direction—and Bill was the only one of the six of them who roused a fox—was to see that none from the other side of the circle escaped between you. It was breathless suspense: you watched the ground before you on both sides, ready to dash to the right or left to stop an animal which would come like a streak of light. . . . As the drivers started toward the schoolhouse, they were so far apart that sometimes, in a valley, or a thicket, or following the line of stream to a bridge or a ford, there would be no one in sight of Derrick and Jack, and only the echoes of distant shouts were carried across the fields; but sometimes, in a level stretch, or on a hill, they came within calling distance of each other, and exchanged news of the chase.

As Derrick swayed precariously on a barbed-wire fence that Jack had not yet reached, she saw that Bill had stopped, at the other end of the fence where it disappeared in a grove of oaks, to hold it for Agnes to cross.

"Fat chance," she thought scornfully, "he'd have to stop anything that came that way!"—then as she scrambled through the thicket of elderberry and sumach that lined the fence, she saw a fox racing across the field toward her. Amazed, and transfixed by the unexpected beauty of color and motion, she could only shout to Jack. By the time he had leaped from the fence, the fox had disappeared in the thicket, and when the two of them stumbled through the bushes and crashed noisily through piles of dead leaves and over dead branches, he darted out, through the fence, away and over the hill they had just descended—like a flame through the grass, Derrick thought. She lamented his escape noisily, but inwardly rejoiced.

When the drive was over and the victims numbered, the feast was prepared: two oxen roasted in a hole in the ground, two iron cauldrons of beans baked above the fire, and coffee boiled. Derrick missed not a detail of the spectacle from then until the last of the slain foxes had been auctioned off from a stump in the school yard. The auctioneer was a tall, red-faced man in a worn beaver cap, a baggy corduroy coat, and faded blue overalls tucked into high boots; he held up the foxes one by one, with superfluous praise of their magnificence, while the wind blew past and stirred the bright hair of tail and back. . . . Around her, for the first time, Derrick saw against their own background people like those she had wondered about in town on Saturday nights. The men and boys were dressed almost uniformly like the auctioneer, the only difference being one of caps or presence or absence of a red bandanna around the neck. Most of them were strangers: uncouth, unkempt, raw-boned farmhands, whom one could not imagine in any other setting than the bleak December fields. The women were almost more interesting than the men; one never saw them in town in anything except their best. Here they wore whatever promised warmth and ease: knitted hoods, black or white, above red-cheeked, red-nosed faces, and disheveled hair; full-hipped jackets that could only have been new in the nineties; long skirts turned up and fastened as high as the knees with safety pins; knitted woolen petticoats, heavy, broken shoes, and, not infrequently, white stockings. Mary and Agnes were in sharp contrast to them: their city clothes seemed none the worse for thickets and barbed-wire fences, and they were the only girls on the field who hadn't red noses, Derrick noted with respect . . . but she couldn't think they were having a very good time, and she still wondered why they had wanted to come.

But when they started back to the Stewarts', late in the afternoon, and she found that they were not to tramp down the road six abreast, but two by two, the pairs widely separated, she knew: it was for this the girls had prepared, and not for the drive. . . . Scornfully, she strode down the road with Jack. They did not hurry, particularly: they stopped once while Jack chased a pig that had broken through a fence into the road, and saw him safely penned up; they lingered now and then to mention the sunset, or the spectacular effect of fence or haycock or leafless tree silhouetted black against the glowing sky . . . and then, after all that, they reached the Stewart house long before the others came. They had warmed themselves by the red-hot little stove in the sitting-room, and had recounted all the news of the drive before the four delinquents came shouting up the lane. Mrs. Stewart and Jack welcomed them vociferously, and pulled up chairs to the fire for them, and in the noise Derrick's moroseness escaped notice.

They were given what Mrs. Stewart called "just a pick-up supper,"—cold meat and salt-rising bread, jelly and jam and cake, pie and doughnuts, and tea. When they had eaten, the girls helped her with the dishes, while the boys went out to hitch. Derrick was pleased to find, when she entered the stable later, that Jack had not finished harnessing Tom. She wanted the others to go out first, and so, although she went around on the other side of the horse to help him, she spent as much time as she could fumbling with the buckles. Jack wasted time, too, turning away to tease the other girls, and it took no further manœuvring to get the carriage started off first down the lane.

She refused to give Jack the reins, because she wanted to overtake the carriage when its occupants had had a few minutes to themselves. She was going to find out how they behaved . . . if she could have presented the idea to Jack as a joke, she would have told him, but it was a serious matter with her. Her conversation with him was limited and rather short-tempered: her grievance against him was the belief that, although once upon a time she could have turned to him for support on any question, now they could hardly talk ten minutes without an argument, and the last thing in the world she wanted was another quarrel with Jack.

When they turned from the side road into the pike and began to climb the hill into town, she saw that they would pass the others with no particular effort on the part of Tom. Probably Bill had twisted the reins around the whip, and the horse was going as he pleased. She watched the carriage as they approached, and saw that that was the case; she shut her lips firmly and stared hard at the road ahead of her, too wrathful and heartsick to join in the noisy repartee that Jack exchanged with them as they passed. When Tom had drawn them away from the carriage, he turned to her fiercely.

"What in the dickens is the matter with you, Derrick? You've hardly spoken a decent word all evening. You act like I'd killed somebody."

"It's not what you've done so much as what you'd like to do." Then she realized with a sinking heart that she was about to quarrel with him, after all.

"What would I like to do?"

"You know perfectly well what I mean."

"Like Bill and Andrew? Gosh, don't you hate yourself!"

"Oh, not me!" She recoiled. "I mean that you'd like to be with Agnes or Mary."

"Well, Agnes or Mary might speak a decent word to me now and then. Honest, Derrick, I can't think what's got into you. Whoever would have thought that you would turn out such a goody-good!"

She was amazed. It had not occurred to her that any one would think her attitude due to any moral issue involved.

"I'm not goody-good. It isn't that. I simply think it's disgusting, that's all."

"You mean you don't think it's wrong? Then why do you make all the fuss about it?"

"Because it's sickening. I simply can't stand it—"

"Well, *why* can't you stand it? You keep saying that it's disgusting, but you don't say why—and if it's not wrong, I can't see why it's disgusting."

"I suppose it's like bad table manners. They aren't *wicked,* but they're disgusting."

Jack admitted her point, but then, after a minute, went on:

"But bad table manners wouldn't be disgusting if there wasn't anybody watching to be disgusted, an' I can't see why putting your arm around a girl isn't the same."

"But it would be disgusting to yourself, wouldn't it?" Jack did not reply, and she continued: "It's bad enough to act that way if you're in love, and you know perfectly well you're not in love. You're only fifteen, and whoever heard of being in love that young?"

It was Jack's turn to be horrified. "Of course I ain't in love. Do you have to want to marry a girl just because you put an arm around her?"

"You oughtn't to want to put an arm around a girl you didn't want to marry." In spite of everything, Derrick found herself arguing the question from a moral standpoint.

"Don't be silly, Derrick. It'll be five years before I want

111

to marry anybody—or maybe ten—do you think I oughtn't to put an arm around a girl for five years?"

"Well, how will you like to marry some girl that's had every-old-boy-in-this-town's arm around her? You know perfectly well you won't. You'll want to marry some one that hasn't ever had anybody's arm around her.

"There won't be any. Shoot! Do you think my father ever thinks about the people that maybe kissed my mother when she was fifteen? Do you think your mother never kissed anybody till she fell in love with your father?"

"Yes. I think so."

"I dare you to ask her."

"You can dare an' dare an' double dare, but I'll *not* ask her. I know she never did."

"Well, from all I hear my mother and your mother say about when they were young, I'll bet you—"

"Don't you *dare!* You can say any old thing you please about your mother, but not about mine!" Derrick still ached with regret at quarreling with Jack, but that did not cool her rage. "And now that you know how I feel about it, you needn't bother to ask me to go anywhere with you again."

"You must think that I have a fine idea of a good time, going with a girl that fights with you all evening! An' just let me tell you this, Derrick Thornton, it ain't your kind that gets married the quickest, but the other kind."

"You act as if you thought I wanted to get married," she replied scornfully. "I don't, an' you needn't forget it."

Thereafter they held their tongues; in silence they drove into the Thornton stable, in silence unhitched Tom, and in silence they parted. Derrick climbed the stairs to bed with a heart full of rage and bitterness, trying to think of ways to show Jack and the others. She must prove that the kind of girl she upheld was worth more than the other kind . . .

Finally, with a sigh, she gave up the problem, and sat down on the edge of the bed, defeated. After all, concerns of this sort were not for her to work out—there were other things for her to think of. Since she was not pleased with the world, nor the world with her . . . then she remembered that it was hardly more than six months since she had renounced the world because she preferred not to know the things that happened in it . . . but this was different: this time her withdrawal would be final. She would begin at once her attack on Fame, and the world could go hang, for all she cared, particularly Jack and the rest of them. Her last decision before she fell asleep was that her first effort would be to write a play. While a poem or a story might conceivably be printed, it might also escape the eyes of Tecumseh; a play, given before the whole town, could hardly be missed, even by Jack!

Derrick brooded over the consideration of a play for a long while before she could think of anything she wanted to write about, and then she turned back to the idea that she had had in the spring, which she had tried to put into a poem: the idea of a land half asleep waiting patiently for man to be done with his toil. One might make a pageant on that theme, the speeches to be uttered by the Spirit of the Land as she watched men come and go. First the mound-builders, then the Indians. It would be more interesting, she thought, if her land were one where men had dwelt longer —Greeks, Romans, knights—but perhaps in such places one hadn't that sense that it would be all over and done with some day. At any rate, she would stick to the truth, as they were so frequently advised to do in the English class; and because she knew nothing about the mound-builders and little about the Indians, she would have to spend some time in historical research. Again Derrick buried herself in the library, this time on the couch instead of beneath it, with books heaped up beside her. She did not hurry to collect material, and succeeded, by reading everything she could find in the public library, in postponing until after Christmas the moment when she felt that she would no longer be justified in her delay—when she knew that she must take pencil in hand or give up the idea. She had decided that it must be written in blank verse, but when she began to put blank verse speeches into the mouth of what she thought of vaguely as "the mighty land itself," she found that her conception of it dwindled, that she must hold on with all her power of concentration to the idea that had grown precious to her . . . with every line she wrote, the "mighty land" became in her imagination less tremendous, and she was filled with regret. She had loved with a sort of terror her idea that mankind was less important and less enduring than the earth on which he lived. She refused to have her conception spoiled, and tore up the speeches, to start over again.

This time she planned the scenes first; this was easier: she could do it and keep her idea unspoiled in the background of her mind. Mound-builders—Indians—pioneers—settlers —the point was that they had all thought that they would live there always . . . and all the while the Land waited, not impatient at their pride, because she knew that time would be hers after the last of them had gone. Derrick was frightened by her idea—it made her shiver with delight and terror . . . if only she could make other people shiver in the same way! The unwritten speeches must do that: but first she planned scenes, background, characters, costumes, action . . . It was difficult to imagine the people who must follow them, for of course it was not reasonable to suppose that they would live longer than the Indians had. She finally modeled them somewhat after the ancient Greeks, who were the most superior people she could think of. This race of her invention was so nearly perfect in her eyes that she grieved over its having to perish at the end. Finally, when the scenes were complete and she did return to the speeches, she made them very brief—merely necessary explanations between scenes and as majestic and dignified as she could achieve.

Once finished, she hid the pageant away in a drawer of her bureau, and by turns she dreamed of its performance and wished she had not written it at all. When, however, there came a chance to present it to the public, she did not hesitate. She remembered that her great aim in life was to vindicate in the eyes of her friends her position as one to whom the world and its ways were nothing.

The High School's need for a new athletic field was made the justification for satisfying the annual eagerness for a dramatic production. It was voted that each class should give a play, on four succeeding Friday nights; the townspeople who saw all four plays should vote as to which one was the best, and the class that gave the most popular performance should have the privilege of naming the field when it was bought.

Derrick and Bill Stewart were appointed on the committee to decide on a play, and they met at once with Miss Herbert, to discuss the question. The classes had decided to keep the names of plays chosen secret from the public until the time for the performances, in order to add interest to the contest. The committee, accordingly, met with the utmost secrecy. Its members, Derrick thought, were very stupid; they had no suggestions to make, although she gave them ample opportunity to mention any possibilities they had in mind. It was not until Miss Herbert's offerings were met by blank ignorance and lack of enthusiasm that Derrick put in her word.

"Do you think maybe we'd be more likely to get the prize if we gave something original? I wrote a pageant a while ago that might do." She spoke with the easy indifference of one who tossed off a play every week or so, hoping prayerfully that her voice would not tremble before she finished.

"Oh, did you?" said Miss Herbert. "Bring it in and let's read it in committee. I think they would take its originality into consideration in voting on the prize. And to-night, all of you, take some of these plays home and be able to report on them to-morrow."

Derrick sat up very late to copy the pageant, with full stage directions, elaborate descriptions of costumes, and with greatly amplified speeches. With fear and trembling she gave it to Miss Herbert in the morning, and with fear and trembling, yet with a compensating sense of her importance, she left the study hall, later, in response to a summons. She found the teacher in her empty classroom, toying with the papers on her desk. Derrick went to the front seat directly before her and dropped into it. Miss Herbert adjusted her glasses, cleared her throat, gave the papers a preliminary rustle.

"This is really very good, Derrick. Surprisingly good. I think we can do it, very nicely."

Derrick's heart leaped.

"Of course, for presentation there will have to be a number of changes. As it stands—"

Derrick's heart sank.

"You planned it to be given outdoors, didn't you? Settings will have to be changed somewhat for the Opera House."

"Oh, yes, of course." Derrick agreed eagerly. If that was all she meant by "changes"—

But it was not all. "You know," she continued, "that anything to be given on the stage must be dramatic. The speeches of the Spirit are almost too calm to hold the interest of the audience, don't you think?"

"But she *is* calm." Derrick was anxious to make Miss Herbert understand. "It doesn't make any difference what happens to her, just so she is left alone in the end."

"I see, of course. But don't you think that to hold the interest of the audience, she had better take sides, and get excited over the result? For instance, here, where the Indians drive the mound-builders out, and you have her say:

'Another day, another race. They come
And go as daisies go before the goldenrod—
Yet winter will one day succeed them all—'

Now, don't you think it would be better to show somehow that the Indians were better than the mound-builders, and the settlers than the Indians?"

"Yes," said Derrick meekly; "I meant to show that I

thought so, but not that she did. If she thought every race was better than the last, maybe she wouldn't want them to go, in the end." She twisted her handkerchief nervously.

"That's just what I was coming to. Don't you think that, instead of having her so satisfied when the last race has gone, it would be pleasanter if she said that these were so far advanced that their civilization would continue?"

Derrick was horrified. Only caution kept her from crying out in dismayed refusal. The point of it all was that the land was left alone in the end. Miss Herbert must be suited, however, or the pageant would not be given. She tried to listen calmly.

"And instead of having this last lot of people a different race, couldn't they be our own race, after it had learned a lot of things? People don't like to be told their country will fall."

"But that's the sad part of it. The mound-builders didn't think of ending, nor the Indians—and now we don't—"

"But is there any reason," said Miss Herbert crisply, "why we should end? After all, you can hardly compare the mound-builders with us—"

"No, but Egypt didn't go on forever, or Greece, or Rome—"

"No, to be sure. But," reassuringly, "they were pagan nations, and ours a Christian—"

Derrick was abashed. To that there was no answer.

"I see what you mean. But the end will have to be changed a lot to make those people seem good enough to be left."

"Yes, can't you work in a sort of Utopia? The brotherhood of man and equality of races—it would be very effective—and of course you'll have to change the speeches of the Spirit somewhat, from the first one, where she says:

'Unwearied I watch mankind, and wait,
Untroubled by his clamor in my ear,
Knowing that in the end alone at last,

With naught but silence in the empty fields,
I'll lie in silence, sleeping beneath the sun.' "

She picked up the papers, handed them to Derrick, then called her back from the door.

"And one thing more. Wouldn't it be better to change it from 'the Spirit of the Land' to the 'Spirit of Ohio'? It seems to me to mean a lot more."

If ever an author suffered, Derrick did, that instant. "But it isn't the same! It isn't what I mean! Ohio began in 1803 and may end in 2003 for all you know, and the land began in the beginning, and will last forever."

"But we had just decided that Ohio will last forever, I thought. You go and see if you can't make those changes in a few days, and bring it back to read to the committee."

Derrick stopped in the cloakroom on her way back to the study-hall, where she could think for a minute with no witnesses. She tried to reassure herself that it would be all right to do as Miss Herbert said. Of course, she knew what people would like, and it was that consideration that must have weight when you wrote a play. But Derrick wished that she had taken an idea she cared nothing about in the first place, because she wouldn't have minded changing it. The "Spirit of Ohio," forsooth! A creature draped in red, white, and blue, no doubt, with the seal of the State painted on the shield, when what she had meant was like the earlier, more shadowy, ancient goddesses—Rhea . . . But of course Miss Herbert was right. That sort of spirit could never be put on the stage. She sighed resignedly and returned to the study-hall.

The pageant, revised by the joint efforts of Derrick and Miss Herbert, resolved itself into a series of historical scenes, and seemed to Derrick a thing so little hers that she could listen without embarrassment to the speeches that she had written when they were shouted and reshouted into the empty depths of the Opera House at rehearsals. She had no rôle in it herself. Mary, whose size and grace and golden hair always won for her the spectacular parts, was the Spirit; Jack was the prophet of the mound-builders, who warned them in vain in a long exalted speech that, if they omitted their sacrifices to their gods, a strange people would come and drive them away and slay them, and who, when the Indians did come, with the conventional war-whoops, led his people in a frantic effort to build with their baskets of earth a rampart high enough to keep them out. Andrew, who had so short a while ago scorned the Indians, now, because of his hawk nose, his crisp black hair, and a voice that could be relied upon as a steady bass with no disconcerting squeaks, was awarded and acted with zest the part on which Derrick had expended most love and effort that of Tecumseh. Even when the rest of the pageant had been so changed as to be unrecognizable, the Tecumseh episode continued to fill her with joy and pride. She was quite convinced, when she heard Andrew recite the speeches she had written, that the Indian warrior was one of the greatest Americans.

If Derrick had, during rehearsals, thought of her intention of bringing her classmates to her feet, she would have been disappointed; every member of the class was too busy and too important with his part to give a thought to its author. Fortunately, she had concentrated so whole-heartedly on the management of it as not to realize that there was anything remiss in their attitude.

The fact that the class was to give an original production was not known outside; Derrick did not even tell her family, but came and went with a great air of mystery. She looked forward to the night of the performance as the moment when her fame would burst upon the world, and she spent a week trying to persuade her father that he must go. He had finally consented, upon her assurance that she had no part in it.

"If I get there and find that you are deceiving me, I shall leave at once," he said. "I cannot sit in agony dreading to see some member of my family make a fool of herself." Derrick's hopes had fallen when she heard him: she had known at once that he would dislike the pageant. But perhaps her mother and her aunts would be nice about it.

When the evening came, she was outwardly no more excited than her classmates, no more in the way behind the scenes, no harder to quiet, and she wasted no more time than the others peeping at a noisy audience through a hole in the curtain. She felt that her future depended on their verdict, and wished fervently that she could hear their remarks when they opened their programmes and discovered her authorship, but she would not for anything have ventured from behind the shelter of the curtain. She decided to hunt for her mother's seat after the Tecumseh episode, and see how much she liked it; that scene was received with so much applause that she was heartened in her resolve, and crept down the fire escape from the stage and slipped around to the front door. But here she had not the courage to face the ticket-seller and the Senior boys who had ushered and she crept up the fire escape again in confusion. Even after the curtain had fallen for the last time on the ringing speech of the Spirit of Ohio commending all her children for their union at last in brotherly love, she could hardly bear to face the outpouring throng. It was not the way for one who longed for fame to behave, but she could not help it. She waited in obscurity on the curb in front of the Opera House entrance for her family, and, when she found them, proceeded home wordlessly on her mother's arm. Her father and the boys were ahead of them.

"Well," Derrick said, finally, to break the awkward silence, "the kids did pretty well, don't you think?"

"Indeed they did!" her mother responded heartily; "the whole thing was very good."

"Did Father like it, or was he mad? I mean, did he think I made a fool of myself?"

"Oh, no! I'm sure he liked it. We were very much pleased."

Derrick waited a minute to see if she would say more, then burst out with—"Mother! Aren't you funny!"

"Well, you're pretty funny yourself, you know. Why didn't you tell us you were writing a pageant?"

They both laughed then, and said no more. They understood each other perfectly. But Derrick was less easily satisfied in regard to her father, and, fearful of his teasing, went immediately upstairs to bed in order to avoid an encounter with him in the living-room.

In the morning, while Derrick was dressing, Mary wheeled up in front of the house on her bicycle, left it against the fence, came in at the front door without knocking, and whistled for her at the foot of the stairs. It was long since she had acted so much at home in the Thornton house; Derrick rejoiced at this evidence that the pageant had had the desired result. Before she went downstairs, she listened for a minute over the banisters to hear what Mary said to any member of the family on the subject of her fame.

Billy strolled into the hall, thinking, perhaps, that it was one of his friends who had come in. Derrick held her breath as Mary addressed him.

"Hi, Bill. Who you looking for?"

"You, of course."

"Listen to him! I didn't know you knew I existed."

"Oh, ye-eh! I reckon Andrew ain't the only one—"

Mary laughed. "How's Dorothy? A little bird told me she was furious because you dropped a note of hers in school, and Miss Black got it."

"Shoot! Dorothy didn't mind. Ol' Black didn't read it."

They went on into the living-room. Derrick did not call down to them, but stood leaning against the banisters while she tried to collect her thoughts. Her disappointment in her discovery that her poetry was not the subject of all conversations on this the first day after its presentation was not so great as her shock at finding how she was apart from and ignorant of the affairs of her friends. Mary knew more about her own brother than she did. She could not even decide which of the possible Dorothys they had referred to; the last time she could remember that Billy had mentioned girls was

121

in the fall after the fox drive, when he had told her what idiots, in his opinion, Agnes and Mary had been to go into the country dressed "fit to kill." He must have changed a lot in a few months. Every one did change, except her . . . perhaps she would have to change, too, to be in accord with them . . . she was somehow less confident than she had been of winning back her place among them . . . she shrugged her shoulders, and slid dizzily down the winding banisters because she knew that Billy would disapprove.

When she entered the living-room, he picked up his cap and left, with a parting reminder to Derrick that if she wanted any breakfast she had better go out and eat it, because Cassie wouldn't leave the things on the table all day. Derrick ignored him and refused to let Mary go, as she offered to do, politely. But, after all, she had only come to say that she had a "tradelast" for Derrick. Collecting compliments, Derrick thought scornfully, on the way she had acted the Spirit of Ohio. It was not hard to twist into quotable form one of the many she had heard the night before, and, in return for what she offered, Mary said that she had overheard Miss Herbert tell the superintendent that "the child is a perfect genius." Once, such a statement would have set Derrick among the stars, but somehow compliments from Miss Herbert had ceased to mean much to her.

"Pooh!" she said, "just the same old soft soap. You don't pay any attention to what she says, I hope."

Nevertheless, that remark of her teacher gave her the courage to face her father at noon. He regarded her solemnly, but with a twinkle in his eye.

"How much did you make last night, Sister?" That was not so very dreadful to begin with.

Derrick confessed that she did not know.

"I walked down street with Mr. Devlin and Jack this morning." He stopped, maddeningly, while he served himself to some hash. It was coming now, she knew. She held her breath.

"Mr. Devlin asked me if you really believed we ought to treat the darkies as our equals."

"What did you say?"

"I told him that I hadn't the slightest idea what you thought . . . that I am kept in profound ignorance of your processes of mind."

"Father! You know perfectly well I don't believe it! Miss Herbert made me put that part in."

"But haven't you learned before this that you must not pretend to believe things when you don't? Now half the town will be down on you for your queer ideas, and the other half, like Jack, will be down on you for being insincere—for saying things for effect that you don't really mean."

"What did Jack say?"

"Why, when I said I didn't know what you thought, he said he knew, and that you didn't believe anything of the kind, but were just showing off."

"He didn't!"

"Yes, he did." The doctor continued, ignorant of the recent breach between Derrick and Jack. "He said you never used to be 'so good an' all'—those being his exact words, as I remember—but that ever since you had been in High School you have been too good for the rest of them. And that, you see, is what comes of taking a high moral stand on questions you have no interest in."

"Dick, don't tease her," Mrs. Thornton interrupted. "You know Jack didn't mean a thing he said."

"Well, darn it, I wish I hadn't written it."

"Why, Derrick! Why?"

"Because—well—because—I liked the idea so much when I started, but when I got through, it wasn't what I had meant to say in the first place. And I can't even think of the idea I started with, now, because the thing it ended up with gets in the way."

"I suppose an artist always feels that way about his ideas," her mother said. "No matter how clear in your mind your thought may be, to begin with, expressing it in words must change it somewhat. That certainly would be true of a young person, anyway. Maybe, when you're older, you can express your ideas without spoiling them by too much handling."

"But maybe people wouldn't like what I thought, really. Miss Herbert thought they wouldn't."

"People around here don't care much for poetry, Derrick. Maybe, when you're older, you can find a place where they will clamor for pageants."

"I suppose, Nell, my dear,"—the doctor teased his wife now, instead of Derrick—"you are implying that I can't appreciate my daughter's poetry?"

Except for the chance unimportant remarks at school, Derrick heard nothing more about her pageant, but because the prize went, not to their class, but to the Juniors, for a riotous production of "Spreading the News," she felt that perhaps they thought she had cheated them into giving a poor thing because it was her own. She realized with a blank dismay that what she had wanted was not fame—she cared very little about impressing people; what she had set her heart on was winning back a place as a leader of her contemporaries, and there she had failed. Fame, or no fame, she continued to be overlooked; they cared nothing for what she thought. . . .

Her outward attitude, until vacation, was one of scorn, her inward feeling one of bitter hopelessness; through the long and lonely summer she struggled with herself. The issues of that struggle were muddled in her own mind, but what it amounted to was that she could not do without her friends; to keep them, she could even bring herself to behave as they behaved—but she did not want to be what they were, inside. . . . Her great-grandmother, Derrick reflected sadly, would say that she was being punished because her love for her friends was greater than her love for God, but her conscience did not trouble her, she decided upon examination, because she loved God too little: she could not comprehend what it was to love God. . . . By the first of September she had decided that her mother was right: that it would be better to wait five or six years before writing another play; in the meantime, she would devote herself to the life that would give her back her friends.

Once she had set out, in the following autumn, in pursuit of her plan, Derrick suffered no qualms as to whether her course were right or wrong, morally. She was not much given to indecision; she might make mistakes, but she made them unhesitatingly, with a firm conviction. For a long while, however, she felt that she was beating against a stone wall . . . she let the girls see her intentions as plainly as she could without deliberately saying that she would do the things they did—that she would not say: she was not particularly anxious to do those things, and would go no further than might be necessary to achieve her end. She tried to take part in the gossip and to play a hand in their small intrigues, but, although they treated her pleasantly enough, they kept the talk, when she was with them, to those things which they would have discussed before their maiden aunts. If she asked them leading questions, they looked at her blankly, and changed the subject.

Derrick felt that she might have made the boys understand her more easily—but it was only when she sat at home in the evenings with the family, and the others were all at parties or the moving pictures, without her, that she wanted them to understand. In broad daylight, when they were at school, she did not see how any person of sense could look at Andrew or Bill Stewart languishingly, over the edge of a book, as Agnes did. . . .

But late in the fall a quarrel between Agnes and Bill gave Derrick an opportunity not to be overlooked. A class party had been arranged for Friday night, and Bill asked Derrick to accept him as an escort to the moving pictures, and to supper at Andrew's afterward. She had no illusions as to his reasons for asking her: he wanted to show Agnes that he didn't care if she was mad, but he didn't want to alienate her affections irretrievably by taking some one to the party whom she could regard as a serious rival. Derrick laughed to herself a Mephistophelian laugh.

On the way to the moving pictures they discussed the weather and the stars, the state of political affairs in the High School . . . but by the end of the evening, she had Bill looking at her in pleased and excited speculation. . . . She had found it easy enough: a meaning word, a sidelong glance. . . .

When she thought back over it afterward, Derrick realized clearly enough that she had not enjoyed the evening; only while she was with them, and knew that she puzzled Bill and annoyed Agnes and amused Mary, could she pretend that she was having a good time. But she had made her plans, and had no intention of turning back from their accomplishment.

All winter long she went everywhere with Bill. She always attempted to convey the impression that she would do anything he wanted, but managed to keep with the others at moments when he might have suggested that he did want something. Jack she dodged: she did not like the cynical curl of his lip, and was afraid that he awaited an opportunity to upbraid her because she had, to all appearances, given up the principles she had enunciated so forcibly. If he had ever begun to dispute with her, any attempt to make him understand would have been hopeless. She could only have said that she had changed her mind. . . . But her equivocal position could not be maintained forever, and when Bill asked her to be his guest at a party at the Stewart sugar camp in February, she felt certain that the time had come. . . .

The night was a perfect one, moonlit and cold; there was snow on the ground still frozen hard enough for them to ride to the farm in a bobsled. Bill did not come into town for her, but entrusted her to Andrew to bring out, along with Mary; the fact that she was a superfluous third relieved Derrick of all responsibility as far as entertainment and witty conversation were concerned. She sat silent beside them, only smiling now and then, or humming the chorus of a song as she considered the moonlight on the snow and the shadows of the bare trees that fell so sharply outlined on the side of the hill, and the beauty of the soaring branches of the roadside elms against the sky.

Bill came to the gate to meet them when warned by their shouts of their approach; he stepped on the runner of the sled and pointed out to the driver of the big team the way to the barn. Only when they jumped down, and stamped their numb feet and clapped their hands, did he single Derrick out from the crowd to ask her how she had fared . . . then he led them into the farmhouse, where they warmed themselves around the stove before they set out for the shack in the woods where the sugar was made.

"You lead the way, Jack," Bill said finally. "You know where the camp is. I'll come along last and see that nobody gets lost."

Jack laughed, with a burst of caustic laughter.

"As if we'd never been through the old woods before! I suppose we've never come here after squirrels, or 'coons. Pretty thin, Bill, pretty thin!"

"You just run along and never mind! You don't know who may get lost in a snowdrift and have to be dug out. . . ."

Bill and Derrick were the last to leave the fire: they escaped finally from the curious eyes of his younger sister into the moonlit night. Already the shouts and laughter of the others came from a long distance through the woods. Bill took her arm and led her through the barnyard and out among the trees.

"Some moon, eh, Derrick?"

"You bet! But you ought to have seen it coming out in the bob. In here the trees are in the way, but we could see about a mile across the fields."

"I know. You can here if you find a place. Look—" He pulled her up onto a broad stump, and put his arm around her waist to steady her.

"Look over there at ol' man Wilson's barns. Don't his

127

silos look like an old castle? I always think of it when I see them on a moonlight night."

Derrick exclaimed with pleasure. The distant barns lay at the foot of a hill, and only the snow-covered roofs and the crenelated tops of the silos could be seen from where they stood.

"It is a castle, Bill! How lovely! The tower on the right is the lookout tower, and the one on the left is the donjon keep—where the Lady Lyonors is in prison. Why don't you set out to rescue her, Bill?"

"Why should I? I don't want to rescue anybody else when I have you."

"Don't be a goose, Bill!" She twisted from his arm, leaped down from the stump, and ran away through the woods. When he caught her, she was standing on the bank beside the creek, which ran with a tinkling noise between snow-covered banks.

"Now I've got you! It's too wide to jump, and the log is way off, downstream."

"Downstream? I guess I can find it."

"Don't bother—it's out of our way. I can carry you across."

"Bill! You can't!"

"Why not? I've got boots on. It won't hurt me any."

"But I'm too heavy!"

"Heavy! About heavy as a feather!" With the utmost care he picked her up and stepped into the water.

"Bill, if you drop me I'll never forgive you!"

"Don't wiggle, then."

"All right," breathlessly, "but don't you slip on the snow getting out."

He ascended the farther bank, put her down, and kissed her awkwardly, somewhere in the neighborhood of her ear. She had been amused, since the instant when he had picked her up, sure that he was wondering whether he dared or not. She looked into his serious face and laughed because he hadn't done it better; then she twisted away again and ran up the hill between the trees. This time she did not run so far; he found her in half a minute, leaning breathless against a tree.

"Derrick!" Every trace of his timidity was gone; with some fierceness he pulled her away from the trunk.

"Bill! Some one will see you!"

"There's no one within a mile of us, silly!"

Derrick, rather to her surprise, found that she did not dislike her position . . . she was willing to stand there, with her head on his shoulder, as long as he wanted her to; she enjoyed the situation, although her feeling was that of a spectator rather than a participator. She might have been in the branches of the tree above their heads, watching two other people; she was conscious of a fantastic throbbing feeling that rose to her throat as they clung together, but her mind did not cease to work. It recorded the fact that she did not find it "simply sickening"; it enumerated the things she liked: his corduroy jacket under her cheek, the strength of his arms, even the size of his hands, that she had once thought of scornfully as "ploughboy hands." She wondered if his mind were at work, too, or if he weren't thinking at all, but had surrendered to that hot, throbbing rush of feeling. That thought revolted her . . . it was disgusting . . . disgusting. She pulled herself away from him, straightened her tam, and brushed the loosened wisp of hair back under it. Then she smiled at him calmly.

"We can't stay here like this all night, Bill. Every one will wonder what's become of us."

"Ye-eh, I suppose so," reluctantly.

When they approached the sugar camp, those in the doorway jeered at them.

"Who got lost in the woods, Bill?"

"Derrick," he answered promptly. "She was playing leap-frog with a stump, and fell in a snowdrift, and I had to stop to dig her out."

They pushed through to the room where the pans of maple sugar were boiling. It was a tiny room almost wholly filled by the square red-hot stove, a stove like an iron box, with no legs, filled with a roaring fire. On top of it were fitted the pans of "sugar water," arranged in succeeding stages of thickness, from the pan at one end which contained the sap to that at the other which held the syrup. The couples around the edge of the room passed from one to another a long-handled dipper from which they drank the thin sweet sap. . . .

When they had eaten their supper, the boys ran out into the snow and made a fox-and-geese ring. Derrick, as she chattered to the girls with what seemed to her an unaccustomed flow of wit, wondered whether she and Bill would have another chance to be alone together. She was curious; she longed to know if she would feel that same queer flood of feeling again, or if she could not overcome her disgust. She had liked it, at first, she admitted to herself. . . . When they had cleared up the remains of supper and burned the papers and boxes, the girls put on the sweaters they had worn beneath their coats and went out to join the game. Almost immediately Derrick offered Bill a chance which he did not overlook: in racing around the circle, she tripped and threw herself headlong into a drift. A dozen hands hauled her out.

"Oh," she wailed, "I'm soaking . . . snow down my neck . . . brush me off. . . ."

Bill was at her side at once, and spoke to her severely.

"What did you come out for in that thin sweater? You'll catch your death! Come back to the fire and dry off—"

He took her by the elbow and led her away. That the others undoubtedly had seen through her ruse she realized; but if they saw through devices like that one, they pretended not to lest sometimes their own subterfuges might be sneered at. A silly performance, every one pretending!

There was now only one dim lantern in the shack, and that and the red line of fire around the edge of the stove door were the only bits of light in the room. Bill closed the door as Derrick went and crouched by the fire.

"Frozen, Derrick? Here, let's open this up."

"No, not really. The snow didn't stick." She shifted her position a little, but did not look up. He dropped to the ground beside her.

"You did that on purpose, didn't you?" he asked.

She laughed, and he put his arm around her and edged a little closer. She wondered at the immediate return of the former flood of emotion, and at her queer relish of any feeling that could make her tremble so. She let Bill hold one hand; with the other, she played nervously with some bits of snow that had dropped from their shoes and that melted in her fingers. As she looked up at him, she longed to know whether or not he felt as she did.

"Don't look at me like that, Derrick."

She shut her eyes meekly. He did feel, then as she felt. Strange that now she did not mind that though:, as she had minded it before.

Then he chuckled. She opened her eyes in astonishment.

"I was just thinking what a funny lot girls are. You, particularly."

"Why me?"

"Why, you always made us think you were different, somehow, and you aren't at all."

"Well—are you glad or sorry?"

There was only one answer to that. He kissed her again. Derrick thought back to see how many times . . . "To any of the others," she reflected, "that many kisses in an evening would be a mere nothing." Then she sat up abruptly.

"Come on, Bill, my clothes are dry." She laughed at his bewildered expression "Help me with my coat, can't you? They'll all be here in a little while after their wraps. It must be getting late."

Bill went back to town with them on the bobsled, to stay all night with Jack. Derrick sat beside him almost as silently as she had sat by Mary coming out. Her own feelings were inexplicable to her. In spite of what had gone before, she could not bear to let him hold her hand, although she knew that most of the others did, under the robes. Bill seemed so much more *Bill* now that they were with the others than he had when they were alone—the Bill of the classroom and stumbling Cicero recitations . . . and to let him hold her hand was unthinkable. Not that he seemed very eager to hold it . . . she wondered again if they felt alike. Perhaps she was too much *Derrick* to him now. . . . It was queer . . . when they were in the woods he had seemed not so much a person whom she knew very well as a personification of something she did not know at all, but wanted to know. That was the best she could do in the way of an explanation.

The next morning she slept very late, and saw neither Bill nor Jack, but in the afternoon the mail included a note from the former. She was paralyzed for a moment by its contents. She read it in a glance, tore it into bits, and in a fury stalked through the house and dropped its fragments into the kitchen stove. The note was brief, however, and it was stamped on her memory word for word. Bill had given no sign of feeling like that while she had been with him. Had he talked to Jack? she wondered, terrified, and if so, what had Jack said? She reconstructed the note in her mind as she stood by the stove watching the black flakes of paper crumble into ashes.

"I couldn't sleep last night for trying to decide whether I ought to apologize to you for acting that way or not. If I thought you had minded, I would, but I don't think you did. I can't help writing to let you know that I am disappointed that you aren't different from the other girls like you pretended to be."

There was not a trace of Jack in that: she decided with relief that Bill had not told. Then, with a sudden flash of understanding, she saw that Bill must have felt as she had when they were coming home. He had wondered how Derrick had ever come to be in that situation with him; he had no feeling for her as a person; she had simply been to him the personification of something he was curious about. . . . She felt strangely old and wise as she stood by the fire thinking it out. . . . But he had had no right to send her the note. At first she thought she would never speak to him again; then she decided to pretend that nothing had happened: neither the sugar-camp party nor the note. That would bother Bill more than if she displayed her anger.

The situation that ensued amused her immensely: they were asked to the next party together, as usual, and Bill could not refuse to escort her without some definite reason. She did not reject his offer, as he had expected, but accepted it in the manner in which she had always accepted his invitations. He was nonplussed, and looked at her occasionally during the evening as if he wondered which of them had gone mad. Throughout the next few weeks they were asked everywhere together; their friends supposed, no doubt, that they continued at that point of intimacy established the night of the sugar-camp party; as a matter of fact, they spent their time when alone in polite discussions of the weather, the stars and moon, and the state of High School politics.

While Derrick still rejoiced at the situation that permitted her to maintain a reputation of being "as good a sport as anybody" without the necessity of living up to it, an earthquake in the shape of a revival shook the town. A vast, unpainted "tabernacle" was erected; there the town assembled, afternoon and evening. At first, Derrick, as she heard of the miraculously sudden conversion of one friend after another, felt that she was missing one of the essential experiences of life, and rebelled against her parents' decree that she should not attend the evening meetings. The afternoon services were out of the question, on account of school

"Every one goes," she told her father.

"No, every one doesn't," he answered with maddening precision; "I don't, you don't, your mother doesn't."

"I mean, every one at school."

"Well, maybe they need it. As for you, I think health is more important than religion. For all practical purposes, you have religion enough."

Finally he gave her permission to go on Friday night, with

133

Mary and Agnes. It was her first experience at a revival; the other girls, who had gone every night that week, ushered her to a seat with an air of importance. She looked around, at once fascinated and depressed. The immense room was hot and overcrowded; it was lighted by flaring gas-jets that whistled piercingly; the ground was covered with dirty straw and the air smelled. Immediately the man began to speak, she became acutely unhappy. He preached against dancing. . . . Derrick felt her cheeks grow hot with shame, and instead of being convinced by him, she could only feel a shocked horror to think that any one should say things like that in a sermon. When he finished and announced a hymn, she sighed with relief, but, unfortunately, the worst was to come. He called upon those who would renounce dancing forever to rise to their feet. Mary and Agnes rose at once. Derrick was stunned. Did they believe those things he had said? It was inconceivable. She folded her arms and sat firm as the Sphinx in the desert while the preacher lifted up his hands and thanked the Lord for the great number of souls rescued from Hell. How silly of Mary and Agnes! She looked at them covertly. Neither of them could live through a summer without dancing, to say nothing of the rest of their lives.

When the lengthy prayer was ended, the revivalist exhorted all who had seen the light and been converted to come to the front and be welcomed by him into the company of those delivered.

The two girls tried to drag Derrick to her feet, but she shook her head stubbornly.

"Come on down in front—every one does!"

"I don't."

"But, Derrick! You're a Christian, aren't you? It's nothing but a public confession of your faith."

"I did that once, when I joined the church. That's enough."

They left her, and moved down the aisle with the singing, jostling mob. It did look as though every one had been "converted"; there were only a few scattered, shamefaced individuals left on the benches. Stemming the tide in the aisles were determined women with workers' badges on their shoulders, who swooped like vultures on the unsaved remnant. Derrick, horrified, saw Agnes stop one of them and point in her direction. She rose precipitately, crept between benches to the opposite aisle, and strode toward the door. Once outside, she ran as if her life depended on it, almost afraid that she would be pursued by some relentless rescuer of imperiled souls.

She lay awake that night and wondered if she had again to face the alternative of losing her friends or schooling herself to accept what revolted her. She could bring herself to a resignation to that idea, in the abstract: she had found that she could not bear to lose her friends, therefore, she would accept whatever must be accepted . . . but that revivalist! Fortunately this time she was saved from having to make a choice.

The next afternoon she spent in the front yard with Margaret and little Henry, helping them make a snowman out of the last wet remnant of a drift. She gloated over the fact that no one could go out Duane Street and not realize that she, for one, did not attend the revivals. A long while after every one had passed, and the street was deserted again, Jack came whistling down the Devlin front steps. He called to her, and she turned, both hands full of snow.

"You're late, aren't you?" she said.

"Late? What for?"

"Why, the meeting."

"The revival, you mean? You needn't think I'm going there to make a fool of myself. First thing I know, he'd have me promising not to go to the movies or automobile riding. . . ."

"Jack! Do you mean to say you haven't been to the revival?"

"No, and I'm not going. But let's not argue about it."

"Heavens! I'm not going to! I don't go either. I'm going

135

to keep on dancing forever, and drinking and swearing and gambling, too, if I want to. Jack—" She came over to where he stood by the fence. "Isn't he *dreadful?*"

They looked at each other for a moment, and all their recent antagonism, that had for so long made them behave to each other as slight acquaintances behave, melted away into thin air and became as nothing.

"He's a vile and unspeakable, blithering idiot. He's a bloodsucker. He's anything you want me to say he is . . . he's a filthy, obscene . . ."

"Jack! Don't you swear at me. I'll wash your mouth out." . . . She threw a handful of soft snow into his face; he vaulted the fence, pursued her across the yard, around the fountain, and up the path to the terrace, where he tripped her into a snow-pile, and scrubbed her face with it.

"Oh, Jack! King's excuse! That nasty, sooty snow! Let me up . . . you can say what you like. . . ."

They leaned, panting and laughing, against the terrace wall. For the first time Derrick saw in the tall boy with the long trousers and slick pompadour the other Jack—the Jack who had played Indian and taken her tramping in the woods. She could have said prayers of thankfulness to a Providence that had sent a revivalist among them.

Jack was the first to catch his breath.

"What do you say, Derrick—let's take the kids to the movies?"

"Oh, I'd love it—Henry's too little, but if Hunter's in the house, he will go." They brushed the snow from their clothes, and went to call him.

The new bond was strengthened by the disapproval cast upon them both, particularly since neither of them accepted this disapproval silently, but spoke sarcastically in defense of what seemed to the others an indefensible position. Derrick delighted in the situation; it was many a day since she had been looked upon as a black sheep and a reprobate.

There was not the remotest chance that either of them

should be moved from their sacrilegious attitude, but, if there had been, an incident that occurred on the following Wednesday would have removed it.

Dr. Thornton had come in to luncheon late, looking white and sick. He glanced at the dining-room table and turned away.

"I don't want anything to eat, I guess, Nell."

She jumped up in alarm. "What's the matter, Dick? What's happened?"

"Come on out, and I'll tell you . . . not before the children. . . ."

They left the room, and the children sat alone and ate their luncheon. Eventually Billy and Hunter went out, and Margaret followed Cassie into the kitchen. Derrick waited for her mother to return, playing peek-a-boo with Henry around his high chair; she had no intention of being dismissed as one of "the children," too young to hear things. Her patience was rewarded, finally. Her mother returned and seated herself before her cold plate.

"What's the matter, Mother? Father looked awfully upset."

"No wonder. . . . Here, Henry, you jump down, if you've finished eating. . . ." She turned back the tray of his high chair. "Run out and find Cassie, sweetheart, and ask her to play with you while Mother eats her lunch."

"Margaret's out there; she can play with him. Here, let me give you some hot potatoes out of the dish. Isn't Father going to eat anything?"

"I guess not. One of the Devins' mill-hands was burned to death this morning, and of course your father is the company doctor."

"Mother! How dreadful! How?"

"I don't know, exactly. An explosion of some kind. His clothes caught fire."

"But couldn't they put it out?"

"They could have if he hadn't dashed out into the yard.

The hose was right there, but by the time they got it outside, it was too late. . . ."

"Where did they take him? Did he die before Father got there?"

"No, but there was nothing he could do. They took him into the rest room and your father said the smell in there of burned human flesh was . . ."

"Mother, stop! . . . Who was it?"

"That I don't know. No one you would know, anyway."

Derrick went out to find Jack, and walked to school with him.

"What does your father say?"

"He's pretty sick. He ought to be. The factory ought to be fixed so things like that couldn't happen . . ."

"Who was it?"

"Ol' man Jackson. That's one of the things makes Dad the sickest. He's worked for us all his life, and so have his brothers and all his sons."

"I remember him: he used to make our stilts for us."

"Yes, that's the one."

But their excitement at noon was nothing compared to what it was when they learned that the revivalist had used the sudden death of "ol' man Jackson" with telling effect in his sermon that afternoon. He had said that only the night before the old man had been at the meeting, and had held back stubbornly, although he had confessed to being "almost persuaded." Now, within twenty-four hours, he was dead, and his soul, that had missed salvation by a hair's breadth, was doomed forever. The preacher had converted his whole audience that afternoon. Who could have resisted such an appeal?

Derrick and Jack exchanged their views heatedly over the side fence.

"Jack, how did he dare to say the poor old man's soul was lost? How does he know? He talks like he knew the Lord Himself. Why, old Mr. Jackson never did anything to be converted from, did he? He was good and kind-hearted, and wasn't he a member of the Methodist Church?"

"Yes—all his life. Went every Sunday. And he was as loyal as the day is long—that's what makes me so sick. He never would let anybody say anything about the firm. Oh, Derrick! I can't stand it! If the preacher had talked about how dreadful it was to let things like that happen, I could 'a' stood it, even if it had hit the company. But to make an example out of a poor old man that never did any harm to anybody on earth—"

"The whole thing would make a good story," Derrick interrupted.

"Story!" furiously, "it would make a darn good sermon, if it was preached *right*—but the only place you could preach a sermon like that would be from a soap-box." He turned from her, strode into the house, and banged the door behind him.

Derrick stared after him in astonishment, then went in and reported his opinion to her father, who shook his head over the boy's vehemence.

"It was an accident, pure and simple, and couldn't have been foreseen or guarded against. But it is unspeakable for that man to be terrifying every child in town by such an example of sudden death. He will have a lot to answer for some day, and I hope he does have to answer for it."

That closed the incident, so far as discussion of it was concerned, but it cemented the bond between Derrick and Jack, and threw them together even more conspicuously as rebels against public opinion. Derrick found that, with support, rebellion was endurable. It was only when you were alone that it was impossible. Even after the town had forgotten Mr. Jackson's death, and had almost forgotten the revivalist, when spring drew on apace, and a few mild parties devoted to games of spinning-the-plate and going-to-Jerusalem were followed by parties less mild where they danced the Virginia reel, because, they said, when they had promised not to dance again, they hadn't considered the

Virginia reel a dance—still Derrick and Jack companioned each other. They viewed with sarcastic amusement the lessening austerity of their friends' outlook on life.

"Wasn't it all tommy rot!" Jack said one night in May when they sat on the Thornton porch. "It won't be a couple of months before they've forgotten there was a revival here. I say, Derrick—" He stopped strumming "When It's Apple-Blossom Time in Normandy" on his mandolin, and sat forward eagerly. "After exams, let's give a rousing big dance, and see how many of 'em come."

"Jack! What a scheme! Only we'll have to draw lots to see which of our mothers must give it—it would be queer for us to give it together."

He pulled two leaves from the honeysuckle vine beside him.

"Which hand do you choose? The big leaf gives the dance."

He held out his clenched fists; she tapped one, and they measured leaves.

"It's yours, Derrick."

"All right, then—the week after exams."

"Your mother will let you, I suppose?"

"Oh, yes—she thinks it's queer of me, anyway, not to want to give parties."

A week or so later, the girls waltzed with each other at a party, saying that, when they had sworn not to dance, they had meant that they would not dance with the boys. Jack and Derrick grinned at each other. And they were quite right in their prophecies. When three more weeks had passed, the winter's debauch in religion had been forgotten: practically every invitation to the dance was accepted. It was an unqualified success; but it meant more to Derrick than Jack realized, for it marked her reception into the world of her equals, not only as a participator in its pleasures, but in her old position as one of its leaders.

And forgotten though the revival might be, on its surface, it did furnish Derrick a weapon with which to defend her leadership. For, as she contemptuously thought, if they did all go back to the old ways, they would not dare let her know it, lest she remind them of all they had said when they had tried to convert her; and if they couldn't let her know that they had gone back, they certainly would not sneer at her for being too good. As for dancing, she was too wise to gloat publicly over the defection of her friends from their loudly announced principles. She had learned that to keep your friends, you must let them go their own devious ways unrebuked, while you conceal from them, if possible, the fact that yours is a different way, and that you are pursuing it alone.

Acting on this knowledge, she lived the next year—her last year in High School—very successfully. Whispers from her conscience to the effect that it was time for her to begin striving for fame were hushed by the recollection of her mother's advice: after all, there was plenty of time ahead of her still, and there was little use in thinking up ideas that were only ruined by being put on paper. She settled down to enjoy her hard-won position in her class, and the year sped on wings, a constant succession of Friday evening entertainments: coon hunts on frosty autumn nights, with hounds and lanterns in the woods; hayrides and ten o'clock suppers at one farmhouse or another; coasting parties with a fire on the hilltop that flickered on the crust of the snow and the flying black figures. . . . At the last, there was the business of being one of the graduating class: the play, the parties and dances, the oration at Commencement.

Derrick was too absorbed in her busy life all winter long to be more than temporarily disturbed at what happened in the family circle. In January her great-grandmother died; she had been so feeble for the last two years that every one whispered that it was better so . . . she had been out of her bedroom so little that Derrick found it hard to remember that she was not still there. Aunt Anne and her family moved into the old house with the great-aunts the Victorian furniture was taken into the attic, the massive old ma-

141

hogany brought back to the rooms where it had been supplanted by carved walnut . . . and the family life went on again smoothly. Derrick was not even particularly distressed by the fact that her mother was going to have another baby in the spring; the responsibilities of housekeeping fell not on her, but on Cassie; she did take the two youngest children under her charge, but Margaret, at eight, was too sturdily independent to require much attention, and Henry, ever since he had learned to walk, had followed Derrick like a shadow whenever she entered the house until she left it, so that there was little noticeable change in the customs of the house. The baby was born in April, with no more tumult than had attended Henry's advent three years before; this time it was a girl, and they named her Rosanna.

At the end of the spring, Derrick named it, sentimentally, the best year she had ever lived. Outwardly she must have borne then the same stamp borne by all ordinary young persons of seventeen. . . . Yet it was some time during this year that she had had what she called, when we discussed it, her "last" intimation of immortality. One night at college, when we should have been studying for an examination in Nineteenth Century Poetry, we had wasted time recounting our own experiences of such intimations, taking for our authority, in the belief that we had known the last of our revelations, Wordsworth's "The things which I have seen I now can see no more."

Derrick told us how she had come down the side street toward home one evening in spring when Rosanna was a few weeks old: Henry was with her, trotting gravely and silently at her side, his hand in hers. She was conscious of the warm clasp of his hand; she reflected idly that the new baby could not be half so sweet; her thoughts went back to the year of Henry's birth. She remembered the sick apprehension she had felt, and wondered why she had not suffered in the same way this winter. Because she had grown up in the meantime, she supposed. There were a lot of sensations she had once been familiar with that she had not known for a long while:

that strange one, for instance, of being lifted out of herself
and the world of finicky unrealities into actual existence
. . . into that consciousness of being one with space and time
that made the world seem like a dream . . . she had fought
that sensation after Esther's death, because she could not
bear to think of Esther, to whom the experience had come,
not in imagination, but in reality; she had fought it so
successfully that now, perhaps, she couldn't let herself go
enough to feel it if she wanted to. Her rambling thoughts
were interrupted by an exclamation from Henry.

"Derrick, look at the birds!"

From where they stood, beside their own gate, they saw,
black against the pale green light of the evening sky, the tall
chimney of their house between the branches of the trees,
and, circling around it, a flock of chimney swifts. They
whirled and dipped and rose again, with an unperturbed
grace in the movement of their long, pointed wings; some
of them swooped into the chimney, one after another, and
reappeared at once, to resume their circling flight.

For one panic instant, Derrick forgot everything but birds
and sky; she did not exist, nor did Henry, nor the house,
nothing existed as distinct, and yet everything existed as birds
and sky . . . for the space of a heartbeat she almost knew . . .
whatever it is we want to know . . . and then she fought it off
. . . she didn't want to know . . . not yet . . . and, fighting, she
welcomed Henry's tugging at her hand.

"What kind of birds are they, Derrick? What are they
doing in our chimley?"

"They're chimney swifts, honey—that's where they build
their nests."

They stood at the gate a minute to watch them. Derrick's
heart swelled in a passionate reaction from that breathless
moment; she could have exclaimed with relief at her restored sense of the reality of Henry, and the house and all
that it held. That one terrible instant must have been like
death itself. It was death that snatched you away from
everything you cared about, and hurled you into an empty,

cold, and undesired eternity. She shuddered, but in the terror was mingled a certain relief. That inside self, with its awful potentialities, had not, after all, been lost in the commonplaceness of the last few years . . . then, all at once, she felt her ridiculousness—all this over nothing but a flock of birds against the sky! But she wondered how she could ever have welcomed that feeling, how she could have invited it, as she had, once upon a time, lying face down on her bed on summer afternoons. . . . Perhaps it would have been better if that hidden self had been resurrected . . .

When she told us about it, we said that what she had felt was an intimation of death, but not of immortality. She was distressed because she had not made clear to us the thing she had known.

"When, just for an instant, you *are* the sky and sun and air, you know that you always have been, and always will be, sky and sun and air, world without end, amen, and whatever else you may think you are is nothing but a dream."

When Derrick cleaned out her bookcase that summer— one of many preparations for departure to college—she found, with the other frayed papers in the old geography, the composition she had written on "Happiness." Amused at the difference four years had made in her handwriting, she stopped to look at it; when she had read it through, she was incredulous. How little she had known! She crumpled it up and tossed it in the wastepaper basket; then, on an impulse, smoothed it out again, took up a pencil, and wrote on the back:

"Unhappiness: What I Think in August, 1913.

"Nothing that I wrote before is true. Education is not necessary for happiness, because there are as many unpleasant things to learn as there are pleasant. Either you have to know nothing, or you have to know good and bad."

She reached up for her Bible to disprove what she had used it to prove in the original: by turning to the Concordance she found what she wanted:

" 'For in much wisdom is much grief; and he that increase to knowledge increase to sorrow.'

"Whether fame makes you happy or unhappy I have yet to find out, but I have already learned that nothing is more important, if you want to avoid unhappiness, than keeping your friends. I did say that before, but now I know that more is necessary for doing so than merely being as nice as you know how. Sometimes you have to pretend that you approve of things when you don't really, and then your conscience makes you unhappy. Here you have to take your choice, too, and be unhappy because you lose your friends or because your conscience hurts.

"It would be all right to say that punishment for sins can be prepared for, and ought not to make you unhappy, if you always could remember, or always knew when you sinned. But sometimes you sin without knowing it, and then you don't expect the punishment, and sometimes, in the midst of what you suppose must be a punishment, you stop and try to think what you did to deserve it, and you can't think of anything. So there is no way to avoid this kind of unhappiness. However, if it is the Lord who punishes you, then your unhappiness is between you and Him, and you need not let any one else see it.

"The only kind of unhappiness you can avoid"—the memory of Esther's death was a torture by fire in Derrick's mind—"is the kind that comes from doing something to your friends. That is the kind of unhappiness that it really seems as if you can't bear, and you must do everything in the world you can to avoid it.

"I intend to find out whether fame makes you happy or not, and to keep from doing anything that will hurt any friend of mine."

She folded the paper again, slit the cover of the geography with a penknife, hid "What I Know About Unhappiness" away in it, and put it on the pile of discarded schoolbooks to be taken to the attic.

145

Part Two

Pleached

Gardens

I

AND THEN Derrick and I were brought together again.

Perhaps, if I had not known her until later, she would have told me from time to time so much about those days that the details would be as vivid, would be held as immutably from receding into the past, as all that she related of the earlier years in Tecumseh. but we went through college together, and Derrick took it for granted that we all saw what she was seeing. My memory is not Derrick's; it is impossible to recapture, by trying, the old feeling. I see in flashes, suddenly, one or another of the lot of us as we were then, particularly Derrick, slender, clear-eyed, quiet, inconspicuous, yet, somehow, subtly, the master of us all; I know that each of us considered the others wonderful and much to be admired, and that our wonder and admiration—almost, our awe, at moments—centered about Derrick. Ours was the seat of the scornful; we were contemptuous of many things; but, when I attempt to portray our attitude, only those incidents come to my mind that serve to show that we were not, ourselves, wholly lacking in sentiment. We subscribed to the popular legend in regard to our cleverness and incomparable wit, but what snatches of conversation I can quote bear little evidence to its truth. Ours was the supreme confidence of youth; we were not much frightened by the spectacle of the futility of most lives;—we were going to accomplish . . . How sure . . . how sure we were of the future!

The most that can be said for us, I suppose, is that we

were fairly intelligent and excellently well read. Derrick was never quite as the rest of us—she saw more clearly, and cherished no illusions . . . but I foresee myself thwarted in the attempt to prove it. It were better, perhaps, to omit any account of those four years; but it was then that Derrick made her friends, and she herself contended that friends were all-important, that upon them depended everything . . .

First, there was Alice McIntyre.

Derrick was on the train that Alice and I took from Cleveland early in September, and we saw her first as she sat opposite us in the diner at the table next to ours. She would have been insignificant enough in appearance had not the red wing on her dark hat, slanting down across her forehead, called attention to the arched black brows and the curiously penetrating hazel eyes.

Alice, who was beside me, noticed her first.

"Who's the girl with the red feather, Sue? She looks as if she thought she knew you."

"She doesn't. I never saw her before."

Then I caught her eye, and she smiled a little as she swayed with the motion of the car. A one-sided smile, aloof, whimsical . . . I remembered, uncomfortably, an ancient, long-forgotten feeling of inferiority—inferiority to an odd child with greenish hazel eyes and soft hair tied with scarlet ribbons and cut in bangs across her forehead.

"Of course I know her," I corrected myself. "Her father's a doctor down in Tecumseh; we spent the day with them once. Good Heavens, do you suppose she's going to college?"

"Why do you say 'Good Heavens'? She looks interesting."

"I didn't like her then, and I suppose I shall have to do something about her. You know—be polite."

"Why didn't you like her?"

"I thought she was queer, and she made me uncomfortable."

Derrick passed us as she went out, nodded and half

smiled. Alice listened in amusement to the story of my Sunday in Tecumseh. When we followed her into the other car, we stopped at her seat and I introduced Alice.

"I thought at first you didn't remember me."

"I didn't at first. . . . You are going to college, I suppose?"

She motioned us to sit down with her, and before I knew what had happened Alice had launched into an account of the weeks she had spent camping in the Rockies. It was not often that she found such an audience as Derrick, who sat wide-eyed, absorbed. We didn't move until the porter came to make up her berth.

"She has Athene's eyes," said Alice, as we stumbled into our own seat. "You know—'glaukopis Athene'—what they translate as 'blue-eyed' Athene, but isn't blue-eyed at all, but the color of the sea when it comes up on the sard and slips back again and takes the sand with it."

"That's not *a* color; it's a hundred colors."

"Yes. So are her eyes."

"Green, I call 'em," I answered shortly. I considered Alice's limited but zealous study of Greek all of a piece with her general unpracticality.

"She looks as if she wrote poetry, too."

"That doesn't take much insight on your part. I've already told you that."

A little later, I met Derrick in the dressing-room.

"I like your red-haired friend," she said. "I didn't know there were people who could talk like that, outside of a book."

Of course, with such conviction on the part of both of them, especially since chance had placed us in the same dormitory, it was inevitable that we should see a great deal of each other. Derrick seemed not at all what Alice thought her, and still less what I had remembered her. I liked her, and did not even hesitate to share with her my lifelong privilege of making fun of Alice. But three was an uncomfortable number, as she pointed out one night.

"Threes always come to grief—consider the triumvirates! We must have a fourth—"

"There's a nice girl," Alice began, "in Chem. Lab. with me—"

"Oh, Al—" we wailed in chorus. "This is a delicate matter—leave it to Sue or me—" Derrick added. She had known Alice at once, with her volcanic outbursts of rage or enthusiasm, personifying by turn Wrath, or Mirth, or Poetic Fire. Derrick, on the other hand, was an enigma to Alice; she sometimes made friends with the right people, but her explanations of why she found them congenial were preposterous. We were afraid to trust her. Besides, I knew that, if Derrick thought we should be four instead of three, it was because she had found the fourth.

"Do you know Frances Higginson, Sue?" she asked, now. "She's in my Comp class—awf'lly good. Short, thin girl, walks like a boy—Norfolk suits and hair skinned back tight, with a ribbon around it behind her ears—red hair, not fiery, like Al's, but pale, a kind of gold-red, and straight. Let's ask her to tea with us at Somerset, and see. . . . The woods along the road are glorious now—"

Frances at eighteen was still a tomboy; she walked with her hands in her pockets if she were alone, or with an arm flung across your shoulders if you were with her, or, if she were excited, she skipped along ahead of you until you despaired of catching her, then she whirled around and returned to your side. But there was no nonsense about her mind: it was swift and keen and direct. . . . She proved her compatibility of intellect and spirit so satisfactorily that we weaned her away from earlier attachments and made her the fourth of us, as Derrick had wished. It was not until later that we found that Edith Townsend refused to let Frances go . . . that if we adopted one of them, we must accept both. . . .

It was Alice who said that we must all be Literary Lights. I was the only one who demurred.

"The only way I can ever be one is to write your biographies when you've been dead long enough for people to be interested."

"Then you ought to be able to write caustic, illuminating character-sketches now, as a sort of practice. . . . Don't you write poetry, Frances?"

"No. I aspire to the novel, eventually, but all I can do now is the New England village, Old Style."

"Derrick, you must write poetry."

"No, I'd like to do plays," she replied loftily

"Just so it's something. Think of the attic of our gloriously uncertain future: curtains of turquoise—window-boxes blossoming with orange and old gold—a deep pool of quietness and beauty with the rapids of New York thundering outside. Very well—shriek derisively, if you must, but you will see— I wish, though, you would write poetry, Derrick. I don't want to be the only one to make a fool of herself that way. I can write the light and graceful essay, peppered with quotations, if I must, but I think poetry a worthier pursuit. And you'll never have time in college to write a play—you'd better keep your hand in by dashing off a lyric now and then. I say, Sue, let's make her write a poem."

"You can't."

"We can. We'll have dinner at the Inn to-morrow night. If you produce a poem at the dinner, we'll go Dutch on it, but if you don't, we'll charge it to you."

"I'll not go."

"Then, of course, we'll charge it to you."

Derrick whistled "Old Black Joe" lugubriously through her teeth as she took down her hair to brush it for dinner. "Ah's comin', Ah's comin', fo' mah haid is bendin' low" . . . Then she broke off suddenly. "Al, I've just thought of how I should have answered you. Let's go back and do that over. Tell me again that I must write a poem."

" 'What, upon compulsion? Give you a poem on compulsion? If poems were as plentiful as blackberries, I would give no man a poem upon compulsion!' "

Alice laughed. "You must learn to have your lit'ry gems at the right moment!"

For a week or more she had been instructing Derrick in the art of when to use the appropriate quotation. Derrick had said that she was too accustomed to the idea that any one who heard her quote poetry would think her quite mad, to be easily converted to its use. To overcome her bashfulness, they had invented what they called the "social bath" —the tubs in the bathroom were separated by thin partitions, and late every evening two of these neighboring tubs were preëmpted and filled to the brim, and while they lay and splashed, they hurled back and forth over the partition scattered bits of Shakespearean vituperation. Any one within hearing then must have thought them "quite mad" . . . To Alice's " 'I'll tell thee what, thou damned tripe-visaged rascal, there's no more faith in thee than in a stewed prune,' " Derrick would reply, in a cold, bitter, knife-edged tone, " 'You blue-bottle rogue, you beetle-headed, flap-eared knave, thou'rt a very ragged wart.' "

Derrick appeared for dinner on the following evening somewhat worn, but triumphant.

"It took me all afternoon to do it, but here it is. I'll read it to you while you eat your soup. I could have written some touching sentiment easily enough, but I wanted to write the sort of thing that would be written by the sort of person that Al would like me to be—you know—"

"Let's have it."

"It's called 'A Colloquy with One Who Would Ride Broomsticks.'

"Cold is the gleaming hair
Crowning your brow,
As if you had been running with the wind in your face.
How can it be when there
Is no wind now?
When there stirs not a breath?"

"I lost my way, blown far down the emptiness of space
By the cold wind of death."

"Cold is the ivory breast
Against my heart,
As if you had been swimming in a bitter sea.
But the shore and where we rest
Are far apart,
As far as earth is wide."
"How should I know until its foam flew over me
The strength of Lethe's tide?"

"Remote are the shadowed eyes,
Once full of light,
As if you had been searching where night and chaos are.
Tell me what dark wing flies
The visioned night?
What is the thing you see?"
"Ah, far enough I flew to learn, beyond the last star
Lies but infinity!"

Alice and I sat astounded, convinced for a moment that
we had captured nothing less than a young Shelley, and I
marveled that any one who could write like that had to be
coaxed to do it. Frances was astonished, too, but with a
difference. She snorted, choked over her soup so that she
had to be thumped on the back, muttered something about
"cosmic consciousness," choked again, was finally restored,
and said, "Why do you give it that title? A broomstick
wouldn't take you so far. Why not the wind, or a comet?"

"But then you would expect to go far. On a broomstick
you would feel perfectly safe, in spite of your friends' warn-
ings, and would be carried farther than you had intended to
go. . . . Don't you like it?"

Alice and I had hardly recovered from our surprise, but
we tried to stammer our appreciation. She waved a hand to
stop us.

"Thanks awf'lly. That's enough. I just wanted you to give

me a chance to shrug my shoulders and say indifferently, 'I'll rhyme you so, eight years together, dinners and suppers and sleeping-hours excepted.' "

She started to tear the paper across, but I stopped her. "If I'm to be a Literary Light by means of biographing you, I must have your Juvenilia." I put the poem away in my desk.

When we realized that Edith Townsend was not going to surrender Frances to us entirely, Alice and I feared the consequences. Edith was a Marylander and a Democrat, conservative in all her opinions, as far as she had any, and she looked upon men with favor, not only in theory, as Alice did, but actually. Boys had been known to appear on the campus and ask for her. . . . We discussed her one evening as we ran up the steps of the dormitory where she and Frances lived, and where we had planned to meet them and Derrick. It was Frances's birthday, but she had said that she could not come with us for dinner unless Edith were asked too. It was her ultimatum, we understood, and we hoped that Derrick would behave. When they had met before, she had been too indifferent even to take the trouble to disagree with Edith; had murmured "yes" and "no" in the pauses of her chatter, her thoughts plainly elsewhere. We dreaded the birthday dinner, and were surprised enough when we entered Frances's room to find that Edith had taken sides in an argument against her and with Derrick.

"We're having a geographical dispute," the latter explained, as we stood on the threshold.

"We've been quarreling about New England and the Middle West," Frances said. She was sitting cross-legged on the end of the bed. "Derrick's foaming at the mouth because I told her I can't remember which is farthest west, Ohio or Iowa or Idaho."

"Ignoramus!"

"And she insists that if anything good can be said for our native State, it's because it was settled by New-Englanders," Derrick accused her.

"And so it was. . . ."

"Lord, Sue . . . your old northern Ohio, perhaps; but that's not the State."

"No!" Edith argued for her. "Maryland made Ohio. It's silly to be romantic about Maryland, when Ohio's just like it—eats just as many fried chickens and waffles . . ."

"And has as many darkies," Derrick added. "Any village of one street in Ohio might as well be in Maryland. Square brick houses in a row at the edge of the pavement, and all the gardens hidden away behind them."

"And it's as exciting to live in as a cemetery," Alice scoffed. "I don't care for the native State, myself. It's a God-forsaken hole. You may go back and be a vertebra in the backbone of America if you like, but not . . . ."

"We can admire the backbone without wanting to be part of it, can't we?" Edith asked, hastily.

"Of course we can," Derrick reassured her. "We'll go to New York and be the rouge on the country's cheek."

After the dinner, when the three of us were on our way home, I said that Edith might be a fool, but that she was at least good company.

"She's not a fool; she's a wily, beguiling little imp—the sort of person who feels a situation and adapts herself to it, manages you tactfully without your knowing it, instead of slapping you on the back, as Al would do. It's all right to be beguiled if you know it's being done. I don't mean that she does it unselfishly—the ministering angel and what-not— she's probably as selfish as can be—so selfish that she wants everything around her to be as comfortable as possible. She may even do it unconsciously . . ."

Edith, then, was to be accepted. Derrick's judgment of people was almost invariably right as we saw the right; all of us but Alice considered it infallible, and followed where she led—she had the authority of a Roman emperor.

"But," she continued, "if we are going to be five, we must be six. Odd numbers are impossible. Do you know Madeleine Van Leyden?"

Everyone knew Madeleine, by sight, at least. A tall, dark, distinguished-looking girl. . . . But I thought Derrick over-hopeful, if she believed that we had anything in common. She said, however, that you could make friends with any one if you worked hard enough at it. I was not surprised, a few days later, to see them come out of the library together. I caught Derrick as she turned toward the recitation hall.

"What is she like?"

"I don't know . . . I haven't got anywhere with her. But she's so good-looking . . . what does it matter what she's like?"

Her next report was that Madeleine was the sort who would be flattered to be told that she looked like an Aubrey Beardsley drawing, but wouldn't like it if she were said to be like a Rembrandt. "Because," she explained, "Aubrey Beardsley is exactly what she isn't, but would like to be taken for—decadent, and ultra-sophisticated, and malicious—and Rembrandt is what she is."

"In what way? You just think that, because of her name. I can't see that she looks a thing like those wrinkled old Dutch women."

"Oh, not the women—the men—the ones with the long, thin cheeks and long noses, the high foreheads with the hair swept back, and the melancholy brown eyes—it's the eyes, I think. Those men who were too intelligent to be contented doing nothing, and too civilized to think that anything they could do would be anything but futile."

"In Holland in the seventeenth century?"

"Centuries have nothing to do with it. There are always people like that, and she's one of them."

"You're being poetical." But I remembered Madeleine as she had sat opposite me in the library one afternoon—the dark somber face, in the shadow of the wide, rolling brim of her black felt hat; the light that on one side touched her hair and her cheek, and the white ruffles of her blouse against the blue of her jacket. . . . "What is she like to be with, Derrick?"

"She doesn't say much, but she has a keen and rather bitter tongue, and what she does say is exactly what she wants to say, shocking or not. In spite of her Olympian poise, I think she is really melancholy, although she gives no sign of it . . ."

"If she is, you will find it out, and why. If you looked at me as you do at some people, Derrick Thornton, I'd blind you with a red-hot poker."

"I'm sorry," she said meekly; "if you're thinking about a person, you forget, and stare . . . If I find out about her, I'll let you know."

And so, in a few days, she came in and told us. She had asked about a snapshot on Madeleine's desk: a woman riding a mule, with the pyramids in the background.

"It looks like an advertisement for cigarettes, doesn't it?" Madeleine had replied. "It's my mother, taken in Egypt three years ago." Then she had explained: her father had been in the diplomatic service, and most of her life had been spent in Germany and the East—Cairo and Constantinople and Athens. Two years before, her mother and father had gone—reluctantly, because it was during her brother's holidays from school in England—on a yacht party in the Ægean, and the boat, with all on board, had been lost in a storm.

We were aghast . . . we who had known only the merest shadows of calamity. This was unbelievable. Some one asked about her brother, and where Madeleine had spent the last two years.

"He's two years older than she, and is at Oxford. She's been living in New York with an uncle, and going to school there."

"Do you like her?"

"She's lots of fun: ironic and disrespectful and irreverent. . . . I'll have her to dinner some night, and afterwards we'll have one of those talks that Al says ploughs up all life, and fertilizes it . . . and we can draw her out, and you'll see for yourselves."

Even now, I laugh when I think of that evening in which Madeleine was to reveal herself to us . . . Derrick and Alice and Frances talked so much that no one else had an opportunity for more than half a dozen observations.

"What are you going to do with yourselves when you get through here?" Madeleine gave them the start they needed.

"We're going to be Literary Celebrities," Alice said firmly. "And you?"

"I think I'll be a scientist."

"A scientist!" We were one in our horror. "But scientists are such cranks . . . they can't speak intelligently of anything but their own subjects—"

"No more can the literati. Ten years from now, a conversation that departs from literature will leave you high and dry."

"That isn't so—we can discourse brilliantly now on politics, religion, the emancipation of women, the race problem."

"All equally dull. I'd almost rather you'd talk about poetry, or nature . . ."

"Let's do nature," said Derrick. "It's spring at home, if not in this ungodly climate. Lilacs around every farmhouse, and, a little later, locust trees in bloom along the road, then honeysuckle on the fences in the moonlight, then clover in the fields, and warm winds blowing the smell of it in your face . . ."

"Stop her," Frances said. "We'd rather talk about poetry. Browning, by choice."

"No," said Alice, "Shakespeare, and old Kit Marlowe, and Shelley . . ."

"Wordsworth," I interrupted.

"And Chaucer and Keats and Coleridge—and Thomas Chatterton," Derrick laughed.

"None of you have named the one I like," Madeleine said. "How funny of you . . . William Blake."

"Blake! How funny of *you!*" Derrick looked at her for a minute with that disconcerting directness. "I forgot Blake, or I'd have said him myself. It sounds well. That's why I said Chatterton, of course. But do you really like him?"

"Most of his I know by heart. Mother used to sing to me when I was little—

> " 'The moon, like a flower
> In heaven's high bower,
> With silent delight
> Sits and smiles on the night.'

"Isn't it entrancing? Then there's

> " 'Never seek to tell thy love,
> Love that never can be told.' "

I don't know why she made us a little uncomfortable. Derrick changed the subject abruptly. . . . When Madeleine rose to go, some time later, she had said hardly another word, but Derrick took it for granted that she had revealed herself to us sufficiently.

"Look here, Madeleine," she said, "we have to put in our applications for next year's rooms in a few days . . . we'd like to have you go with us."

Madeleine looked around the circle questioningly.

"It's unanimous," Alice assured her.

"Why, then, I'd like to . . ."

We asked to be put together in one of the less popular dormitories, where there was a chance that there would be six rooms empty; and we were given an end of the third floor corridor. There we dwelt in amity for three years.

II

IT was during that first summer vacation, when Madeleine was abroad with her brother and the rest of us were at home, that the War began. We went back to college full of it, the five of us; Madeleine was not there for the first three or four weeks. It was supposed generally that she had encountered difficulties in the way of her return; Derrick thought that she did not want to come back, and fretted over the possibility. We talked of nothing but the War; we talked of it, the natural human insistence on the relation of it to us, as people talk of an accident: where they stood when it happened, what it looked like to them, and how they felt . . . at first, we spoke more of what we had said and thought when the news first came than we did of the things that were happening at the moment; it was hard to recover from the surprise to even the shadow of a realization of the state of affairs.

To me, a reference to the outbreak of the War will always bring to mind not a picture of armies taking the road out across Europe, but one of hot stone steps before a hot city house on a dusty afternoon in August, where lay a newspaper, half open, with blatant red headlines. To Derrick, in the same way, it will no doubt bring always the recollection of an August thunderstorm, and a quarrel with Jack.

The "Times-Star" had brought the news of England's ultimatum to the Germans. Every one had clamored for the paper, the boys in the furious excitement of youth that caught Derrick and roused her to a fierce partisanship of France; they, on the other hand, under the familiar and too-long-fostered impression of England as a tyrant, hoped that Germany would give her a good drubbing. Derrick had not thought much about England, but would not have them wish any misfortune upon France. . . . Into their angry dispute, which they had carried to the dinner-table, their father's voice had come quietly.

"Don't talk about it as if it were a history you were reading, and could read, right on to the end, as if it would not affect you at all. Remember: we're one blood, England and America, and we'll never stand aside and see her beaten, if it should come to that. And if it doesn't come to that, our sympathy must inevitably be with her."

He explained more fully to the wide-eyed, astounded boys. Derrick listened . . . and thought, not of why, but how. . . . She tried to imagine what it was like, her eyes fixed on the sky and the tree-tops through the dining-room window. The day had been sultry, and now there was a thunderstorm rolling up from the south, low black masses and churning billows of cloud that swept toward her eyes. The sun, low in the west, still shone across branches and over the vivid grass with a lurid, pale, copper-tinged light. There was a remote roll of thunder; she winced involuntarily. Little Henry, who sat across the table from her, and who had watched her face, fascinated, saw her shudder, and he whimpered, frightened.

"Oh, Derrick," he said, "is it guns?"

"No, Bruddie," she laughed, "the fighting is a long way off."

Her mother interrupted her, sharply. "Heaven be praised for that, anyway. . . . Run upstairs, and shut the windows on that side of the house, will you, Derrick, before it rains? . . . It's across the ocean, Henry, the War . . ."

But Henry's words touched Derrick's imagination. She pretended, as she went upstairs, and afterwards, as she sat in the living-room, her eyes closed, that the tumult of the thunder was the roar of guns . . . it was not hard to imagine it, so long as she kept her eyes shut so tight that she couldn't see the lightning flashes. Henry came and put his hand on her knee.

"It's only lightning, Derrick. You aren't afraid of it, are you?" Then he himself dodged as a particularly wicked bolt shot past the window and lighted the dusk: the tossing green of the branches, the driven sheets of rain, the grass and the street. When Henry uncovered his ears, she took him on her lap and offered to read to him.

"No," he said, "I want to know about the War—"

But before she could tell him, Jack ran up on the terrace and in at the porch door. She rose with an offer to take his coat, but he held it from her.

"Whew! Isn't it a night! . . . No, it's dripping—I'll leave it on the porch and spare the floors. . . . How's that, Mrs. Thornton?"

"Well, the floors have been dripped on before this . . ."

He came in and shut the door, and he and Derrick walked back through the hall to the library.

"Isn't it awful, Jack! The War, I mean, not this . . . tell me what you think."

He had come over to talk about the War, but was strangely reluctant to begin.

"It wouldn't have happened, of course, if . . . well, if . . . oh, I don't know—"

"If what?"

"If they hadn't kept up their enormous silly armies, and their silly old systems of government. With their armies all ready to fly at each other's throats, of course there would be war as soon as there was an excuse for it. If only the armies had refused to fight!"

Derrick stared at him in amazement, and plunged into an angry argument. Jack, it seemed, was a Pacifist. . . . There followed the most bitter quarrel they had ever had. . . . His reasons, given as she gave them when she repeated the discussion to us later, seemed weak and unconvincing, but she was perhaps not quite fair to Jack. . . . At any rate, whatever his reasons, she must have listened to him with horror. . . .

While they talked, the storm, which had promised for a while to die down, swept back with redoubled noise and fury. Derrick broke off in the middle of a hot speech and stepped to the window to listen to the continuous roll of the thunder.

"I can't bear to stay in here like this," she said, over her shoulder, "if it has to storm, let's go out on the porch and watch it. . . ."

They stood on the porch as far back in the corner as they could crouch, and watched breathlessly for each lightning flash. One bolt followed another so rapidly that almost without a pause there were revealed to them, brilliantly and terribly, the threshing tree-tops, the torn clouds, and the roof-line of the Devlin house, miraculously untouched and stable. They made no attempt to speak above the tumult, and their anger passed as they watched, mute and awestruck. Through the midst of it, with no heralding pause to warn them, shot a terrific flash that seemed for an instant to shatter the foundations of the world. Derrick threw her hands before her face and cowered against the wall of the house.

Jack laughed at her, but breathlessly and jerkily. "It struck somewhere that time, for sure. Where can we go to see?"

"Attic."

They reached the screen door simultaneously and together raced through the living-room—where Derrick flung a word of explanation over her shoulder as she passed—across the hall and up the stairs. They peered through low windows across the neighboring roofs, stumbling from one side of the attic to another while Jack held matches to light them around boxes and trunks and broken furniture.

"Must have been a tree or a telegraph pole," Jack said, just as Derrick from her side of the house exclaimed in a sort of horrified delight:

"No—it did strike—look—down in the corner, behind those trees. See the red light?"

"Sure enough . . . must be in the country . . . Lord! I thought it was just around the corner! They'll never get it out—this is the first rain we've had in weeks—the barns are full of hay, and dry as dust. Shall we go?"

"Let's."

With one accord they clattered down the stairs.

"If your father doesn't want you to drive, I'll dash over and get the Ford sedan"—Jack seized the opportunity to say so much as they rounded the stairs in the second-floor hall. Below, to the family, Derrick's explanations were of the briefest.

"There's a fire in the country. Going to need the car tonight?"

"I might. Besides, it's too dangerous for you to drive on a night like this."

"Father! What a nuisance! It's almost over."

"Over! Listen to it!"

"Never mind, Derrick. I'll get the Ford. You won't mind if I drive, Doctor?"

"Don't go for ten minutes, anyway. If a branch should break in this high wind and fall on you, it would smash the Ford to flinders."

"Jack goes too fast for a branch to fall on him," Billy interrupted from where he sat, book in his lap, his long legs crossed over the arm of the chair. "He'd be out from under before it hit the ground."

"It'll take ten minutes for him to get it started." Derrick brought his coat from where he had left it on the porch. "Run on and tootle for me at the front gate when you're ready. Want to go, Billy?"

"Can't, darn it. I've got a date."

"How about you, Hunter?"

He leaped to his feet. "You bet I'll go."

"No, Hunter." His mother, who had just come downstairs after putting the younger children to bed, stood in the doorway. "I'd rather you wouldn't. There's no telling how soon they'll get back—though I do beg of you, Derrick, not to be late—besides, something might happen, and one member of my family wrecked would be enough."

Jack returned, and Derrick snatched up her raincoat and leaped from the steps to the curb. . . . The glow in the sky had increased; there was no doubt as to the road they should take: south of town, along the river road, in the shadow of the hills. There was little attempt at conversation. Mud and water rose in sheets about them as Jack drove without swerving down the flooded road. Except for the yellow fan of light thrown by their lamps and the angry red glow in the sky ahead of them, they were racing through a profound, almost tangible darkness. Occasionally the lightning glimmer showed them the foaming river and the troubled boughs of trees on the one hand, on the other, the solidity of the hills; continuously there sounded in their ears the tumult of the wind and the rushing noise made by their wheels in the puddles. Once Derrick shouted that it was as well that they had not taken the big car . . . once when a lightning flash showed for an instant a black, shadowy mass of roof and wall beneath the tree-tops, Jack blew his horn as if in salute.

"The old stone mill . . Wheeler's house is on the hill on the other side." He leaned down and looked out across her lap. "All dark—they've gone to the fire, too, I reckon. . . ."

"Our first High School party was there—do you remember? And I wouldn't go with you."

"Yes—you were mad—you were always mad at me then. It's over four years ago . . . don't seem that long, does it?" Then he exclaimed in horror, "I see where the fire is, Derrick: it's Mr. Sutton's dairy."

He increased his speed until he came into line with the automobiles of neighbors who had come to help; there they sat for a moment to watch. The rain had stopped, and the lightning came only in intermittent flashes, but the fire in the barn loft lighted the whole neighborhood—roofs, tree-tops, and sky—with a wild red light. There was a turmoil of running black figures; above their shouts sounded the frightened neighing of the horses that had been rescued and the noise of their stamping. As an accompaniment of all the confusion there was the roaring noise of flames in the wind.

"Look, Derrick! The dairy barn's caught, and they haven't got all the cows out. I'm going to help them—they'll never stop it in this wind."

He was out and away before she could reply. The flames from the barns mounted higher. The glare was so bright, so tossed by the wind, so wild and strange, the cries of the horses so weird and unnatural that Derrick was terrified, aghast, shaken by the old childish fear of things that could happen and did happen, breaking suddenly now and then into the midst of everyday living . . . that reality beneath the shell, a glimpse of which stripped from you all thought, all feeling, except horror. And this was not even the shadow of that other reality—War!

Hot and acrid on the wind was borne the stinging smell of smoke, obliterating the clean fragrance of the rain. One fire grew less as the other mounted, until finally the roof of the barn that had been struck trembled, sank slowly toward one side, again hung motionless while the smoke swirled above it, and then fell, with a volcanic eruption of sparks and fire and a singing roar of the wind . . . then the flames fell back and settled themselves to devouring the wreck in less spectacular fashion. Derrick watched the other barn whence they led, one by one, the terror-stricken cattle. She tried to pretend that this was Belgium . . . with every fiber of her intelligence, she wanted to know the meaning of war, but she could not concentrate on her make-believe; she had too breathless an interest in the scene before her. She attempted, each time a black figure entered the barn, to decide whether or not it was Jack . . . she relaxed a little whenever a figure emerged. The flames burnt with ravenous rapidity . . . this roof, too, might fall at any moment, and some one would be caught beneath it . . . she clenched her

fists, and then let them fall limp in her lap when the dairy-
man forbade any one to go back. But after that, the crying
of the cattle became an agonized, strangled bellowing that
rose above the noise of wind and flame; she could not bear
it, and stuffed her fingers in her ears and twisted around on
the seat, so that she could bury her face in her lap. She
wanted not to know when the second roof fell . . . she lay
that way until Jack came back, and shook her arm.

"Ready to go?" he asked.

"Any time. It's almost over, isn't it?"

"Yes . . . poor cows . . . we didn't get them all . . . did
you hear?"

"Jack, you weren't burnt?"

"Of course not. All smoked up, though. Can you stand
the smell?"

"I don't mind. The roof might have fallen in any time,
and caught you in there."

"He wouldn't let us go in after there was any risk." He
scoffed at her fears as they drove homeward, and recounted
details that she had missed. Before he had finished, she
interrupted him.

"Jack, I always did think you were one of the queerest
people I knew. Why do you feel the way you do about the
war, if you have the courage to risk your life for nothing but
cows? I mean—cows and country don't balance very well,
do they?"

"Crazy! How often do I have to tell you that I didn't risk
my life? Besides," he added coldly, "it isn't a question of
courage. I'm not afraid—at least, I don't think I'd be afraid.
But you must admit there's some difference between risking
your life to save cows, and risking it to kill men . . . and men,
at that, that never meant anything to you, one way or another."

"Oh, well, of course there's no sense talking about your
risking your life . . . but I should think you could understand
how other people could risk theirs, for their country."

"If I could see that one was right and one was wrong, I

suppose I could understand those that risked it for the right."

"But they all think they're right."

"Of course. That's just the damned senselessness of it. They think they're right because their governments tell them so. And, really, it's six to one and half a dozen to the others." He broke off abruptly. "I may as well tell you, Derrick, I'm a Socialist."

"A—what!" Then she laughed. "A Socialist!"

"Yes. What is there funny about it? Upon my word, Derrick, I can't make you out. I hardly dared to tell you, you've been so furious against all my opinions . . . then, when I tell you why I have the opinions, you act as if it was the greatest joke in the world."

"No—it's only that I'm relieved to know it's that and not lunacy. There's so much more chance of your recovering from Socialism than from madness. It's all because of that University you go to . . ."

Jack was chagrined and angry . . . but, before they parted, she turned to him in a conciliatory mood and said that they must not quarrel, because there was so little left of their vacation; and she promised that she would not argue with him again about the War.

That promise she broke just once, one day when she met him at the Devlin gate as she passed. It was when the papers had begun to be full of stories of German atrocities in Belgium. She could not forbear a little flourishing of her triumph.

"I hope you don't think it's immaterial which wins, Germany or England?"

"Why not?"

"But, Jack! The things the Germans have done!"

"English lies. You don't believe them, I hope?" He half smiled in a superior way, yet there was a look of dread in his eyes . . . it was as if he had deliberately determined to infuriate her, but at the same time hoped she would not take up the gauntlet. She was bewildered by this expression, and said nothing, so that he continued.

"If I should want one side or the other to win, it wouldn't be the side that could think of lies like that to print about a civilized nation." He put on his hat and turned away, and left her there, staring.

Derrick said, when she told us of their encounter, that she had felt worse then than on the night of the fire. And she looked troubled as she told us about it.

"It's so queer . . . I can't help thinking he doesn't want to talk that way, but thinks he has to. There was more excuse for it, at first, when no one knew how Germany would behave. But now . . . to have him refuse to admit the truth! I can't tell you how I feel . . . you see, he's the only friend I have at home that I can really talk to. The others aren't interested in what we're interested in, and Jack used to be the fairest-minded, most honest person I knew, and had the sanest judgments. He's the sort of person whose opinion you accept almost before you accept your own, because you can depend on his fairness to the bitter end, and you know that you yourself are prejudiced. And now!"

"How do you know you aren't the prejudiced one, now?" Alice asked her.

"I don't." She replied shortly "I only know that I understand the feeling of the English and French. That I could fling myself with a bayonet on an alien hand that threatened to touch a country that I loved It goes back, I suppose, to the idea that I think I must have been born with, that the earth is more important than the people who live on it. Why not? It's more beautiful. . . . That may be prejudice, Al, but I'm afraid I could never think a person was right who didn't feel it. . . . *Feel* it, I mean, whether he believed it or not. . . ."

As she ended the discussion Derrick came from Alice's window-sill, where she had stood, and sat down at the desk, her fists clenched, her eyes black with emotion. . . . It is easy to draw the picture, to hear again the passionate conviction in her voice . . . but impossible to recall, to rouse again the old emotion. Who would have thought that it could have been forgotten? Yet—a long while after that night, when Derrick's sister Margaret was in college, she petitioned to be allowed to spend the summer abroad. Derrick sighed over the trend of the times.

"It never occurred to us to go abroad in the summer, did it?"

"Good reason why," I replied. "You forget there was a war on. . . ."

"So there was . . . so there was . . ." She looked at me blankly. "Who would ever have dreamed it could have slipped my mind, even for an instant? . . . and after all the hours we spent rolling bandages!"

When Madeleine finally came back, we tried to get her to tell us her experiences. She thought she did tell them, I suppose, but she was always a silent person. However, the very fact that she accepted the situation, that she put so little drama into her account, made the War to a certain degree more real to us, and so great and so dreadful that it seemed presumptuous in us to think at all of ourselves in relation to it.

When she and her brother had reached England from Italy, after the declaration of war, they had spent together the time between the day when he had enlisted and the day when he had been sent into training. If it had been Derrick, we should have had the story of those days in detail, but Madeleine said nothing beyond the statement of the facts and the brief assertion that Bob had been corking, and that, of course, even if she had wanted to keep him from going into it, she couldn't have answered his arguments. How could he have gone on at Oxford, alone? She herself had wanted to stay: to take nurses' training and follow him to France, but he had been so determined for her to return that she did not insist.

And so, because she did not speak of how she felt, we did

not either; we knit furiously against the coming of winter in France, read the newspapers, listened to lectures and tried to believe what we read and heard, while, so far as our daily life was concerned, we went on as we had gone the year before, only talking while we knit, instead of while we walked.

It was Derrick who learned most clearly from Madeleine what the War meant to her. In a search for her one afternoon, she had climbed to the newspaper room in the library —a room we all loved, because so few went there, and it seemed so far removed from the world when the late sun shone across the littered tables, and the sound of voices on the campus came intermittently, as from a great distance— and she had found her there, the tears heavy on her lashes as she stared at the pictures in the "Illustrated London News" of young English officers killed in battle. Whereas Madeleine would not have shown the slightest sign of personal grief, she was not ashamed of this. She had dried her eyes openly, and blown her nose, and had explained to Derrick.

"It is worse for England than Moses' curse was for Egypt. That took only the first-born. Before this ends it will take all the boys that are fairly grown up out of every family. And, of course, England can never be the same again. Even if they win, those who made England England will be gone." Then she had stopped abruptly. "There's no use talking about it . . . you can only repeat the platitudes that have been in every newspaper since the War began. But think of all those light-hearted, clever, rollicking boys—who didn't believe anything much, except that life was intended for pleasant ends—having the courage to go like this."

"They must have believed in things they didn't talk about."

"I suppose so. After all, they were brought up on the battles of Marathon and Thermopylæ and Salamis, and on stories of good old English pirates like Drake and Raleigh.

173

And I suppose mighty few of them ever heard any doubt cast on 'Dulce et decorum est—' ' "

The fall passed rapidly, nothing happened that touched us, and the War became so much a part of the background of our lives that we were conscious of it as we were of the weather, no more, no less: it was something over which we had as little control as we had over the elements, with which it divided honors as a topic of conversation. Only now and then, in some chance moment, we were brought up sharp.

One afternoon shortly before the Christmas vacation, Derrick and I went in town to do our shopping; we spent most of the daylight in second-hand bookstores on Cornhill, and in the dust of antique shops, and just at dusk cut across the Common to Boylston Street. Here the sidewalk was thronged with shoppers, eager, careless, with sprigs of holly in the collars of their fur coats; we struggled against the tide, laughing, carefree as any, while the strong wind from behind blew us on, lifting and twisting our skirts. Ahead of us, against the dull, smoky gold of the western sky, were the low roof of the library and the spire of the New Old South Church. . . . As we passed a certain lighted window, Derrick seized my arm, led me from the gutter through the crowd going the other way, and drew me to the glass.

"Look, Sue! That Rembrandt print. . . ."

Suddenly, before I had had time to answer, there was a sound of distant voices, singing . . . we both heard at the same time, and turned. Far off, across the Common, the great Christmas tree was lighted with a thousand lights, and somewhere in its neighborhood a crowd of men was singing . . . "It's a long way to Tipperary . . . It's a long way to go . . ." Only a few in the hurrying throng so much as lifted their heads. Derrick and I said nothing; there was no need . . . we stood quite still in the bitter wind until the last note had been sung. Finally Derrick shook my arm, and turned again.

"What I was going to say about the picture was—doesn't it look like Madeleine? You never would admit it—"

It was the portrait of a thin, mournful-eyed cavalier with a broad-brimmed hat turned down over his face. I laughed. "I can see how you think so, with considerable aid of the imagination. Would you like it? I'll get it for your Christmas present."

We turned into the shop hurriedly, the song on the Common already forgotten—that pitiful, silly song that we had heard then for the first time. But I cannot look at the print to-day—and it is mine now—without remembering how we were moved. A grotesque and whimsical association—Rembrandt and Tipperary!

One afternoon in January, when there was no one at home but me, the maid came up to look for Derrick, with the word that there was a caller for her in the parlor. Derrick was at the library; I went down to offer my services as a messenger, and found a tall, blue-eyed boy, with crisp, curly black hair and strong, aquiline features. Andrew MacLauchlan, he introduced himself—I said that I had heard of him; I did not add, as I might have, that I knew him as well as, or perhaps better than, if I had grown up in Tecumseh myself. We walked across the snowy campus to the library, talking casually of the difference in climate between New England and southern Ohio, and of the general state of affairs, political and social, in the latter commonwealth. He interrupted me nervously as we approached the library steps.

"What do you people here think of the War, anyway? You aren't Pro-Germans, are you?"

"Pro-Germans?"

"Well, I didn't know . . . I didn't see Derrick when she was home Christmas, and I wanted to see her before I go —I'm on my way to Canada to enlist, and every one at home thinks I'm crazy. I thought Derrick, maybe, might see how I felt. That's why I came, but then, all of a sudden, I was frightened for fear she might be rooting for the Germans."

I reassured him.

"Of course, I might have known she wouldn't, but the thought took my breath for a minute. I don't know why I should think she would understand, anyway—Lord knows, she worked hard enough when we were kids to make me forget I was a Scot."

Derrick, who sat habitually in the window of the Literature Room, for no more poetic reason than that the radiator was concealed under it, saw us coming up the path, waved, disappeared, and an instant later ran down the steps to meet us.

"Well, Eagle-beak," she cried, as she shook hands with Andrew, "what are you doing so far from the native heath?"

"I'm on my way to the native heath . . . the real one . . ."

"Scotland, you mean? I'd forgotten it was your native heath, it's been so long. What under the shining sun are you going to Scotland for, now?"

"Well, not exactly Scotland. I'm on my way to Canada. That's the quickest way to get to England . . ."

She understood at once, and her laughter and her pleasure at seeing him died, frozen. . . . I spoke to them hastily, murmured something about my work, and departed.

Derrick came in, after an afternoon spent with him, and found me alone at my desk. She dropped on my bed and talked, half to me, half to herself.

"Andrew's a nice boy, isn't he—and so good-looking. Why do you suppose he felt he should go? He is sure he won't be back . . . but I suppose they all think that. But he talked about it dreadfully, and I couldn't let him see how sick it made me . . . he had to get it off his chest . . . all he asks, he says, is for it to be over quickly. He told me he had read an account of a man who had had his face shot off, but was still alive when some first-aiders came along and found him, and was still able to make them see that he wanted a drink—when he couldn't possibly drink . . . Oh. . . ." Derrick buried her face and quivered. "Oh, how could he! And he spoke in such a dull, matter-of-fact way about it. Do you suppose he hasn't imagination to *see* things, or is he deliberately twisting the knife?"

"Why did he decide to enlist?"

"He says people at home, some of them, still believe in the Germans, and he couldn't stand hearing them any longer. He was sure I would understand how he felt, he said, because I tried so hard to make him a thoroughgoing Ohioan, that he thinks if I had left Ohio when I was eleven or twelve, I would still be willing to fight for it. . . . Of course, every one at home thinks he's lost his mind . . . I wonder about Jack . . ." She paused and bit her lip meditatively, then continued: "Of course, he may not know about it—he's up at the University . . . Andrew didn't say anything about him, though he's the best friend he had at home, and he didn't say anything about Mary, either. She's in Tecumseh, this year, taking care of her grandmother. Queer, isn't it, how things change in your relations with people . . . For years I've been nothing to Andrew, in comparison with Mary and Jack, and now he took all this trouble, just because he remembered what I was like ten years ago . . . And all for a bleak, rocky country he hasn't seen for so long that he's forgotten what it's like. Gone off to fight in kilts, and, once upon a time, he cried because he had to wear them. . . ."

In May of that year, the *Lusitania* was sunk; from then until the vacation in June the War filled our minds almost to the exclusion of everything else, until the moment of parting came, and we said good-bye until September. We talked of nothing else, but it had not actually touched us—yet.

One morning in August, I had a note from Derrick in which she said that she would not meet Alice and me on the usual train in Cleveland; she was going to New York for several weeks, to stay with Madeleine, who had had word that her brother had been killed in action in Flanders. We had said very little to each other about his chances to escape; it looked in the spring of 1915 as if the War would go on forever, and the only men in the English armies whose lives would be spared would be those so wounded as to be discharged. I should have said that I was prepared for the news of his death, but when the letter was handed up to me over the banisters one morning as I went down to breakfast, and I glanced over the brief sentences in Derrick's familiar hand, my knees trembled so that I could not trust myself to go on down, but sat there on the steps, thinking of Madeleine . . .

~~~~~~~~~ III ~~~~~~~~~

WHEN WE RETURNED for our Junior year, that fall after the death of Madeleine's brother, we found her more than ever morose and silent; we talked little of the War, on her account, and our conversations centered upon ourselves. We spent time that we could not afford to waste on discussions of our characters, intelligences, probable futures: we were noisily outspoken in regard to our likes and dislikes, noisily intolerant of stupidity, sentimentality, and piety. To a casual observer we must have seemed, in habits of speech and thought and action, as like as six twin peas. The language of one became the language of all; our vocabulary contained Madeleine's pet name "lamb of God," "p.i.,"—the abbreviation of Derrick's "pernicious influence," with which she damned anyone of whom she disapproved—"p.f.," Frances's "poor form," by which she judged the world, Edith's "cryptic," with which we dismissed what we did not understand. . . . But Derrick wrote poetry and the Prize Play, and became the Literary Figure of the college. That was later in the year; when we first came back, we devoted ourselves to making things easy for Madeleine; to distract her thoughts we centered our attention on Alice, who fancied she had fallen in love that summer. There was need of all our forensic powers to prove to her that she had not, and that to marry would be to throw her talents away.

One afternoon, when we walked to Weston Hill and came back to the society house for supper, our discussion by

179

the way was less facetious than it had always been—I remember it, because, at the end, Derrick spoke with such vehemence, such unwonted seriousness. . . .

It was a warm day for the middle of November, and we strolled down the road, kicking through the leaves that still lay ankle-deep on the path. Frances and Madeleine had been recently to an exhibit of etchings, and now they maintained that all before us could be interpreted by needle better than by brush: the line of the stone wall around a curve in the road, the grace and lightness of bare elm boughs lifted to the sky, the delicacy of the birches, the dark evergreens and their shadows on the hillsides. We tried to convince them that, without color, half the beauty would be lost: we pointed out the varying greens of pine and tamarack and spruce; the reds from scarlet to russet, in the leaves; the browns in grass and hillside, gray in the stone walls, amethyst on the horizon, and the clear, brilliant turquoise of the sky above us. We had almost reached the top of Weston Hill before the subject languished; it was not until then that Derrick cut in with a remark on a different topic.

"We are so nice as we are—how can Al think of marrying? Do you see, Fran?"

"I'm not sure that I'd be willing to take an oath of celibacy. Life is too hard for women who don't marry."

Derrick regarded her in amazement.

"Are you thinking of matrimony, Fran? I thought that I was going to be edified by watching you develop into the typical New England spinster. You know the type, Sue—spare and stooped, with a sardonic sense of humor. Didn't you always wonder what they were in their youth? And they were Fran, of course—tomboys up to the last minute, then suddenly, overnight, old maids. That accounts for their walk: that stride that sends their long full skirts swishing around their heels is simply Fran's hop-skip-and-jump grown up. And here is the young lady, instead of accepting her fate, aspiring to—to baby-carriages! Can you imagine anything funnier than Fran stalking behind a baby-carriage?"

Frances laughed with the rest of us, but demurred, nevertheless.

"I don't see why it's so funny! Why is it funnier to think of me with baby-carriages than Derrick?"

"Because, my lamb, I've wheeled baby-carriages all my life—and am therefore all the more sure I shall never wheel one of my own. How can you be bothered with marriage?"

"But why don't you want it?" Alice questioned her. "Think how much of life you miss if you don't know anything about love or having children."

"That's the damnedest silly attitude," Madeleine struck in. "Married women all have it. They know all about life, because they've spent a night or so in a man's arms, and unmarried women don't know anything, because they haven't."

"Madeleine!"

"It's true. Why not say it?"

"You're right, Lin. And I can't for the life of me see why those who marry and give up writing books or painting pictures don't miss as much as those who don't marry and give up love and babies."

"But not every woman can write books or paint pictures," I reminded her.

"I'm not talking about them."

"Some women want to give them up," Frances said, but her murmur was lost in Alice's more belligerent outburst.

"I can't see why you have to give things up when you marry. You can combine them."

"No, Al. Marriage is a life-work. If you decide in favor of writing books, you may be able to work a combination by running in a love affair now and then, or even a baby or two —perfectly good babies. But try to interrupt a married life to write a book, and it is sure to be a rotten one—or a rotten married life."

As we returned from Weston after tea, we went back to the question of etchings; we were walking along the stone wall at the edge of the campus, when Alice flung out her arms in a great sweeping gesture that shook most of the berries from a branch of juniper that she had carried back from the hill.

"There's so much color it fairly chokes you. 'Put one hand on your diaphragm,' as the elocutionists say, 'breathe correctly and repeat with me in deep chest tones: Life! Life! Life!' " She paused as Frances sat down on the stone wall to tie her shoestring. "Fran, you're a dull lump of clay! Etchings! Look at the trees!

" 'Crimson and gold and russet on the boughs,
And on the distant hill, unmoving flame.'

What is it that I'm quoting, anyway?"

Frances looked up, quivering with mirth. "It's from that sonnet on 'Autumn' you wrote last week."

Alice shouted in pure exuberance of spirit, and seized her hair with another theatrical gesture.

"Idiot! Never mind—look at the sun behind those trees, and I'll quote:

" 'While barred clouds bloom the soft-dying day,
And touch the stubble plains with rosy hue.' "

Off to the left, beyond the tawny meadows where the long grass bent before the wind, lay the cobalt-blue expanse of the lake. To the right, the road beneath the elms was empty except for an old wagoner who drove his stolid horse from one pile of leaves to the next and lazily pitchforked them into the dingy blue cart.

"How bucolic!" Alice exclaimed. "When we get home, we'll see who can write the best 'Lines to an Old Wagoner Seen Gathering Leaves from the Elm Drive When Returning from Weston Hill!' "

It was not until after we had washed our supper dishes and were gathered around the hearth at the society house that we returned to the question of marriage, and then it was by a roundabout way. Frances had recovered her novel from behind the davenport cushions where she had hidden it. She ran through the pages impatiently as she asked, "Why is it that in books, men are so nice and women are such fools? It isn't true."

"It is," Edith contradicted. "Women are spiteful and mean and trivial. Men are generous and broad-minded and magnanimous."

"Who said so?" Derrick looked up at her from where she sat on the floor, knees under her chin. "Don't take some man's word for it. Look around at us. Could men be as nice as we are?"

"But you must admit that men have qualities that women haven't." Edith was stubborn. "Honesty and straightforwardness and straight thinking."

"Nonsense. It's the convention to say so. But either the men who write books are wrong, or they act like such fools when they're with women that we see them at their worst. Of course, we can only judge them by the way they act with us."

"How do they act with us? What qualities do they show, I mean? I like the way they act with me."

"Did you ever know one who isn't conceited? One who didn't know all about whatever subject came up? And who didn't lecture you about it, simply because he was talking to a female?"

"Or," Frances interrupted, "if it was a subject he couldn't possibly pretend to know all about, he ignored its introduction into the conversation, and talked about something else. Did you ever know one who let you tell him anything?"

"Of course not. And naturally," Derrick concluded, "being so conceited, they make themselves out nicer than they are when they write books."

"Perhaps," Edith ventured, not so crushed as she should have been, "they don't let some women see how nice they are, really."

Frances ignored her remark.

"It works the other way around, too, Derrick. Men are nicer in books than out; women are nicer out of books than in. Why?"

"Because," Edith retorted, "they don't let men see how nice they are, and men write them as they see them."

"Nonsense."

"It isn't nonsense. Is there one of us that you like as well when you're with men as alone with you?"

"You may be right," Derrick weakened. "I'm either dumb with them, or quarrelsome. I didn't mean that was nonsense. I mean the bit about men writing what they see. They only do that when they see villainesses like Becky Sharp. If they intend to describe an admirable woman, they make her up out of whole cloth, and she's always a fool. That's because in their eyes the admirable woman is the one who depends most on a man. Look at Dickens's good women, and Thackeray's. . . ."

"When they imagine ideal women, they imagine them fools because they like fools," Frances said.

Edith scorned to answer her, but Alice joined the battle in her stead.

"You aren't being fair to Dickens. Lots of times his women have more backbone and brain than the men. What's-her-name in 'David Copperfield,' and Esther in 'Bleak House.' "

"But they aren't alive. You remember Dora in 'David Copperfield,' but not the other one."

"Then there's De Morgan."

"Yes," Derrick admitted. "That's one of the reasons you can't help loving De Morgan."

"And what about Meredith? There's Diana . . ."

"There's no greater fool in literature than Diana. She has my vote for the prize idiot. He says she's clever, and quotes conversational gems to prove it—then it takes him a paragraph to explain the humor in the remark that sent her suitors off into convulsions of mirth. And the things she did! A moron would have known better." Then Derrick turned to Edith. "You know that if Tom Whitman—to take any one of a dozen possible examples—put you into a book, he'd make you a much bigger fool than you really are. Or, at least, if he had been a Victorian, he would have. As it is—in the works of previous novelists the women were all fools, in those of to-day, they're merely animals."

"S.g., Derrick."

"Oh, well—you can't even attempt to be clever if you're not allowed to generalize. Naturally, once in a while, a man of genius realizes that a woman is a human being and endows her with a little common sense: Shakespeare and Thomas Hardy. I've just read 'Jude the Obscure. It's tremendous; the most impressive portrayal of the growth of a man's intellect and the degeneration of a woman's, caused by exactly the same battering by circumstance In the beginning she has a mind, and the spirit to use it—and every bit of it she loses, through one blow after another, until at the end she's beaten to a pulp . . . it's dreadful . . . but you would no more marry a man who could see like that than one who thought you were a fool."

"Derrick," Madeleine asked quietly, "do you really hate the idea of marriage as much as you pretend?"

"I *loathe* the idea of marriage." She sprang to her feet, and, turning her back to us, stood staring down into the fire. "Loathe it! And I don't know why, unless it is the sight of my mother's wasted life. She's thrown it away. Any animal can produce children."

"Does your mother call it wasted?"

"I don't know." She turned around and faced us. "You know, I think even if I fell in love, I'd deny it to the bitter end. It's only your body that falls in love—your mind knows better, all the while . . . No, don't exclaim in horror . . . Go and play the piano, won't you, Edy? Let's not argue any more to-night."

No one who heard us talk would have guessed that we were a little awed by Derrick. An unexplainable feeling, but genuine. We heard her describe without reserve the events and emotions of the past, yet were not altogether sure that we knew the Derrick of the present. We laughed at her, and at what she wrote, but felt an invisible wall beyond which there must be no trespass; we were with her morning, noon, and night for four years, yet never gave her a nickname. . . .

She pretended not to take seriously the writing of poetry; perhaps that is why we dared to laugh at her and it. She said that she wrote it because Frances and Alice did, and because it was fun to have it to read and discuss at our supper parties in the society house or in canoes on the lake—and because she liked the thrill of exultation that came always, whether the verses were good, bad, or indifferent, with the writing of the last word. She called herself a Pantheist that year, and most of her writing dealt with that subject.

Whatever her motives in writing it, whatever our estimate of her poetry might be, certainly she began to make for herself an enviable and amazing reputation in the college. It is hard to tell which of her poems, printed in the "Magazine," so marked her and set her apart . . . there were some War poems, better than most . . . one had to write War poems then if one wrote at all . . . but I think it was more probably the one that she called "Swallows' Wings."

At mid-year time we had set aside an evening to review for our literature examination, and had determined beforehand, Madeleine and Edith and I, amused yet resolute, to keep all attention on the business in hand. We had decided that the best way, and undeniably the most pleasant, to do our reviewing was for one to read selections to the others and have them guess the authorship, giving reasons. . . . Those of us who dreaded that examination banded together in a conspiracy to keep the others from talking. Derrick lay on the bed with Page's "British Poets" on her chest, and read to us as she skipped through it. We learned then what determined conversationalists they were: discussions of style led so easily to discussions of philosophy, and discussions of philosophy came to no end. In spite of all we could do, they were misled by the Immortality Ode into a relation of their own experiences of intimations of other existences; we who had never had any intimations of immortality, but had firm convictions as to the limitations of the human mind when confronted with a sheet of examination questions, sat and listened to them, three unwilling martyrs.

When we came back to the dormitory the next afternoon, after the examination, Derrick said that she had written a poem about the swallows and the chimney and immortality . . .

"Old warden Life, waiting at the door
   The hour that sends me away,
Do not so solemnly finger your beard,
   Nor bid me kneel and pray.

"For I am not a craven, and
   Of prayers I have but one;
I shall not fear if I but think
   Of wind and sky and sun.

"I only pray thee, Life, release me
   While in the green-gold sky
About the cold black chimney, at twilight,
   The fleet-winged swallows fly.

"The birds who came with whir of wings
   Beneath the elm-tree boughs
To nest above me while I dwelt
   Alone in an empty house,

"Whose beautiful wings awakened in me
   Memories of wind and sky,
Sun on the hills, and windy grain, when
   But one were wind and I.

"Fain would I see those wings again as
   I go out to sky and sun:

137

Then shall I have no fear at all of
    Our being eternally one."

After the news came, in May, of Andrew's death in France, she tore up all that she had written about the War, except one that I found in her notebook, and was allowed to copy before it was destroyed:

"Winds blow south on August nights,
    In September, north;
August nights are myriad-voiced
    When the winds go forth;

"August nights are sweet with scent
    Of mown clover hay,
Noisy with the locust and
    The light leaves at play.

"From the south September winds
    Blow but listlessly,
Nothing speaks, September nights,
    Save a whispering tree.

"August nights are nights to sleep;
    The north winds are cool;
Warm September nights (the moon
    Is very gold when full)

"Are nights for lovers to remark
    Shadows of the leaves,
Moonlight on the bannered corn,
    Grain in silver sheaves . . .

"But south and north unnoted
    Night winds come and go;
We only turn our troubled ears
    When the east winds blow,

"As if the sound of guns could come
    With them from afar . . .

And what are the names of months to you
    Where the battles are?

"August nights are myriad-voiced,
    September nights are still . . .
But how should you remember them,
    Entrenched upon your hill?"

It was in the spring that Derrick wrote the Prize Play, but she had to be driven to do it. She came in one night disgruntled because she had been rebuked for her attitude toward her work—she neglected determinedly all that did not interest her—with the admonition that she could not go through life in such a way.

"How does she know how I should go through life?" Derrick grumbled. "It's my life, not hers."

"Is there any quality or virtue that one could be sure would carry one through? It would be easy enough to cultivate it."

"Courage, this man thinks." Frances looked up from her book.

"Fortitude?" Derrick peered over her shoulder. "Corking, isn't it? But you know, Fran, it isn't courage we need. With us, it won't be a struggle against things that terrify, but against things that smother. We'll always be comfortable— we don't need money—" Frances groaned and Alice tore her hair. "You know what I mean. Don't be geese, just because you've spent your allowances. We'll never starve in a garret—it wouldn't be common sense, when we've families to provide for us, and brains to provide for ourselves. Perhaps it's courage for some people . . ."

"Perhaps it's love?" Edith smiled. She knew she would be teased . . .

"No, that's too easy. There's not one woman in a hundred that doesn't love something, if it's only a dog—and I can't see that it helps them to get through life."

189

"Not if 'getting through life' means getting happiness out of it—or getting through it with the least possible amount of unhappiness. You are foredoomed to lose the thing you love, and then where are you?" Madeleine was abrupt in her speech. "It is beauty that never betrays you, and that you never lose. And, really, it's a watchword that answers for achievement as well as for happiness. The world is a beastly place, but one might make it a little less beastly for other people. That's the one answer I can think of to the threat of futility."

"Lin! I thought you were the complete cynic, and didn't believe in any answer to that threat."

"Sometimes I don't."

"Beauty is no battle-cry for me," Derrick continued. "It would only make me go home and be placid and good-tempered and social. I need something to drive to action—and so do you, Alice McIntyre. Sloth will undo us, if we haven't some charm to defeat him."

"I said 'beauty of achievement,' " Madeleine repeated.

"Too high-sounding. Love of fame might do—but what fool could go around shouting about fame? No—there's only one word—in the language of every day, 'persistence.' " She sighed. "My pathway so far has been strewn with three-page monuments to my lack of persistence."

At that opportune moment the president of the dramatic club appeared in the door.

"It's you I'm looking for, Derrick." Frances rose and offered her the Morris chair. "Why haven't you written a play for the contest?"

"I meant to, but other things were more important . . ."

"Important!" The presentation of the original play was the event of the spring term. "Look here, Derrick—you know you can write a better play than anyone else in college—"

"How did you guess it?" Derrick grinned.

"You've got to write one, for the honor of the college. There's another week before the contest closes—"

"I don't believe in doing things for the honor of the college. That's an outworn ideal. I'm an individualist."

"Do it for yourself, then—" she laughed. "Or don't you believe in fame, either?"

"I'm a glutton for it. But I have decided against 'fame' for a watchword, in favor of 'persistence,' and I can't persist in what I haven't begun, can I?"

"Derrick," I reproached her. "You began a play a month ago—"

"Sue compels me to be frank, Bess." She laughed. "I meant to pretend to be superior to your old contest. I began a play, and it was so rotten I put it away. I never wrote a play before—"

"No matter how rotten it is, you finish it. We've got to give a play in public, and we don't want to blush for it. Any you write will be fit to produce, which is more than can be said for most that have been handed in. And the judges are strangers—we don't want to be ashamed for the college."

"I'll finish it, Bess—but it doesn't promise well."

For the rest of the week Derrick buried herself in the stacks in the library, with reference books piled up about her. The play was "Catherine de Medici." I thought she would have done better to write about Tecumseh, and said so.

"I'm sick of Tecumseh," she defended herself. "I've done it for every theme I've written in this college. Besides—girls are impossible in modern men's costumes—they're better in velvet and lace."

Late on Friday afternoon, wan and exhausted, she came home with a monumental heap of manuscript; that night she prepared to read it to us, for our criticism. Before she had gone far, Alice took it from her.

"You're not dramatic enough. Let me read it . . ." And she and Frances proceeded with a riotous burlesque.

When they had done, Madeleine turned to Derrick in amazement.

"Do you mean to say you intended that to be taken seriously?"

"You mustn't mind us," Alice hastened to say. "Of course, it's serious. I mean to try out for Henry of Navarre, myself. It's a magnificent part."

"Thank you. . . . We bit our thumbs at you, Lin. It's a tragedy: Catherine's fear for the theme, that led her to the extremity of Saint Bartholomew's. Blood and thunder combined with the subtlest psychology—"

"What do you know of subtle psychology?" We laughed at her . . . but we knew in spite of our mirth that it was better than any one else could do, and it was with no surprise that we heard that it was the one to be presented.

Alice was chosen for the part she wanted, and for the next two weeks the two of them were absorbed in preparations. Derrick went to rehearsals, helped to make selection of costumes, and even painted scenery when it was discovered that there was nothing at hand that would serve as walls of a sixteenth-century palace. She was worn to a shadow when the day came for its performance. Madeleine watched her critically at lunch, and followed her upstairs.

"You'd better sleep this afternoon, Derrick. You look sick . . ."

"Sick! Sick! I should hope I was sick! So would you be. I'm so ashamed of Catherine I could crawl into a hole and die, and instead I've got to go to-night and pretend to be pleased. Pleased!"

"The girl has lost her mind." Frances stared at her. "You didn't mind when Al made fun of it, and we all laughed."

"Of course not. That was you. But to have the whole damn public see me blush—"

We could have told nothing about the play, afterward, except that Alice played magnificently her "magnificent part." We sat with hearts of ice, afraid that some one would forget a line, and when it was over, and Derrick did not respond at once to the calls for her—"We want *Derrick Thornton!*"—we wondered uneasily what had happened. Only Madeleine remained calm, as always. We hated her. "She's probably gone off somewhere to be sick," she said.

Strangely enough, when Derrick stood finally on the edge of the platform, she seemed as unknown, as unfamiliar, as if we had not seen her for ten years—as remote as the north star. She could not speak, for the clamor, the cheers and applause . . . she merely stood there, laughing, her arms full of roses, vivid against the dark curtain. It was not until the cast joined her on the stage, and Alice, still bearded, in ruff and doublet, stood whispering in her ear that she became ours again . . .

One could not have asked a noisier fame. Frances seized my arm in her excitement. "Think of the dozens of times Derrick will do this! Aren't you glad we saw her the first time?"

We battled our way to the stage, through those who crowded around her, and finally bore her home. In her room we puttered around her uselessly but affectionately, helped her out of her evening dress and put her flowers in vases collected along the corridor.

Frances, sucking a finger that she had torn on the thorn of a rose, regarded her curiously.

"How does it feel to be famous?"

"It isn't worth the agony."

"Don't you think you could get used to it in time?"

"No. My name's my own, and I can't bear to hear it shouted. . . . It leaves you with such an empty feeling to find out that you don't like what you've always wanted—as if the bottom had dropped out of everything." She sighed heavily as she dropped on the edge of the bed, her feet in bedroom slippers, her hair-net standing off rakishly from her tumbled hair. "Don't laugh at me, Sue. My triumph is dust and ashes in my mouth!"

But I could afford to laugh, remembering how she had looked alone there on the stage, smiling at the tumult.

THE WAR NEWS grew worse and worse that spring, and we were tense with eagerness to be out and away; we regarded with envy the class to be graduated in June, whose members would be free to do something. . . . Do Something, we said in exasperation, seeing it spelled with capital letters. We threatened, each of us, not to return for our last year, but to go into nurses' training, or the Red Cross. But scattered broadcast as we were, we spent the summer in unwarlike talk, parties and excursions, and all the normal activities of any summer vacation. We returned in September to relate what we had done, rather than what we intended to do; Alice was full of a camping trip in the Canadian wilds, Edith had been in Maine, Frances on Cape Cod. Derrick had seen that summer the wedding of the first and best of her old friends: Mary Graham had married Bill Stewart. She laughed over it, and told us the story of her one romantic encounter with Bill.

For the first week in September after college opened, we suffered triumphantly the martyrdom of caps and gowns and stiffly boned collars. Madeleine was magnificent in hers; amazed Freshmen whispered together in her wake when she had passed . . . but the wise Sophomores watched for Derrick and pointed her out to them when she swept through the library reading-room, her books under her arm, her gown floating out behind her, her cap aslant above the clear hazel eyes. Derrick and Alice and Frances were supposed in the popular mind to be known favorably to members of the faculty; the first two in their advanced literature courses played at being scholars, and spent hours in the library stacks; Frances, it was rumored, had been said by her professor to have made a contribution to philosophy in her June paper, and she was quite generally regarded with awe . . . But still we found time to argue the old questions, morning, noon, and night . . .

Derrick came in one time with a book of verse she had been given to review for the "Magazine," and asked us to discuss it. Our communistic life was carried even to this point; we covered labor problems for Madeleine, poetic philosophy and all questions of art for Derrick and Alice. Frances came in once and said, "You must talk about God to-night—I've a philosophy paper on Him due to-morrow—" But this evening we balked; we had not even seen the book.

"It's the Princeton boys' stuff," Derrick explained, "and it's so much better than ours that it's pitiful. Why should it be? Their brains are no better than ours."

"Perhaps they are."

"Now, Edy! We've settled that, once and for all. Why is it better, Sue?"

"Perhaps it's because they concentrate more—don't try to do anything but write poetry."

"No committees, you mean? No boards, no theatricals? No shouting about college spirit? We entered on a crusade against college spirit last year, as I remember, but haven't got very far."

"Think what the crusade has done for you, Derrick," Madeleine scoffed. "You refused to have your name put up for 'Magazine' editor last spring, because you wanted to devote this year to art—"

"Only partly because of that, and partly because I knew I shouldn't be elected, and if my name were up it would have split votes and kept Elizabeth out."

Madeleine did not heed the interruption. "And so you

present the perfect picture of a lady devoting her life to art. You write your papers the day before they're due, and your Poetry Club things you postpone doing so long that you have to go without dinner the night the club meets to get them done. What do you do with all the time you gained by staying off the 'Magazine'?"

"I think," Derrick laughed, "and converse. . . . But to come back to the subject. Why is the male superior?"

"I tell you," I insisted, "they care more about it than about anything else. You may care a lot about it, but not so much that you don't waste energy on other things."

"I don't care for anything else in the world."

"You may be willing to admit that to us, but you wouldn't take such a stand publicly for fear of being laughed at."

"And," said Madeleine, "you know perfectly well that if we told you that we didn't want you to write—that you couldn't—you would never write another word.'

"I suppose not. Alack-a-day! I've a poor, weak, palsy-stricken will, and I may as well renounce my ambitions first as last. Think how peaceful life would be if you made that decision and never had anything on your conscience about that."

"Don't be a fool," I rebuked her crisply. "It's not true that your conscience would be free—"

"Sue—" she frowned upon me severely—"you're going to be what the novelists call a 'dominating personality.'"

We renewed the discussion afterward with less exchange of personal remarks. Derrick and Frances had received wedding announcements from a girl who had been, our first year of college, the conspicuous literary hope of her generation, editor of the "Magazine," an example to the young . . .

"And now," Derrick wailed, ' married! A girl might as well be dead as married! I refuse to admit that men have better minds than women, but they certainly aren't victims of marriage as women are."

"Women accomplish mighty little, but it's no more true of married than of unmarried. Think of all the gifted girls we've known that haven't done anything—maybe they haven't had time yet; but think of all those whose names have come down to us—how many of them have done anything?"

"Perhaps a lot of girls, because they're clever and precocious, seem gifted when they're really not." This was Madeleine. "Sometimes I believe I'm the only girl in these United States who doesn't think she can write."

Derrick laughed, but Alice rose belligerently and ran her fingers through her hair.

"It's because women have been under man's heels for so many long centuries." Of course we shouted her down, derisively; she chuckled, but when we gave her a chance, continued. "I mean it. Think of all the centuries when it has been man's part to do and woman's to be done to—or simply, done! It's different now, but how long will it be before a habit of mind like that can be broken?"

"But, Al! Think!" Derrick remonstrated. "The proportion of women who accomplished really great things to men of achievement was every bit as large while women were trampled under man's heel, as it is now that they're free."

"Don't you think, Al," Frances knit her brow—"that it may go deeper than that? It may be instinct rather than habit. It is not only woman's habit to live passively, rather than actively, but it is also her instinct. Psychologically and physiologically, I mean. You talk about a woman's creative desire being satisfied with children—about her not needing any other outlet for the creative instinct; but, really, how much creative instinct does a woman have? Isn't it man's creative desire that gives a woman children? She merely submits—"

"You mean that women haven't the will to create that men have? That in the case of art, women may have as much creative imagination as men, but aren't driven by the force that makes them use it? Why not? Is it a biological distinction that can't be overcome?"

"Yes, something like that. Of course, I may be talking perfect nonsense. But you know they aren't driven by love the way men are—they may be restless and unhappy, but not absolutely driven. At least, not normal women. They submit to men and have children. It's too bad there isn't something they could submit to to make them use their mental creative powers."

"But if it's a biological distinction, evolution ought to do away with it"—Alice stuck to her original point. "I maintain that it's a habit more than anything, and that we'll grow away from it as women grow more independent."

"I agree with Edith," Derrick broke in. "It's because women—"

"But, Derrick! I haven't said a word!"

"I agree with what you would have said if you hadn't been 'fast asleep' behind the arras, snorting like a horse.' . . . There's no way to get around it. Woman can't fix her mind on abstractions as a man can—Fame and Glory and Art—because her mind is intent always on the people she cares about and wants to please Love, I mean—love in the broadest sense. A woman's life is governed by the desire to win some one's approval—not just a lover's or a husband's, necessarily, but the person's she cares most about. Perhaps the approval of a group of persons—but only in rare cases, of the multitude."

We were indignant, of course, but she was roused to her theme.

"Why do you write poetry, Fran?—Al? Because you're simply bursting with something that has to be said? Pooh! You write it because you want my approval, I write it because I want yours—or because I want to surprise my family pleasantly some day."

"You're a cynic, Derrick. It's a terrible thing to say about us—and I thought you were a stanch defender of the sex. Won't you allow us any higher motives than that?"

"The theory fits the known facts admirably."

"It doesn't," Alice contradicted. "If women did things for the sake of winning some one's approval, then married women would accomplish more than unmarried."

"Oh, no!" Derrick shook her head. "It's women who demand things of each other; women who accomplish do it because they are driven by sisters or aunts or frank and brutal female friends—like you! But the minute a woman cares only for some man's approval, she's lost, because no man demands intellectual attainment of a woman—he doesn't even like it—it makes him uncomfortable because it endangers his feeling of superiority. A man demands comfort always, and love sometimes, and all obstacles removed from him while he does his creating and follows his intellectual endeavors. Of course, it's a terrible weakness in women to need to be driven—"

"But, Derrick! There must be exceptions. Some men demand intellectual attainment. There's George Eliot."

"And Lewes? Yes—the one example in a thousand—but it really proves my point—she would never have written a novel if he hadn't absolutely made her. She said so herself. He's the rare man who does want the woman he loves to amount to something. And then, the Brownings—the best things she did were for him; but I don't suppose that he really thought that his superiority was endangered—"

"We don't think there's anything in your old theory." Alice moved to the couch where Frances sat on the edge beside the drowsing Edith, as though to declare that together they would stand. "Think of all the women who did things, and didn't do them because anyone drove them to it. What about Jane Austen and the Brontës?"

"I don't know. Perhaps the Brontës hounded each other, I know very little about Jane Austen—but she did have an older sister she was devoted to. How do you know they didn't work to please their sisters?"

"You think Jane Addams and women like that aren't devoting their lives to an idea—or an intention, or whatever you call it?" Madeleine asked.

"No. They're devoting themselves to a lot of dirty little ragamuffins they have seen in the slums. But, of course, that's different—that isn't creative—they may simply be inspired to do the most useful thing possible with their lives."

"Look here, Derrick—don't be so damned superior about your old creative work—the most a lot of us can hope to do with our lives is something 'merely useful.' "

"Oh, Lin! I didn't mean to be superior. People who talk most about what they expect to do are nine times out of ten mere cumberers of the earth. I'm not worried about your life, but about Fran's and Al's and mine. Think of the women who have had minds capable enough, but either wasted them utterly, or used them to help some man who got all the credit."

"For instance?"

"Well—Dorothy Wordsworth. Why should William have sucked up her mind? He had enough of his own—"

"I doubt it."

"At any rate, it wasn't fair. Then, Jane Welsh Carlyle—what mightn't she have done if that old curmudgeon she married had given her a chance to use her brain? Or if she hadn't married him?"

"She was probably happier married to him, in spite of her complaints, than she would have been writing in a garret to please some female friend."

"No doubt. We weren't talking about happiness. What artist is happy? I'll wager the Lord Himself was pretty sick when He had finished creating the world and saw what it was like."

"Derrick!"

"Speaking of happiness, Derrick, there's another point." Alice was still combative. "Don't you think that generally a man creates because he's unhappy, and either wants to forget his unhappiness, or to express it—a sort of divine discontent. Which has been said before, I believe. Women aren't so apt to be restless and unhappy—they slip so easily into content, and are made comfortable with so little—"

"What is it that satisfies them? That's my point—approval of the person they care most about; and if they get that without working for it, so much the better."

"No. Other things satisfy them—physical comfort, wealth, society. I'm more of a cynic than you are, Derrick."

"You're wrong if you are. You think a starving woman in a garret, who cared for no one, would be more apt to do something great than the comfortably well-off woman who was keen about some one who insisted upon her achieving? No—the woman in the garret would get herself a safe job at so much a week and live on it."

"Then you think it behooves us all to attach ourselves to those who demand Great Works?"

"Exactly."

"But you can't say to yourself, 'I will love this person, because he will make me work. I will not love this person, because he won't.'"

"Of course you can't, Al," Madeleine said. "Don't pay any attention to her. If there isn't something stronger than yourself inside you to make you do it, no one else can."

Edith turned over on the couch and almost pitched Frances off onto the floor.

"Let's not get started talking about each other—we should never come to an end. I was trying to keep awake because I thought you were 'most finished.'"

"We are, Edy." Madeleine rose, gathered to her her trailing blue bathrobe, and picked up from the desk a water-stained copy of Keats. "Come bathe while I do, Derrick, and we can finish learning the 'Ode to the Nightingale' while we soak."

When they had gone out, Edith rose, yawning.

"You don't agree with that theory Derrick expounded, do you? Because, if you do, I don't see how you could like much the idea of her living with Madeleine in New York next year."

"Why not?" We stared at her.

"I should think you could see with half an eye . . . Madeleine's so fond of her that she doesn't care a rap whether she does anything or not . . ."

Everyone knew that winter that our entrance into the War was unavoidable; we were tense with expectation. Through January and February and March we spent our evenings knitting, our Saturdays and holidays making bandages and surgical dressings—hundreds of us, around long tables set in endless rows, experts, after infinite repetition, in the manipulation of gauze and linen.

When the six of us were at the shore during spring vacation, the news came that war had been declared. When we had read the papers, we climbed the highest rocks above the water and lay for hours in the spring sunshine showered with spray from the waves that pounded in, that thundered into the caverns beneath us and twisted themselves into great sucking whirlpools. With our eyes on the horizon, on a smoke-hung steamer or a distant, sun-touched sail, or on the low clouds, we wondered whether the Government would send an army or merely the navy and supplies . . . whether all the boys we knew would go . . . whether we could go, ourselves . . . we fumed at the necessity of returning to college for those last ten weeks. It seemed immoral to be as light-hearted as we knew that we should be. After Commencement—Derrick said that she would take a course in motor mechanics and drive an ambulance, Alice that she would train as a nurse, Frances that she would learn to typewrite and go as some sort of secretary. Three insane ideas, but we did not jeer; people must do insane things in an insane world. Only Madeleine discussed no plans, but said quietly that she intended to go—she didn't know how—

There was a sudden gleam in Derrick's eye as she watched Madeleine.

"Look here, Lin, have you done anything about getting there?"

"No—not a thing. Did you think I shouldn't tell you?"

"I know you wouldn't, unless I made you promise before-hand."

"I hate to talk about what I'm going to do until I'm sure."

"But we've caught you now. Promise to tell both of us . . ."

She promised, and so we two knew when she applied to her uncle to find something for her to do that would take her to France, but it was weeks later before we heard of any result of her petition.

On a Sunday night two or three weeks before Commencement, four of us were enjoying the comfort of Alice's corner room, with its full bookcases, its etchings, and copies of solemn old Italian paintings; our consciousness of incomparable and never-to-be-surpassed contentment was due partly to the sound of the June rain that fell noisily outside, partly to our satisfaction in each other's company and to the realization that we must make the most of that companionship before it came to an end.

Frances sat at the desk with heavy philosophic tomes piled high about her, the desk-lamp turned low over the paper she was trying to write: "The Influence of Parmenides on Plato." Her thin legs were twisted about the chair; her Pre-Raphaelite features, always so adequately rendered Bostonese by her severe style of neckwear and coiffure, to-night glowed pale and picturesque under her tumbled red hair. Alice was beside her in the Morris chair reading "Changing Winds"; she chuckled over it now and then, or thumped it in disgust, or shuffled her feet. Madeleine had put up the card-table and had strewn her papers—notes, quotations, scrawled page-numbers—across its surface. She was about to attempt to collect them, to evolve from chaos a dissertation on "Browning's Conception of the Freedom of the Will." She looked tired: her long legs were thrust far out in front of her, under the table, her hands lay listless in her lap, and she scowled at the thick volume of Browning which lay half on the edge of the table, half on her chest.

The windows were open, and the voices of those on the

way to Sunday-evening chapel floated in. The wind blew into the room in little gusts, the curtains fluttered, and rain spattered on the window-sill. Madeleine sighed profoundly, and the Browning slid from her chest to the floor. She glared at it.

"Browning pains me. I can't tell whether or not he believes in the freedom of the will."

Alice closed her book, hitched her chair closer to Madeleine, and flipped over the Browning pages with accustomed hands.

"Look—he says he believes it," and she ran her fingers down the lines of "Prospice," quoting here and there:

" 'Fear death—to feel the fog in my throat,

Yet, the strong man must go:

For the journey is done, and the summit attained . . .'
No, he doesn't either, does he? But it's rather nice."

"Nice, but not helpful."

"Isn't there any place where he says yes or no?"

"Plenty—plenty where he says one, and plenty where he says the other. That's the trouble. I think he does, though. You can't get around

" 'One who never turned his back, but marched breast forward.' "

"Why do you want to get around it?"

"I don't believe in it much myself, and it's so hard to get the point of view of anyone who does."

Alice thumped on the table with her book. "How can any one be so witless as not to believe in the freedom of the will?"

"I don't see how any one can reconcile an omnipotent God with freedom of the will."

"I don't. I don't believe God is omnipotent."

A whistle sounded just then in the corridor, and Edith and Derrick opened the door, soaking wet and dripping little pools on Alice's threshold.

"Hello—put your wet coats in your own rooms, not in here, and come back, *vite*. We're talking about God."

"We'll be right in. Come, change your things, Edy—you look like the Poor Little Match Girl." Derrick hustled her off.

"Didn't you bring a paper? I thought you went for that—"

"They were all gone—sorry." They closed the door behind them.

"Edy *is* a lamb of God, isn't she!" Madeleine shoved back her Browning with a sigh.

"Yes—but why so demonstrative all of a sudden?"

"I was just thinking of my fondness for her—for us all. Aren't we nice?"

"We are, but let's not tempt the jealous gods. Commencement is week after next."

"Here they are, back again—that's it—sit on the bed"— I moved over to make room for them—"and don't say a word until they get started again."

"I suppose Al was talking? She hasn't told us her idea of God this week—" Derrick chuckled.

"It seems just now to be something like that of H. G. Wells in 'Mr. Britling,' eh, Al?" I prompted her.

"Yes—I don't think He is omnipotent at all. I think He grows with the ages, develops, advances toward Perfection —you know."

"I know." Frances came to her assistance. "You believe just the opposite of Berkeley. Instead of thinking that we have ideas because God has them, you think God has ideas just because we have them; that is, if men have an idea of a God that has ideas, there will be a God that has those ideas. In other words, God is man's idea of God, neither better nor worse than He is conceived by man. An idea projected into space. Not a very active God, is it?"

"A remarkably lucid explanation, Fran," I scoffed, and Derrick murmured something about that being what Thomas Hardy believed if you could say that he believed anything . . . but they continued with no notice of our comments.

"No, not active at all—merely an idea," Alice agreed. "It's all very well to say that God must be omnipotent and omniscient and perfect, because we have an idea that He is all those things. But I don't believe it. We haven't any notion what Perfection is, although our idea of it progresses all the time. See what I mean? I don't think God is ever any more perfect than our idea of Perfection, and that He is growing all the time just as humanity progresses."

Madeleine put Browning on the table and sat up eagerly "I'm getting awfully mixed, Al, but if you mean that God has always been man's idea of God, wouldn't it have been fun to have lived in the days of the old Greeks, and actually to have run the risk of meeting Diana in the woods!"

"How absurd!" Derrick jeered. "Like the mediæval idea that Jupiter and Hera and the rest of them really existed, but were devils and not gods. . . . Do you think, Al, that there are as many Gods as there are different ideas of God, or do you jumble them and take the general average?"

"Alice, what I don't see is this—" I tried to recall them to the point. "If God is an idea, created by man, who created the world in the first place? If you have to conceive another creating force, then it is your creating force that is God, and not your old idea—"

"There's a practical soul." Edith smiled at me, head on one side. "Tell us, Al: who created the world?"

"There you have me. I don't know . . ."

"What about immortality, Al?" Madeleine wanted to find some one who believed what she wanted to believe. "If God is only an idea, you can't believe in immortality, can you?"

"No, I don't. That is, I don't believe there is any except what exists on this earth—art, and influence, and that sort of thing. Do you believe in it, Lin?"

"I don't know, honestly. One's religion—one's faith—is a constant struggle between reason and emotion, isn't it? If I thought Mother and Father and Bob would be waiting for me somewhere on the bank of a river when I died, I

207

shouldn't mind dying at all. But I don't. It's—it's preposterous!" We sat silently a minute, while the clock ticked hurriedly. Then Madeleine laughed. "Sometimes I can make myself believe in reincarnation—that one goes from life to life in a struggle for perfection. But then, of course, if the people you're fond of die first, they get a step ahead of you, and you can't catch up, so what's the use? Sometimes I don't believe anything, except that it's all a colossal, ghastly joke —no God, no anything, except chance . . . What about you, Derrick? Do you believe in immortality?"

"You know that I do. I don't know any philosophy, so you can batter my arguments to pieces; but I do believe that the fragment that is in you that is your soul is immortal—that it is God, whatever God is, and always will be. Of course, that doesn't mean that I believe in personal immortality . . . how can any one, when all that makes a person— character, individuality, personality, appearance—depends on the flesh—either is what you inherit, or what your environment makes you—and so must perish with the flesh, in fact often perishes before the flesh. . . . But there is something that can rise above the flesh once in a while, and know that it is infinite and eternal . . . you know: sky and air and wind and earth and stars . . ."

She hesitated a minute in embarrassment, then leaned forward, clasped her hands in her lap, and continued:

"Do you remember how last year at exam time we talked about our last intimations of immortality? Well, I have had it since, twice . . . I don't know why I am telling you this . . ."

"Go on, Derrick. Don't be a fool."

"Once was during the holidays, when I had taken ether to have my wisdom teeth pulled, and, coming out of it, I positively knew . . . I thought, while I was still unconscious, I mean, that I hadn't been unconscious at all—that I was being dragged back from the plane where you were conscious of most—of everything, really—to the one where you were conscious of least. The first thing I remember was an existence penetrated by air and sky and sun, particularly sun, and greenness, as if it were summer, and in that instant I thought, 'I haven't been unconscious, I've been conscious on a higher plane than this, even,' but I couldn't remember what it was . . . but it was tremendous, and I rebelled at being dragged still farther back, to a still lesser plane—and then, suddenly, I was back. . . . Now, Fran, don't call it a common experience, and say that all psychologists can explain it—I don't want it explained. . . . It sounds silly to say 'plane,' as if I were a swami or a spiritualist, or something, but it's the word that was in my mind at the time. Isn't it interesting?"

"It is," Madeleine said, doubtfully. "But I can't see that it *proved* anything. You weren't actually over the border . . ."

"You said you had felt it twice, Derrick," Frances reminded her. "When was the other time?"

"A couple of weeks ago. You remember, Sue—the day you and Al found me in the woods, and asked me what I was doing there, so disconsolate—and I said I wasn't disconsolate, but had gone out there to think?"

Alice and I, walking one afternoon in a remote part of the campus, had come upon her where she sat at the foot of a pine tree, her knees under her chin, her arms around them.

"It had happened in class, and I went out there to try to hold on to it. We were reading Keats—or she was reading to us, and talking as she read—and I can't think why—I don't suppose it was what he was trying to say, nor that that was why she read it to us exactly in that way—but suddenly, again, for an instant, I knew . . . 'Are then regalities all gilded masks'—that was the passage. You know it."

"Of course." Alice quoted:

" '—there are throned seats unscalable
But by a patient wing, a constant spell,
Or by ethereal things that, unconfined
Can make a ladder of the eternal wind.'

I suppose he meant something of the kind—then, and in

> 'Be still the unimaginable lodge
> For solitary thinkings, such as dodge
> Conception to the very bourne of heaven.' "

Alice was puzzled. "It is thrilling poetry, but it never proved anything to me."

"Don't misunderstand me. I didn't mean that it was a reasoning process." Derrick paused a minute, to consider. "It was as different from a reasoned-out conclusion as looking out of a window on a pitch-black night is from looking out when it is lightning. On a dark night your reason tells you what may be there, but you don't see it. Then a lightning flash comes along and you do see it. I heard the lines, and for a tenth of a second I absolutely knew. Truly, for that instant—that you are part of eternity, and immortality, and everything—you know that nothing else in the world matters—that there is no point in wondering whether a you that doesn't actually exist ever amounts to anything or not. . . . I suppose that what I'm saying sounds like drivel, but I can't explain it any better."

"I suppose no one who hadn't experienced it could understand," Madeleine replied. "I must stick to my belief in an omniscient and omnipotent God. And, perhaps, a malevolent one. But that doesn't matter. I'd hesitate to go out that door, if I thought that not even the Lord knew what would happen to me next. Of course, I don't believe in the freedom of the will, and I'm utterly inadequate when it comes to a Browning paper."

Some one knocked just then, and, in response to Alice's call, the maid opened the door.

"Is Miss Van Leyden here?—Oh, yes, I see—telegram for you on Mrs. Pearson's 'phone, Miss."

Madeleine rose, nodded significantly in answer to the question in Derrick's eyes, and left the room. Frances watched suspiciously.

"What is it, Derrick? Do you know?"

"How should I know? Something about Commencement, probably. She doesn't know whether her uncle is coming or not. When do you expect your family, Sue?"

"Heaven knows. They're motoring through, you know. This bad weather will hold them up. It will be great to have the car here—"

"We'll paint the place red. It will be our last week together, and we'd better make it worth remembering." Derrick sighed resignedly.

"I hate you, Derrick," Edith groaned. "Fran and I are going to be perfectly miserable all that week, aren't we, Fran? Madeleine will never show a sign of feeling, because she never does, and it is plain to be seen that Derrick is planning to meet the end with a jest on her lips, but we aren't—"

"Lin's coming back—isn't that her step in the hall?" Frances put down the papers she had been fingering nervously.

Madeleine flung the door open.

"Uncle Jim wants me to come to New York on business right away. What time is it?" She was a little breathless, and exultant. We sat stunned, gaping at her. Derrick fumbled for her watch.

"Al's clock is never right. I say half-past eight."

"I can take the nine-forty into town, and catch the midnight to New York, if Mrs. Pearson will chaperon me in and put me on the train. I'll ask her, and then pack. Will you help me get my bag ready, Derrick?"

"Can't I do something?" Edith scrambled to her feet. "I'll call a taxi, then you won't have to bother with that." She ran ahead as Madeleine, Derrick, and I went out into the corridor.

"Well, Lin?"

"My dear! Uncle Jim said to come at once, and to bring photographs for passports!"

"Really? Oh, wonderful, wonderful . . ."

"Sh-sh!"

"It is wonderful, and I hate you for being so calm about it." We reached Madeleine's room and closed the door. "Aren't you going to tell the others now? They will be hurt."

"Can't help it. Nothing is positive, and I'd hate to have it get all over college, and not go, after all." She flung her hat and suit out on a chair. "My word! This has been such a nice room, and in no time at all it will be some one else's, and ruined, with wrong pictures in the wrong places."

Derrick had thrown herself face down on the bed, silent.

"Don't be silly, Derrick. You've known for ages that I've wanted to go." Her voice trembled a little. "A lot of help you're being to me, aren't you?" Then she added, a bit more gently, "Nice girl! Don't stop to think about it till you get into bed, and come and tell me what I'll need in New York."

Derrick rose, threw her a kiss almost gayly, and was hauling blouses from the bureau drawers when Edith came back. Mrs. Pearson was quite willing to go in town with her, and the taxi would come for them. . . . Madeleine ran down the stairs buttoning her gloves as the horn sounded at the door. We leaned out of Alice's window to call good-bye. Then Alice took her novel again, and Frances returned to the desk, where she sat and stared at Plato and Parmenides. Edith picked up Madeleine's papers that had been left on the table, and arranged them in neat little piles.

"It leaves such a hole in everything when Madeleine is gone," she complained. "When do you think she will be back, Derrick?"

"She'll come up on the midnight Monday, and get here Tuesday morning."

Frances eyed her severely. "What I want to know is— what is that girl up to? What wild thing is she planning? No —'ye needn't attempt to deny it!' I know it's something."

Derrick looked uncomfortable. "Can't tell, Fran. Sorry."

"Derrick Thornton!" Alice sat up straight, and pounded the arms of her chair. "Is she going to France?"

"Why? What makes you think of that?"

"Just happened to remember something she said to me not long ago. We were talking about some one who had gone over, and she said, 'I am filled with a desire to go and do likewise. Futility is too great a bore to be endured.' Them were her werry words, and she meant it too."

"Don't be silly, Al. She can't go to France. She's too young. They've made twenty-five the age limit, haven't they?" Edith put the Browning away in Alice's bookcase.

"She is going! Derrick cannot tell a lie! My soul! Think of the submarines! Tell us about it."

"She doesn't know for sure. If she goes, it will be as secretary to a hospital unit. Her uncle is influential enough . . ."

They regarded her in shocked silence. The clock's ticking reëchoed in the room, and the rain beat on the window-pane . . .

"But the training—how—" Edith stammered, finally.

"She went to business school last summer. You knew that."

"So she did." Alice crossed the room to the window, and, shielding her eyes with her hands against the pane, looked out into the darkness. "Think of it! Madeleine! And ships torpedoed . . . I wonder if she would mind . . ."

"She certainly would! Don't be a fool!" Derrick's voice was harsh. "I lay with her once on the rocks at Marblehead, watching the waves that came banging in, and she said that she would rather die any way than by drowning. But, of course, the fact that she doesn't want to drown won't save her from it. Sometimes I think Fate has marked her . . ."

"Derrick! Fate! You, too!" We laughed at Alice's disgust, and she turned and asked Frances what she thought.

"I don't know, Al. It depends on whom I am with. With you and me—and Derrick—I think it's up to us—we'll achieve what we go after, if we go after it. But some people can't escape their destinies. I remember the first time I ever saw Lin—she was so different from the commonplace herd

213

that it made you uncomfortable. Something in her eye, as if Fate had marked her . . ."

We laughed at her. "Oh, rats! You would say the same about us, if we were sailing . . . Parmenides has gone to your head . . ."

Madeleine came back on Tuesday morning . . . to be ready to sail she had to be in New York by Friday, and so planned to ride down on the midnight train again; so short was the time between Tuesday morning and Thursday night, with the multitude of things to be done, the last examinations to be taken, and papers finished, that there was not a moment for lamentation along our corridor. The Browning paper had to be written, clothes packed, curtains and books taken down; the Dean had to be interviewed concerning the degree to be taken *in absentia*. Late on Wednesday night, Madeleine put the finishing touches to her paper, during pauses in the conversation, while the rest of us sat about her on the floor, in a chaos of clothes, books, and pictures.

Breathless with the suddenness of it all, we had not done asking her questions as to how it happened . . . She was sailing on a French liner, and she wasn't much afraid of submarines, because they hadn't got many French boats . . . only once in a while, in the middle of the night, she had qualms . . . No, she wasn't sailing alone: the French teacher from her old prep school was going on the same boat, and had been no end nice to her . . .

Edith was the most persistent in her cross-questioning.

"Did they find out all the years you lived in Germany? Wouldn't they have been suspicious?"

"They didn't say anything. Of course, the State Department knows Father was there—it wasn't his fault. But I don't dare to tell Ma'm'selle how fond I am of German still. It's funny, isn't it?" And she watched Alice wrap her battered old German books in newspapers—she handled them as she would have handled red-hot coals. "All these things haven't made any difference about that. Do you know the

song 'Wenn Ich ein Vöglein wär'? Mother used to sing it
to us:

> " 'Bin ich doch im Traum bei dir,
>   Und red' mit dir,
>   Wenn ich erwachen tu',
>   Bin ich allein.'

That and the 'Erl-König': 'Wer reitet so spät durch Nacht
und Wind?' That was Bob's favorite. We lived for two years
in Munich when Bob and I were tiny children, and the
governess used to drag us to an art gallery that we loathed.
I wore a huge flopping red straw hat, and Bob used to amuse
himself by walking round and round me, biting nicks out of
the brim."

Alice had packed the German books and took Descartes
and Berkeley from the shelf.

"By the way," she interrupted Madeleine. "I have found
out about the creation of the world."

"Oh—you have?"

"Yes. I don't think it ever was created."

We all whooped for joy, except Frances, who stopped us
with a superior air.

"She's all right. It's a perfectly justifiable belief. Infinite
regression, you mean, Al?"

"Yes. Why not? Evolution takes us back beyond measur-
able time—why not believe that it takes us back infinitely?"

"But, Al—" Frances took the part of a Socrates, intent
to trap her. "If you believe in going back infinitely, you have
to believe in going ahead infinitely."

"Yes—nothing can end."

"What about immortality, then?"

"After death, the body—and everything—goes back to its
elements—is reabsorbed, as it were. Immortality, as I said
before, is just influence."

"But what about the soul? Does it end? Nothing can end,
you say."

"I suppose I don't believe there is such a thing as the soul."

"Then you're nothing but a blooming materialist."

"I'm not! I shan't be a materialist!"

"You're an inconsistent idiot, Al."

"Of course you are." Derrick laughed. "Whatever may be wrong with Lin's philosophy, she's at least consistent."

"Consistent! Consistent!" Alice, spluttering, rose to her feet. "She's the most inconsistent girl in the world. Here she professes to believe that her life is all laid out for her, and that all she has to do is wait for the next thing that is foreordained to happen—but she digs around with all her energy, and pulls wires here, there, and everywhere, to get to France!"

"Al! I flatter myself that the Lord has predestined me to an active life!"

Derrick interrupted them. "Do you want to take your evening clothes?"

"Of course not. Send 'em home—unless you can use them. They'll be out of style before I'm back again. And my books—Derrick, if you and Al and Sue are really going to have an apartment in New York next year, I'll lend 'em to you. Uncle Jim won't want to be bothered—"

Derrick sighed. "Of course, we want to go to France, but I suppose we'll never get there—the chances are we'll be in New York. Pack them and leave them here for the summer, and we'll write the janitor in the fall where to send them."

She fingered lovingly the richly bound old books. Edith and Frances swooped upon the treasures that the luxury-loving Madeleine had gathered about her during the four years.

"Your pictures, Lin—can't I have them, and your book-ends, and candlesticks?"

"Sh-sh!" Madeleine covered her ears. "I'll leave them with you for the duration of the War, but I hate to have you rejoicing over my obsequies. I'll take this cornfield-in-a-mist with me—put it in the trunk, Sue. I'm fond of it, but it isn't worth anything, if it should happen to be smashed. You can have the Whistler bridge—" She pointed to the etching that hung over her desk. "And Edy and Fran can scrap over the others. I'm afraid to take this vase—I'll leave it with you, Derrick, if you will swear to take care of it faithfully."

Derrick promised, solemnly, and we were silent as Madeleine handed the slender turquoise vase to her. She had carried it back and forth in her suitcase in vacation times, refusing to trust it to a trunk, because it was the last thing her mother had given her.

At midnight the boxes were ready to be nailed; the trunk was packed, except for the last few things. Madeleine jested with us as she wearily prepared for bed. . . . We had unearthed an old snapshot of her, taken after she had typhoid, and had lost her hair. Half-mocking, she held it up before us and said, "I may look that way again. They say the lice—"

"Lin! Oh, horrible!" Edith flung her arms about the tall girl's shoulders and buried her face. "I can't bear it! Nice, clean Madeleine!"

"There, my dear! I was joking . . ."

"A vulgar joke, I should say." Derrick's voice was cold, or tried to be—cold and unshaken. She pulled Madeleine free from Edith's clutches, and continued, "I had a thought, Lin—an inspiration—when you take your paper down in the morning, ask Miss Harcourt if she will chaperon us into town tomorrow night. It is absurd to think of chaperons, when you are about to go to War, but I suppose we must mind rules while we are here . . . We can take Sue's family car, and go to Durgin and Park's for supper, and then put you on the train."

"I'd love to—if Edy will promise not to weep and unnerve me—" And beginning with Edith, Madeleine kissed us all good-night.

The last things that we had to do were finished so soon on Thursday that it was still quite early when we drove away. The shadows had just begun to lengthen out across the green and to creep up the walls; the roofs and towers were still sunlit. Through the cool, deep-green shadows of the wooded parts of the campus, and across the bright grass of the hills, passed groups of girls in gay-colored dresses and sweaters. Derrick turned back to watch them, but Madeleine stared ahead of her, down the road.

Uphill and downhill, in Boston and out again, we drove out along the North Shore, where the wind blew in from the sea into our faces. In the harbor great ships came and went, and, silver-white in the last sun, small sailboats caught the gleams of light and reflected them from the dim horizon. We talked as we rode, of everything and nothing. . . . I wondered, absolved from conversational obligations because I was at the wheel, about what would happen to us all—to Edith, chattering as swiftly as she could about nothing, to avoid saying anything; to Alice, on the other side, holding down her flying hair and quoting poetry about the sea to Frances, on the little seat at her knees; to Derrick, on the other folding seat, silent, with Madeleine's gloved hand back on her knee; to Madeleine herself, beside me . . .

In the dusk, we turned back to the city, left the sea behind us, with all its war-time mystery of restless searchlights; we threaded the narrow, crooked streets of the old harbor edge of Boston, down past Faneuil Hall to Durgin and Park's, where we clattered merrily up the dingy, narrow stairs. It was an old hunting-ground of ours, that noisy, low-ceilinged dining-room, with its odd assortment of habitués: ruddy marketmen, in long white aprons, who talked politics and prices; sleek business men in groups of threes and fours, or paired with strange-looking women; suave Harvard youths; a group of the town's Bohemians. Here we had always come for our first celebration after long vacations—Christmas holidays and the summers. Edith reminded us of it.

"It's funny, isn't it? We can never come here after a vacation again. It will never be the same—never!"

"Shut up, Edy! We'll meet here again some day. Let's

swear it, shall we?" Alice splashed her glass of water above us.

"We can't, Al. Six is a lot to get together from the four corners of the earth, and we may hate each other when we do meet. Some of us will be fat and sloppy, and some of us will have babies that we'll insist on talking about."

"Edy—remember what I said, and, for Heaven's sake, brace up!" Madeleine looked so reproachful that Edith relapsed into silence, and thenceforth the meal was a noisy, if not a genuinely merry one. When we had finished and escaped from the importunate friendliness of the fat waitress, we took the automobile and rode about Boston for two more hours: through the empty, echoing streets along the water's edge, then uptown, around the Common, out Beacon Street . . . we rode in silence, patting each other's knees occasionally, and now and then mentioning incidents of long ago, or not so long ago . . .

In spite of all the hours left before midnight when we turned toward the station, our good-byes were hurried and incoherent. Madeleine gave us barely time to shake hands with her before she turned to follow the porter who had taken her bags. She stumbled a little, hesitated, then went on, as though to turn back now were to be lost. We watched her stride down the long walk beside the train, behind the red cap, until she climbed into her car . . .

We rode out of the city in silence, in silence arrived at our own door, and climbed the stairs to our corridor. Alice was the first to refer to Madeleine.

"She is 'One who never turned her back,' and all the rest of it—and isn't it funny that she honestly thinks that her own choice had nothing to do with it!"

Derrick stopped at her door, and paused doubtfully on the threshold for a minute.

"I don't think it was her own choice. The funny thing isn't that she should go over there, but that she should ever

219

have been here . . . we have lost her for good, but it's something to have had her . . ."

She went into the room, and closed the door behind her . . . the rest of us went on to the end of the corridor, and, from force of habit, dropped on Alice's bed.

"If you are as tired as I am, you won't invite yourselves in here," she scolded. "I suppose you're relieved, Edy—you don't have to worry now about Lin and Derrick living together . . ."

"I wasn't worried. I just wondered . . . of course, Derrick may not do anything, anyway . . . well, she may not," she reiterated, as we exclaimed indignantly.

"Why not? She has shown that she can . . . and there's nothing to keep her from it . . ."

No doubt every one's recollections of Commencement are scattered and kaleidoscopic; I can recall it as a jumbled series of pictures: the orderly and impressive march into the chapel, the mad outpouring, the greetings and congratulations; at the end of the day, the class supper: lights and songs and flowers, and immoderate laughter; the snakewalk around the tables, when we all shook hands with each other for the last time (and, in some cases, for the first, but we did not think of that—we forgot that there were those in the class we had never bothered to know). When the ordeal was ended, we sought retirement in a kitchenette halfway upstairs. Edith laid herself face down on a zinc table and wept hysterically; Alice took the radiator and spread her handkerchiefs out beside her to dry; Frances and Derrick leaned arm in arm against the wall, half laughing and half crying. Frances was the first to control herself.

"Brace up, Edy! We've only a few minutes until we have to get our lanterns and go down to step-singing."

"Commencement is an unspeakable institution." Derrick blew her nose violently. "You get so tired, you've no more control over your emotions than a rabbit. Get up, Al, and wash your face."

"Yes," Frances urged, "wring out your handkerchief and reflect upon the fact that this time next year we'll think all this was awfully funny!"

"But that," wailed Alice, "is the most damnable thing about it!"

Almost before we knew how we got there, we were in line again, capped and gowned, with lighted paper lanterns; we marched to the chapel for the last time, singing. We were near enough to the front of the line to find places on the top step; once there, Derrick, who was beside me, blew out the candle in her lantern, sat down, and leaned wearily against the chapel door.

"They'll have to sing without me," she said. "I was never so tired in my life—I hope I may die if I have to move again to-night!"

In the morning Edith left hastily, afraid to try her spirits further, but the rest of us packed our four years' accumulation in a more leisurely fashion, and lingered until we had recovered our cheerfulness, we had dinner together at the Inn the night before we left, and met the end with mirth . . . Over her coffee Alice adjured us solemnly to listen to her last words.

"This merriment is all very well, but we must remember that this is an important moment, and we must close with due gravity. Are we going to amount to something or not?"

"We are—"

"Then clasp hands around the table and swear this solemn oath: 'Down with Matrimony, up with Art, Fame before Forty or bust!'"

"And our motto—" Derrick hesitated.

"Go on, give us one—"

"The only thing I can think of is, 'Now is the winter of our discontent made glorious summer by this son of York.'"

"Idiot!"

"Is this better: 'Thane of Glamis, thane of Cawdor, King of Scotland'?"

We received her suggestion with the silent scorn it deserved; it was Alice who had another idea.

"Let's wager on our futures—bet on the first one to publish, and make it worth while: a new hat to be contributed by the losers to the winner on our fifth reunion—and I bet on Fran."

"I bet on your poems," Derrick responded promptly.

Part Three

The
Sky That
Holds Them
All

In July I came down to Tecumseh, as I had promised
Derrick I should. Ten years had passed since the Sunday I
had spent there as a child, but I found unchanged the town
I remembered—a remote little county-seat, buried fathoms
deep in dreams and dust. The court-house stood in the shade
of motionless elms and bony sycamores, the clock in its
tower half concealed by the tree-tops. Beyond this square
the central part of the town had no protection from the sun;
it blazed down the length of Main Street with a brassy glare,
and the heat hung above the brick pavement in visible
waves. No one stirred out-of-doors unnecessarily, except for
the few Negroes who slept all day in the shade of the elms
on the court-house lawn.

Derrick had said one time that when I came to Tecumseh
again she would show me how it was possible to love the
sleepy town, but now she had forgotten, or thought of other
things. She offered no comment as we drove down Main
Street one morning, past a few empty, dust-covered automobiles at the curb, past the grocery-store on the corner where,
on the yellow brick wall above the awning, were painted the
signs of the trade: on one side a mammoth bunch of bananas
against a white oval background, on the other, a fish that
stood on his tail in a similar oval. In the window between
a slatternly woman in a soiled kimono leaned out across the
sill. There was a livery-stable on the opposite corner, where
a few men sat with their chairs tipped back against the wall,

or lay with their legs crossed on the slope that led up to the door; all had battered straw hats over their faces.

"Mark them well," Derrick said, "and you will see when we come back that they will not have stirred."

"What a Rip Van Winkle town!"

"It is this accursed heat—it withers your ambition and blurs all outlines, so that everything seems fantastic, and all your thoughts quite mad."

I looked at her sidelong under her hat: her eyes were hidden beneath its deep black brim, but I saw with sinking heart the morose twist of her mouth. It was not the heat that made her so. I remembered the apprehension I had felt when I read her appeal to me to come to Tecumseh as soon as I could . . . an apprehension for which I had been unable to find a cause. I remember now how I watched her and wondered, that morning, as we drove slowly through the deep dust out into the country. The road ran straight before us between two high rows of hedge, neglected in the prevalent fashion until they had become impenetrable walls of trees. Ahead of us there was nothing to see but the road, the unclouded, metallic blue sky, the gray strips of grass at either hand, the converging lines of gray osage-orange hedge.

Strange moods of restlessness and disillusion were easy to explain that summer: the country was stirring itself to go to war, and the sight gave rise to long thoughts. But my fear for Derrick was fear of something worse than that . . . and I tried to think . . .

It might have nothing to do with the War.

It might be a sudden agony born of the sight of her mother grown irrevocably middle-aged. I had come to Tecumseh expecting, unconsciously, to find Mrs. Thornton as she had been on the Sunday when I had seen her first. She was not. The old vigor was lost, and she seemed almost dangerously easy-going. She had grown heavier; the shadows beneath her eyes were sunk deep; she moved more slowly, the old fire was burnt out, the black eyes paler and softer. And her hair . . . with a pang I realized that the gray had so prevailed in the smooth twist of braid that no one who saw her now for the first time would describe her as a black-haired woman. . . . I had seen her once and had remembered her always as the very substance of life, inviolable . . . and now, like a melancholy refrain, there sounded through my mind "That time of life thou may'st in me behold." . . . But I could not see that Derrick looked upon her mother with anything of the dismay I felt. it was trite enough, my reflection that a change so slow as that, so inevitable, is not noticed if it takes place before your eyes. but only when you come upon it suddenly.

It might be that Derrick was haunted by fear for Madeleine. Her first letter had come only the morning before; we had read it together as we sat in the window-seat in her room, while she, at her mother's request, watched the quiet street for the approach of a huckster. Madeleine had written from Paris, where the hospital unit had gone: they had seen one submarine on the way over, but had not been fired at; during her first night in Paris there had been an air raid— and she had stayed in bed all the while, because she had not realized, until she heard the explosion, why the whistles had blown, and she had decided then that it was too late to run, and that, at any rate, it would be as silly as to run from lightning: if you were to be hit, you would be hit. She thought that they would not be in Paris long, but would move up behind the lines. . . . It was true that Madeleine's friends could not think of her that summer with any degree of comfort, but surely fear for her would not make Derrick want me with her in Tecumseh.

It might be Jack. He had clung tenaciously to his ideas about the War. Derrick would not forgive those ideas, and the violence of their opinions had limited them to the most casual intercourse since I had been there. Derrick, by her own account, had always quarreled with Jack; they had always been only too willing to engage in combat. It was not like her to be morbid on such an account, to be afraid of argument, but here was a difference so fundamental, so all-important, that to begin a dispute would be almost fatal. How much would Derrick care if that dispute could not always be avoided?

I liked Jack: liked him for his serene good-humor, for his immediate acceptance of me as a friend and an equal, for the steel in him that held him loyal to Derrick and the others, and, at the same time, to his own beliefs. I liked him for his quietness, for the mirth that twitched his mouth and the affection that sounded in his voice when he teased the children . . . and for the clear sapphire of his eyes above his tanned cheeks. If the situation held terror for Derrick . . . I sighed . . . only the sheerest perversity could lead them to a quarrel . . . but there are moments and moods when there is pleasure in hurting even your oldest friends.

Whatever it was that Derrick feared, whatever the reason why she had wanted me to be there, she obviously did not intend to speak of it. We rode without a word through the dust down a road as straight as an arrow; without a word she sounded a raucous clamor on her horn when a waddling sow climbed from the ditch beside us and crossed in front of our wheels; without a word she stopped the car beside a wagon gate set in the hedge.

"Now you see . . ." she said, finally, and lifted her hand toward the field that had been hidden from us by the long hedgerow. "There is Bill's wheat he was talking about cutting."

The grain was so high that our eyes were hardly above the level of the wide, unbroken sea of burning, dusty gold; motionless, windless, an intense color in the hot sun, it swept from the gate beside us back to the edge of town, where in a blurred line were trees, roofs, spires, and a thin haze of smoke. At one end of the field were the harvester with their machines reaping and binding the sheaves.

"Yes—whatever he meant when he said it would register a high percent, it certainly looks it." Then I broke from the matter of fact. "How lovely it is! I never really believed before, that it was half so beautiful as you made it seem."

"It isn't color so much," she said reflectively, "nor light nor length nor breadth, as it is something intangible—the peace of it, past understanding. Everything slips away from you, and you are left with it. . . ."

"You are conscious of it before anything else, and after anything else, first and last."

"Yes. Lifted on a wave, borne off from your thoughts—as though the earth itself said, 'Peace I leave with you, peace I give unto you—not as the world giveth, give I unto you.' Do you suppose that men who go to War, those who have gone to other wars, and those who know that they must go to this one, are thrown back on this feeling? And that what we are conscious of is not the beauty of the earth alone, but of the mind of man that remembers it, and that remembering, makes it a more transcendent beauty? . . . What is the feeling of a shadow of sorrow that is part of the beauty? A consciousness of impermanence? The fields have their glory, but it is brief enough. Already the wheat is being cut."

"But you never lose the feeling of peace; it isn't a thing of seasons. 'The beauty of the earth is never dead.' "

" 'Poetry,' goose, not 'beauty.' " Derrick laughed. "But you mustn't contradict me before I finish. I was going to wonder about the unescapable sadness that is part of the peace . . . a sort of foreboding . . . either of the loss of the beauty of the earth by our own deaths, or by destruction of the beauty itself. But you say it is your own sadness."

"No. It is just your own mood, colored by what you know. The War will hardly touch us enough to cost us the beauty of the earth, by death or destruction, either one."

We sat in silence for a minute. There were only distant sounds of rattling machinery and men's voices in the fields and the regular monotonous moaning of a dove in the hedge. In sudden irritability, Derrick exclaimed, "Do be quiet, ol' Mr. Rain-Crow: they don't want rain until the wheat is cut." She pulled the gear lever and we slipped forward slowly in the dust. "You didn't see Bill in the field, did you? We might pick him up."

We were on our way to have lunch with the Stewarts.

"He might have been there—I should never have known him beneath a hat like theirs."

"He wears one, of course, but would be embarrassed if we caught him in it—at least, he always used to be. Mary loves everything that has to do with the farm, or that smacks of the soil, and she may have laughed him out of it."

The young Stewarts had gone to live after their marriage in the old farmhouse, which stood a few yards back from the road on the lane that led to his father's late-Victorian dwelling, and which had been used by tenants after Mr. Stewart had built the new house. From the main road one could see only an occasional glimpse of white through the thick grove of maple trees, but from the gateway in the lane there was visible from end to end a low house of whitewashed stone, a patchwork that had been added to by each generation: at one end was the square cabin of hewn logs, gray with age, now used as a summer kitchen, and at the other, the last mid-century addition of high-ceilinged parlors.

We found Mary beneath the maple trees on the lawn, the baby-carriage beside her, with a mosquito net over the wide-eyed baby. She would not let us play with him.

"It's a wonder to me, Derrick, that your mother's babies lived to grow up, the way we handled 'em. I'll wheel him around to the kitchen door and ask Carrie to see that he doesn't choke to death while I show you around."

She pushed the baby-carriage across the lawn to the open kitchen door, and called to the rawboned, jaundiced woman beside the stove, who grunted wordlessly in reply.

"Tenant's wife," she explained, when we turned away. "No good, but you can't get a darky to come into the country to work. What shall I show you? Gardens? Chickens? Barns?"

"All of it. Sue must see one good farm—"

Mary led the way to the barns. She strode ahead of us, a sun-blessed figure, and the light glinted in her smooth spun-gold hair as she turned to talk to Derrick about the farmyard. From the fence I looked down across oak-shaded slopes where stood rows of shelters for the pigs, with their peaked roofs, like so many small wooden tents. Through the wide pastures at the foot of the hill a thin line of water, edged with willows, circled in and out; here the cattle grazed in the shade. The more distant hills were great patches of black, green, and gold, separated by lines of hedge. Over the dark mass of trees on the horizon hung a white haze of clouds, only vaguely distinguishable. A hawk soared lazily, tilting on one wing, above a field of gray-green oats. A picture finished, complete—smooth and gentle—"an endless quiet valley"— the heartfelt things, past speaking dear to unknown generations of dead men—dead men who had found the land a wilderness and who had wrought of it perfection. Here was a tranquillity not to be touched by foreign wars.

Nevertheless, at the luncheon-table, we did discuss the War for a moment. Bill had come from the house to the fence corner where we stood to call us to the meal; if he had been in the harvest field, he had changed his clothes and was immaculate in white trousers and dark coat. The signs of his calling, however, were plain upon him: the deep sunburn on the bridge of his nose and high cheek-bones, his broad, sloping shoulders, the size of his hands, so noticeable when he carved. We spoke, while he filled the plates, of the pleasantness of the low-ceilinged dining-room, its grateful darkness, green-tinged because the sunlight fell through cracks in the closed green shutters, its coolness due to the impenetrability of stone walls a foot thick. Derrick cut sharply across our meandering talk.

"Bill, how do they really feel here about the War? You don't hear . . . Oh, I know, the minister preaches about it, but almost as if it were no more a concern of his than the wars of Saul and David; and Billy and Hunter fight for the newspaper, but only so they can argue about what the generals are trying to do, as though they were reading a serial detective story. And our National Guard Company leaves to-morrow for training, and they say that almost every one who could has enlisted, but you would certainly never guess it. People think of everything in the world to talk about but that."

"It isn't that, exactly. Some of us have to go on doing the same old things, and it's only natural that we should go on talking about them. On the other hand, it doesn't seem possible for it to go on so much longer, after all these years, that our men will have time to train and get over there, and train some more, and still find fighting to do. I don't suppose half the fellows who have gone into the National Guard expect really to get into it."

"Why not? I feel as if it would go on always, like elections or taxes. Even if they won't take any woman under twenty-five, I expect to get there."

"You!" Bill threw back his head and laughed. "Oh, Derrick! The first good strong wind that came along would blow you away!" Almost contemptuously he looked at her thin body. "If it were Mary, now!"

Derrick surveyed his wife's blonde, imperturbable person. "She is magnificent, I admit, but—"

"Don't be silly!" Mary was unembarrassed. "When we used to play until we were ready to drop, Derrick never dropped before I did."

"Thanks, Mary!" Then she changed her tone, and began a little defiantly, "But there are lots of boys, Bill, that aren't planning to go who could as easily as not. I mean those, not like you, who haven't any ties. What's the matter with them?"

"I reckon that lots of us have figured out that since the Government's passed the draft bill, the ones will be chosen that way that ought to go, and it may as well be left to chance. But if you mean Jack Devlin," he added, "I don't know anything about him. He has ideas, and you may as well believe that he's going to stick to them." Then, just as I was afraid that Derrick might enter into a controversy with him, he changed the subject. "Are you folks going to the Country Club dinner to-night?"

"I can't get used to thinking of Tecumseh with a Country Club. Isn't it funny! In the fields where we used to trap muskrats. Yes, we're going: Father and Mother, and Sue with Billy, and Jack and I. Even Hunter: his crowd is going to wait on the tables at dinner, and is allowed to stay and dance. . . . That's why I wondered about Jack. How does he dare to go to a farewell dinner for the soldiers? People might be so unpleasant!"

"Who would be unpleasant? These are enlisted men who are going because they have chosen to go; there will be others there, like me, who are waiting to be drafted. That's nothing to be unpleasant about. Besides, there won't be any one there who isn't a friend of Jack's—who doesn't know as well as you and I know, Derrick, that he isn't a coward—that he is absolutely sincere, if he is absolutely wrong."

"It is hard to respect any one who is as wrong as that."

"Nonsense! Jack Devlin is incapable of doing anything that would cost him your respect. As a matter of fact, I think he half regrets the stand he has taken and wishes he could see things differently."

"Perhaps. He is so fair-minded that he must always see both sides of the question. But all the same, I do think he's just inviting unpleasantness by going to the dance."

After luncheon, we moved to the grass beneath the maple trees, and spent several hours in gossip and discussion of agricultural questions; it was not until late in the afternoon that we returned to town. Derrick drove the car into the garage—the transformed stable—and we entered the house through the kitchen, where we stopped to speak to Cassie.

"Are there lemons enough in the pantry to make lemonade? It's so hot. Who all's home?"

"Ma'g'ret's 'roun' some'e'es, an' mebbe the boys. Yo' maw's down street at the Red Cross, an' the babies a' spendin' the day down to yo' Aunt Anne's. Ah reckon they's lemons a-plenty, but tak' kyeer how yo' use up the ice. Ol' ice-man ain' been 'roun' yit to-day."

"I'll be careful. Sue, call around the house, will you, and

233

see if the boys are at home? Then let me know how many glasses to make. . . ."

I found Margaret sitting in uncomfortable dignity on the side porch, a novel open on her lap. She was, at fourteen, calm, steady, and easy-tempered, except on the one point of the disrespectful treatment of her by her brothers. She closed her book as I came to the door.

"Have a good time? I should think it was too hot to do much running around in the sun."

"It is hot. Derrick stopped in the kitchen to make lemonade. Are Billy and Hunter home?"

"Yes—upstairs getting ready for that dance. Hunter has to go early, because he's going to wait on tables at the dinner. Takes him ages to dress, these days, he's so duke-i-fied. You'll be lucky if you don't get soup down your back, with that gang of rough-necks handing it round! . . . If Derrick's really making lemonade, I'll fix a place." She pulled the wicker table out from the wall, moved the magazines, and went into the dining-room for a table-cover.

"I called the boys," she announced as she returned, "and they said they'd be right down"—and at the same moment that Derrick came out with the tray, they appeared in the door behind her: Billy, the perfect Princetonian, with his superb air and spotless white flannels, and his sleek hair parted in the middle; Hunter, taller and not so heavy, lazy, lovable, and handsome, with his sleepy black eyes and olive skin, his slender grace and teasing manner—at seventeen one of the gods of the town high school. He took a "Saturday Evening Post" from the chair where Margaret had put the magazines, spread it open on the porch step, and lowered himself upon it carefully in order to prevent the possible contamination of his white trousers.

The conversation turned at once to the dance of the evening. Billy was patronizing . . .

"What will it be like to-night, Hunter? Any good girls going?"

"I reckon a few," he drawled. "Peg's friend Jean Dennis, I shouldn't wonder."

"Don't you dare call her *my* friend! . . . Derrick, you can't think . . . that boy!" She pointed the finger of scorn at Hunter.

"Who is she? Not one of the Dennises?"

"One of *the* Dennises." Margaret nodded emphatically.

"Dennis or not," Hunter defended her, "she's a darned good dancer."

"I'd be ashamed, if I were you, to admit that I knew how she danced."

"Oh, see here, Peg!"

"Still harping on that, Margaret?" Mrs. Thornton had come to the door behind us, market-basket on her arm. "I'm a little tired of hearing about it."

Billy rose to take her basket and to pour a glass of lemonade for her.

"Sit down, Mother. We were kidding Hunter."

"So I gathered. Margaret's never forgiven him for the night he took her to the basket-ball game, and when it was over, left her at the gate, and told her to run on in to bed —that he was going to the dance—" Mrs. Thornton laughed, and Margaret flushed.

"The dance was at that terrible dance hall down on West Street, and a public dance. You wouldn't have had me take Peg, would you?"

"Certainly not. She's too young for any dances, let alone one of that sort."

"He had no business to go himself, then," Margaret insisted. "If it's too bad for me, it's too bad for him. And to take Jean Dennis!"

"There's nothing against the child, is there, except her family and her lack of manners?" their mother asked. "She's loud, of course . . . but she's a pretty little thing now, though I suppose she will coarsen dreadfully. I can remember when Mrs. Dennis was as pretty as any girl in this town."

"Mother! That fat vulgar Irish woman?" Hunter whistled through his teeth.

"Vulgar! What could be more vulgar than Jean? You should see her dance, Mother."

"I don't deny." Hunter moved uneasily on his magazine. "I don't mind taking her to a dance on West Street, but I wouldn't take her to the Country Club. I'm taking Marjie Fay, if you must know." Marjorie was the pretty little pink-and-gold cousin of the Devlins who was visiting Jack's sisters.

"You're going to be the kind of fellow," Billy said scathingly, "that has one girl for Main Street and another for the back alleys . . ."

"Boys! Stop it!" Derrick's angry tone startled them so that they all turned to look at her. "What immeasurably contemptible things you do find to quarrel about! Have you forgotten that you're going to a dance that's supposed to be a farewell to the soldiers? It may be the last time in their lives that some of these boys will dance a step in Tecumseh . . ."

Hunter was instantly sympathetic.

"Poor devils! You don't hear a word about them—they're just an excuse for best clothes and a good time. It makes me so sick I think I'll run off and enlist myself."

"Fat chance they'd take an infant like you," Billy retorted. "Besides, you wouldn't dare after Father made me promise to wait until I was twenty-one before I went."

"And if we don't talk much about the War"—Mrs. Thornton rose and put her glass on the table—"it's because we've thought so much about it that our nerves are stretched taut, and it wouldn't take much to snap them." She turned to Margaret. "You'd better telephone for the children, dear. Cassie has your dinner almost ready. Send them to bed early, and don't sit up for us yourself, though your father and I don't plan to stay for the dance . . . And you girls had better go dress. Billy's all ready now."

"I had to dress early—Hunter says I have to take him out

and come back for you. It's what comes of having only one car for a family this size . . ."

"You're lucky to have any, my son."

"I'm going with Jack, anyway. Six of us couldn't go in our car without mussing our dresses." Derrick collected the glasses and had carried the tray to the door when Billy stopped her.

"See here, Derrick! You light into us for not thinking or talking about the War—how do you think it looks for you to go to a dance for the soldiers with a pacifist like Jack Devlin?"

"What do you mean?"

"I mean, considering the things Jack says and thinks about the War, and the country and the soldiers, you should be ashamed to be seen with him."

Derrick's eyes hardened, her face was like a mask, but her wrists must have trembled, for the lemonade glasses clinked together. She waited a minute . . .

"What Jack thinks is his business, not mine or yours, and I am not going to give up a friend because he does not think as I do."

I followed her upstairs, a little amused by her contradictory spirit: she had forced Bill Stewart to defend Jack against her accusation, but when her family attacked him, she herself went to his support. . . . While she dressed, she gave no indication that she had on her mind anything more serious than the question of whether or not to wear her topaz earrings in an attempt to make her eyes look less green than they would otherwise look above her organdy dress, whose color was that of apple leaves in April.

The Tecumseh Country Club was a remodeled brick farm-house a few miles from town; the acres of the original farm had been tamed and tended into the semblance of a golf course—a piece of madness in the eyes of the farmers of the country. It was a course bounded, not by gentlemen's estates, but by the fields of grain and hay, by a swampy pasture where grew clumps of willows and a long line of sycamores, by a heavily rutted country lane, and by a creek whose banks were a wilderness of walnut and ash and tulip-trees rising above thickets of wild roses and blackberries and a tangle of wild grapevines that hung in loops between the trees. The house was on a slight elevation, and the wide porches overlooked, in long vistas between patches of wood-land, an unlimited rolling country, one low slope beyond another, to the world's edge. As I stood there for a minute before dinner, a cloud of blackbirds came up from the fields to settle clamorously in the great trees along the creek. I remembered again the poem that had been in my mind that morning:

> "An endless quiet valley reaches out
>   Past the blue hills into an evening sky;
> Over the stubble, cawing, goes a rout
>   Of rooks from harvest, flagging as they fly."

But within, there was nothing of the quietness, the tran-quillity that, outside, was a part of the evening. The porches and the lounge of the club were hung with flags and bunting, two battered rusty sabers were crossed above the fireplace, but in the dining-room there was no decoration except tall vases of midsummer flowers. Their sharp, hard colors and acrid scent assaulted the senses as did the shrill laughter and the high, strained voices of the women and the vividness of their summer dresses. The room was so crowded with small tables that the boys who served could hardly squeeze be-tween them with their trays, and there could be little con-versation at one table that would not be overheard by others. Our talk was as meaningless as any; there was a certain restraint upon us! Jack was visibly uncomfortable, although he did not once dodge a reference to the War. Derrick was silent, and looked tired, but there was a blaze of excitement in her eyes as she watched Jack, or turned from him to watch the room.

We danced after dinner in the lounge and on the wide

porch that went around three sides of the house; the space was thronged, although many of the older people, Dr. and Mrs. Thornton among them, left soon after the dancing had begun. Billy was summoned to drive them home, but was so distressed at the thought of leaving me squireless that I offered to go with them, saying that I liked to ride better than to dance. When we returned, Bill Stewart met us on the steps.

"You're just in time; this is the dance we swap."

Billy Thornton took Mary's arm and led her away to a bench beneath the trees; we two danced into the lounge at one end, down its length, out the opposite door, and around three sides of the house on the porch.

"Did you see Derrick?" Bill asked, when we had completed the circuit.

"No. I looked for her. Is she dancing?"

"She's sitting in the corner inside, with Jack. I think they're fighting—that's why I asked if you saw them. It's the corner opposite the orchestra. When we go past again, you watch—"

They were in two wicker chairs behind some palms, in the corner. Over Bill's shoulder I saw them: white-cheeked, furious, staring at each other. The apprehension that I had felt as a shadow closed around me like a dark and choking fog. There was in the two quiet faces a white fury incarnate . . . and in Derrick's, a shadow of horror. Her eyes flamed in the pallor of her face. Before we turned, Jack began to speak—I did not hear him, of course, above the music, but I breathed more easily.

"You see?" Bill said, when he had swept me away and down the room.

"Yes. They must be quarreling to look like that. Derrick has been so—" I hesitated, not sure how much I could say to Bill.

"You don't think she cares about Jack, do you? *That way*, I mean?" he asked bluntly. "Mary says she does—always has—"

"Oh, no! No!" I recoiled, tripped, threw him out of step. "I'm sorry, Bill. My fault. No, I don't think so—" But my heart throbbed in my throat.

"I'm glad you don't think so. It wouldn't do at all. There never were any other two friends who could get so bitterly angry with each other and still be friends—and even they mightn't be friends, married . . . But Jack—you see . . ."

"You think he feels *that*, for her?"

He was silent for a minute as we rounded a corner thick with other couples.

"We might go out under the trees, but I'd like to stay where we can see them; we might need to save the situation by going to talk to them. Yes, I think he does . . . not that he ever told me so, mind you. I think he's deliberately torturing himself, quarreling with her this way so that he won't give in to what she thinks is right and he thinks is wrong—and enlist. I may be imagining it, but I've been thinking ever since she came home that something was going to happen."

When the music stopped, we went out to the porch for a glass of lemonade, and talked with the others around the punchbowl until Billy Thornton came up with Mary. The Stewarts said good-night then, and departed. I went out on the floor with another partner, but Derrick and Jack had left the corner behind the palms. I did not see them again while the dancing lasted, though I watched, heartsick. When the orchestra played the last tune, and Billy and I crossed the floor together, I asked him casually if he knew where Derrick was.

"They haven't gone—Jack's car's still there, next to ours" —he nodded toward the row of motors on the drive below —"but we don't have to wait for them—they've wandered off together somewhere—they can take care of themselves. Let's drive down to the river and watch the moon come up. It's too nice a night to go in."

He drove down the road to the middle of the bridge, where he stopped the car, and we waited until the pale gibbous moon rose above the line of willows along the river-bank, and its reflection was a faint, wavering streak of gold between the deep shadows of the trees. But Billy was not one to dilate on the loveliness of the night, beyond a curt word or two . . . we talked of the men who were to leave for camp in the morning: how the old members were "riff-raff," whose families would have to be taken care of by the town —but how the ranks were filled out with the boys every one knew—those Derrick's age and a little older.

"Jack's the only one of that crowd, except the married ones, that isn't going. Even Pete McInnis is leaving the meat-store." Billy laughed scornfully.

As we drove into the Thornton garage, we heard the sharp slam of a street door, somewhere.

"Sounds like Devlin's door," Billy said. "They've just got back, I suppose."

"Do you think so? I'll run on in, then."

But there was no light in Derrick's room, nor in mine, next to it. Her door was ajar, and thinking to get out her nightclothes and open the bed, I entered and switched on the light. Derrick, her hair disheveled, the skirt of her organdy dress crumpled beneath her, lay face down across the foot of the bed. I went over and sat beside her.

"Derrick, why did you get into such a row?" I spoke in as matter-of-fact tone as I could command. "You might have known you would feel like this."

She sat up and pushed her hair back from her forehead. "It wasn't that"—then, suspiciously, "How did you know we were having a row?"

"The way you looked. If that isn't the trouble, what is?"

She drew a sharp breath.

"That started it . . . Jack! For *Jack* to say such things! I couldn't bear it . . . I was so angry . . . I couldn't think of anything but how angry I was. How dreadful to have let every one see it!"

"No one saw it but Bill and me."

"Bill? I'm sorry. . . . Sue, were you ever so angry that you felt the scorching blood go through your veins? . . . I felt it, but gritted my teeth and made myself sit there without stirring while I listened . . . and only half listened, because I was thinking what a terrible thing anger is. It flung us apart and split the earth between us into a bottomless chasm that widened and widened . . ."

"But you knew before what Jack thought."

"Yes, but not *all* that he thought, until then. He said that there was no such thing as patriotism, no such thing as courage, no such thing as heroism . . . that all the men in all the armies have to be drugged to make them fight . . . that all the officers are cowards, and never let themselves get into dangerous situations, but send their men to be killed . . . and on and on and on, like that, worse and worse . . .

"It was like having some one you've known always changed before your eyes into a stranger. I wanted to cry out to him and tell him to stop before I had lost him entirely, but I couldn't, I was too angry. I told him . . . I don't know what I told him . . . that he was degraded—that he wallowed . . ." She shivered, and was silent a minute.

"And then he grew as furious as I was. The veins stood out on his forehead. And I—if I looked as I felt . . . At any rate, he said we'd better go out on the golf course and finish, away from every one."

"I missed you, and wondered."

"Did you notice the night?"

"Yes. Billy and I went down by the river and watched the moon come up."

"To change from the heat and glare and noise to *that!*" Derrick drew a long breath. "The earth went on and on forever, one field beyond another, and the night was so warm, and sweet with clover, and quiet, except for the music behind us. And the stars . . . How in the face of the stars could you think that anything mattered, really? I could regard the chasm quite coolly—it was still there, mind you—" Derrick lifted her white face, and smiled grimly.

242

"And I thought a melodramatic writer would say that an old friendship had died before our eyes . . . and that was so ridiculous that I tried to tell myself that this quarrel was no worse than those we had had before. . . . I knew quite well, you see, that I was angry with Jack when we didn't think alike because I cared so desperately that we should think alike. (What a fool, Sue—did you ever know such a fool?) That has always been true. I thought of Jack when he was a little boy—how stanch an ally he had been, and how bewildered he always looked when I turned on him like a vixen, and how comfortable it was after we had been almost like enemies all through high school, to have him back again, that last year. I wanted to reach out and touch him, and ask him if he were thinking about the same things. Two people do, generally, if they are really conscious of each other."

She broke off, crossed to the dresser, and began to unfasten her clothes. I hoped she would not go on—but she did, after she had recrossed the room and stood in the window playing with the cord on the blind.

"Then, do you know . . . he turned to me and said, 'I was just remembering what a funny little thing you were—let's talk about that instead of arguing.' And because he had been thinking just what I had, I knew what was coming. I think I knew before he did." She laughed shakily.

"Don't tell me, Derrick, don't—"

"Of course not. Just enough so that you will keep me from making a fool of myself."

"Why," I asked sharply, "should you make a fool of yourself?"

"Suppose my emotions should bewitch me into thinking I wanted to marry him? I don't, really."

"But, if you love him—"

"I don't, not with my mind. I knew long ago that in case this day should come, I must prepare what to say, so that at the crucial moment I shouldn't have to think . . . No one could think, then . . . but could just say over what I had learned by heart. So I said it."

"He didn't believe you, did he?" I laughed. It seemed so improbable.

"Yes, he did. He began by saying we shouldn't quarrel if we didn't care so much what the other one thought. I admitted it, and he went on. 'I didn't mean those things I said. I couldn't have explained, then, why I said them—but I was afraid of my feeling for you. Afraid you would persuade me out of the things I believe—I think—' and he said it quite deliberately, as if he had to make himself say it—'that I wanted to make you so angry that you would say things that I could never forgive.'"

Derrick came back to the bed then, and sat down beside me. I stared at her. She had thrust back from her clear eyes all trace of emotion, but her mouth trembled.

"Don't look like that, Sue. What does it matter? We'll all forget it soon enough. . . . He went on from there and said all the things I hoped he wouldn't say." She leaned back against the bedpost, her eyes closed. "I said that we couldn't tie ourselves together disagreeing as we do. And he said— he was so hopeful, Sue—that if he knew I loved him in spite of his ideas, he wouldn't try to convince me. I turned my back on him, and went and leaned against that old oak tree that marks the turn in the golf course. After a while he followed me, and said that he was a fool, and that, of course, I couldn't care for any one who felt about the War as he did, and was bound to be branded as a coward. I didn't say anything, so that was all."

"Oh, Derrick! Derrick! You let him think that?"

"Yes. He couldn't think worse of me, could he? I felt filthy and contaminated, but if it made him despise me, so much the better."

"There was nothing more?"

"No. We sat down under the trees to watch for the moon. The fields went on and on, to the horizon, and the wind was warm and clover-scented. I sat looking at my hands in my lap, wanting to put one on his knee. I never wanted anything so much in my life, but I just sat still, and tried to think it didn't matter whether I did or not, and that in a little while my hand would be dust and worms in the earth, and there would be no one to know or care whether I had done such a simple thing as move it from my knee to his. So I didn't, and after a while we got up and came in."

"Derrick, what makes you so morbid? Why didn't you tell him the truth?"

"He wouldn't have understood, any more than you do——" She smiled at my bewilderment.

"You haven't told me why, yet."

"I have. . . . I knew this was coming, and I thought and thought . . . and I am right about it. I am fond of him—but not fond enough to give him myself. I don't mean my body—that is so unimportant. I mean *me,* what I think and am and know, 'way down inside. That I am not Derrick Thornton, really. If I married him, I should have to keep all that from him—so it won't do. Don't you see? You couldn't marry a man and hide from him all the things about yourself that really matter. For your own sake you couldn't . . ."

"You have a very romantic and exalted idea of marriage. After all, if you're happier together than apart——"

"You couldn't tie yourself *for life* to anyone unless you cared for him with your utmost power of caring . . ."

"But how can you measure that? You're making something very involved out of what should be perfectly simple."

"I knew explaining it would do no good." She smiled at me coolly. "Do run on to bed, Sue, and don't mind me."

The soldiers left the next day; in the car we followed the straggling marchers, some of whom were in uniform, some in their ordinary business clothes. It was a desolate scene: the dirty station, its grime accentuated by the glare of the sun and by the heat waves that rose from the pavements; the knots of people, the few whom I knew lost in the larger number of factory hands and small store-keepers and clerks; the men seedy and morose, the women tear-stained, their hats slipping back, their skirts slipping down, their wailing children clinging to their hands. The train, when it finally

245

came, was filled with soot-and-sweat-streaked men, who leaned, some curious, some apathetic, from the open windows of the dirty coaches. The band played while the train was there, but its lugubrious strains roused no spirit, no enthusiasm, in any one. We turned away in silence, heavy-hearted.

That night after dinner the Thorntons, with the three youngest children, went driving; the boys had engagements, Derrick excused herself on the grounds of weariness, and I stayed at home with her. We were out-of-doors all evening: Derrick sat on the edge of the porch and I was behind her in the corner, where, after the twilight waned, the light from the window fell across my knitting. It was not until I was almost ready to suggest that we go to bed that I saw Jack cross their lawn and step over the low iron fence between the two yards. Derrick went down to the edge of the terrace to meet him, and I rolled up my knitting and went inside to the library, where I could hear nothing but the click of the needles in my hand. . . . There was a nightmarish quality in the silence. . . . The family came in and went upstairs to bed. I did not know the time, but my sweater had grown perceptibly when Derrick came in search of me.

I looked at her, and found myself drawn more helplessly into the nightmare. The room was unreal . . . its glassed bookcases, the globes in the window, the ship model over the mantel—all a dream: the only reality, Derrick. She stood for a moment in the library door, intensely alive, as straight, and still—as vivid—as a candle-flame where there is no wind. Her eyes glowed like stars, but the hand held at her throat trembled, and the heartbeats throbbed beneath her finger-tips.

"Sue, dear—" She came to the couch and dropped beside me. "I told him yes, after all."

I was swept with a wave of relief. "But why—"

She hesitated, looked about at the lamplit room, began to shiver. "Come outside and I'll tell you."

I followed her to the porch door, down the terrace steps

to the lawn beneath the trees. We walked the length of it twice before either spoke. I finally repeated my question.

"How did you happen to change your mind before it was too late?"

"I didn't until after it was too late. He went to the city this morning and enlisted in the artillery."

"Derrick!"

"Yes, I know. He couldn't have done worse. My lie has cost me my immortal soul."

We were silent for a minute as we stopped beside the fountain; I feel again its spray blown in my face as I remember. There was nothing I could think of to say. I waited for her to resume.

"Do men really believe that women care for a person for what he thinks and not for what he is? He said that, when it came to a choice between what he thought and what he loved, he would take a chance in having been wrong in what he thought: that every one he most respected believed he was wrong, anyway."

"And you explained?"

"How cruel I had been, and why? Yes, I tried to, but he didn't understand, just as I knew he wouldn't. He still thinks it was because he hadn't enlisted, and he will think so, to his dying day. It's no more than I deserve for letting him believe it, in the first place. He ought to have been very angry with me, but he was so glad to find how much I did care that he didn't think about anything else. At any rate, when I said I had made him act against all the principles he believed in, he said—I'm afraid he said it to reassure me—that he had honestly decided that he could do nothing but enlist: that it was like building a wall along a river to prevent a flood: you might think there would never be a flood, and that, if there were, the damage would be less than the cost of preventing it, but that, if you were in the minority, you couldn't stand aside and watch others build the wall—you would have to pitch in and help."

"It's a feeble enough argument, but after all, he would have been drafted!"

"Yes, but in that case I shouldn't have been responsible."

"Then you are going to marry him?"

Once more we walked the length of the garden in silence; I was about to apologize for having asked, when she spoke again.

"I'm sure I don't know. I didn't say I would. He said that he couldn't even ask me until after the War, and, in the meantime, all that we needed to take us through anything was the knowledge that we could be absolutely sure of each other . . ."

As we approached the fence, we heard the boys at the gate; they started across the lawn, and Derrick slipped her hand from my arm.

"I'm going upstairs to bed. You don't mind? I don't want to see them."

She sped up the terrace steps and into the house. When I followed, I found her lying on her bed where she had thrown herself in complete abandon, the pillow clutched in her embrace, her face buried in it, while she murmured over and over again, "Oh, Jack, Jack . . . my dear . . ."

She had not heard me. . . . I turned and crept silently from her door, once again swept with that black apprehension. . . .

In the morning she came into my room before I was up.

"What have you planned for to-day?"

"Golf with Billy this morning."

"May we pretend to go with you, and slip off driving somewhere? In the afternoon Jack has to go with his mother to say good-bye to all his relatives. He's so funny about his family—says they're broken-hearted to have him go, but are awfully relieved, on the whole, to be able to be broken-hearted, because they were going to have to be ashamed for him. He'll have dinner with them, of course, but we can manage the evening. To-morrow he leaves."

"But just to go into training. You'll see him again."

"I doubt it. What would ever take me to Alabama? And I'll not be here if he gets home on leave. In New York, perhaps, if he really goes. But, Sue: what I wanted to say . . ."

"Yes?"

"Don't let the family see, will you? I'm too uncertain in my mind . . ."

"They won't think of it; they're used to Jack."

Nevertheless, I admired Derrick's skill in dissimulation. She came down to breakfast dressed for golf—white flannel skirt and silk sweater of a strange color like old dull gold that, reflected in her eyes, made them a transparent hazel. . . . She told the family at once that Jack had enlisted, and they waited in the living-room until he came up on the terrace, where Derrick met him and brought him in; they gathered around him, slapped him on the back, shook his hands; and Derrick gave no sign that she felt anything beyond pride and a frank and justifiable affection.

Afterward, when the two of them sat together in the back seat of the car, her animation vanished; there was something saturnine, ironic, in her expression. She had thrown a purple scarf around her shoulders and had put on a hat of the same dull gold color as her sweater, faced beneath with purple; she had pulled it down over her forehead, so that what I thought was a look of fear in her eyes might have been nothing but the shadow of the hat. At any rate, I noted as I looked back over Billy's shoulder that they were holding hands behind the golf-bag set against the seat between them—and Jack smiled at me triumphantly: there was no suggestion of regret or doubt or dread, nothing unfathomable in the light that shone in the blue eyes.

At the Country Club, Billy and I took the golf-clubs and left them; they stepped over into the front seat and drove off on what Derrick explained to me afterward was a sentimental pilgrimage. Jack had wanted to walk out the creek-bank to the spot where they had once believed the Indian chief was buried, where they had always gone, in October, to look for walnuts. He had wanted to see again the giant poplar trees. They had left the car at the end of a wagon track beside the creek, and had walked from there. . . . The poplar trees were taller than all others along the creek, so that they were visible from a great distance, from the beginning of the open pasture lands to the short ascent where the path led into the woods. . . .

"From away far off," Derrick described them, "you could see only the motion of branches the color of water in sunlit air. Nearer you could see that they had form and substantiality, but they were still glorious. All silver and shimmering gray in the sunshine when the wind slipped along beside them and lifted their leaves. I had never thought, before, that Jack had any feeling for things like that. It made me feel surer of him, to find that the same things are the same to us. He is sweet, Sue," and she smiled a little secret, one-sided smile, while she stared at me. "It seemed dreadful for him to have to go with nothing more from me than I had given. I half wanted to offer myself to him, entirely, to do as he pleased with, for the day. It seems to be the fashion in England, judging by all the contemporary novels. . . . I can imagine his horror at the suggestion. . . . Besides, I found, that time I let Bill Stewart kiss me, that there's no satisfaction to be had out of that sort of thing, nothing but shame, and disgust—and you don't want shame and disgust mixed up with your feeling for some one you care about most awfully."

When Jack had gone, she said nothing more to me of what had occurred; she gave no sign of what she must have been feeling, except that, at times, she was extraordinarily absent-minded and rather sad, and in the mornings, when she first rose, her eyes burnt like a black fire in the white mask of her face. She missed Jack, as we all missed him; that would have been true had there been nothing between them beyond what there had always been; but the days were devoted to the same old amusements: we golfed, drove the car, went on picnics, strolled down street in the evenings for sodas at the Greeks' . . . until after the time we stopped at the Stewarts' to invite them to Sunday dinner. We had hardly crossed the lawn to the chairs beneath the trees before Bill attacked Derrick.

"I've been meaning to ask you, Derrick, if it was you that persuaded Jack to enlist?" His manner was friendly enough, but Derrick stiffened at once.

"I didn't ask him to enlist; I didn't even suggest that he should. As a matter of fact, I don't think he should have, with his convictions. . . ."

"I'm glad to hear it—it would have been a pretty low-down thing to do. I don't see how some girls can do it—they must feel like murderers when anything happens to the men they've forced to go."

"But you don't think anything will happen to Jack?"

"I'm sure I hope not. But I don't see how you're going to know—"

Derrick choked back a rising terror in her voice.

"But it was you who said that our men would never get to the front. . . ."

"I thought so, but I don't know . . . the Allies are hard up for men. I'd hate to bet much on any of their chances—and I know I couldn't sleep at nights if I were to blame for any one's going."

"But there's the regular army to go first . . ." Derrick rose at once, forgot that she had come to the Stewarts' with an invitation. "How can you talk so, Bill? I refuse to believe that any one we know will be hurt. We've already lost Andrew—by the law of averages the rest ought to be safe. Come on, Sue—we must get back before dark—our tail-light is broken." And she led the way back to the gate in the lane, where she had drawn the car up on the grass by the fence.

As we came from the country road to the end of Tecumseh's paved streets, there were shrill-voiced children playing hide-and-seek in the dusk beneath the long rows of maple trees. She slowed down to avoid them.

"All Tecumseh was snarling at Jack's heels because he wouldn't fight—now I suppose they're yapping at mine because they think I made him go . . . a vindictive lot, aren't they?"

After that, while I was there, she refused to go out in the car, refused to go on the street, unless it was necessary. She explained that the sun made her head swim, that it felt like a blight on an accursed land. It was true that the heat grew more and more unendurable, so that we sat day after day in the close-shuttered library. She forgot that she had promised to show me how one could love the country, and even Tecumseh; I did not remind her. We knit interminably heavy gray sweaters while we discussed our immediate futures. Derrick had given up all hope of getting to France, what with her father's dictum that she hadn't the strength to be of any service, and the Government's that no woman under twenty-five could go; she had decided to join Alice and me in New York in the fall and hunt for a position . . .

However, the two of us were not left much alone; the house overflowed with children, to no one of whom was it conceivable that any member of the family could want to escape from the others. They collected late in the afternoons in the library or living-room, or on the porch when it was not too hot, for lemonade and cakes, or iced tea—and again in the evenings for watermelon, or berries and cream. And all day long, between times, a wail from the distant part of the house would send Derrick running, with dark threats: "If that is Hunter, teasing the baby . . ." Mrs. Thornton would come in with the sewing she was doing for Rosanna, while the latter played on the floor with her rather disreputable dolls; grave-eyed, solemn little Henry would sit on the floor beside the window, where the light fell through the shutters in narrow lines across the book he tried to read, or the paper on which he drew grotesque pictures for Derrick's admiration. It was a very pleasant commotion to one who had neither brother nor sister. I wondered how Derrick, in spite of the change in her feeling for Tecumseh, could regard calmly the prospect of leaving them all, permanently; I asked her, one day, and she frowned upon me in surprise.

"It's all very well to be home, Sue, but I couldn't do anything here, and I shall go mad if I don't do something soon. I'm holding my breath until I have a chance to get away."

When we parted, therefore, early in August, it was with the expectation that we should meet in New York in the fall, and that we should at once set out to win for ourselves both fame and fortune.

~~~~~~~~ II ~~~~~~~~

IN THE MIDDLE of October, Derrick wrote us the date of her expected arrival. Alice and I were ready and waiting for her: we had found an apartment and had gone to work. I was so much more forehanded than they, and had so much less faith in Providence, that the previous spring I had applied for and been given a position to teach at a private day-school on the West Side, uptown; Alice had come into the city a penniless fortune-seeker and had found at once a place as clerk, for a few dollars a week, in a bookstore—one of the conventionally unconventional sort, west of Washington Square. Derrick, just as reckless, with little idea of what she would do, but armed with a diploma from the secretarial school she had attended since I had left Tecumseh, came into the Pennsylvania Station from the West, late one Saturday morning.

Alice had asked for a couple of hours off—if her position paid hardly enough to buy her handkerchiefs, it at least offered her almost unlimited liberty—and we had gone up to meet the train. We stood one at the top of each of the flights of steps that lead from the track level, but, as always happens in that madly planned station, Derrick followed the porter to whom she had given her bags by some other way, and we missed her. We were hardly surprised when the last straggler had climbed the steps, when the gates were pulled shut before our eyes, and we had had not a glimpse of her—one expects to miss one's friends there—it is the accepted fate. We turned at once and hastened through the crowd toward the taxi-stand; it was Alice's suggestion that we should go up on the stairs at the end of the concourse and look for her inside, first, from that vantage-point, since she must have stopped to check her baggage. . . She was halfway across the noisy hall when I saw her, shrunken, like all the elbowing throng, to a pigmy by its vast proportions, and yet, somehow, as I realized when I saw her for an instant as a stranger might have seen her, rather distinguished-looking. The navy-blue suit and black hat were inconspicuous enough, but she was unhurried erect, unhesitating; she walked with a light, quick stride that somehow set her apart—like a swallow, I thought, that circled across a chattering host of English sparrows. I was suddenly uncomfortable, as always when I saw Derrick for the first time after a separation, reluctant to go down and approach her. But when Alice saw her, too, she seized my arm.

"There she goes! She has a new winter suit—what a spendthrift!"

We darted after her. She turned as we came up.

"Why didn't you look for us? Didn't you think we should meet you?"

"No, I didn't know that any one ever met any one else in New York. It was rather fun, not being met: I was practicing looking like a real New-Yorker, and knowing well enough there was no one paying any attention to me, to be deceived. But it's a thousand times more fun, being met. I haven't had any lunch—where shall we eat?"

We took the bags from the porter and went across to the Pennsylvania Hotel, where Alice gave them to a bellboy to check. She told him to bring the tickets to us in the dining-room, but there was some mistake, or he could not find us, and he did not appear, so that, after we had eaten, when we had looked for him in vain in the lobby, we were confronted by the necessity of identifying the bags. The man behind the counter looked at Derrick sternly as she explained her plight.

"What's the article on top, ma'am?" he asked, when he brought out the bags she had indicated.

"The hat-box is locked—this is the key—" She dropped her jangling key-ring on the counter. "That ought to identify it. The suitcase—" Her eyes twinkled, the hauteur she had assumed as the outward and visible sign of the New-Yorker, melted suddenly. "Right on top, you'll find a mason jar of preserved cherries."

The man relaxed a little, condescended to look amused. He opened the bag and lifted out the cherries.

"I guess it's yours, all right, ma'am."

Derrick turned to us as he replaced them and shut down the lid.

"What a joke—just when I was doing my best to look like Somebody! Mother sent them, for us to put in pies."

When we came out of the hotel, she signaled to a taxi, but we restrained her.

"You must learn at once that the day for such extravagances is past. We walk—or take a Broadway street-car."

"In that case, considering the bags, I vote for the car."

The apartment we had taken was in a converted brownstone front near Third Avenue on a cross-street not far below Gramercy Park. In pride and elation we led her across Twenty-third Street, down to and around the little square patch of park, with its forbidding high iron fence, within which nursemaids on benches watched little boys on velocipedes and little girls with hoops. Alice capered—actually capered for joy, despite the fact that she was weighted down with Derrick's suitcase.

"Careful, Al—those cherries will come smashing right down through the bottom of that."

"What does it matter? I'm so pleased to see you—and so pleased to find that the fires of youth still burn in my veins, and that I am not so old that my spirits can no longer soar aloft—"

"You lambs of God!" Derrick herself, for all her assumption of dignity, skipped across the street between us. "You couldn't possibly know how glad I am—how glad I am to be here! When I got on the train yesterday, I felt seventy-five, and so melancholy—leaving home this time, really and truly, for good, forever—you know how it is—and when I got off the train this morning, I felt at least forty—and now I feel fifteen."

When we turned down our own street, which was to a large extent a street of warehouses and wholesale dry-goods stores, we made a ceremony of it.

"Think how often you will walk down these blocks, in rain and shine, summer and winter—"

"When you return weary and worn from your day's labor, through snow and sleet, through rain and hail, through waves of heat, when the fumes of gasoline stifle you and scorch your lungs—"

"You're getting too realistic, Al. Which is our house? Show me—"

"This isn't—nor this—nor this!" We swept her past houses that had been remodeled, stuccoed, painted in pale pastel shades and shuttered with solid green shutters. "But this is it—"

Outwardly, our brownstone mansion had not been changed since its erection: a flight of eight or nine steps led to the front door; the iron railing of these steps continued to the right along the pavement's edge as a fence for the little bit of grass and the ground-floor entrance. Above the basement windows was a balcony, with similar railing and window-boxes, where, in the spring we explained we could plant vines or nasturtiums—for the windows behind the balcony were the windows of our apartment.

We led her into the hall, which was narrow, bare, and uncarpeted, and which never quite lost a reminiscent odor of boiled cabbage, but from which you could enter our rooms by any one of three doors; we unlocked the first of them, thrust her in, and waited for her exclamations of delight. And I, I must admit, felt some trepidation and sudden misgiving: I had not realized until that moment how much I cared whether she liked it or not. But Derrick could always be depended upon to behave well in an emergency. She put down her bag and looked about her.

"Lucky dogs! . . . Lucky dogs! It is magnificent." She tossed off her hat, and paced the length of the front room, which had been the drawing-room of the house in its earlier and more prosperous days, from the windows to the folding-doors that shut off the rest of the apartment. "Books are so silly—things never turn out like them. I came with the picture of the conventional garret in my mind."

"You wouldn't rather have had a garret?"

"Heaven forbid! Comfort first, space next, and romance last. What a room this must have been, in its day! The ceiling is as high as ours are at home—I didn't know there were others like them still left in the country—and once it took two chandeliers to light it."

There were in the ceiling, parallel to the two great white marble mantelpieces, two white rosettes of leaves and twisted vines, but the chandeliers had been taken down, and the room was lighted with lamps.

"Of course, it's rather dark here in the daytime," I ventured to suggest. There were only the two windows in front, long windows, to be sure, that reached from the floor almost to the ceiling, but they faced north, and the room was very large.

"It doesn't matter." She refused to recognize the drawback. "We'll never be here in the daytime, anyway. . . . Isn't it too bad for a nice old house to come to this, though . . ."

"What do you mean, 'come to this'?"

"All split up. What are the people upstairs like? And in the basement?"

"Our landlady lives in the basement. We don't know the others."

"Don't you suppose the house feels rather let down, full as it is of waifs and strays?"

Alice doubled her fists and placed them on her hips, belligerently.

"An' who're ye callin' waifs an' strays? Three fine young women like us, tastin' the intoxicatin' wine of independence for the first time! The house should be proud of us—will be proud of us—will become a shrine. In this humble room will foregather the Great, of whatsoever. creed or nationality, or party—" Then she added, with a seriousness even more amusing, "I'm sure I don't see why they shouldn't. They all live in New York. We'll invite them to tea and dinner, and they'll come, whether they know us or not. They don't mind that sort of thing."

"They may not," Derrick said haughtily, "but we do. Come, show me the rest of the place, and where to put my things, and wash my face."

Behind the large front room, separated from it by folding-doors, was a smaller one, with French windows that opened onto a porch above a neglected and rather dirty back yard. At one side were bath and kitchenette, both overfull, one of clothes and chiffoniers, and toilet articles that, somehow or other, persistently and maddeningly succeeded in getting themselves spread all over the floor—and the other of dishes, sometimes clean and sometimes not, of pots and pans and tea-towels and dish-mops . . . I showed Derrick her bureau drawers and her closet, and helped her with her bags.

"You were lucky to find a place furnished, Sue, since we have no money, and no possessions more substantial than books and cushions and pictures." Then she dropped her voice to an awed whisper. "And may I ask how much we're paying for it?"

Later we went out to Third Avenue and brought back our dinner, and Derrick made a cherry pie: with an apron over her suit skirt, her sleeves rolled up, and her hair in her eyes, she recounted the latest of her family anecdotes, and delivered the messages they had sent to me, while Alice showed her where we kept the pans and our new rolling-pin, while she buried her arms in flour to the elbows, and shook it to the left and right, recklessly, and while she rolled the dough with loud thumps . . .

When we had washed the dishes, and had explained to her all the housekeeping arrangements, even how (and she was horrified) the garbage had to be wrapped in a paper parcel and left by the front steps every night; we built, of coal borrowed from the landlady, a fire in the grate to make her feel at home, and, stretched out before it, we talked for a while of the delights and difficulties of earning a living.

"Now, Al, tell me—what kind of a bookstore is yours?"

"A madman's. It's the front room of a house, much smaller than this, with shelves around the sides, and books piled helterskelter everywhere. It's heated with a fireplace, and the windows are never opened. You can get tea there in the afternoon if you want it—and you would be surprised at the number of people who do, considering the lack of air. The amount of business that man does is unbelievable. I suppose it is largely due to his madness. All sorts come in to gossip and to sit and read, even if they haven't the money to buy a book. Of course, I'm paid practically nothing, but I can live for a while on atmosphere. Every one you've heard of drifts in sooner or later. That's why I'm there—I want to know them—and, Heaven knows, it's easy enough to do—'every man his own press agent' seems to be their motto. After a while I'll cut loose and hunt something more profitable and less wearisome. This daily bread business is no merry jest. Sue comes home every night limp as a rag."

"Nonsense. I'm not used to it yet, that's all. My children are harmless enough, as children go. How about you, Derrick? What are you going to look for?"

"I'd like something like Al's, where every one important is sure to turn up sometime. Do you suppose there's a newspaper editor anywhere who needs a secretary? I haven't any preferences in the way of newspapers, just so they're Republican, so I thought I'd look them up in the telephone book and begin with the one nearest here. The shorter the distance between me and my office, the longer I can sleep in the mornings."

It was not until we were ready to start to bed that Derrick showed any disposition to criticize. Once more she walked from the folding-doors to the windows and back again, clad in her trailing kimono, with comb, curlers, and toothbrush in her hand, and stopped on the threshold, whence she could survey both rooms.

"What am I to do with my pictures? I have a lot of them, and you haven't left me much wall space. Do you mistrust my artistic judgment?"

Alice's desk was in the smaller room, above it her Brangwyn etching; mine was in the corner at the back of the larger room, and scattered above it and about, on neighboring walls, were an aquatint of birch trees and a river, a little etching of a New England hillside road, deep in snow; alone beside the door was the circle of angels from the Fra Angelico Last Judgment. In the opposite corner were two couches, in the smaller room another, and beside the front fireplace still another. Over them, and over the bookcases that stood on both sides of the door, we had hung the pictures that Madeleine had left with us "for the duration of the War."

"Which is my desk? You've got so many couches in here, the place looks like a seraglio."

"Only one more than enough for us, and we must have a bed for at least one guest. The one in the back room is yours, and the desk between the window and the fireplace."

"And you've been generous enough to leave that wall bare, so that I can hang a picture! Was the atrocity over the mantelpiece rented with the room? If it was, it can come down, and I'll put The Knight and Death and the Devil there." That was one of her Dürer prints that she knew I most disliked. I had no feeling against the friar telling his beads that she hung over her desk, nor against the Saint Jerome that she stood on the bookcase.

Sometimes, even now . . . and *now* is many years since

that night . . . I get out those pictures that she gave me when she left, and rehang them as they were, and my affection for them is only a shade less than my affection for the Rembrandt print that has always hung between the windows where she had it—the print I gave her on that Christmas when we heard "Tipperary" sung on the Common. It is easy to remember the apartment as it was then, down to the minutest detail—it has hardly changed at all since. Derrick and Alice were not here long, but I stayed after them, sharing the rooms with others while I needed help with the rent; the original furniture has long since been replaced by my own, but desks and bookcases and beds are in the same old corners, many of the same pictures are still on the walls, and on the desk that is now in Derrick's corner stand the squat bronze lamp and a bit of carved ivory that she had there. . . . If sometimes the long, dark room seems haunted, it is because I have invited a ghost to walk there—not Alice's nor Edith's, because they are too comfortably middle-aged, the mothers of children whom they bring in to show off to me when they are home from their schools; not Frances's, because she comes down, once in a while, eminent and distinguished and much-to-be-admired, and lifts an eyebrow at me because I have grown narrow-minded and stodgy; not Madeleine's, because, although she stays with me when she is in this country, she has hidden from me even more successfully than before all indication of warmth and affection; she seems cold and impenetrable, and I see little of the old Madeleine in the handsome woman with the melancholy dark eyes and graying hair. . . . But of Derrick . . . I sometimes pretend still to expect the sound of her foot on the step, of her hand among the dishes on our shelves, to find her at her desk when I come home. . . . It is perhaps because I saw her so infrequently in the last years of her life that I have no trouble in seeing her as she was, that there is no mist between me and the Derrick of those three winters. . . . In and out of the apartment, quiet, competent, taking from me the meal I had begun, awkwardly, to prepare, or from Alice, with unkind mockery, the pressing or the sewing or the cleaning she had undertaken with characteristic clumsiness; at her desk, the light of the lamp full on the thin cheeks and the lines around her mouth; leaving for the office in the morning reluctantly, swift but unhurried; returning at night, the paper under her arm, and the new books to be reviewed, weary, but eager to recount the day's gossip. . . .

When I reached home late on the Monday afternoon after her arrival, I found Derrick unpacked and settled: her trunk had been taken to the cellar, her pictures were hung, her books on the shelves, her clothes in her drawers, and she sat at the desk we had allotted her, writing home. I had left the house that morning under the impression that she intended to spend the day searching for someplace to work.

"Have you been here all day? Or did you go out? What luck did you have?"

"Excellent luck, my dear—got a place the first paper I went to—sort of sub-sub-secretary to the people who do the weekly Literary Supplement. They don't pay much, but it takes me only a few minutes to get there. I begin next Monday. The only recommendation they cared about was my letter from the business school; I suppose they are awfully short-handed on account of the War—at any rate, they seemed to need some one badly. It only took me a few minutes to settle my future, and since then I've been exploring the city, which I'm going to continue to do all week, while I have dimes for bus fares and soles on my shoes." She turned from the desk, hooked her heels over the rung of her chair, and clasped her hands while she chanted to me, city-bred, a litany of delights. "You look at the city with such different eyes when you know you're going to live in it. You never told me it was like this. I never have come up the Avenue on a bus when it didn't lift my heart with a great bound, and almost take my breath away; but now, when the street is hung with flags that shake in the sunlight above your head, it is magnificent beyond belief. And the sky is such a color, and the line of white stone cornice against it is clear-cut as a piece of carving. . . . I do hope you will want to go with me to look around sometimes. I haven't got so far as to notice the people yet, but I suppose we can find amusing ones."

When Alice came in, Derrick repeated to her an account of the day, with added detail.

"I think I'm going to be the slave of them all, but supposedly I'm working for the head man. He's corking: tall and stooped, lean in the cheeks, quizzical, gray-haired. You know the type."

"Yes," I said. "Sentimental. Romantic-young-ladies man."

"All men are sentimental, but he has a sense of humor."

"What's his name?"

"Matthews. Edward, I believe."

"I knew it! That he edited that Literary Supplement, I mean." Alice was excited. "His second wife's a cousin of Edy's—don't you remember? She used to come down for Thanksgiving and week-ends. They have four young children, and he has a son by a first wife that finished at Yale in '16. Edy went down to the Prom with him. Surely you haven't forgotten?"

"Of course not! A round-faced, auburn-haired youth that Edy said she had set her cap for. He took us all to dinner at the Inn once. How stupid of me not to have thought of it! Of course, he's the son of my Mr. Matthews. What do you suppose he's doing?"

"War, of course."

On Saturday I went with Derrick on what she called a tour of the city. I have forgotten now where we went and what we saw that first time we walked together, for afterward most of our Saturday afternoons were spent in the same way, and many evenings. We walked aimlessly, as a rule, but in whatever unpromising corner of the city we found ourselves, we never failed to be rewarded, never failed to stumble upon some dramatic fragment of an episode. We wondered, ourselves, if our eyes were better when we were together, or if it were purely a matter of luck. Neither of us ever called the other's attention to a face, a figure, or a scene; it was a kind of game to wait until we had passed on to make our comment, and it was a delight to discover each time that we had seen the same thing, and had seen it alike. Not that we ever called it a game—that would have spoiled it. Sometimes Alice walked with us—then all was different, and we saw little of what happened before our eyes, because we followed with such concentration the conversation in which she led.

Every inch of Fifth Avenue became as familiar to us as the college campus had ever been, from Washington Arch to the upper end of the Park. We saw buildings come down, and buildings go up; we watched parade after parade march down the street beneath an unending succession of the flags of all the Allies, for that was the winter when it was a poor day that did not have its parade, and when every one who could found work in an office that had windows on the Avenue. We knew all the types that walked there: soldiers in an infinite variety of uniform; bizarre little Jewish stenographers, stunted, bow-legged, clad in silks and furs, painted like Pierrot, with flaming cheeks and chalk-white chins and noses; sleek and pompous clubmen, middle-aged, admirably turned-out, who walked with a lofty pride before the shop-windows, but who crossed the streets warily, a little timidly, cherishing an imperiled dignity.

Sometimes there were faces that defied you, that were not to be placed. Once, on a Saturday noon, we saw a workman in blue denim, a battered felt hat beside him, kneel to pray in the center of the pavement before Saint Patrick's, while a crowd that seemed not to notice the nature of the obstacle, turned out of its way to pass.

Lexington Avenue was a different world. Here there was none of the glory of its neighbor, none of its blatancy, but queer little shops, hospitals, dingy houses made over into apartments, and a succession of great Roman Catholic churches, one after another, so that you had hardly passed the steps of one before you walked into the shadow of another, thrown from across the street. The name of the saint revealed, not infrequently, the nationality of the congregation from Saint Patrick's uptown to the church of Saint Ignatius Loyola on Park Avenue, where there dwelt in the neighborhood many French of what we supposed, cautiously, to be the bourgeois class. These churches exerted on Derrick the fascination of horror; she lingered always to peer into their dim interiors to the distant glimmer of rows of candles on their altars.

When we had walked up Lexington Avenue for several miles, we turned through and came down Third, or, farther over, along the river, as close as we could get to it, past the ancient and honorable but long forgotten neighborhoods, like Sutton Square, which had been lately rediscovered, and were about to be rescued from their melancholy but rather poetic decay. Third Avenue was still another world: a business street, lined by stores, roofed by the Elevated, yet echoing to the noise of the exuberant and hearty life conducted by the clamorous people who lived in the tenements above the tracks. In one block, one race, in the next, another, but all shrill, all excitable, full of a love of life that poverty had no power to restrain. Even on winter evenings, gross women, with fat arms folded beneath their breasts, stood in the open doors, arguing, scolding; children played hop-scotch in the gutters, or pressed their noses against shop-windows whose displays for Christmas were pitiful, tawdry, glittering; ragged vendors of hot roasted chestnuts stood on corners with their carts, while their gas-flames flared, and the air whistled in their little stoves. Below Fourteenth Street were districts populated to the saturation point. We knew Grand Street, and Allen Street, where, in the spring, the children followed, as did those of Hamelin the piper, minute merry-go-rounds drawn by horses from one narrow, crooked street into another. We knew Chatham Square, where we lunched, when we were poor and in need of a lot of food for a few cents, at the unquestionably dirty but generous Port Arthur.

Always there were strange and incomprehensible faces: on the Subway and the Elevated, on the street, and on the ferries when we rode to Staten Island and back, past useless forts and the great ships in the harbor painted in zigzags and cubes—and in the parks, huddled noon and evening on the benches. Derrick peered at them, that maddening, speculative gleam in her eyes, and looked from them to me, as if to ask if I had seen behind the masks what she saw. . . . I always smiled, and nodded a little, deceitfully.

When winter came, and the streets were too bitterly cold for walking, when the snow fell and traffic became hopelessly muddled, and you had to stand first on one foot and then on another, ankle-deep in slush, while street-car after street-car, full to the steps, crept past relentlessly, when the subways were so crowded that there was constant danger that your breastbone and backbone would be pushed together like an accordion—then we no longer sought the far-flung city streets for strange sights, but kept to museums and art exhibits and shops. On Saturday nights we went to the free concerts in the Metropolitan Museum, and while we wandered up and down the aisles in the Hall of Armor, and back and forth past Egyptian statues to the strains of the "1812 Overture," we reflected sentimentally on the "unimaginable touch of Time" as we noted how, unheeded, the stirring echoes of the "Marseillaise" rang down the corridors past the motionless Jewish couples who leaned, amorous, vacant-eyed, against the cases in which the mummies lay.

After her first Monday at work, Derrick returned to confirm Alice's belief in regard to the Matthewses, father and son.

"It's the same one: he has a picture of Ted on his desk, and he's in an aviator's uniform so that's what he's doing. I wonder if he's across."

"You might ask."

"No—I'd have to say I knew him, etcetera, etcetera, and

it would be unbusinesslike. The only person there I can imagine being sociable with is the office boy. The girls are either too important, superior, or they are flip little gum-chewing chits; but he's a bonny, blue-eyed child with a curly golden pompadour, a Scotch name, and a tremendous ambition to become a reporter."

Afterwards, she learned that Ted Matthews was at a flying field in this country, one of those disgruntled youths kept on this side to teach other luckier boys who were sent on in a few months to actual participation in the War. Because of her resolve not to mix friendship with business, she made no acquaintance that winter that carried over from office hours into our common life. Later, when a young artist who had been sent with the army as a kind of illustrator extraordinary for the Government came home gassed and penniless, and brought into the office some sketches that he hoped could be used in the Literary Supplement, they struck up a friendship at first sight, but it must have been midsummer when she brought him to the apartment for the first time.

But Alice had no such compunctions, or those who came into the store were more interesting than those whom Derrick saw. She brought her acquaintances to the apartment, and often the front room resounded with the noise and confusion of many people, from whom Derrick remained a little apart, quietly amused, tolerant with a tolerance half consciously acquired, half mere indifference. Sometimes we dined with them at Henrico's, or at any one of the dozen subterranean restaurants in the neighborhood of Washington Square, or went for coffee late in the evening to Romany Marie's, and afterward to one of their studios. We preferred, however, to have them come to us: it was more comfortable, and we could be more confident of a dinner that we ourselves had cooked. They dropped in more and more frequently as time passed; they came, starvelings as they were, to help us cook the dinner, and they stayed to wash dishes and to argue with us afterward. We bought coal for our grate, and gathered around it after dinner with our cigarettes

and coffee. Even when we had eaten alone, we were rarely
left so for an evening: Sam or Max or Frank, or all of them,
would whistle on the doorstep until someone went to let
them in. There were two girls whom they brought with
them, sometimes, but who never came alone—Theresa and
Rose—vivid, dark, shabbily dressed, with bérets pulled on
over untidy short hair, a queer foreign look in their features,
a fire (often a blaze of resentment), not to be quelled,
in their eyes. Their avidity and intentness and lack of
humor, their thin, sharp, suspicious faces, bothered us, but
we liked their daring, their awareness of all that passed
around them, distorted as their interpretation of it sometimes was. I watched Derrick stare at them, sometimes,
curiously; they were creatures of an alien world, one that we
had long wondered about, but had never been particularly
eager to enter.

It was Max whom we liked the best—and feared the most
—and now I cannot even remember his other name! Derrick asked me once, euphemistically, if I thought Alice could
be really interested in him. . . . He had a pudgy, muddily
pallid face, and small, beady eyes, but his hands were beautiful—long and white and slender; and he had a most flattering way of breaking off suddenly in the midst of a brilliant
declamation to make an admiring comment on your person
—Derrick's feet and ankles, which were undeniably comely,
or Alice's hair. . . . But I reassured Derrick: I had not seen
that Alice was particularly attracted to him, and I hoped not,
because he would certainly make her most miserably unhappy. She said, "I hadn't thought so far ahead as that, but
I can't bear to see Al with anyone who makes her take a
place in the background, who throws her into shadow. She
must marry one of those strong, quiet men that you find in
Zane Grey—products of the Great Open Spaces—who will
be content to sit and smile and smile while she holds the
center of the stage."

"You must find him for her, then: she hasn't any followers
of that description."

It was certainly true that Max played the ringmaster: he snapped the whip of his wit, and we all responded. We talked Socialism and Anarchy and Pacifism and the New World Order, and they smoked one after another of our cigarettes while we stirred our sluggish brains to action, Derrick and I, usually, against the others. He seemed able, always, to hypnotize Alice into agreement with him, but however late the hour of his departure, we never let her go to bed until we had argued her out of any mistaken ideas that might have been left in her mind. One night even Derrick withdrew from the debate, and argument languished. Max delivered a furious tirade against Capitalism and Militarism, and a plea for the necessity of a new day, then broke off to a discussion of art and the theater, and, finally, disappointed in his desire for combat, departed with his cohorts.

When Derrick had said good-night to him, she dropped moodily into the low rocker by the fire; when Alice and I turned back from the door, we found her hunched over the hearth poking the coals.

"Jack has never argued so well as that. I wish he could. If I had ever seen that he had a good reason for thinking as he did . . . he never convinced me that his ideas were founded on anything but false information."

"Neither are Max's. You don't mean to say that he convinced you?"

"No—hardly that. I still think that we couldn't stay out and let all the things we've stood for go down with England and France, or be saved by them, without our having a share in it. Civilization is worth nothing if it isn't worth fighting for. But I see now that it is possible to believe that civilization can be worth nothing if it has to be fought for—that there are those who would let it go with a loud, resounding crash, and start over again. Can it be true that there are two rights: one for me because I believe in it, and the opposite for some one else because he believes in it? If it is, I certainly was born wrong—the shadows of my ancestors hang over me with the admonition that right is right and wrong is wrong, now and forever, amen . . ."

The weeks were so full of what was exciting and newly discovered that it might have been easy to forget that Derrick was in love, and separated from her lover, had you not seen her, sometimes, follow with her eyes a uniformed figure on the street, or watched her, on an evening at home, rise from her desk, leave unfinished the letter she had begun to write, and lie on the couch to dream above a book whose pages she never turned.

Jack had a day and an evening in New York before he sailed. Twice Derrick allowed me to see what she felt for him—or the shadow of what she felt—once in the summer before, once again in the following autumn. This time she said little that she could not say coolly and casually. I came in from the theater on that night after he had gone; Alice was asleep in the bed in the corner, behind a screen, but I found Derrick waiting up for me, sitting on a stool beside the fire, her arms clasped around her knees. She looked up as I entered, tossed my gloves on the table, and crossed the room to warm my hands.

"It is cold, isn't it?" She moved over to make room for me. "But it's a glorious night—the snow all creaky underfoot. Did you have a good evening?"

"Fairly. It was a silly play. How do you feel? Partings are such ghastly things—"

"Not ghastly, exactly. Queer. Afterward you feel your aloneness around you like armor, setting you apart from other people, no matter how many you are with." She looked up at me, and I saw, belying her matter-of-fact tone, the white lines across her cheek-bones, beneath the shadows around her eyes, and the still whiter lines around her mouth. "Besides, Sue, I said I would marry him when he came home. . . . And if anything happens to him, I will . . . if he is wounded or sick . . . and I should never let him suspect my doubt. But nothing much can happen: our men, outside the regular army, don't know enough to do any fighting: they'll build railroads and that sort of thing. . . . If he comes home safe, I don't think I shall. I didn't mean to lie to him again—it seemed a little thing to promise in the face of life and death. . . . But truly, I am not sure enough of my feeling for him to make it right for me to do it—and I don't see how anyone can deliberately do what he knows is wrong and is sure to mean unhappiness in the end."

"You're a Puritan."

"Perhaps. . . . It's strange that your body can feel so strongly while your mind stands off to watch, and knows that it can't last . . . but I do know it."

When Jack had gone, she became more and more restless; she grew impatient with the life she was leading; she refused to join any suggested expeditions abroad, but, when we stayed at home with her in the evenings, she could not settle down to a book or a magazine. She wandered about the room, she ran her finger listlessly across the backs of the volumes in the bookcase, but did not take one out—or she stood in the window and watched the street, indifferently, or played solitaire at her desk in the corner. There came a night, finally, when she burst out with an exclamation of dissatisfaction.

"This is a footless life we're leading, Al. Why don't we do something about it?"

"I like it. What does it matter if it is footless? Everything is. I intend to go right along as I have been going—get a new job whenever I'm bored with the old one, and write a poem every once in a while until I have enough of them to print in a volume. What more could you want to do? Working in an office from nine to five isn't exactly a sybaritic life—"

"Compared to what the boys are doing, it seems so. Besides, I don't work very hard at the office—there honestly isn't enough work to do to keep me busy. I think I'll write a play."

I must have looked my surprise: her expression reflected as she turned upon me.

"Why, Sue! Didn't you think I would, after all?"

"Well—I don't know—not this year—you have written so much poetry—"

Since we had been in New York, I had played secretary for Alice and Derrick—had typed their poems and had sent them from magazine to magazine, while they evinced not even enough interest to ask questions. Derrick was even indifferent when hers appeared, now and then, tucked in unimportant corners of the papers and weekly reviews, or when—more rarely—there was a check for her. But despite the extreme casualness of her attitude, she had never ceased writing them. Now, however, she was scornful.

"You know I don't really care particularly about writing poetry. I don't mean that I don't like to do it, but that it isn't a consuming passion. What I want to do is something really important—and if you stop believing that I can, I'm lost."

"What's it going to be like, your play?"

"I don't know. I haven't got that far yet. Only, of course, it must be dreary and realistic, and not get anywhere."

After that, as Alice said, life with Derrick, while she stayed in New York, was like playing with the petals of a daisy . . . "she will, she won't, she will . . ." We laughed at her behind her back; it is hard to believe, now, when I remember her poetry of that winter—but we did. We should have been wise enough to manage her, to keep her at work on the verses she wrote in a few minutes, curled up on the cushions on the couch, or with her feet over the arm of a chair, and to persuade her to take some interest in getting them published. Others, whose productions would not bear comparison with hers, pushed and clamored and shouted, advertised themselves; there was a whole group of slender young ladies—some younger than others, but all slender—who read their own works from the platform, and in the press praised each other. But the very fact that there had never been a winter so favorable to young poetesses (there was a new one discovered each week and thrust upon the public, a finished personality, poems, picture, and past —invariably a dubious past—all complete) held Derrick back from any effort to reach a similar pinnacle of fame. She watched them with an amused and scornful eye, and preferred to remain unpublished.

At the very beginning, we had been excited when the literary gossip of Alice and her friends, their tales, to which Derrick often contributed, had made us feel that we were on the fringe of a Circle. After Alice had made the acquaintances she had desired at the bookstore, she moved on from there to a radical publishing house, where her salary was no higher, but where she got a firmer hold on that fringe. As the winter passed, we led more and more the life of the literati: we knew where to eat and where to walk, what to expect of forthcoming theatrical productions, and when to buy tickets for first nights. Then, just as I began to grow uncomfortably suspicious that the desire to be in the circle rather than on the edge of it would not be particularly stimulating, Derrick reassured me by expressing her opinion of what she called the "School of Push and Praise." It was not that she did not admire the young poets—the work of those whom she had read but not seen, the persons of those who came into the office—she admitted that she would have given her eyes to know any one of them, but she was so afraid of imitating their vices rather than their virtues that she almost fell over backward in her uprightness. Her poetry went into the waste-basket, unless I rescued it, and she treated distantly and with hauteur the girl who was the verse editor of the Literary Supplement.

After her first suggestion of a play, however, she applied herself diligently for several nights. Before she had worked out the plot, there came the first of those interruptions that made Alice and me more and more doubtful as months passed and the play was not finished. This first time, it was the War news that made us forget everything else: as the spring advanced, it grew worse, almost hopeless. Billy Thornton joined, as stretcher-bearer or ambulance-driver, a medical corps made up of college boys; he sailed from New York before Easter. Jack had written that he was in training far from the battle-line. It was not for them that we trembled, but for the fate of the world, while that dreadful Easter came and went. Appalled, shadowed by calamity, we lived from one edition of the newspaper to the next, from moment to moment, while Paris was shelled, and the French line was broken, and the English retreat seemed neverending. Paris and the Channel ports . . . no other thought could hold the mind, until finally the English came to a halt, their "backs to the wall," American engineers helped to fill a gap in the line, the Germans were stopped, and we knew some faint shadow of the relief and thanksgiving of those who had been more immediately endangered.

So long as you felt, unconsciously, that *thinking* for the French and English would help them—that going to sleep at night was a betrayal of the cause—you could not really go about the ordinary day's business with undivided attention. You might be making beds or washing dishes at home, or writing letters or typing at the office, or teaching ancient history, but there was never a moment when you were not, at the same time, listening for the newsboys to call the next "Extra" in the streets. Derrick could not think of her play. When the worst was over, and your conscience no longer reproached you for being able to forget the War at intervals, then you could resume your private life. Derrick returned to her work, and, in the little leisure that she had, held her mind to the task of twisting things that had happened, or might have happened, in Tecumseh, into a drama: a drama that would involve the revivalist, the old man who had been burned to death and lost his soul, and Maggie Seddon and Bill Sheehan.

In July, she cleared off the top of her desk and went home for her vacation. Alice left for Cleveland just at the time when Derrick was to return, but I stayed in New York all summer to study at the University. When she came back, therefore, she found me alone in the apartment, and consequently just so much more rejoiced to see her. I did not conceal my pleasure, although I expected her to regard the city and everything in it with loathing, after so brief a vacation. She was undeniably delighted to get back, however. I wondered if she really could not bear to be separated from her play before it was finished; but it was not that, I soon learned: it was a revulsion of feeling against Tecumseh, the family . . .

For the first time, she had seen her mother changed, had realized how she was tired of the life she had to lead: tired of housework, tired of children, impatient. She said to Derrick that if she could not get away from them now—not actually, but in mind—have herself to herself for a while, return to the sculpture that she had never once dreamed that she would not do, sometime—if she could not do it now, she never would. Derrick, I think, must have been not altogether sympathetic: she said, rather unkindly, that she could not see why her mother did not make some effort instead of only talking about it; she persuaded her to fit up a part of the attic as a studio and made her promise to work there.

A letter that had come from Billy while Derrick was at home proved to her how genuine was her mother's indifference to them all. She who had always been the last authority could not stir up interest enough, now, to lift her hand.

Billy had decided, he wrote, that he would not be a doctor, after all. It had never occurred to the Thorntons that he would want to do anything else, but here he expressed his determination: he was going into something peaceful, the manufacture of soap, or production of tobacco; he would make an attempt to supply the world plentifully with some one of those things that they, as soldiers, suffered the lack of. He could not face going on to Johns Hopkins; he never wanted to see any one's internal organs, never again. Thus Billy, at twenty . . . it made them heartsick to think that at that age he had seen so much horror . . . it was impossible, according to Thornton standards, to imagine any one less sensitive than Billy. Of course, there was no question of trying to persuade him to change his mind: he had earned the right to choose what career he would; moreover, as they well knew, heaven and earth would not move him, once he had determined on his course. And, as the doctor said, it was not as though Billy were the only son in the family: one of the other boys could just as well carry on the family tradition.

That casual suggestion of her father's roused all Derrick's opposition, and she looked to her mother for disagreement as strong. Mrs. Thornton had always had a firm conviction that the children should be left alone to choose what they would do. But now Derrick found her mother resignedly in acceptance of the situation, although troubled: she suspected that Hunter had set his heart on something else, and no one could imagine little Henshi ever being a doctor . . . but, in the end, they would have to do as their father said. . . . Derrick was amazed, puzzled . . . sometimes she thought that her mother no longer cared what became of them . . . then sometimes she feared that there must be something dreadfully wrong with her. . . . It was not as though Dr. Thornton were a tyrant—Derrick smiled at the absurd suggestion when she talked to me about it. He would not insist, if he could be persuaded that neither of the boys would be satisfied in his profession. But Mrs. Thornton did not rouse herself to resist. She was sorry for Hunter, but her attitude was that of one who looked on at an unhappy situation in which she had no part. She had long enough devoted her life to her children: that she was unconsciously governed by that reason was the impression that she gave. But Derrick was willing to fight. First she wormed out of Hunter the confession that he had applied for admission to Sheffield instead of Princeton. In the face of her amazement, he insisted upon it: he wanted to go to Sheffield because he wanted to be a marine engineer. It was hard for

Derrick to believe that this was anything but a small boy's
lust after the sea, due to the influence of Conrad, but ar-
dently she supported him in his cause, and gave him new
courage to resist when there was danger that would give way
to his affectionate desire to please his father. The latter
insisted that Hunter was a born doctor, but Derrick would
not let the boy be convinced.

"If he gave up and went to medical school," she said, "it
wouldn't make any difference how good a doctor he was,
he'd always be discontented with that other ungratified desire at the back of his mind. He would always feel ill-treated.
Let him try what he wants—he'll probably come back to
medicine."

"And in the meantime, he's wasting years of his life."

But Dr. Thornton gave up all attempt to persuade him,
and Hunter looked forward to Sheffield after another year
in high school. He had been graduated that spring, but his
father said he must have another year of mathematics before
he even tried to go to Sheffield. It was not his strong point.
. . . All this was settled before Derrick came back to New
York; it was not because of the escape from family disputes,
therefore, that she was glad to be away from them, at work
again. It was because she could thrust into the background
—selfishly, as she said—the thought of the change in her
mother . . . except when she wondered vaguely why she had
that strange lump at the end of her breastbone, then remembered. She tried to explain her feeling.

"It is bad enough when you grow up and see that your
mother is not, after all, the wisest and most beautiful woman
in the world, but your foundations are shaken on the day
when you discover that she is less strong than you are, less
to be relied on than yourself. Now I see so clearly that she
is unhappy, but there is nothing I can do. When I am at
home, I lie awake at night, sick with dread and a feeling of
helplessness . . . and so I'm glad I'm here, where I can
persuade myself it's all imagination, mine or hers."

While Alice was still away, Derrick took out her play

again; when she returned and found her engrossed, she badgered her to tell us the plot. Finally, on one of our rare evenings at home alone, she consented; we could tell her, she said, whether or not it would do, whether or not it were possible. She seated herself cross-legged on the couch, cushions piled behind her, her hands folded quietly in her lap.

"If I can't make you believe it, I'll not write it."

She began in a deprecatory fashion, apologetic in her tone, but she believed herself, and after a sentence or two, told it as something she had seen.

"The shanty stood in a little triangle of field, swampy bottomland, with three willow trees rising out of the weeds beside it. The roof sagged in the middle, like the back of a broken-down old horse; there were two windows in the side, and beneath them a path which showed that only the back door was used. This led from the cabin to a creek in the background, across a rotten, shaky footbridge that had some boards missing, and holes in some of the others; beyond, the ground rose in a steep bank of muddy red clay, and the bridge was continued in a flight of rickety steps."

In a moment, it was not Derrick we saw, lounging on the couch, but—as she had often made us see it before—Tecumseh on a warm Saturday afternoon, the sun shining through a haze of dust in the air; the rank smell of a wilderness of weeds, of mud, and stagnant water was in our nostrils.

"There a boy and girl appeared against the sky, above the steps. The girl was perhaps eighteen, pasty-faced, towheaded, dressed in a skirt that sagged and a blouse that would not stay with it; she was awkward, unclean, unintelligent, but full of life and good spirits, laughing continually. An ebullient creature, like Al."

"So long as you don't give her my hair, I don't mind. Go on."

"It was probably because of her laughter—so flattering in its implication—that the boy thought he was in love with her. He was a street-corner loafer—thin, stooped, shuffling, his cap pulled down over a pimply face—who spoke with the crude, revolting wit of that type. He begged her to go out with him to the moving pictures that night, but she refused: it was prayer-meeting night, she would have to go to church. He asked her, then, to sneak out after her mother had gone to bed and to sleep. She consented, without much reluctance, and he went on to make love to her: uncouth but fluent, and somehow, in spite of vulgarity, pitiful and rather sweet, which" (Derrick admitted in an aside) "is easier said than done! She stopped him when she saw her mother coming; he kissed her good-bye and departed hurriedly. Maggie ran across the bridge, but had not entered the shanty door when a woman reached the top of the steps and called out to her. . . . A huge woman, barefooted, a mound of quaking, unclean flesh, in a long skirt that draggled in the dust, a man's jacket and a man's felt hat; a virago who scolded the girl brutally, coarsely, because she had let that 'loafer' come home with her. Maggie leaned against the door, saying nothing; her mother approached and screamed in her face until she was out of breath, when the girl asked, indifferent to all that had been said, 'Hain't you brought nothin' home to eat?' Then the woman took from a basket on her arm a newspaper-wrapped package. 'Mis' Schuler' had given her a piece of roast, left-over; she had offered her, too, an old hat, but she wasn't going to be seen in 'none of ol' Dutch Gertie's hats she'd wore ten years herself!' She spat on the ground vindictively, and launched into an account of her day, the late storm soon forgotten. She was a 'cleaning woman' who scrubbed porches, weeded garden borders, and washed windows—and she was a member of the church of the Nazarenes." Derrick stopped for a moment to consider. "I don't know that I can explain the Nazarenes. It is a perfervid religion, whose chief doctrine seems to be that, if you can achieve a state of holiness, you are forever after holy, and can do no wrong—a sort of poor-white Methodism. And they believe that the Second Coming is to be in their lifetime, and that they will, therefore, have the pleasure of witnessing the doom of the unholy. Of course, Maggie's mother had no doubt as to her own holiness."

As she continued, Derrick condensed more and more her synopsis. She admitted that it was hard for her to get it clear in her own mind—"But there would be the scene that night . . . the boy was followed to the bridge by his father, an old and respectable widower, a mill foreman, whose older sons were industrious and God-fearing, but whose youngest, he was beginning to suspect, was worthless. In vain he tried to persuade the boy to go home with him—he was called an old granny and pushed aside. The boy whistled from the bridge, Maggie crept out to join him, and they went up the steps and away together.

"And another scene the next afternoon: inside the shanty —rough board floor, stained walls, a broken-down rusty stove, a table, two chairs, and, in the rear, the door that looked out on the field, the willows, creek, and bridge. The girl and her mother are there; the boy's father comes to tell how Maggie had been out with his son the night before— couldn't she do nothing to keep her in? . . . Then he is appalled at the tempest he has raised; he intended no harm to the girl, only hoped to save the boy from her. In terror he retreats to the doorstep while the woman rages. Behind him appears the preacher of the Nazarenes, a man for whom nothing could be said, except that he was passionately sincere, a man hard, coarse, cruel. The woman, when she sees him, becomes at once submissive, oily, sanctimonious. She tells him about Maggie and the boy; Maggie, to save herself, protests that she had only talked to him on the bridge for a minute . . . the old man, who knows that it is a lie, says nothing. . . . The preacher turns to him, quotes the Bible, 'the sins of the father,' exhorts him majestically to see the light, to seek conversion, so that through him the boy may be saved. . . . The honest soul had heretofore resisted all such pleas, unable to see the beauty of holiness, but now he hesitates, promises to come to the revival meetings when they begin, and goes away pondering.

"Another scene: the five-and-ten-cent store, where Maggie works, on a Saturday night. Counters on both sides, candy, peanuts, earrings, beads, postcards, hat trimmings . . . tables down the center, with ribbons, embroidery, kitchen utensils. Aisles thronged with farmers' wives, pushing, shoving, exchanging jokes with Maggie, behind the peanuts, her laugh ringing out above all the noise and confusion. The boy is waiting for her, against the counter. It is after closing time; the crowd drifts out, urged by the sight of clerks spreading white cloths on the counters. Maggie says the manager thinks it is so late that none of the banks will be open . . . even on Saturday night, when they open especially to receive the money that the farmers have spent in town, they close at nine-thirty. The money will have to stay in the store until Monday morning. When the last customer has gone, the boy and girl follow. The store-manager, who has no intention of leaving the money there, telephones a bank cashier to ask him to go back and open up for him; he empties the cash-register drawers and departs with his money bags. . . . And that same night, the boy, with a friend, comes back to rob the store. He boasts of his conquest of Maggie's virtue . . . he has promised to buy her a diamond, but he ain't going to be caught going to work for it . . . he knows there's money enough here to buy a ring. But, after all, the cash-drawers are empty except for a few silver dollars and small change. The boys take it and climb out the alley window. . . ."

Derrick stopped and sighed. "This part is so difficult . . . I am not sure how to manage it. The boys are caught and sentenced to the workhouse; Maggie is blamed for betraying them—hadn't she said there would be money when there wasn't? Hadn't it been for her that he had wanted the money? Her lover swears never to forgive her. And, although she is ignorant of his belief, she is a different person after he has been jailed, as low in spirit as she always had been cheerful.

"Then the revival. That is easier. The barnlike building, flaring lights, no floor, but straw on the ground, rough benches of unpainted wood . . . the impassioned preacher, the boy's father, broken by his disgrace, trying to believe, the unhappy girl, her mother. . . As the revivalist paints the tortures of hell, the torments of a guilty conscience, the happiness of repentance, the girl is convinced. It is because she has sinned, because of her conscience, that she is unhappy. . . . A revival can be an orgy, a thing of insane ecstasy, of frenzy. The contagion sweeps over Maggie. She knows the Bible . . . 'harlot' and 'scarlet woman.' She thinks that her mother would probably kill her should she ever know the truth, and yet . . . the madness of the congregation, singing, shouting for joy, because their sins are forgiven, because they are safe. . . . Her head reels. The preacher beseeches them to come to him after the meeting, those who are in sin, to confess to him, and ask for forgiveness. . . . With a score or so of others who have been swept off their feet, she waits her turn after the hard of heart have gone . . . and tells him. When, after her stumbling confidences, she dares to look at him, she recoils in terror. He trembles with a holy rage, beside himself. He half lifts his arm, and, with his hand raised, his finger pointing, he calls to those who are waiting . . . and while he holds the terror-stricken girl, he repeats her story to them all, holds her up as a reproach, a shame, an example, calls her 'Magdalen.' When he has done, he flings her from him, strides down the aisle and away. She stumbles toward her mother, while all those around draw back in loathing. And her mother, still in the frenzy of holiness, blowsy, bloated, her unkempt hair falling across her face, lifts two fists in the air and screams at her. She forbids her ever to come home again. The girl is left alone, huddled on the end of a bench . . . alone except for the boy's father, who comes down the aisle to her. He knows that his son must be the one responsible for her

283

downfall. At first he cannot get her to admit it—she has not forgotten that he tried to keep them apart—but now he says that she must come home with him. The girl, faced suddenly with the realization that she has nowhere else to go, nevertheless stubbornly refuses. He says that he will not leave her, that he is a widower and has no daughter-in-law in the house, to take care of it, that he needs some one . . . and that it will not be long before his son is home to marry her. She somehow understands his pride, and is grateful for his kindness, and finally submits to be led away with him.

"Then the last scene, in his kitchen, Maggie and the old man having their Saturday noon dinner together. They talk of the day when the boy will be back, and of how, of course, he will straighten up when they are married, and how in the end nobody will ever think of anything wrong. This Maggie does not quite believe—'men are so funny,' she says . . . they all treat her as if they thought that now she was common property . . . but she will not let the old man express his indignation. 'It doesn't matter.' And, indeed, it seems to cast no shadow on her restored and abundant good spirits. . . . But after he goes 'up-street' for the Saturday afternoon gossip, a truck-driver comes with a load of coal; at the kitchen door he asks where it is to be put. He is grimed from head to heel, only his teeth gleam . . . Maggie, forgetting already her own account of her mistreatment, jests with him —when he tries to kiss her, she slaps him, wipes her face on the roller-towel, and tells him what she thinks of him—of him and of the grocer-boy and the livery-stable man. He withdraws, abashed . . . but when there is another knock at the door, she peers out cautiously, before she opens. It is, this time, her lover, come home unexpectedly, with some days off his sentence for good behavior. With passionate joy she welcomes him; with surprise at finding her there, with anger, he throws her off . . . he does not say why, she does not know, but does not ask, accepting as reason enough the ruin of her good fame. She sees at once that the end that she and the old man had so confidently counted on is, after

all, impossible. She can stay no longer in his father's house
. . . She goes off upstairs to collect her things. When the old
man comes home, he finds the boy alone in the kitchen;
there are explanations . . . when he has heard what has
happened, he says that Maggie is not to go: either the boy
will marry her and they will both stay, or she will stay and
he will go. After bitter words which are of no effect against
his father's determination, the boy leaves the house. Almost
before the girl can be told, however, he is back, and with
him the preacher of the Nazarenes. He has come to upbraid
the old man for turning his son out of the house for a woman
of the streets—his son who has sinned and paid, and is
repentant, for a girl who has sinned and not paid—who has,
indeed, sunk only deeper in sin, living with the father of her
lover. . . . The old man listens in ominous quiet; when the
preacher has finished, he rises and says that there is one way
to make the matter straight: whether the boy goes or stays,
he must marry the girl; if he does not, he will make a will
leaving the boy's share of his savings account to the girl. The
boy surrenders at once in the fear of that eventuality. The
preacher is taken aback . . . but the girl, for the first time
that afternoon, is roused to a show of spirit. She is ready to
quit. She will not marry the boy, now, nor will she stay with
the old man, if people are going to talk about him. She can
earn her living, all right, all right . . . and she laughs. The
laugh that had once had in it only high spirits is now hard
—hard and revolting. She doesn't care how much they talk
about her. She has been called a bad woman so often that
enough men believe it . . . the livery-stable keeper has even
asked her if she would not like to live in a room he has, over
the stable. She will go ask for it. . . . She takes her bundle
of clothes and leaves the house. For a moment they are
dumbfounded, then the old man turns on the preacher: his
boast is that he saves souls—here is one that he has sent to
the devil. She had trusted him as a man of God, and he had
rewarded her faith by calling her a 'harlot' until she had
become one. The preacher does not admit the justice of the

reproach: the old man has forgotten that it is his son who had made her a harlot. Then the boy accuses him: 'There wasn't no harm in whut we done. We was gonna be married, an' didn't see any reason to wait. There wasn't anything wrong until you made her think it was wrong . . . an' then your blabbin'. If you'd kep' your mouth shut, she'd be as decent a girl now as any in town. It was the whisperin' an' gigglin' behind her back, an' to her face, wherever she went that made her a bad un, an' not what we done. We liked each other, an' liked bein' together. She hadn't no one else to like: look at 'er mother! An' you've gone an' drove her into the streets.' The boy seizes his cap and rushes out after her . . . almost at once the preacher recovers his self-possession and turns to the old man with a few selections of his patter: eternal damnation for those who harden their hearts, the end of the world—the coming of Christ, when they will be rewarded for their scorn of him, one of the servants of Christ . . . with which the curtain falls, leaving him untouched, hard, cruel, confident . . ."

Alice at once suggested her opinion when Derrick had stopped.

"Cheerful little thing you propose to write."

"Yes—one of those nasty but fashionable bits of grim realism."

"Realism!" She scoffed. "There never were people like that."

"Indeed there were. I knew that old woman when I was a child. I shall never forget her fat, dirty, bare feet, although she's been dead now for years. And the revivalist—I've longed to do that revivalist, although, of course, the one I knew was of a different class socially—I should hardly say intellectually."

"Do you think you can write the dialogue? How do you know how people like that talk?"

"I can try—of course, I don't know whether I can do it or not. But I do know how they talk—I went to school with them for twelve years, and, besides, I've watched them, and listened. What about it, Sue?"

"Well, I must say, it sounds perfectly dreadful—but if you can do it, you will knock them cold."

"But you think I can't?"

"I'm sure I don't know. I think you can do almost anything if you try hard enough, but you didn't pick an easy plot, exactly. It would be better for a novel. There are too many scenes, for one thing."

"I know. I must meditate on it. But the idea and the characters."

"All right. And the background. It's a wonder to me how you can keep a feeling for it in the midst of the hurly-burly of New York . . ."

She promised me faithfully to forego the theater and all evening social gatherings, and we promised to let her alone. But the next interruption she brought on herself.

She had spoken to us frequently of Silas Faulkner, the young war artist who had come into the office so constantly; she had promised to bring him to dinner, but it was not until almost the end of the summer that he came down with her one evening. We knew little about him, beyond the fact that he had been gassed and consequently sent home, that "home" was in Kansas, where he had not gone—he had preferred to stop in New York to find something to do with his drawings. All summer Derrick's Literary Supplement— as we called it—had published every week one of his black-and-white sketches, terrible but profoundly moving portrayals of battle and bravery and sudden death. We admired his work, and Derrick liked him, so we prepared for him our most elaborate dishes, and welcomed him in our best clothes —welcomed, to our amusement, exactly the sort of boy we had known always, at home. He was tall, broad-shouldered, and blue-eyed, with a cow-lick in his rather coarse yellow hair; his wide tie was the only affectation of the artist that he displayed, the thinness of his cheeks and the lines around his mouth the only sign of the warrior, and they by no means counteracted the seal of her possession of him that Kansas had stamped on body and countenance and speech.

We were none of us uncomfortable on our first encounter; he said at once that Derrick had told him we were all from Ohio, and if we were all Middle-Westerners, we knew exactly where we stood. After dinner, he and Derrick talked about summer in the country: picnics on moonlit nights beside a river, long drives when you stopped by the road and bought melons from a farmer and ate them at once, with no implement except a penknife; they so whetted each other's appetites that nothing would satisfy them but a slice of watermelon, and they ran out to the nearest fruit store on Third Avenue to look for one. Completely at ease as we all were as we divided the quarter of a melon and opened our last bottle of ginger ale, there was a shade of astonishment in his eye as he watched Alice. Derrick had probably not said much about her, and she was at her best: her amazing hair a blaze of glory in its upstanding disorder, her wits on fire, her laughter bursting like a flood from behind a dam.

Max came in that same night, with a friend, too late to share the watermelon, but not too late to find Silas still there. He made himself unpleasant at once: when he had asked where Si was from, he sneered at Kansas in the tone of one who believes his to be the accepted opinion, and in his manner if not his words he congratulated Si on having escaped.

"Have you ever been there?" Si asked.

"No. Do you expect ever to go back?"

"No." Si laughed, but from that moment his dislike for the man was obvious; he made no attempt to conceal it in the argument of the rest of the evening.

Max saw his eyes on Alice, and maliciously introduced a discussion of Pacifism—as though we were not all sick unto death of the subject! He knew that Alice would support him, and, when she did, with keenness and violence, the amazement with which Si had looked at her deepened, and he threw himself into the discussion, headlong. Derrick withdrew and listened, relieved, for once, from her duties as the Opposition. But it was plain that Si argued, not for the sake of the argument, but because he honestly wanted to convince Alice. They were so absorbed that they became more frankly heated, more stubborn, more contradictory, than people usually dare to be on their first meeting.

Si came often for a while after that, and it was evident that it was for Alice that he came. Derrick need not have been distracted from her work: if she had gone into the back room and closed the doors, she would hardly have been missed. Neither she nor I, however, would have foregone the pleasure of witnessing the combats that ensued. Alice no longer supported Max in their controversies, but listened in silence, only shouting with laughter now and then while he and Si snarled at each other like angry dogs on leashes. . . . When Si asked her, she let him draw her portrait: it was only a sketch done with red chalk, but it was full of fire and life. Derrick set it on the mantelpiece, and after that Max came less and less frequently, and when he did come, he talked not politics, but literature, a subject on which he could be sure Alice's opinions were his. Finally he came so seldom that after Si told us, early in September, that he had decided he must humor his mother, after all, and spend the winter in Kansas, he did not hear of it for many weeks. We were left alone, after Si's departure, to spend our evenings as we pleased. It looked as if Derrick would have solitude enough that winter to write a dozen plays.

III

RAIN FELL in the city steadily all day long, the first of the fall rains. It beat down from the curb-side sycamores the few yellow leaves that had survived the summer's heat, plastered them on the sidewalk, or drove them in a soggy mass into the gutter. It made the horses hang their heads as they plodded through it, and the curtained automobiles slither dangerously at the corners. Pitiless, rain in the city is, blown against sterile concrete and brick; there is nothing in it to remind one of the unending cycle of change and death, decay, and in decay the promise of a new life, as there is in the country, where the drops carry the fragrance of wet earth, rotting wood, the soaked bark of the trees, and the fallen leaves.

It was late in September, the week before my school was to open; I had seen Alice and Derrick depart in the morning with self-congratulation: I had no need to go out in the rain, but could spend the day at work on plans for lessons—dull enough, but a better lot than theirs. Derrick had come back once, from the doorstep.

"Sue, darling," she pleaded, "we shouldn't hate you quite so much if you would promise to have a good supper all ready for us when we come home."

"Of course I will. Beefsteak and mushrooms. You can look forward to it all day . . ."

I hummed "How firm a foundation" contentedly while I washed the dishes, and almost enjoyed the sound of the rain;

290

but afterward, when I had taken out my books and there was no sound in the apartment, it began to seem portentous, unendurable; as the hours passed I grew more and more acutely aware of the manner of its falling: how it did not waver, did not slacken—more and more conscious of the emptiness of the rooms. After lunch I picked up a novel instead of going back to work, but I could not shake off an indefinable dread; I looked continually over my shoulder around the apartment, like a nervous old lady. Finally, reduced to counting the minutes before it would be time for Alice to come in, I decided to read until five, when I could go out for the steak for supper with some hope that when I got back they would be in the house. This programme was followed to the second: when the clock in the Metropolitan Tower struck five, I slipped on a raincoat and ran out to the nearest grocery on Third Avenue. When I returned, they were not there, after all . . . but it was hardly time, really. Supper was to be cooked. I listened to catch above the noise of the beefsteak in the skillet the sound of a key in the door, but they still had not come when everything was ready to be taken from the stove.

At first I was cross, as one always is—they were inexcusably thoughtless; then I tried to think of some reason why they might have gone out to supper—but there was my promise to Derrick to have a good steak for her. If anything had happened. . . . For a long while I stood in the window and watched the tireless rain that still fell steadily, and the passersby, all strangers . . . countless strange people, one after another, huddled beneath their umbrellas. It was only seven, and I was unreasonable: nothing ever did happen to people you knew, and the same thing could not have happened to both of them, since they had not been together. Nevertheless, I started to telephone Alice's office—then stopped at the sound of the outside door being opened. A second later Alice's hand was on the doorknob.

"Where under the sun—" I began indignantly—but stopped at sight of her. The coppery wet hair was plastered to a white cheek, her hand trembled as she laid her key on the bookcase. "What is it, Al?"

"Where's Derrick? I didn't come home because I thought she wouldn't want me—but I didn't dream that she wouldn't come herself."

"What is it? What has happened?"

She held out the evening paper.

"Jack Devlin on the casualty list. Killed in action."

So that was it, I thought, and not merely the rain, that had made the day so dreadful . . . my knees trembled, so that I dropped on the couch. When had this nightmare begun? When would it end? I shrank from the thought of the hours ahead. Derrick—poor Derrick! The paper in my hand rattled deafeningly, as paper can. I looked at it . . .

"How did you keep this so dry? You're dripping, yourself."

"I had it under my coat, wrapped up."

We stared at each other. There was no volition, no reason in what we said. Then I caught my breath.

"Are you sure, Al? She hasn't come in yet. Do you suppose she's seen it? It might be another person of the same name."

"No. They list them under state and town. And if she isn't here, she's seen it. It would have been better if she had heard any other way first. Heaven grant that she was alone! Can you imagine finding *that* when you were with strangers? Where do you suppose she's gone?"

Alice paced the floor. I sat with the paper in my hand, my eyes on the name. She turned upon me suddenly.

"I can't stand it, to wait here like this. I'm going out. . . . Look here, Sue—she won't want me to be here when she comes in. She's never told me how she felt about Jack. Of course, I know—but it's only because I've seen, not because she's said anything. I have to get out before she comes. I simply haven't the courage to face her."

For a minute after she had gone, I listened. . . . There was no sound except that of the rain and the dulled life of the street. . . . I had no more courage with which to await her than had Alice. If only it were really a nightmare! Alice hadn't half an idea how bad it would be, if it were true: she did not know that Derrick would hold herself responsible for his death as surely as if she had fired the cannon. . . .

I rose to take from the back of the stove our forgotten dinner and to put the kettle on to boil water for tea; I brought in a few lumps of damp coal from the back porch, built a little fire in the grate, and sat before it, lighting and relighting bits of kindling until the coal had dried and the blue flames crept up. All the while I reasoned: one expected soldiers to die in battle, the ones you knew as well as the others. Andrew MacLauchlan, Robert Van Leyden. They had been killed, and the world had not stood still. But this was different.

I thought of Derrick face down on her bed, the pillow in her arms, of Jack and Derrick in the back seat of the automobile, holding hands behind the golf-bag, of Derrick's somber, frightened eyes . .

Again I went to the front window and over the bars of our balcony railing watched the street, the wet sidewalk, and scanned the figures of the few passers-by who came under the glare of the light on the corner. As each umbrella appeared, I held my breath; as each in turn proved not to be Derrick, I was left weaker and more frightened. I thought: could it be possible that in all these months she had not foreseen that this might happen? With her imagination that did not wontedly stop short of the ultimate possibility, could she have been so blind?

And then I saw her. She crossed the street so wearily that she seemed to struggle visibly for the strength to lift herself from the gutter to the curb. Paralyzed, noticing how the silence and emptiness deepened, threateningly, behind me, I stood in the window and watched until she had almost reached the steps. At the last minute I went to the closet in the other room for her kimono and bedroom slippers; as I returned with them to the fireside, she entered and stood on the threshold, the folded paper clutched in her hand.

I could not move toward her, but with a word, after all, one could put an end to the silence and the terror . . .

"Derrick, come take your wet things off, and I'll get you a cup of tea."

She crossed the room carefully and slowly, from the support of the door to the support of the chair; she pulled her wet hat off and dropped it on the floor, sat down, leaned back, and looked at me dully.

"You've seen the paper, then?" Her voice was hoarse, hardly above a whisper, but perfectly steady.

"Yes, we saw it." I knelt and took off her shoes. "Where have you been? Will you eat some supper if I bring it?"

"I couldn't."

"A cup of tea, then. Unfasten your wet clothes and put this on, while I get it."

She fumbled with her belt obediently. I brought back the tea, and, while it was still too hot to drink, helped her slip her clothes off and wrapped the heavily embroidered silk kimono around her. Her white face and sunken eyes were pitiful above the brilliant flowers. . . . While she drank, I took down her hair and brushed it.

"Where have you been since five o'clock, Derrick, to get so soaking wet?"

"Walking, for a while, then on top of a bus, riding up and down." She shivered. "It was so queer. . . . Oh, Sue . . . you've no idea how queer it was. There was no one else up there—it was raining, you know—and it was like being alone in a boat in the middle of the ocean: the whole street went up and down like the floor of the sea, and all the hundreds of umbrellas bobbing along beneath me were in another world. It was unreal and terrible, but I couldn't bear to make the effort to ring the bell and get down. It was the way you behave in a dream, not actually." She shivered again, and spoke more and more hoarsely. I took the teacup from her and carried it out; when I returned, she continued.

"The bus conductor thought I was crazy: he looked and

looked at me whenever he came up for the fare, and the third time he said, 'You ain't sick, Miss?' And I couldn't be haughty, and I knew it wouldn't matter if I told him the truth—I looked up at him to see if he looked kind, and he was a grizzled old Irishman, so I said, 'No—but I've just heard that my best friend has been killed in France.' I had the impulse to be really low and say, 'my boy friend,' because I knew he would understand then, but I couldn't. Anyway, he said, 'Oh, Miss, I beg your pardon,' and tipped his cap, and when I did get off, he looked the other way while he helped me down."

She stopped . . . and a convulsion of agony racked her. Her head she held rigid against the back of the chair, her arm thrown up before her eyes. I looked away and waited . . . it was better to hear her talk, even in those unnatural tones.

"You must get to bed, Derrick. You've caught cold now. Take a hot bath and then let me bring you a hot-water bottle."

"I never catch cold. Don't worry . . ." She spoke quite simply and ordinarily . . . then, like one awakened from a dream, when the horror of it comes flooding back and cannot be shaken off, she turned to me. "Oh, Sue! Think of those amazing blue eyes of his, with the life gone out of them—part of a dead body, cast aside like a suit of old clothes . . ."

"It may not be true. There are often mistakes, and if you haven't heard from home, probably the newspaper is wrong. His name got in by accident, or it is a case of mistaken identity."

"No. It's true enough. It would have to be: we are bound to be punished, just as my great-grandmother used to say. And she was so peaceful about it, sitting in front of a fire, like this, rocking, with her skirt turned back over her knees. And now, it's the second time for me . . . it wouldn't be so bad to be punished by dying yourself. I never meant for him to go off and enlist. See, you know I didn't."

"Of course you didn't. You had nothing to do with it."

"Yes, I did. But how should I have dreamed he would do it, after all he had said?"

A matter-of-fact tone, only unusual because of its uncanny hoarseness. She broke off and watched me as I turned away and poked the coals.

"Sue, dear! Don't look like that! I beg your pardon for this vulgar display of emotion." She rose and steadied herself against the chair. "I'm going to bed. Don't let Al—will you? She won't mind if I don't wait for her?"

"Of course not. I'll wait, and warm up the supper."

"Haven't you eaten? I'm sorry." She picked up her clothes and started for the back room, where she slept, then turned again at the door. "Where do you suppose Al is? Walking Brooklyn Bridge to keep me from leaping off? I've caused you a lot of trouble . . ."

Alice came in presently, and nodded her head in understanding when she saw the door closed between the two rooms.

"I knew she was home: I came along awhile ago and climbed the steps to peek over the balcony, but I hadn't the courage to come in."

We had our warmed-over supper, and in silence went to bed. Alice I could hear as she tossed and turned on the other side of the room; I lay tense and wide awake, watched the patches of light thrown about the room by passing automobiles, noted the noises of the city that rose and fell: the roar of the Elevated trains, the horns of taxis, the measured stroke of the clock bell in the Metropolitan Tower, while, with all my power of concentration, I listened for some sound from the room where Derrick lay . . . but I heard nothing, not even a creaking of the bed, so that finally I listened no longer, but relaxed and fell asleep.

In the morning she rose at the usual time and breakfasted with us.

"Don't you want us to telephone the office and say you're ill?" Alice suggested. "You don't want to work to-day—"

"Why not? Nothing could be worse than sitting here with nothing to do."

"You look—worn-out—you'll expose yourself to the curiosity of the whole office."

"Nonsense. A little rouge will prevent their noticing."

So she went and came as always; she looked that night white and tired and drained of all vitality; we did not let her wash dishes, but sent her to bed, and then over the dishpan discussed what could be done.

"The sight of her makes me ache," Alice said, "but there's nothing I can say. Hasn't she talked to you?"

"Not but a little last night, and then she was almost hysterical. I feel so helpless. If she wants to be let alone, now she's got hold of herself, we'll have to keep hands off."

"Of course. But to have her feel like that, and shut herself up with it."

For several days Derrick went through all the motions of our ordinary life, unapproachable, armored against us by her remoteness. We could only pretend that nothing had happened. But night after night I lay in bed and listened: surely sometimes there would come a moment when she would want some one . . . there was never a sound from her room until after almost a week when I was roused by the opening of the door between us, and looked around to see her standing in the crack.

"Are you awake, Sue?"

"Yes."

I sat up, groped for my slippers, and followed her into the other room. It was a hot night: the full-length windows were open as far as they would go, but there was not enough air stirring to move the curtains. Derrick pulled a chair over beside them.

"Sit with me, Sue, and talk—or say over all the poetry you know. For a little while, anyway. I can't sleep." She threw a cushion on the floor and crouched there, her shoulders against my knees. "I couldn't bear to lie there alone a minute longer. All these nights go back, somehow, to that other night when I knew that Esther was dying—I think I feel sorrier for myself then—that miserable child—than for myself now—but it is impossible to be quite sane when you are alone in the night, even at the best of times." She twisted her long thin fingers together. "You don't mind my calling you?"

"You know that I don't. Shall we talk or say poetry?"

"Poetry, if you don't mind. Anything to get out of my head 'Reading Gaol.' 'For each man kills the thing he loves.' Horrible!" She drew a sharp breath.

"What shall I say?"

"Anything. The old things that you've always known— like 'The white plumes of Navarre,' or 'A soldier of the legion,' or 'Up from the meadows rich with corn—' "

But I had not been brought up on McGuffey's Readers.

"I don't know them. I only know the new things, like 'Is there anybody there, said the Traveller—' "

"That will do."

But it was an unfortunate choice. She interrupted before I came to the end.

> " 'And he felt in his heart their strangeness,
>   Their stillness answering his cry . . .' "

"Feeling the strangeness isn't enough to make you know they are there. Would you rather feel it, and be in doubt, or be quite sure they aren't—that the house is empty, and the Traveller is imagining them?"

"I think—" I hesitated; "I'm afraid I think I'd rather be quite sure they *aren't.*"

"But, Sue! That makes it so much worse. To have set him free to be immortal—that would cost only your own happiness—the loss, I mean. But to have made an end to everything for him, too . . ."

I hastened to change the direction of her thoughts.

"Why do you talk of your loss, when you said you were not going to marry him, anyway?"

"Because. Do you know how once in an æon you look some one in the eye, and you really see each other for a breathtaking instant? It isn't true that you can prove only the existence of yourself in that instant you know the existence of the other person, too. It happened once or twice to Jack and me, and might have happened again, whether we were married or not. You know—

" 'One hour, or two or three, in long years scattered,
    Sparks from a smithy that have fired a thatch—'

And to know that it can't happen again . . . it leaves one most awfully . . . awfully . . ." Her voice trailed off into silence. Stiffly she sat withdrawn from me, and stared out through the open window. Then she sighed, and recommenced. "I exist, alone. If you exist, no one can be sure of it except yourself. . . . Oh, Sue, Sue, my dear: hold on to me, and prove that you are really there!"

I held my hands still on her shoulders.

"Hush, Derrick! I know I exist, you know you exist, and so there we are—"

"And Jack doesn't, so there we are, too. One hour and then emptiness, afterward. One year after another, and

" 'to make amends
    One flaming memory that the death-bed ends.' "

I did not say that she was young to talk about the emptiness of life. I do not remember that I thought so then. I asked her if she were sure that the memory would end

"What is your belief in immortality? You used to say that you *knew*."

"Yes. There were those moments. But it was a pale sort of immortality. It was not I who would go on, but the thing in me that isn't I, that would go back to what it was before. . . . That isn't the kind of immortality Jack wanted—but perhaps he believed in his kind so absolutely that he attained it. To think of him as immortal . . . But it would have to be the other way for me. Perhaps if I try hard enough to remember those moments, there might be another one. But they come so unexpectedly, not by taking thought. . . . It makes you feel like an ancient pagan challenging your god for a sign. Give me the sign, and I shall believe—otherwise, I shall believe nothing. If I could only know, again, then things wouldn't matter so much. Magnificent terror and magnificent certainty . . . that was it." Then for the first time she lifted her white face and stared at me out of cavernous dark eyes. "But it is magnificently lonely, too, and just now that is the worst of all—"

"Derrick, my dear!" I felt for the first time in my life the heartbreaking helplessness one always feels in the face of grief. "Don't we count at all?"

She turned and threw her arms around my knees.

"So much that I almost forget, in the daytime. That's why I called you to-night."

Then suddenly, in a revulsion of feeling, she denied the truth of what she had just said. And afterward, I never knew . . .

"Don't pay attention to me, Sue. Let it go in one ear and out the other. I don't think I meant a word of what I said, really. I was just being melodramatic. I mean: the more I moan over having lost him, the less capacity I have to think of the other, the real thing—that I killed him. I was just getting myself into a pretty state, and not being honest, either. If Jack had lived, I should have been alone, just the same. So much alone that it is inconceivable to me that I could ever have let him know me, entirely: that inner secret self, I mean, that is really nothing but wind and sky, yet is the whole cornerstone of my being. I tried to tell you before, and can't, without talking perfect rot; but this is the point: I think I couldn't have married him, because it doesn't seem decent to marry and keep yourself hidden. Yet, I suppose that is what women do who marry, for certainly no one has ever been able to get through to another person, wholly.

And if you did, you would have to go alone, at the end, after all. Isn't it despicable to be afraid of death! And yet—that smothering, black sensation that chokes you when you think of it. . . . It can't be so bad, really, so many people have died —and Jack—*Jack* knows—and still I am afraid. 'The dead praise not the Lord, neither any that go down into silence.' I hated that Psalm as a child. 'Neither any that go down into silence.' " She rose then and went and stared out of the window. "I suppose I shall never have the sign I want—it would be fitting punishment for me never to be able to believe, again: for me to know that we have nothing but this life, and that I have ended even that for Jack . . . Say me another poem, Sue, then we'll go to bed . . '

I struggled frantically in my mind for words . . Had she unburdened herself of all that had been in her thoughts that long week, only to be left with this most bitter self-reproach? . . . Somewhere, among those sonnets, there was one . . I stumbled upon the middle of it, and went on through to the end:

" 'It may be that the loosened soul may find
  Some new delight of living without limbs,
  Bodiless joy of flesh-untrammeled mind,
  Peace like a sky where starlike spirit swims.
  It may be that the million cells of sense,
  Loosed from their seventy years' adhesion pass
  Each to some joy of changed experience,
  Weight in the earth, or glory in the grass;
  It may be that we cease; we cannot tell.
  Even if we cease, life is a miracle.' "

But she was where she could not be touched. When she finally replied, she spoke with a flippancy that jarred on me harshly.

"Good old Sue! How well we know our Masefield! But I am not sure that I am not afraid of life, too—I have taken the count so often!"

I rose and went to the kitchenette for crackers and apples, which we munched as we stood by the window. Beyond the empty square of city back yards rose the walls of the buildings that faced the other street: walls blank and dark, except for one lighted window high toward the roof, where, beneath an unshaded light, a group of men in shirt-sleeves were playing cards. Above, remote and thinly veiled by motionless clouds, hung the moon. As always, at intervals, came the rising and falling roar of the Elevated trains. . . . Derrick made some light comment on our gambling neighbors, and then, as the clock in the tower struck three, she turned away to go back to bed.

IV

ALONG WITH the rest of the world, we had the influenza that
fall, and nursed each other for weeks. Derrick was the last
to catch it; it was after she was up but before she was able
to go out, that the Armistice was signed. We stood together
in our window over the balcony, to listen to the distant mad
clamor of rejoicing; I remember how I thought that not even
the end of the world would rouse Derrick from her apathy.
Of course, it meant that Billy was safe—he had come
through unscathed, and would be home in a little while
. . . it was of that she spoke that afternoon, not of how, if
it had come only a little sooner, Jack, too, would have escaped.

After the Armistice, the city was in high holiday mood:
the War was over. Christmas drew near, a Christmas such
as had not been known for five years, with no soldiers in the
trenches to be thought of—it was a time to celebrate. Derrick affected a feverish gayety that it hurt you to see.

The one real interest in her life was Madeleine's letters.
She had written frequently, always, but it was not until
now that she could tell us much of what she was doing.
Heretofore, there had been long descriptions of the countryside in which the hospital was located: the great forests,
the woodcutters' huts, the flower-bordered paths, the ancient château with its mirror-like moat, the deep-shadowed
green of the rolling sward that reminded her of the college. She was the only one of us—Madeleine!—who had

303

admitted homesickness for the time when we had been together. But now there were accounts of the hospital, of the men, of the armies, all that she had not been able to say before. Derrick, I think, nursed a secret hope that surely in the next letter she would say that she was coming home; when she wrote, instead, that she was going into a canteen for the American troops in Coblenz, Derrick's disappointment was plain to be seen.

It was that disappointment that made me say in a letter to Edith, shortly before Christmas, that Derrick needed something to rouse her, and that I wished Madeleine would come home. I said also that Frances, who had plunged into work for her doctor's degree at Yale, had written that she would spend Christmas with us . . . and that Ted Matthews, when he had sufficiently recovered from his recent attack of pneumonia, was to go into the newspaper office under his father. Edith's reply was short, but full of matter.

"You're a hospitable lot, telling me Fran's coming down, but not asking me up. Would you turn me out if I appeared before New Year's, prepared to spend a month or so with you? As for stirring Derrick up, I think Madeleine's your best bet, but if she isn't coming home—well, it's an office I have taken upon myself before."

Frances came down from New Haven the week before Christmas, severely and smartly tailored, her red-gold hair elaborately coiffed, thin, alert, energetic, but without the familiar boyish restlessness. Derrick twitted her with having changed.

"You've settled the quickest of any of us, Fran. It's so unexpected. What's happened to you?"

"I like what I'm doing, and don't expect ever to do anything else, that's why." She leaned forward in her chair, her hands around her knee. "Psychology is developing so rapidly —that's why it's so interesting. People are finding out new things every day, and it keeps you on the jump, especially if you hope to find out something new yourself sometime."

"What are you going to do when you have your degree?

Teach, or get a job on some important bureau to investigate the feeble-minded, or do some kind of research?"

"I'm a long way still from my degree—but I think it will be research. I couldn't teach—"

"Oh, Fran! Aren't you going to apply your psychology to the 'old New England village' and write the novels you used to talk about?"

She laughed. "That was a pleasant dream of my youth . . . no, I've given up the idea. I suppose that's why, if it's true, that I seem settled. You've no notion how much more at peace I've felt since I've renounced that ambition. Before, my conscience was always nagging me to be doing something that I was not doing. Now, I'm free, with only one idea in my mind."

"Fran! We've lost you to science, then?" I reproached her.

Derrick chanted:

"Three little niggers, boasting what they'd do.
One turned scientist, then there were two."

"Exactly," Frances replied. "The bets have narrowed to you and Al."

We had a fantastic but strangely merry Christmas: Alice's friends from the Village came in in the evening and we had high tea and violin music and shrill conversation. A few days later, Edith came: Frances and I cooked supper while Derrick went over to the Pennsylvania Station to meet her. At the sound of the taxi, we hurled ourselves at the front door, and on the top step, while Derrick paid the driver, she and Frances flung themselves into each other's arms. We dragged them into the living-room, pried them apart, stood Edith off from us and surveyed her, top to toe: soft gray silk hat, soft gray squirrel coat, suede shoes. . . . She tilted her head on one side, her eyes danced.

"Well?"

"Very well, indeed. You might be straight from Paris."

"I'm so glad you like it. But the coat's all I have. I've come up for an orgy of shopping." She looked from one to another of us. "And, Derrick, you're going with me. I'd trust your judgment anywhere. Consider yourself engaged for Saturday afternoon."

"I'd love to go. The next best thing to buying clothes for yourself is helping others to buy them. You should have had Madeleine. She spends money superbly."

"You'll do, if you can manage to be interested. Three guesses as to why I'm visiting you this month."

"Well," Derrick teased, "Teddy Matthews is going to be in town."

"That's it exactly," she replied, with perfect composure.

"You behold in me the deadly female. And, Derrick—you are to conspire with me. Have you seen him at all?"

"Not to speak to. He has come into the office several times, but I've dodged him; besides, I've been fairly busy. I don't think it has occurred to his father that I might know Ted, although his consciousness of my college education has increased since the day I located a quotation for him."

"When was that? You never told us—"

"He was reading an article in which Shakespeare was quoted, and said he thought he knew his 'William'—that's what he called him—'William'—fairly well, and didn't believe he wrote the lines given. And I said, 'Yes—Henry V,' and told him which Prologue it was in—of course, it was just luck that I remembered it. He looked politely incredulous, and went and hunted it up, then he came back to my desk and glared at me and said fiercely, 'Look here—did you know that, or merely guess it?' Isn't it funny how the male hates to give you credit? . . . What do you want me to do for you, Edy?"

"When Ted comes in, find out, if you can, what state his mind is in. Of course, if it is full of some one else, it's hands off for me. If it isn't—'Lay on, MacDuff!'"

"Hasn't he written you?"

"Oh, yes—but he might be concealing 'most anything."

For the next few days we lived in a welter of suit-boxes and hat-boxes and a froth of silk and lace. Monday night when she came home, Derrick found us in the midst of a scene of "trying on." With all the airs of the most correct model, Edith appeared in garment after garment, revolving on her toes before the long glass in the back room. Derrick, bedraggled and weary after a day in the office, threw herself on a couch to watch.

"Do they admire our selection, Edy?"

"We admire, but disapprove," Alice replied. "Think of the starving Belgians! You must have brought the wealth of the Indies with you. I didn't know any one in the world could buy an entire wardrobe from the skin out, at one time."

"I thought we didn't have to think of the starving Belgians, now the War's over," Edith protested. "But it does look like more than it really is. Besides, I haven't had any new clothes since college, to speak of."

"Are we eating to-night?" Derrick asked. "It doesn't look much like it."

"Of course, we are. The Chinese place on Fourteenth Street. Change your clothes, Edy, queeck's a feesh—"

It was not until we descended the Chinaman's stairs after dinner that Derrick volunteered the information she had wanted Edith to ask for.

"Ted was in the office to-day."

"Red-headed as ever, I suppose. Did he know you?"

"Yes."

"Derrick! You're too provoking!" Edith shook her arm. "Tell me every word he said and you said and how many times you laughed, and what color necktie he had on."

"It was a sort of Alice blue. I was going out of his father's office as he was going in, and we met in the door. He said, 'Miss Thornton, upon my word! Why haven't I seen you before?' And we shook hands violently, and his whole moon-face burst into radiance. He was so glad to see me that I'm not sure you have a chance. I murmured something, and his father rose uncomfortably behind us. He said, 'Do you mean to say you two know each other?' And Ted said, 'Of course. She was one of Edith's best friends in college.' And I said, 'Edith's here for a month, visiting us—we've an apartment, you know.' "

Derrick broke off there, and turned to Frances to indicate a disreputable two-story building on the corner where we had crossed.

"Yonder dive is O.Henry's saloon, Fran. He spent his evenings there, and when he sobered up, made it immortal."

Frances surveyed it—roof, doors, gutter.

"They've had a Christmas party there—look—they've just thrown out their Christmas tree." She pointed to the rubbish barrel, on the curb down the side street, across the top of which a dead brown cedar tree rested drunkenly.

"Sue—you were complaining about not having kindling for the grate—help yourself—" Derrick strode to the barrel, pulled the tree down, and dragged it behind her.

"Derrick! You wouldn't!"

"Why not? We need it, and they've thrown it away. Take what the gods provide."

"It's like Elijah and the ravens," Edith supported her. "I'll help you to drag it, if you'll go on about Ted from where you left off."

"I can't remember. Had I got to where his father came and stood by us? He did, at any rate, and I told him about the night Ted took six of us to dinner, and he said he was glad to know that some of his bank account had been spent honorably. Then he allowed that your Cousin Rose would be hurt to know that you were in town without having let her know, and that you would have to go out for a week-end."

"I intend to—but not just yet. This has to be led up to gently. Go on."

"That's all. Ted asked me to go lunch with him, and I pleaded a previous engagement—which I did have, with the office boy. We go Dutch together at Child's, most noons, or around at the Brazilian Coffee House. When I declined, he asked us both for to-morrow, and I accepted for you. So you're to meet us at one-fifteen at Maillard's."

The luncheon on the following day, to which Edith departed in the full glory of squirrel coat and gray silk hat, was the beginning of a full social month for all of us. While Frances was still there, we asked Ted to dinner, along with Max and one or two others—Ted looked, beside their swarthiness, round, red, and rosy-cheeked, but was not a more lusty trencherman than they. At other times there were theater parties with Ted and some of his struggling young lawyer friends: the boys were in a reaction of high spirits from their experiences abroad, or, as in the case of Ted, from the dullness of camp life, and there were never merrier evenings than those spent with them, but I could not see, in spite of the air of conspiracy worn by Derrick and Edith, in spite of their whispered colloquies and sudden bursts of noisy laughter, that Edith's case was being very rapidly forwarded.

She asked us one night if we would mind going out to dinner the next evening, and let her entertain Ted with supper in the apartment: she wanted to present herself to him in a domestic light. We were laid waste by our laughter when she made her preparations the next day. Derrick insisted that we should stay concealed in the kitchenette to see that the chops and peas were fit to eat, but Edith, face flushed and hair disheveled, swathed in one of Derrick's gingham aprons, pushed us out of the front door, and waved us away disdainfully.

"You know I'm a better cook than either of you, you hypocrites! You forget how many of my *eggs au Beauregard* you have eaten in the dear dead past."

Derrick looked up at her from the pavement.

"The apron's very becoming, but how are you going to stage-manage it? A lady takes her apron off when she comes to the table."

"He's going to have to help me: set the table, and that

sort of thing. Run along, slow-pokes! It doesn't matter where
you go, just so you don't come back too early."

When we climbed the steps again, some hours later, I said
that I wondered how many of our friends we should have
to see through this, and looked at Alice suspiciously.

"I am amused by this spectacle, myself," she said coolly.
"What do you bet he did or didn't?"

"A dinner that he did."

"Good—Sunday dinner at the Brevoort."

We entered and looked, from Edith where she lay on the
couch with a magazine, to each other, with secret laughter.

"You win," said Derrick. "What's the matter, Edy?
Wasn't it a good party?"

"Excellent." Edith flung down the magazine. "The food
would have melted the heart of a Chinese idol, and we sat
over it and talked and talked, without ever approaching the
fringe of sentimentality."

"That must have been hard for you."

"No. We had an awfully good time. I didn't exactly want
him to be sentimental. I don't know what I did want."

"Then why are you so down?"

"Well—I'm going home next Monday."

"But we're spending the week-end out at the Matthewses', aren't we?" Derrick reminded her. "Probably
Ted's planning to do a little stage-managing himself."

Edith laughed, so spontaneously that we looked at her in
amazement. With difficulty she controlled herself. "Perhaps—" she said, her eyes lowered, her shoulders quivering,
"perhaps he is—"

She and Derrick had been asked to drive out with the
Matthewses to the suburb where they lived, directly from
the office on Saturday noon, so that I did not see them after
Saturday breakfast until Monday evening, when I came
home from school. Edith flung herself upon me when I
entered.

"He did, Sue, he really did!" She bounced up on the
couch, her feet under her. "We spent all this morning

looking for a ring, and this is it! Honestly, my head whirls so I don't know where I'm at."

From her I could get nothing more coherent, but from Derrick, when she came home, I drew a connected story.

"You know, I thought, when I was introduced to those children in the limousine, that the joke would be on Edith. Four of 'em, stocky, blonde, rosy-cheeked young things, with steely, contemptuous blue eyes, and no softness or affection in them. I was under the impression that she had planned to melt Ted's heart by mothering his half-brothers and sister—and you could mother four blocks of granite with as much hope of a response as you could those independent young brats."

"I didn't plan to do any such thing. I've visited them before, and I knew what they were like. You never saw such children, Sue—"

"Go on, Derrick, about Ted and Edy. I don't care about the children."

"But they're important," she insisted. "At least John—the baby . . . Well, on Saturday afternoon, Edy and I were alone in the living-room—her cousin Rose had gone to a Red Cross committee meeting, and Ted had driven her over, and Mr. Matthews was in the billiard-room, and the children were upstairs with the nurse. What do you suppose your cousin would think of our house, Edy, with children swarming all over it, instead of tucked away nicely upstairs?"

"Go on, Derrick, don't wander."

"And John took that opportune moment to escape from the nurse and try to slide down the banisters—and fell off—most fortunately for Edy—"

"You heartless wretch!"

"It didn't hurt him—only knocked the wind out of him, and frightened him to death. Of course, we rushed out, and Edy picked him up and laid him on the living-room couch, and, when he had stopped yelling, dried his tears—just as Ted appeared in the door behind them. Then the inspired infant threw his arms around her neck and kissed her. I don't suppose he had ever voluntarily kissed any one before—and you should have seen the expression on Ted's face! After that there wasn't a chance that he could hide his feelings. I admire you, Edith, for being able to regard tenderly as unnatural a child as John. It was that that did it."

Derrick stopped there.

"Go on! You're too provoking."

"That's really all. After dinner I played pool with Mr. and Mrs. Matthews, and left Ted and Edy to fix it up beside the fire. And Sunday we didn't see anything of them at all."

At moments during the narrative, Edith had chuckled delightedly, but she refused to explain, beyond saying that she guessed she was excited. When I went with her and Ted to the station the next morning, however, they looked at each other and at me with the same glimmering amusement in their eyes. I accused them of incipient madness. Not even being in love excused their behavior.

"It isn't that, Sue," Edith said. "Oh, if you only knew how gullible you are!"

"Gullible?"

"Did you really think I needed to pursue Ted?" She slipped her hand through his arm, and he looked at me pityingly as he patted it. "You must swear on your honor not to tell Derrick—I was engaged to Ted before I came."

"Why! You deceitful little baggage!"

"I wasn't, really, at all. I never once said I wasn't engaged to him, now did I? You asked me if we wrote, and I said yes. I wrote him when I sent you word I was coming, and that he must play up . . ."

"But why?"

"Because you said Derrick needed something to rouse her, and I wanted to show you that I could do it. And you must admit that for a month I've given her something to think about."

Of course I did tell Derrick, that evening . . .

"The little minx! And to think that all my labor was

unnecessary! And when she came, I was just ready to go back to work again . . ."

"You can work now. I find matchmaking such strenuous business I hope the rest of our friends can manage without us."

Alice and I had discussed before this the probability of her returning to her play: I thought that she might, but Alice said she never would; she was sure that any attempt to get her started would be in vain. Nevertheless, one night when she had risen and gone quietly to the couch in the corner, and stretched out there, face down, Alice could restrain herself no longer. She rose, too, and walked to the end of the room and back again, her eyes on Derrick, who, even with her face hidden, was conscious of her scrutiny. She stiffened rebelliously, then turned over and stared back at Alice.

"What's the matter? Can't I come and lie down without attracting attention like an animal in the Zoo?"

"I'm sorry," Alice said meekly. "It bothers me to see you so restless."

"You're the restless one."

"I'm not, except from wishing you had something to occupy your mind. Why don't you get out your play and go to work?"

Derrick looked at her in a kind of dull surprise.

"Oh, I couldn't Al. I haven't thought of it for weeks. I'd forgotten there was such a thing. Besides"—she took her book up from the table—"I'm too interested in this to stop reading in the middle of it." She read determinedly for the rest of the evening.

The apartment seemed very empty after Edith had gone: the reaction from our weeks of comparatively riotous living was perhaps responsible for Derrick's listlessness. Alice was seriously intent on getting enough poetry written and printed to warrant her in collecting a volume. Derrick, on the other hand, would do nothing: she was glum and silent, and read continually, all the new novels, one after another. It was at that time that some of the poems of the previous winter, which I had sent from magazine to magazine until they had been accepted, were published, but when the papers that contained them were sent to her, Derrick refused even to glance at them. They looked very well in print, I assured her, but she was stirred only to contempt.

"Drivel and rot!" she said. "I can't see why they ever took them. What is the sense in going on with it, if everything you write is bound to seem wordy and trivial and meaningless when you have forgotten the mood in which you wrote it?"

But one night, when Alice, at her desk, struggled, noisily and with some vituperation, with her recalcitrant rhymes, Derrick took pencil and paper, curled up in an armchair, scribbled for perhaps a minute or two, and then called to Alice.

"Here's a pretty little rhyme, Al—listen while I read it, just to show you how easy it is to do:

" 'Outside the windows, only the night,
    Laughter, within, at some one's clowning—
    Song that rings false, and garish light,
    Noise made the noisier, for drowning
    Fear of the nothing, fear of the night.' "

"That is the most childish thing you have ever written," Alice said, with some acerbity. "You know you don't mean a word of it."

"Indeed I do. Every word. Either there is nothing, or, if there is a God, it is the God you used to talk about—the God that is the creation of man: his idea. And how man pays for being cruel, when the God that he has made is cruel, too, and turns around and crushes him! . . . And I am going to say so, and say so, and say so, until people believe it. Half the trouble with us is that we *will* go on being hopeful, and people *will* write misleading optimistic poetry that sounds well and isn't true. I'm going to found a new school—the School of Feminine Pessimists!"

After that she wrote poetry as assiduously as Alice, and when she had finished, turned it over to me: what she had done with she had no more interest in. The new poems cost her less for postage: to her surprise and amusement, they were accepted promptly, and, once printed, they were noticed, reprinted, spoken of. . . . Derrick was referred to with adjectives . . . delicate, mordant, caustic, graceful . . . by the next winter one or two critics wondered when she would have a volume ready to publish. In truth, she did say bitter things beautifully, briefly, trenchantly, the only hope in them the courage that dared to face nothing and persist. They stung to the brain, and haunted the memory. We recognized the quality of the poetry, Alice and I, but we could not take Derrick very seriously: she spoke lightly, always, of what she wrote, jested about her secret sorrows; her pose was that of the youthful cynic, and she invited us to laugh at her. It is only now when I read over what she gave me that winter, that I realize that the lightness was a pose, the bitterness genuine the cumulative effect of pages of that poetry is overwhelming. She could not have written it had she not meant it, every word: all the world and life itself must have seemed a colossal joke, devised for torment. In truth, after Jack's death, her only comfort was in the thought that:

> "Apart as dusk and dawn are,
>   We'll sleep as all men must.
> When all whom we have known are
>   Irrevocably dust,
>
> "When only wind-blown grasses
>   Take root in rotting brain,
> Not even he who passes
>   Can mourn our ancient pain."

In the spring that followed there was a constant succession of friends and guests who came and went in and out of the apartment: Si returned from Kansas, sick of it, and jubilantly glad to be back; Billy Thornton landed in New York from a transport; Hunter came from home to meet him, and the boys spent a week-end with us. They had hardly left us when we had a letter from Madeleine written in a strange mood of homesickness in which she said that she would be back about the first of July.

"Al's writing me as though I had bought a house and lot and settled in France for life is what decided me. You may think I have an iron countenance and a heart of stone, but I love my friends and native land, and can't wait more than a couple of months longer to see you . . ."

But between her letter and her arrival there were another visitor—Derrick's old friend Pete McInnis, who spent an evening with us—and Derrick's vacation and Edith's wedding . . .

On one of the many nights when Si had come in for a game of bridge, Pete called Derrick on the telephone. We three listened in silence to her startled exclamations. She put up the receiver with an unsteady hand.

"He wants to come around," she explained. "*That* Division has landed."

"That Division" was, of course, the one Jack had been in.

"To-night, Derrick? Did you say he could? We'll go into the other room—"

"Oh, no, don't! I'd rather you wouldn't. There's no reason why—"

"It wouldn't be decent not to—"

"Stay awhile, then. It's so awkward, meeting people for the first time after—after—so long."

"We'll stay a few minutes," Alice consented, "then pretend we have an engagement and go out."

Almost instantly, before we had finished putting the card table away, the doorbell rang; Pete must have telephoned from the nearest drug-store. He was in his khaki still, of course, his face bronzed to the same shade, a tall, ungainly figure, extremely ill at ease At first, when I saw his discomfort, I was inclined to leave them at once, but he gave no sign of wanting to see Derrick alone; it was the presence of Alice and me that made him unhappy: he and Si were at home with each other at once. After all, if he had lived in Kansas, or Si in Ohio, they might have grown up with each other: both the young soldier home from foreign wars and the young artist had about them an ineradicable flavor of the rural Middle West.

Si asked him where he had seen action, and they began to exchange stories of their experiences that were, in the beginning, only amusing, or, at the worst, grotesque. In a moment, however, it was "in this attack" or "in that attack," followed by tales of horror that held us fascinated, spellbound, sick—until finally Pete said, "That was the morning . . ." hesitated, floundered, came to a full stop, and looked at Derrick miserably.

"That was the morning Jack was killed?" she asked, indifferently. "Tell me about it. I have never heard . . ."

It was the moment when we should have gone, but we could not, without some awkwardness, interrupt; we sat silently and uneasily on the edges of our chairs, waiting for a pause that would let us escape.

"There ain't much to tell. Nothing, I don't reckon, you don't already know. The artillery was layin' down a barrage, gettin' ready for our attack, an' one o' them shells come along an' ripped up the battery. Buried 'em, mostly, it blew such a hole in the ground, but Jack was hit in the chest with a piece of shell. Never knew what hit 'im, I reckon."

"I'm glad. That's something. I wonder if he thought, beforehand—"

"Queer thing about that. He never had thought so—or, anyways, never said he thought so, until the night before. Of course, I didn't see him all the time, but we was gen'rally quartered in the same dump, an' when I talked to him he never give no sign. The rest of us was always sure we was gonna get ours the next engagement, an' Jack, he'd been carryin' around for weeks a copy of the will I'd made, an' a letter for Denah Van Tassel. Remember Dene? She's kinda waitin' 'round for me to come home. Well, I needn't 'a' wrote that letter: all I ever got was a touch o' gas. But that night before we had to attack, Jack come around to me with a letter for you. An' he said I wasn't to send it, but to give it to you when I got home. An' I was to say that, whatever happened, you was to remember that he knew it was right for him to go, an' that he'd found out more about livin' an' dyin', an' what a man was equal to, than he'd 'a' knowed if he'd lived to seventy if he hadn't went, an' that findin' out about things was all there was to life, anyway."

"And I know just as well"—Derrick spoke with a sick quietness—"that it was all wrong for him to go—"

"Ye-eh—I kinda thought so, too. He took things hard, not the way the rest of us did. Lord knows we all hated it bad enough."

Si rose to reach the match-box on the mantelpiece, and changed the subject abruptly.

"What are you going to do now, McInnis?"

"I reckon I'll go back into my father's meat-store. He's gettin' along, an' needs me there. Butcherin' hogs is a peaceful kind o' occupation, 'longside o' butcherin' humans. About the peacefulest thing I can think of is weighin' out bologny."

He stretched his long legs out before him and lighted the cigarette Si offered. "Lord, Derrick, I remember waitin' on you across that counter when we couldn't hardly reach—"

"Yes—we used to count the change over and over to be sure it was right. And I was always so impressed by the carcasses of butchered pigs sliced open, or cut in half, and hung up on hooks in a row along the side of the store."

"We talked about hardly nothin' but them old days, Jack and me. Whenever we struck one o' them God-forsaken, muddy little French towns, we got to goin' on about Tecumseh, an', mostly, about you. It was always, 'Do you remember this' an' 'Do you remember that,' an' he said once that the longer he was away, the less he thought of you like you are now, an' the more like you were then."

"It must be funny, the things that come back to you, times like that. What did he remember?"

Derrick reached for a cigarette: it was a long Russian one, with a cardboard tip. Si rose with a match, but stood beside her laughing.

"I can't light that—you've got the wrong end out."

She laughed, too, and turned it around, but with a hand that trembled.

Pete continued without heeding the interlude. "I don't know's I can think of 'em all. Once it was the way we took you trappin', an' once it was the time you pretended to burn him at the stake, an' was just gonna light the excelsior around his feet when your mother came out an' caught you. Then once it was the way you used to swing in that rope swing in the Devlins' front yard—you always 'pumped,' he said, an' went so high you brushed the leaves. There was one night he told about when you swung like the two of you was bewitched an' couldn't stop or couldn't talk, but just went on an' on—an' the li-lox was in bloom, an' you could smell 'em, an' your hair blew acrost his face. He said it was funny he should remember about the li-lox an' your hair, because what he was thinkin' about was what if the rope should break, an' you should go floatin' off into space. He said it was the first time he knew what dyin' would be like, but he'd knowed ever since—swingin' off into space, he meant, with nothin' to stop you, never comin' down again. Ain't it queer! Did you ever know he thought o' things like that when we was kids? Of course, when you're goin' into battle you do, but that's different. Ain't that so?"

He turned to Si, who brought the conversation back to general topics, and then, after a few commonplace remarks, explained that the three of us had promised to go to the moving pictures with some people at nine o'clock.

We went to a show on Fourteenth Street, and it was so

late when Si brought us back to our door that we were sure that Derrick had been given a long enough time in which to compose her feelings, if she had needed to. We found her with a book on the couch, but her eyes were red and swollen.

"Did he stay long?"

"Only long enough to give me this." She showed us, still unopened, the letter he had spoken of, grimy, crumpled, but with the superscription still clear and firm. "Jack's letter. Isn't it silly to be so undone by the sight of handwriting . . ."

She rose and laid it on the bookcase, and sat down with the evening paper; it was not until she started for bed that she picked it up again and took it with her into the back room.

In the morning she was pale and heavy-eyed, and admitted that she had not slept.

"I couldn't stop thinking about it—that letter. It was so queer of him—not at all the sort of letter you would have expected him to write. I wonder if he would have been different if he had come back! He quoted poetry in it, and Jack never read poetry. He said he found it in a book in a Y.M. hut, and learned it—and guess what it was! In a letter that was really a farewell to life, and to—everything—a *beau geste*—that silly little poem!"

She did not open the letter to read the lines to me, but rose to get a volume of de la Mare from the shelf.

"This is it. I suppose it reminded him of the things he wanted to remember:

" 'Speak not—whisper not;
Here bloweth thyme and bergamot;

.   .   .   .   .   .

Breathe not, trespass not;
Of this green and darkling spot,
Latticed from the moon's beams,

Perchance a distant dreamer dreams;
Perchance upon its darkening air
The unseen ghosts of children fare

. . . . . .

While, unmoved, to watch and ward,
'Mid its gloom'd and daisied sward,
Stands with bowed and dewy head
That one little leaden Lad.' "

Derrick closed the letter in the book and replaced it; I
never saw her open it again; it was not moved from the shelf
until the day she packed her books.

"There—there's no use thinking any more about it.
. . . Not that I could forget. The lines he didn't quote are
the lines for me:

" 'Hides within her bosom, too,
All her sorrows, bitter rue.'

But there's no use lamenting. The time to die is when you're
not afraid of death—and he wasn't—"

When Derrick was asked at the office when she preferred
to have her vacation, she spoke for the first two weeks in
June. Her mother wanted all the children home at the same
time, as they had not been for two years—wanted Derrick
to come before Billy, who had already tired of doing nothing, left to take a position he had been offered by a Cincinnati manufacturer. Moreover, if she went to Tecumseh
then, she could stop in Baltimore for Edith's wedding on her
way back to work, and she would be in the city again long
before Madeleine. For my own part, I rejoiced for her when
the first of June drew near, glad that she was to go then,
before the heat of New York could wear her any more nearly
to the bone. I told her so, one evening, when we had gone
out together for a bus ride.

When we reached the Museum, she suggested that we get off and walk in the Park. We wandered idly along, north of the Museum, until we came to the bridge above Eighty-Fifth Street, and the steps that lead to the path around the reservoir.

"Let's walk around it, Sue. It's a long way, but we can cut off to the nearest Park entrance when we get tired, and I'll have a farewell view of the city."

"I'm glad you're going. The country is so lovely this time of year that I envy you."

"Why?" she asked perversely. "What could be lovelier than this?" She indicated the horizon with a twist of her hand. " 'The city now doth like a garment wear the beauty' of the evening—"

We had walked to the eastern rim of the reservoir across the smooth sheet of water, behind the blown spray of the great fountain in its center, the irregular roof-line of the West-Side apartment houses was black against the pale color of the evening sky—so black that it lacked perspective, and lay flat on the dull gold. Even the rounded, bright-tipped clouds might have been painted. To the north-west, above all the other roofs, rose the dome of the Cathedral of Saint John. Higher in the sky the gold of the west deepened into green, and that above our heads into a clear blue, where already a star or two showed dimly on the zenith. Behind us, in the east, above the trees that line the bridle-path, the color faded off again into a soft amethyst, where hung, untouched by any wind, a few lines of cloud, gold and deep rose.

"If one could watch the sky, always . . ." I resumed after a while. "But think how blessedly quiet it will be in the country, and no smell of gasoline."

"But think of all I have to face: the talk about Jack—and his family—and the sight of all the places where we've been together. It seems more peaceful here, to me."

"No, it isn't. You know what I mean, Derrick. Just think of not being able to look in any direction, for instance,

without seeing green trees. When you have been in the city
for a long while, that is the first thing you are conscious of,
in the country—that all-pervading sense of greenness, and
moving light and shade—"

"Sue, I never heard you so poetical! . . . But I know what
you mean. I've been trying to write some sonnets about that
very thing, at the office, when I didn't have much to do, and
there was no one around to be curious but the office boy. He
comes to gossip with me, and I have to slip them under the
blotter until Mr. Matthews calls him to run on some errand.
I brought them home to-night—let's go down, and I'll touch
them up a bit, and read them to you. This path will take us
out somewhere in the Nineties, won't it?"

Alice and I were ready for bed when she turned off the
lamp above her desk, and brought the sonnets to read to us.

"There are some inexcusable rhymes, I know—you don't
need to point them out to me. But cheerful poetry is never
so good as cynical." She sat cross-legged on the foot of
Alice's bed and cleared her throat:

"And so your brief life ends. To still my grief
  To numb despair, I climb the hill again
  Where long ago we fashioned our belief
  From old philosophies. I ease my pain
  Remembering the courage of your thought
  That sought always a faith to satisfy.
  Your 'Death is Life's high meed' some comfort brought
  Even to one who loved the earth as I.
  So I have come again where the old quiet
  hanging above June fields may transmute death
  To peacefulness, may hush my wild mind's riot
  To a renewal of that ancient faith:
      The faith that made you talk of going free
      When Death released you from mortality.

"What vague conception of eternity
  Seems fairer than the earth? Below the hill

A breeze moves in the thicket lazily,
Whitens the breath-stirred willows, and is still.
There grow all fine and feathery-leaved trees:
Locusts and thorn, and where they shade the flowers
Of wild rose and the elder, come the bees;
Beyond the ripe gold wheat are village towers.
How can I turn my mind from earthly things?
These beauties of the hill we loved the while
We spoke in praise of death. . . . A red-bird sings,
A quail calls from the long grass by the stile.
    What has death for you that will compensate?
    A hill, with willow trees, at Heaven's gate?

"When dusk has fallen on the windy field
Then I may find some echo of our faith,
Remembering nights when great Orion wheeled
Down to the dark world's rim, and shadowy death
Seemed to your daring spirit but a way
To bold adventuring beyond the sky—
For earth, enwrapt in peace the livelong day,
With its green hills held sturdily and high
Seemed in the dark an empty desert place
Whence we could time the circling of the spheres.
My faith may meet the test a moment's space:
Orion climbs the sky as in old years—
    But nights like this, heavy with clover scent,
    Make of philosophy bewilderment.

"If you have held your faith, you are to-night
Where swirling mists form some new, fairer earth;
Beyond our sky where ancient stars are bright
One are you with the hand that guides its birth.
But I shall grow too old, and love too dear
Beauty of earth that I have known, to yield
The hill where summer came, year after year,
Bringing the wheat and wind-blown clover field;
Here I may sleep unstirred, while locust trees
Lose all their fragrant bloom, and spring is dead,

While briar-roses wither, and the leaves
Are drifting gold that blows above my bed—
    Until the winds, in some far distant age
    Bring me, you loved, your tale of pilgrimage."

We were silent when she came to the end. "Well?" she insisted.

"The rhymes don't bother me"—Alice rose to the occasion—"but you can't put Orion and clover blossoms into the same night. Don't you know that Orion is a winter constellation?"

"Yes—but I'm sure I've seen it as late as April. But what does it matter?—you don't expect scientific truth in poetry, do you? I know they aren't much good, anyway, and I couldn't do anything with them if they were, but put them away and let them moulder."

She laid them away in her desk drawer, and I was left wondering at her idea of "cheerful poetry":

    ". . . nights like this, heavy with clover scent,
    Make of philosophy bewilderment."

Derrick gave me an account of her vacation when I saw her at Edith's. The house was full of guests; the night before the wedding Derrick and I shared a bed in an attic bedroom, and talked until morning. We discussed first Ted and Edith, their past and future—the trousseau, the wedding presents, the other guests. Finally, after we had exhausted even the most trivial aspects of the immediate situation, Derrick began to tell me about her two weeks at home. Almost at once I realized that all that had happened that winter, since Jack's death, was of no importance in her eyes compared with those things of apparent insignificance that she was describing.

For a while she had grown more and more depressed. She had gone home with the idea that because Mrs. Thornton had wanted them all there at the same time she must have recovered from the strange mood of the previous summer, when she had been so indifferent. At first, because the house was so full, and every one so noisy, Derrick had no chance to observe her mother when she was not in action; but she did ask, when she had a moment alone with her, if she had kept her promise to fix up a studio in the attic. Mrs. Thornton answered her briefly, but in her reply Derrick had seen the whole story: she had arranged a table under the north windows of the attic; she knew that if she didn't get to work now, she never would—and it was now that she had first had time for it, for Rosanna had just that year started to school; she had "fiddled" for a while with her old tools and a pile of modeling clay—but she found that she had forgotten all that she had ever known—it was too late for her to start again—or, at any rate, with her life practically ended, she could not hope to become anything but a muddling amateur. She could not re-create, after so many years, the old Reneltje Derrick; she had been too long dead. One Saturday afternoon she had climbed the stairs listlessly and had found Henry, his Airedale pup asleep on the floor beside him, shaping in the clay a recognizable figure of the dog. Since then she had given him a lesson once a week, but had ceased to do anything herself: she was done for (her bitterness and Derrick's sorrow were mingled in the voice of the latter when she quoted the phrase); there was nothing left for her but the old age of a worn-out housekeeper, mother, grandmother—she supposed, grandmother, although she hoped that Derrick would not marry and "give up her life to a pack of babies."

She must have seen that Derrick understood even more than she had been told. The clairvoyant power that had once been her mother's was hers now: the two had changed places; Derrick was the stronger, and her mother turned to her. She saw how her mother's ambition had been always the secret force of life, how she had loved her children passionately, unreservedly, but always with the expectation that they would be out of her way in time—how she knew now that she had waited too long. Derrick was weighted down by the desolation of the knowledge that her mother shrank with fear and loathing from the approach of old age; that she considered her life over and done with, herself gone, her body a shell, a shadow, useless, except for keeping a house and clothing a family. And she was depressed for her father's sake. He gave no evidence that he saw anything amiss; he came and went very much as he had always done, satisfied, genial, teasing, delighted to have her at home. . . . Whether he knew or not, Derrick's heart ached for him.

Her depression reacted upon her until she was, most of all, unhappy on her own account. She had nothing to hold on to: she seemed to have lost herself—the real self—as irrevocably as had her mother. The foundation of the life of the younger Derrick was her idea of her mother: slender, young, vivid—it was a new Derrick whose mother was a sad-eyed woman, whose father was a man grown rather heavily middle-aged, a little pompous. Any one was a different person, she explained to me whimsically, after she had dared apply to a parent the adjective "pompous."

She was most depressed by the strange idea that she had lost herself (she never made it quite clear to me—and I am still less capable of explaining it) on the birthday of her great-grandmother Ferguson, when she and her mother had gone to the cemetery with flowers. It was a warm day; birds twittered sleepily, hidden in the weeping willow trees; the soft grass gave beneath their feet as they walked between the graves. The cemetery was on a hill; it looked down upon a creek and the "Bottoms," where the "poor whites" lived, and across to the town beyond. On the hill opposite was a school-house; there a bell sounded, its echo drifting to them across the intervening valley; in an instant the yard was full of children who circled about one another noisily, purposefully. Derrick watched them as she stood in the sun beside the tombstone, while her mother arranged the roses and peonies they had brought—and she carried away with her a more profound sense than she had ever had before of the futility of human life. She remembered how, to her great-grandmother in her old age, very little of all that had happened, of all that had been done and endured, had seemed of importance. If she in her turn lived to be as old, there were sixty years ahead of her. How many changes in all those years? Two generations of nieces and nephews would grow to look upon her as a waxen image, aloof, hovering like a ghost among them; that figure would be to them the only Derrick. Her forgotten griefs would not matter to them, nor their present ones to her, and in the end none of them would matter to any one. But that Derrick would not be herself, any more than she, now, was the old Derrick. Was it impossible to keep the self immutable? Was there no unity beneath the changing externals? For that she sought, groping in her mind—for some core of being more vital than mere memory. One should be able to find it in feeling, if at all—but how was it possible to find one's feeling unchanged, if not one of the objects of that feeling was the same?

Then she had been ill—she laughed at the illness—a "bilious attack"—but it was while she was still in bed that she found in the sensation of a moment what she had sought. Once, while she dozed alone in the sunlit room, she pretended, for an instant, that she was the child who had lain there, face down, on summer afternoons, attempting to separate soul from body in her intense curiosity. And as suddenly as the feeling had ever come upon her before, she knew it again. From outside of her body, she surveyed it, thin, listless, feverish, a straight line in the center of the wide four-poster bed. It had nothing to do with her: she was not Derrick Thornton—there was no such person, really: it was all a queer make-believe—queer—queer. Then she had laughed. She had come back to the real Derrick only in the moment when she knew, as she had known so often, before, that there was no Derrick. She repeated to me, to make it clear, her thesis: "You're never sure of yourself except when you know there's no such person."

After that, on other afternoons, as she lay half asleep, she

called before her the images of things known immemorially
—changeless things—and in the feeling they roused in her
she knew herself unchanged. The house: she could have
gone through it blindfolded; she could feel beneath slippered feet the curve in the stairs; beneath her finger-tips the
deep scratches in the banisters; she could feel under her
knuckles the shabby carpet in the back hall where they had
been allowed to draw chalk rings for marbles on rainy Saturdays; and again her mother became what she had been in
those early years, when, as Derrick grew up, the house had
impressed itself on her consciousness. There was, too, her
own room, with the bed in the corner where it had always
been, the white bookcases built around the windows, with
"Little Women" and "Treasure Island" and "Huckleberry
Finn" on their shelves—the dark green, smooth and shining
floor, cold to her feet, with the faded rag rugs lost in the wide
expanse, like small boats on a sea—the windows that overlooked on one side the street, on the other the yard, where
the yellow flowers of the tulip-trees were falling into the
fountain, and where, in a little while, Jack would come and
whistle for her. It was not possible that he would not come
. . . a thin, tanned boy, with sapphire eyes and a shock of
sunburned yellow hair.

There were images too poignant to be dwelt upon, but
there were also those not intermingled with grief for frail
and changing human beings. The last snowdrift, in a corner
of the fence, melting away from the wet brown leaves beneath it, and the pungent smell of those leaves rain splash-
ing in puddles, dripping from gates that left your hands wet
when you opened them; thin wisps of grass and a clover
blossom between the bricks in an old path; snow, piling up
on the arches of the iron fence, and above the window-sill,
against the glass. In no order, but swiftly, one after another,
these things passed through her mind, and because she had
seen them before and would see them again, tomorrow or
another day, she felt safe, in a world where the things that
mattered did not change.

Before she was out of bed, she wrote a sonnet which she gave to me; she explained that it was the feeling she had had even when she was most in love with Jack—that only the feeling, and not the circumstances, were true:

"At last she reached the end and signed her name.
Black on the white, it stared at her. Quite strange
How suddenly fantastic it became,
And how unreal the room . . . but with the change
She knew: the name was less a part of her
Than night winds howling down the empty street,
Than the unending rain, and ghostly stir
Of heavy boughs against the roof, and sweet
Music of water on the ground—and yet
The fate that had imprisoned her had made
The name her prison's title, and by it
She here had signed herself away. Afraid
To look again at the familiar scrawl,
She tore the note and let the pieces fall."

V

MADELEINE LANDED in New York on the first of July. Derrick and Alice and I went to the dock to meet her, and afterward, with her uncle and his family, to their house uptown, where we had been asked to luncheon. In her short, squirrel-trimmed, wine-colored suit, Madeleine seemed taller and more slender than ever; in spite of her tan, she looked very tired, but there was nothing in her manner to indicate weariness. She was brisk, self-possessed; there was in her manner that constraint that you feel when you see a friend in the flesh again at last, and realize that you have counted too much on his understanding and have unburdened yourself too freely in letters.

When we left the house, she walked to the corner of the Avenue with us and stood while we waited for the bus; Alice asked if she were not ashamed to be seen with us, drab and insignificant as we were beside her. She scorned to answer but I saw Derrick's quick glance from one to the other of them, as though she had thought of the same possibility. . . . It was not until the bus lumbered toward us that Madeleine pulled Derrick to her and spoke with something like tenderness.

"When I can decently, Derrick, I'm coming down to stay in your apartment with you, if you will let me. Aunt Julia will want me to do the social life with her, and I can't stick it."

"Lin! Let you!" Derrick scolded her, laughing. "We'll be down on our knees to get you!"

When summer school at Columbia came to an end, I went home for a vacation, but a few days before I left, Madeleine moved into the apartment, and settled her belongings into our already crowded quarters.

"And now, what?" Derrick asked her, when she had unpacked.

"Nothing. Absolutely nothing, but sit and sit and sit, until I take root."

"How long do you think you can stand it?"

"As long as I have your company of evenings. You don't know how starved I am for intelligent intercourse."

"But all day long? Sue's going home, and Al and I have to work."

"I can read. I have two years to catch up on. Show me what you have on your shelves that I should know, and make a list of what you haven't got, and I'll go up to Brentano's in the morning. Of course, there were some of the new things to be had at Brentano's in Paris, but not all, and there wasn't any time, at any rate."

It was not Madeleine's way to talk about her experiences: she parried our questions, and came back at us with others of her own, so that we spent hours discussing with her Alice and Si, Edith and Ted; Derrick, squatting on the end of the couch, was at her best as she embellished her stories. It was only by the most persistent questioning that we learned anything at all about what Madeleine had been through, and even then, anecdote merged so speedily into discussion that, without realizing how it happened, we found ourselves, not listening, but arguing over Gallic and Anglo-Saxon ideas of morality and religion, of art, government, politics. . . .

While I was in Cleveland, both Derrick and Alice wrote me at length of afternoons and evenings with Madeleine: tea at Sherry's new place at Fifty-Ninth Street, or at Henri's; of hurried half-hours, before closing time, in the shops and art galleries. They enjoyed the feeling that the city, in the

summertime, was empty except for themselves—a feeling
that did not desert them even when they were elbowed by
the throngs. But Alice did not enjoy unqualifiedly, as Derrick did, the companionship of Madeleine. She wrote, with
indignant splutters of ink, that Derrick was fairly
obliterated. She took Madeleine to task, and told her that,
if she would be content to spend her evenings at home,
Derrick might amount to something. She answered coldly
that she was not responsible for Derrick . . . but soon after
that, she asked to be allowed to read the unfinished play. It
was Derrick who wrote that she had given in to her en-
treaties, but that she had handed the play back without a
word. She was too honest, Derrick thought, to praise what
she did not admire, and too kind to tell the truth. She had
never pretended to be, as the rest of us were, confident of
Derrick's powers.

A short while before I was due to return to the city,
Derrick said that Madeleine was getting restless. It was to
be expected, of course—no one could do nothing forever.
After having rejoiced in New York for all these weeks, she
had turned against it, and was homesick for Paris . . . "And
she doesn't belong here—she is out of tone—and we can't
expect to keep her. She is talking about being futile, and
reading the Want ads in the 'Times' every day—but it isn't
there that she will find anything to suit her."

When I had come back, when school had begun again
and I had settled down to work, Madeleine still talked
vaguely of hunting some kind of position, so that, when she
came in to dinner one night and announced that she had
found one finally, we knew to what she referred, although
we were mildly surprised.

'With whom?"

"Near East Relief."

"In the Madison Avenue offices?" Derrick asked. "That's
conveniently near home."

"No. In Athens."

It was too cruelly sudden. Derrick was stung to remonstrance.

"Lin! You might have told me, so that I could have gone, too."

"That's why I didn't tell you—because I knew you would want to go."

"And you didn't want me?"

"You know better than to ask. But you couldn't stand it. Malaria and typhus."

"But to have gone with you—"

Madeleine shook her head. "It's a good place for me and no place at all for you. It would have been fun to show you Paris, but we'll do that some other time. This is the place for you now. When I'm gone, you can get to work again."

"You're all in a conspiracy against me. You used to say that you didn't care whether I accomplished anything or not."

"I don't. But if you went, not having done anything, it would be with an uneasy conscience, and that is the worst of traveling companions."

Derrick sighed. "I suppose it is one of those things one might as well be philosophical about, but I have an awful feeling that we are going to spend most of our lives being philosophical about you. We'll never have you for any length of time. It's what comes of being so afraid of futility."

On the first of October, Madeleine sailed. I never knew whether Alice's plea to her in regard to Derrick had anything to do with her departure or not but if she had stayed only a little longer, she would have had the pleasure of seeing Derrick distracted by Alice herself. Alice and Si. It was a diverting spectacle.

Si was forever at our apartment, but beyond his constancy in attendance, Derrick and I could see nothing in his attitude resembling the lover's. Alice blew hot and blew cold: she hung on his every word with a kind of adoration, or she contended with him, angrily, peevishly. We speculated as to whether there was really any doubt in their minds, or whether they were teasing each other, and incidentally, us. Si came every evening, and buried himself comfortably in our one big chair; if Alice's other friends came in at the same time, which happened only infrequently now, Derrick and I stayed with them, and by the most constant flow of chatter that we could command tried to keep their attention from the glowering Si. When there was no one else there, we withdrew, the two of us, and went to a moving-picture show, or walked down Third Avenue, or east and south to Saint Mark's in the Bowery, or west and south to Washington Square. Sometimes we pleaded work as an excuse and shut ourselves up in our own back room. The latter was a great strain on our nerves: on many a sleeting cold December night we tried to concentrate, I on my school-books, Derrick on the novel in her lap; tried not to listen to the murmur of voices in the front room. Such an evening never passed without some expression of exasperation from Derrick.

"If only they'd settle it! You don't suppose, do you, that he thinks she won't? She could bring him to the point by showing him the poetry she's been writing lately."

"Heaven forbid! If he saw it, he wouldn't want to marry her."

"If he saw as much of her as we do, he wouldn't need any sign. Any one who goes around like Al, waving her arms like a windmill, with no thought of the furniture, bursting into guffaws of laughter when not a word has been said by any one for half an hour . . . and she is too unreliable to be trusted to boil a pan of beans without burning a hole through a pan . . ." She paused, and we both harkened, involuntarily. The murmur of voices in the other room continued, unexcited, without a break. Derrick tossed her book on the table.

"You must come out with me . . . I can't stand this."

She brought my hat and coat, and through the door of the back room we slipped into the hall and went to the nearest moving-picture show, always a refuge when the apartment was not large enough to hold us all. As we returned, we met

335

Si on the corner; he did not pause in his jubilant whistling as we passed, but smiled and raised his hat. Expectantly we dashed up the front steps, only to find Alice drooping moodily before the fire, her feet on the fender.

"Well?" Derrick said.

"Well, yourself? And where have you been? I hope you brought in some cigarettes. Ours are all gone."

"As a matter of fact, we did—" Derrick tossed her the box. "But it's a pity you couldn't pick a beau who would keep you supplied."

"Not I! I haven't any luck. I have to supply my beaux."

"You don't look as if you'd had a very exciting evening."

"Duller than dishwater. We talked about Art, in which I'm not in the least interested."

Derrick and I crossed glances, groaned in spirit, and went to bed with no more ado.

Several hours later I was awakened by whistles and catcalls on our front steps. I opened my eyes to see, in the dusky room, lighted dimly, as always, by the street lamps, Alice, her mane of red hair tossed wildly back, sitting up in bed to listen.

"Some one thoroughly drunk," I said sleepily. "Do you supposed he's lodged on our front steps for the night?"

"Something tells me," Alice replied warily, "that it isn't that. Listen."

There was a familiar twist to the whistling. As I was about to say so, a plaintive voice called, "Alice!"

"It's Si! Shut him up, Al! The first policeman who wanders past will arrest him for disturbing the peace."

Alice slipped her feet into her shoes—she never had bedroom slippers at hand for midnight crises—and put on a long coat over her bathrobe. With her hair tucked inside the coat collar, and her shoestrings slapping, she stumbled across to the window. Stealthily, I crept into the other room for Derrick, and brought her back; we sat on the edge of my bed to listen, where we could stifle our mirth in the pillows.

The balcony outside the window was only a foot or so higher than the railing of the front steps, and only a hand's breadth removed from it, so that conversation between step and window was easily possible, although, unless one or the other stepped onto the balcony, the parties to it were invisible to each other.

Alice, from the window, hissed a loud "Sh-sh" then called, "I know thee as the blind man knows the cuckoo, by the bad voice—"

There was an exclamation of pleasure from the step.

" 'It is the east, and Alice is the sun,
    Arise, fair sun and kill the envious moon—' "

Alice flung high her arms—we could see her, silhouetted against the window—and shouted—

" 'The moon sleeps with Endymion!'

And if you're not careful, Romeo, you'll be sleeping in the Tombs. 'Doff thy name . . ' "

" 'Call me but Love, and—' "

"Shut up, you idiot!" But this was a game at which she was not to be outdone. She returned, " 'How camest thou hither, tell me, and wherefore? The place is jail if the landlord find thee here—' "

" 'What love can do that dares love attempt,
    Therefore your landlord is no let to me—' "

"Si, how can you! 'If you be not mad, be gone; if you have reason, be brief—' "

' Here," he reproved her, "you're mixing your sources—"

" ' 'Tis not that time of moon with me to make one in

337

so skipping a dialogue,' " she continued. "Do behave yourself, Si. You're acting like a perfect ninny."

But Si was irrepressible. Back came his booming bass:

" 'How silver-sweet sound lovers' tongues by night,
   Like softest music—' "

He swung himself up over the railing, and stood on the
balcony.

"Come here a minute, Alice. I've got something for you."

"I'll do nothing of the kind. It's three o'clock in the
morning and my teeth are chattering with the cold. Besides
—you may think we're alone, but we're not—we're well
chaperoned."

"Let me have your hand, anyway."

She thrust her hand out of the window, and then broke
into a loud exclamation.

"Si, if you mean all this, why couldn't you have done it
decently—"

"I have no courage until after the clock strikes three.
Won't you come out?"

"No. If you want to ask me anything, come around for
breakfast in the morning. We have it along about ten
o'clock on Sundays."

He laughed, murmured something we could not hear, and
climbed back from the balcony to the step; Alice waited
until his footsteps could no longer be heard, then stepped
to the table to turn on the light. His ring blazed as she
twisted her hand under the lamp. She called to us with
excited cries of pleasure.

Derrick crossed the room and leaned her cheek against
Alice's shoulder.

"Can you tell me why you haven't settled this long ago?
Why you have kept us in such suspense?"

"Humph! It was Si who kept me in suspense! Besides,
we've had such a lark playing at it—why should we have
hurried?"

"Oh, Al! You remind me of how you used to mimic the elocution teacher. 'Put your hand on your diaphragm and repeat after me, in deep chest tones—Life! Life!' What fun you are!"

"No doubt. I suppose matrimony won't be half so much fun."

"In your household? I think it will. How soon do you expect to enter upon it?"

"How should I know? He hasn't even asked me yet."

Si came up our steps late the next morning, and rang the doorbell like a law-abiding citizen. Alice gave him his breakfast in the front room; it was not until noon that she called us from the litter of Sunday papers in which we were buried to come in and advise them. It was not really advice they wanted, but approval of their plans.

"I'm going to give up my job, first," Alice said.

"That's one of the easiest things you do. And next?"

"I'm going home."

We exclaimed in dismay.

"I'm sorry. But if I go right away, I'll be there for Christmas, and perhaps at that sentimental season I can persuade the family to welcome Si to its bosom, and let us be married right away."

"And if you can't?"

"We'll step to the Justice of the Peace, and be married, anyway. We must be back as soon after the first of the year as we can, so that we can move into that studio apartment on the top floor when it is vacated."

"Sue, we're going to have the fun of watching them!" Derrick seized Si's hands, shook them vigorously. "We can watch you paint and Al write poetry—"

Alice left almost at once, and in a week or so Si followed, to be welcomed, we presumed, by her family, who opposed no obstacles to their immediate marriage. In the meantime, Frances came down again for Christmas, so that the apartment did not seem so empty without Alice as it might have done. Edith and Ted, who had a small house in the suburb where the senior Matthewses lived, joined with us in our teas, dinners, and theater parties, and we three went out to spend Christmas Day with them. We spoke that day as if we had settled into the life that we were forever afterward to follow. "What could be pleasanter?" . . . "When only Al got back—what more was there to be desired?" . . . "Now that we were all fixed . . ."

It was Frances who reminded Derrick that she had a family. She asked if she heard from Hunter often.

"I? No—he doesn't write to me. How is he? Do you ever see him?"

Frances looked rather uncomfortable.

"Yes, occasionally—he comes around and lets me cook a meal for him once in a while in our apartment, and then he takes me out to dinner somewhere, in return. He looks very well—and isn't he a handsome young blade!"

"Too handsome. All the looks of the family. I've been disturbed about him since he came down for a week-end in the fall. We saw nothing of him, to be sure—he stayed out so late both nights that he was here that we had the pleasure of his company only at breakfast. But I thought he was awfully gloomy—sunk in one of his fits of depression. He hasn't got into any trouble up there, has he?"

"Oh, no—unless you call a condition in mathematics trouble."

"So that's it! Lazy young rascal! Begged and begged, and had us all pleading for him, until Father let him go there, and then lets himself get into academic difficulties! I refuse to worry about him."

"It may be more serious than you think. I suspect it isn't only mathematics. He told me to warn you to warn the family that, if he didn't work a condition off, they wouldn't let him stay after mid-years."

"Hunter Thornton! Father would never forgive him! He's gone home for Christmas now, and he can warn them himself. I'm fonder of Hunter than I can tell you, but he's been

riding for a fall for some time, and I shouldn't be surprised
if this were it."

She wrote to him after the holidays, to expostulate; he
replied that he was afraid it was too late . . . and he was sure
that he never could have understood the stuff, anyway, even
if he had worked harder. Then in February he sent her a
note: it was true, as he had feared; he did have to go. He
did not send her word when he went through New York; she
did not blame him for not wanting to see her.

Her mother's letters gave Derrick the only information
that she received as to how the family had taken this blow
to its pride. Her impression was that it was Mrs Thornton
herself who showed plainly how she was hurt. The attitude
of the doctor was admired by his wife: he could have been
exceedingly disagreeable; instead, he concealed his rage, if
he felt any, and his chagrin, and merely teased. If the teasing
stung, that was no more than the boy deserved. He told
Hunter that he could go to work in Tecumseh and earn his
own spending money for a while; that perhaps by fall he
would be grown up enough to know what he really wanted
to do. Through her mother's words, Derrick felt her father's
contempt, and wondered if that would not be harder to bear
than any amount of scolding. . . . At any rate, Hunter found
work in the Devlin mill, and the family saw little of him
thereafter: the whistles blew to summon him at seven-thirty
in the morning, he came home for a few minutes for luncheon and dinner, and in the evening went out with the
young people who had been his friends in school. It was the
last which Mrs. Thornton hated: she did not like them; she
did not want to see him, too, grow hard and cheap and
flippant; she wondered if, truly, he could do anything well
besides dance and play tennis and ornament a front porch,
clad in his white flannels, and win with ease the affection of
anyone for whom he cared.

Something of her mother's bitterness showed in her letters. Her blame of Hunter was born of her blame of herself.
"One failure in a family is enough," she wrote; and again,

"It is my fault, I suppose—my own fatal lack of—whatever it is that I lack so fatally—that I have passed on to you all."

But I think it must have been early in the year, before Hunter's disgrace, that Derrick received the letter from her mother that so dismayed her. Because Mrs. Thornton's letters were always full of gossip, anecdotes of the children, of the town, with rarely a word of herself, Derrick had been able to forget, when she was not at home, that her mother was unhappy. But when she saw it in black and white, it was less easy to thrust into the background. I remember how she dropped into a chair when she had finished reading that letter, how she looked at me in dismay.

"This, from Mother! And there has never been another like her, before this, for letting you alone to do as you pleased with your life. . . ."

"What is it? What has happened?"

"She wants me to come home. She's lonesome . . . she has said so, right out, with pen and ink." Derrick was aghast. "And she wants me to keep her company. I've 'no idea how she misses me.' Imagine missing one, with five others there—"

"You're the oldest, of course."

"It can't be as one of her children that she wants me. It isn't that she can't bear to think of our being scattered—it's simply that she wants some one to talk to. She must want it badly—she's deluded herself into thinking I could get more work done there than here."

"Can't you?"

"You know perfectly well I can't—and so does she."

"You aren't getting a great deal done here."

She tossed the letter onto the desk as though she dismissed the subject as not worth her consideration, but evidently it was not so easily dismissed from her mind as she had wished. The next evening she did not take out her play, but sat down instead to read "Jean Christophe"; she was still reading it when her mother's next letter came, and in the intervening week she had not written a word. I could see that she opened the letter with some misgiving, but her face cleared as she read.

"She's changed her mind about my coming home. She says she didn't feel very well last week when she wrote. She can't remember what she said, but I'm not to pay any attention to it. Father and she have set their hearts on my being Somebody, and I must stay in New York until I am. And if I don't want my life to be wasted, I must be resolute in refusing to devote it to a husband and family. . . . How funny of her! I can't make it out. But at any rate, no matter how much she wanted it for her own sake, she would be disgusted with me if I did go home. I suppose I must get to work in earnest, now, and show her that I can do it. It wouldn't do to stay away and still do nothing."

Nevertheless, she went on with "Jean Christophe" in her evenings. It was not until an evening in February that she went to her desk and turned its drawers out in the middle of the floor.

"Is this merely a housecleaning fit, or are you looking for something?" I peered around at her from my desk as she seated herself in the midst of the papers.

"Looking for distraction, merely."

She sorted the letters and snapped rubber bands around the piles of those she wanted to keep; after a lingering re-reading, she tore the others into scraps. Stray sheets of paper with lines of verse scribbled on them she collected into a pile.

"If I could rewrite these things, I'd have enough for a volume in quantity if not quality." She picked up the pages and with a relentless hand tore them across.

"Derrick! How could you!"

"That was only a histrionic gesture. You know as well as I do that everything even my partial judgment could see any hope for has been copied in my notebook long ago." She threw the torn bits of paper into the waste-basket, and picked up the portfolio that contained what she had written of the play.

"Now, Derrick—no more gestures!"

She laughed at me. "It's no good. Hadn't I better start a new one?"

"For the everlasting good of your immortal soul, you finish what you have begun. If you've forgotten how you planned it, I can tell you."

With the sheets in her hand, she pulled herself into the nearest chair, stumbling as she stepped on the hem of her skirt. There she read over what she had written, oblivious, for the moment, of the clutter on the floor.

"It's pretty feeble, Sue. . . . But I can fix this place. Where's a pencil?" She moved to her desk, scratched and scrawled for a minute, then read on in absorption. She presently exclaimed: "How do you suppose I thought of that? I'm sure I couldn't have, now, if I were doing it . . ."

She left the portfolio on the top of her desk that night, and on the next evening, when we had finished the dishes, she went to it at once, and, after some preliminary fussing with pencils and pencil-sharpener, went to work. When Alice and Si came back to the city that same week, to set up housekeeping in their studio apartment, I told Alice that she had gone to work again.

"All that was necessary was to get started. She'll do it now: nothing will happen to stop her, because everything that could possibly happen has happened already. We'll have her famous yet—"

And the very next day I came upon her in the bathroom staring miserably at her reflection in the mirror. She was standing motionless, almost in a trance, and had apparently forgotten that her arms were in a bowl of soapsuds halfway to her elbows.

"Derrick! If you must day-dream, why not make yourself comfortable first? What on earth were you thinking of?"

"If you must know," she answered shortly, "I was making fun of myself for wanting to go home."

"You're not homesick? For Tecumseh?"

"Yes—for Tecumseh. I know—you really like the city, but you're city born and bred. I hate it."

"Derrick—you don't, any such thing. Think of—"

"Oh, yes, I know. There are things about it I like—but no one could stand it forever—the clamor and the dirt, and no room to breathe."

"But your work? At the office, I mean? You couldn't get a job like yours anywhere but here." She had risen in the estimation of the editors of the Literary Supplement until now she wrote reviews, refused manuscripts, accepted poetry . . .

"I'm sick of it. I've found out all I wanted to know about them. I see through them, I mean. It's a clique, made up of prodigiously conceited, precociously clever young newspaper men. To be anything, you have to be boosted by the clique—to be boosted by it, you have to know them all, to belong, and be willing to boost them. New York is the worst place in the world for the literary aspirant, for, unless you're middle-aged and level-headed, you get pulled into the turmoil. And then where are you?" She shook her head solemnly as she sat on the edge of the tub to dry her hands. The released water gurgled lugubriously in the pipes.

"But you've always said you wouldn't do anything at home."

"No. But I'd have a better time doing nothing there than here."

"Why don't you go, then?" I asked in exasperation.

"I can't—don't you see?—until I have done something. I've talked so much, the old hens would cluck for joy if I came home with my tail between my legs."

"What's happened to you, Derrick? You never used to be so indecisive." Then suddenly I thought I understood. "You don't mean what you've said. You are worried about your mother."

"I suppose that's it. It is so upsetting not to be able to think even of your mother without apprehension."

"But there's no sense worrying if there's nothing to worry about, and there isn't, really, is there?"

I reported this conversation to Alice, who said that it was nothing but common, ordinary discouragement.

"If we could only prove to her that what she's done is good. But our saying so wouldn't satisfy her . . ." She ran her hand through her hair, with consequent disaster to her net—then she exclaimed: "Eureka, old bean! Edith!"

"Edith? How?" Edith was going to have a baby in the spring, and was at that time immured in her suburb.

"Through Edith to Mr. Matthews. Derrick wouldn't have mentioned it to him, would she?"

"Of course not."

"Edith can write her a note expressing indignation that she hasn't been allowed to read the two acts that we have read. Derrick will send them to her—she always humors Edith. Then Edy can show it to her father-in-law, and, if he has anything good to say about it, we'll tell her—or he can —otherwise, we'll never confess."

With no hesitation, Alice took a sheet of note-paper and wrote to Edith. A week later Derrick came in with a roll of manuscript in her hand.

"You fraud! Base deceiver! Broth-boiling hag! You know you deliberately schemed to have Mr. Matthews see this—"

I wavered, unable to decide whether to blame Alice entirely, or whether to accept some responsibility myself; before I answered, Derrick laughed and continued:

"It would serve you right if I refused to tell you what he said."

"Oh, Derrick! We did it for your own good"—I dodged the end of her umbrella, poked at my ribs—"because we think you're the coming Shakespeare."

"He didn't mention Shakespeare. What are we going to have for dinner? It's my turn to cook—" She went into the kitchenette, and I ran upstairs to Alice's top-floor apartment.

"Hello," she said. "Have you heard about Si? No? I thought that was what had taken your breath. . . . He's sold that group of pencil sketches of New York for a fabulous sum—"

I shouted my congratulations to Si, who hovered about the stove with an apron tied around his neck, and then turned back to Alice.

"Derrick's got those two acts back—Mr. Matthews brought them in himself. She hasn't told me yet what he said."

"Then don't let her until we can get down there, after supper . . ."

When we all drew up around the fire, after the dishes had been washed, Derrick looked around the circle in mock indignation.

"Vultures! Waiting to pick a dead man's bones! I shan't tell you a word he said."

"Come on—" I handed her the manuscript. "Page by page. Every word. If you don't, we'll think it's modesty, and believe the most flattering things."

She turned over the pages to indicate where he had marked it.

"This must come out, he says—it is impossible. This is rotten, through here—and whatever made me think a person of that class and type would do or say anything like this?" She put the pages on the floor and laughed at us.

"But didn't he think it was *any* good?"

"He said that it *would do*. That it is written in the accepted spirit of the age, and, that if I work hard enough on it, he doesn't doubt but what it would be produced. So, of course, I shall go ahead and write the third act."

Uncomplimentary as he may have seemed, he had said enough to set Derrick to work again, doggedly. It was plain to be seen, however, that she had to force herself to sit down at her desk every night, that she had to exert all her will power to keep herself at it. . . . I wondered if she were still thinking of her mother, and asked her, one evening, when she had thrown down her pencil and gone to stand in the window, if she were reconciled to New York, or still weary of it. . . . She peered out into the twilight, her hands around her eyes to shut out the lights of the room.

"Reconciled to it, in the spring? As if any one could be anything but weary of a city then! I was thinking of how things must be in the country now . . . I feel as if I were defying a certain fate, staying on here this way."

"What fate?"

"I haven't the slightest idea. A large, black, unescapable, unnamable fate. But I will stay, until I have finished." She went back to the desk. "I haven't seen spring in Ohio for years. . . . Honestly, human beings are the greatest lot of fools, shutting themselves off from the things they care most about for the most grotesque reasons."

"It's all a question of being able to decide what you do care most about."

"Yes—and sometimes you're so sure you care about something when you don't, really, that you let yourself in for it for the rest of your life."

"You should have the courage to admit the truth, however silly it seems."

"But if you have talked too much about the thing you think you care about, you haven't that courage. Your pride insists that you must show people that it isn't because you couldn't get the thing you wanted that you've changed your mind. You have to risk your neck climbing for the grapes, even if you have found out before you start that they're sour, and you'd rather have the ripe persimmons that you've only got to shake the tree for!"

But in spite of her protests of indifference, even of distaste, she did persist, and early in March told us that she had finished. She hushed our enthusiasm with deprecatory explanations.

"I only mean that I've written the first draft. It will have to be done over again, but I can't do it now. I'll put it away, and have another go at it later."

"Read it to us."

"Not now." She was obdurate. "Not until it's been rewritten. But I thought you might suggest celebrating by going to the first night of that new play next week . . ."

"Of course . . . and since you're the celebratee, I'll be the one to stand in line for tickets."

"You won't have to . . . Ted has ordered them. The manager sent Mr. Matthews a card, offering him a chance to get his tickets early, and he didn't want to go, so he gave it to Ted. If they think he's his father, we'll have good seats."

The seats proved to be excellent, as it turned out: in the front row of the balcony, in the midst of some, looking down upon others, of the critics. We had been to many first nights before this, but had been content with last-row seats generally, where little that made the excitement of the occasion, except the drama itself, was visible to us.

This play was a dramatization of the novel of the season, and all the reviewers were out to see it. The author was in a box, a slender, gray-haired woman, with excited dark eyes. She waved now and then to one or another in the audience whom she knew; the theater was packed, a sounding confusion of voices; dozens of self-important gentlemen in evening dress bustled in and out. Derrick and Ted pointed out to us all the critics whom they knew by sight.

"The more important they look, the less weight they have with the public," Ted said.

"You'll be sorry you ever asked to see them," Derrick warned us. "You'll never be able to take seriously again anything they say. But they'll be nice about this."

"They should be. See how they're swarming in and out of her box."

It was just as I spoke that she happened to look up at us: I was embarrassed to be caught staring, and slipped back into my seat, but, to the infinite surprise of us all, she smiled and bowed to Si. We all turned on him.

"You know her? And never said—"

"Look here, you're keeping something from your wife—"

"I supposed she'd forgotten me long ago. I used to know her: I illustrated some magazine stories of hers once, before she was important enough to have really expensive artists hired for her. She liked my drawings, and asked me to tea, and we got almost what you might call clubby. It was before I went across, and I haven't seen her since I've been back."

"So you consort with the Great and keep it from the girls—" Ted teased him. "I go around boasting of my high connections—" As a matter of fact, he knew writers and critics because he was his father's son, not because he had a literary thought in his head, nor because he was ever anything but bored in their company. He sat through the evening's performance in serene indifference.

The applause after the first act was uproarious.

"I suppose," Derrick said, "if the question of her fame were wavering in the balance—"

"By fame, you mean the morning papers, of course?" Ted mocked her.

"Of course. If it were in the balance, it's settled now. They'll shout her name to the heavens. Isn't it fun! I'm as excited as she can possibly be. Look—she's gone out. Let's go down—we may see her in the lobby."

"How childish of you, Derrick!"

"She's probably behind the scenes."

But we did go down, and, as luck would have it, did pass her as she stood at one of the entrances in the center of a group of men. She looked up, caught Si's glance on her, and stopped him to shake hands. He introduced us, and we stood a moment while she spoke to Alice of her husband, and reproached Si because he had not brought her to call. As we turned away, we heard her say to the men with her, who had exchanged greetings with Ted, something about the "young war artist."

Alice glowed with pride.

"You're on the road to fame, my boy. They have heard your name."

He snorted.

"I've met them all before. It's all bunk. They know nothing about art, whatever they may know about literature. All that matters is whether you're passably witty and so anti-Puritan as to be damned near depraved—and absolutely unsentimental."

"You are, aren't you?"

"Which? . . . But there are other qualifications that are more essential, for the real thing, that I haven't got, that they'd never miss. I know 'em."

"You're so casual, Si," Derrick laughed. "I know 'em, too. I have even typed letters for two of them—they have a great way of dropping into the office and using whatever secretary is handy; but just the same, I'm all in a twitter, hoping they will recognize me when I'm dressed in my best. And as for her—she can have my heart flung at her feet whenever she asks for it. You needn't laugh, Al; I mean it. It almost makes me think respectfully of fame, seeing her."

"She has something better than fame, and that is brain enough to have won it honestly. There are other ways of getting it with those fellows—"

"I know, Si. You can push and shove until they wake up in surprise to the fact that you are one of them, and must be treated accordingly. It's a sort of bargain. You praise me and I'll praise you. And here I am, free to say what I please about them, because I've written nothing, and so can't be said to be speaking from malice. But Si is right about her —she has a mind. However, so far as that's concerned, they all have brains, if they would use them."

When the fortunate playwright made a curtain speech after the close of the next act, and was received with a thunder of clapping hands, Derrick was more than ever reduced to unthinking admiration, although she said nothing further about either author or critic until after she and

I had reached home, and were alone. She put down hat, gloves, and purse and stared at me in silence.

"Well?" I insisted.

"I'm all undecided again. I have a strong feeling for New York on a night like this. I think I'll stay in it forever."

"Of course you'll stay—and a year from now, we'll be at your first night."

But the next morning was damp and rainy; she arose out of sorts, weary and reluctant. There was no slightest sign, no lingering gleam, of the previous night's excitement. She sat down to breakfast with a sigh.

"I'm oppressed with the feeling that I shouldn't have had such a good time last night. Something unpleasant is about to happen."

"You're always having that feeling."

"And something always happens, doesn't it?"

"Nonsense. You revert once in a while to your Covenanting ancestors who thought it wasn't safe to be happy. Or else you are suffering the punishment you richly deserve for having eaten that heavy chocolate thingummy at Huyler's last night when the rest of us were contented with lemonades."

She grunted, picked up her hat, and started out, then returned with the morning mail.

"This, I suppose, is what I was dreading. It is awful to be afraid of opening Mother's letters, but I never know what to expect any more—"

When she had finished reading it, she tucked it in her pocket.

"I can't see what is the matter with her—it can't be only Hunter, or her own disappointment and loneliness. . . . But I can't stop to think about it now—I'm late already."

When she came home that night, she announced that she was going home for the week-end.

"The week-end!" I echoed. "But it takes you eighteen hours each way. You could hardly have Sunday dinner at home."

"It isn't quite that bad. Mr. Matthews has given me Saturday and Monday mornings off—I'll go Friday night and not have to leave home until Sunday night, which will give me a day and a half there. It will be enough. I must find out about Mother, Sue. I can't stand this any longer. Either something serious is the matter with her, or she is imagining things, or I am. It may be her health—but if her happiness actually depends on my being at home, then I'll have to go, whatever any one thinks."

"Of course," I granted. I thought I was perfectly safe. "But after warning you not to give your life up for a husband, your mother would hardly let you give it up for her. She isn't a selfish woman . . ."

"Mother?" she echoed in disdain. "I should say she wasn't!"

Because I was so confident, I could not believe my eyes when I reached home on Monday night, and found Derrick's trunk in the middle of the room, practically full, her books piled on the floor beside empty packing-cases. There were a few dresses hung on chairs and a litter of gloves and handkerchiefs beside the trunk-tray. The fireplace was full of scraps of paper.

"Derrick!" I called her, my heart fairly in my throat. She came in from the bathroom with an armful of clothes.

"I'm sorry to be so sudden, Sue, but I must go. Mother is ill, after all—"

"Really seriously ill? Why hadn't they let you know?"

"She hadn't told any one—she only suspected it, herself —but I don't believe she cared much. When I came home, she broke down and confessed, and Father rushed her right off to a specialist, but it was too late to do any good. And so I have to get home as quickly as I can."

"But why do you take your books? You'll be back as soon as she's better—"

"She isn't going to be any better . . . don't stand there with your mouth open like a fish. . . . I thought I said so at first . . ."

"I'm so sorry . . . no, you didn't say so. Derrick, does she know it?"

"The doctor didn't tell her, neither did Father, but I'm sure she knows. I can only be thankful that I went out when I did, to see. If I hadn't known—but I really have known, all along—I only pretended not, so that I shouldn't have to go. I can't tell you how thankful I am!"

"But you can come back afterwards . . ."

"And leave the children?"

"But with all your aunts, couldn't one of them—? Will they need you?"

"It isn't that—it's a matter of self-protection. I simply can't run the risk of anything happening to any of them, and I not there."

"But your being there wouldn't prevent—"

"No. Can't I make you understand at all? If I were there, and anything happened, I should have done all that I could do. No—I must go for always. I've broken the last bond, and all that sort of thing." She indicated the bits of torn paper in the fireplace. With an exclamation I crossed the room and pulled out a handful. They were the pages of her play.

"Derrick!" I held out the paper to her, accusingly, as one would hold a broken dish before a guilty child.

"Exactly. I'm about to burn it." She took a match from the box on the mantelpiece, lighted it, and dropped it on the papers.

"Derrick!"

"Not a word, Sue! Weighed in the balance with other things, it isn't worth sighing for."

"But remember how, to your mother, in the end, her work outweighed everything else. Aren't you afraid you are letting yourself in for the same kind of torment?"

"No. Mother nursed her ambition, instead of renouncing it. She loved us all, but she expected us to be out of her way in time. It was finding out that she had waited too long that made her so bitter. But I have given up mine, having seen before it was too late that I could never have done anything very great. I shall build my life on something else."

I wanted to say that I thought that it was already rather late for her to do that, but instead I watched the flaming bits of paper, the crisp edges turning to black ash, the smoke curling out from a thick handful that the flames had not reached.

"Don't look that way, Sue. It doesn't matter."

I turned away to fold the dresses she had not packed.

"Did you go to the office at all?"

"Of course. I had to tell Mr. Matthews, and resign my position."

How calm she was! . . . While the thought of her mother was in her mind, she had no emotion to spend on anything else. She could give up without hesitation the life she had chosen to live for three years . . . she was driven by a terror that made every half-hour precious, that swept everything out of her path. . . .

I laid her dresses in the trunk and closed down the lid.

"Have you everything . . . ?"

"I think so. You can have my pictures; we already have more at home than we can hang. If you will help me with the books—and when they've been nailed up, have them sent by express collect."

"I'll get Si—he can do the nailing—"

Alice came back with me, too, and on her way opened the door to the man who had come for the trunk. We sent him off with it.

"Derrick—give me your ticket, and I'll clear along and check your trunk for you. The boxes of books can wait until afterward."

"It's in my purse on the bookcase. We'll take a taxi with the bags, and meet you at the gate. The train leaves a few minutes after seven."

"How about dinner?"

"They run a diner to Philadelphia. How about you?"

"We'll get ours all right . . . Have you 'phoned for a taxi?"

On the ride to the station, Derrick prevented our broken

attempts at condolence; we murmured comments on the traffic, the dirt, the villainous cast of countenance of the taxi-driver. . . . She gave her bags to a porter when we alighted, sought for Si in the throng before the gate, took her ticket and baggage check, and thanked him. She shook hands with us.

"Of course, whatever happens, I'll see you all before so awfully long." Then a sudden thought struck her. "Sue—I've upset your household arrangements terribly—I never thought—but I'll pay my share of the rent until you find some one else to live with you."

"You know you will come back—"

"No, really . . . I mean what I say."

"Well, I'll not have any one else in there in your place. I'll pay all the rent myself . . ." Which was sheer braggadocio.

The gate was opened, the porter thrust himself through the crowd, and she followed at his heels. We watched them down the steps.

"She burnt the play, Al, before she left."

"Of course. If she didn't it would always remind her of this. And however calm she acts, you know as well as I do how she feels."

"Sometimes, Al, I think you're not the fool you seem."

"Of course she's no fool." Si stepped between us as we emerged from the crowd. "But Derrick will soon get sick and tired of Ohio. She'll be back—"

"I wish I thought so. I wish she hated Tecumseh—but she doesn't, you know—she really likes it."

"She won't for very long. And if she does, what does it matter? If she has it in her to write, she'll write, whether it's here or at home."

But not even Alice, for once, could bring herself to agree with him. They went off, disputing, to a dinner engagement. I walked on down Seventh Avenue and across Twenty-Third Street, slowly, reluctant to return alone to an empty apartment.

Part Four

Herbs

and

Apples

Mrs. Thornton died in May, after weeks spent in a hospital in the city—weeks when Derrick lived in a room in Billy's boarding-house, and went every day to be with her mother —and after some time at home in a hushed and empty house. The two younger children, terrified and heartbroken, had been sent to stay with their Aunt Anne. It must have been a period of torture for Derrick. She never spoke of it afterwards. I did not see her until a year from the following August; she told me then all that had happened after her mother's death, but she did not go back to the weeks that had preceded it.

On the train I took from Tecumseh to New York after the month spent with her, I had my first chance to go back over all that she had said, and to ponder the question of whether she had changed in the year and a half when I had not seen her. Of course, I had expected to find her changed, and for the worse. I tried to decide, while I thought how her clear hazel eyes had regarded me tranquilly. . . . Once, you had felt that she withheld from you, consistently, what was the most important thing, the thing that was going on in the back of her head at the time. This was still true: she had told me while I was there what had happened in the year past, but little of the hour or the day whose sun then shone . . . but was she guarding her present, or was there, now, nothing to guard? The old mockery, the mockery of a fugitive who knows that she has escaped you, was gone. Her eyes held the light of an untroubled, shallow pool where the sun strikes it. Once I had resented her aloofness, now I drew back from my own simile. Who could want Derrick to be a sunlit, shallow pool? If it were true, what had done it?

Margaret was on the train with me, on her way to visit us before she started to college a week later. I watched her a little rebelliously, as she sat staring out of the car window: it should have been Derrick there on the seat opposite me, on her way back to the city. But she had refused to come. I saw her again as she had stood on the station platform beside the train, rattling off messages to Alice and Edith which I must be sure not to forget; Rosanna had clung to her arm while she watched with an expression of friendly triumph in her wide black eyes. The family had known well enough that I had hoped to take Derrick back to New York with me, but they need not have worried, for she had not the remotest idea of going. . . .

I noticed how closely Margaret watched the country that revolved past the train. Was it possible that she had some of Derrick's old feeling for it—that she felt some reluctance on being carried away? I turned to the window, too, and watched.

Outside stretched the flat fields of central Ohio. It was September, and the farmers were cutting their corn, in an unvarying, deadly monotonous, never-ending succession of fields. The distant straight horizon was broken only by the occasional flashing past of a small village, like all the other villages, with bells on the crossing-gates that rang beneath our windows as the cars clicked over the rails. We were only a short way north of Columbus, but already the low, rolling hills of the Miami Valley had vanished. I turned from the window wearily, and wished that I could sleep all the way to New York. Then, with the flat country shut from my sight, my mind slipped back to Derrick.

What of her passion for those fields, those low hills and wide horizons? Was it in truth enough to make her content, to quiet any uneasiness? She had insisted that it was. . . . I lifted a languid eye to the cornfields once more, and shuddered . . . then began to think back over all that she had told me. In the minutest detail she had given me the story of the first months after her mother's death, as though she had sought to make clear in her own mind the way she had taken from grief into security.

At first there had been innumerable things to keep her busy, and she had been forced to thrust her sorrows out of her mind. The family, always rather undemonstrative, had disintegrated, fallen apart—they were gentle and quiet, but afraid to speak of their mother; they masked themselves against Derrick. She had stayed at home for them, but there was nothing to be done until they ceased to regard her as a transient. She had been a stranger to them for so long that she was, for a while, helpless against their attitude.

The time came when Billy, who had been their support through the awful days of the funeral, must go back to Cincinnati to his work. Only Derrick went with him to the station; he said good-bye to the others at the front door. Dr. Thornton walked to the car with them and put Billy's bags in the back seat.

"I'm sorry I can't see you on the train, but I have to go round to old Mrs. Wilkins's." He put his left hand on Billy's shoulder as he held out his right. "I hate to see you go. It's a pity you couldn't find something to do here."

Derrick looked off down the street while the two men shook hands; she tried not to see how tired her father looked, how heavy.

"Never mind, Father. I'll be home so often you'll think I'm a regular nuisance."

"No . . . no, no danger. But I reckon we'll not see much of you. Judging from the number of life-size photographs you brought up, your week-ends must be pretty full."

It was the first time he had made an effort to tease any of them; it showed that it was Billy who could have roused him. Derrick said as much as they drove off

"Father depends on you, Billy, not on the rest of us. Come as often as you can."

"I will. Lord! It's harder on him than on all the rest of us put together. All those years, and never a thought but for each other . . ."

It was inevitable, Derrick thought, that her father should turn to Billy rather than to her. Billy did not know that their mother had died convinced that her life had been wasted; neither, of course, did the doctor . . . but do what she could, the shadow of that knowledge came between Derrick and her father.

Afterward, she grew very confused and melancholy, thinking of these things. Dr. Thornton was outwardly composed, matter-of-fact, and as much at ease as always, but he paid little attention to the children, to their comings and goings. . . . She had some sense of his hidden agony, but she could make no attempt to cross that barrier of the matter-of-fact with her mother's outcry against marriage ever in her mind. And it was not fair to him, she reflected one night when the two of them were alone in the living-room, and when she watched him dozing, or pretending to doze, the newspaper across his face. How could it have been marriage, family, the house that prevented her mother from doing the things she had wanted to do? After all, there had been five years between Margaret and Henry, and in that time her mother might have carved any number of imperishable statues. Perhaps, when she had known, subconsciously, that she would never do it, she had gone on having children as an excuse that would justify her in her own eyes. One's mind played queer tricks. . . .

Perhaps she, Derrick, was being tricked in the same way. Had she come home from New York to afford herself an excuse not to do what, subconsciously, she knew that she never would have done? But New York was already as fantastic as a dream in her memory. This was the only reality she had ever known: the house, the town, her father, with the newspaper over his face, her mother, living or dead.

She remembered how winter had used to come on, while they had sat night after night in this same room; how, finally, it would snow, and she would see it snowing, her face pressed against the glass of the long windows: soft rolls of it that piled up on the iron fence around the terrace, on the frozen honeysuckle vines; how she would turn then—"Oh, Mother, it's snowing! The first snow!" . . . how the boys would come to stand beside her and stare at the flakes that fell into the square of light cast by the windows . . . how her mother would put down her sewing or her book and run upstairs to see that it did not blow too hard on the baby.

Then Christmas, then the coming of spring, each day longer than the last, until one evening when it would be still light after dinner, and they would beg their mother "It isn't dark yet! Let us play outdoors to-night—please, Mother, just till dark!"

The background of her childhood had been the presence of her mother—as the sky, that sweeps from one low edge of the horizon to the other over a flat country, is in the minds of the children of that country, not realized when they are young, nor when they leave it, but only when they return after a long absence, and find it again, above them, and draw a long breath at last. . . . Then Derrick reproved herself for the high-flown figure. How silly she was getting! But, nevertheless, it was true that she could not create for herself in her imagination a childhood without her mother; and what was impossible to her was the reality for Henry and Rosanna.

No one could in any way make up to them for their loss, but she could at least appreciate it, and her staying with them was not an excuse to herself, contrived by a cowardly subconscious mind. It was the only thing she could do. What satisfaction could she find anywhere else if they were less happy than they would be with her at home?

But it was a fond illusion to assume that her presence would prevent their unhappiness. They might be just as happy without her. Perhaps it was an excuse. . . .

Her mind pursued its intricate circles endlessly, until she rose to go to bed—and pursued them again, many times after that.

After Billy had gone, Derrick was alone in the house; Hunter went back to his work in the Devlin mill, the children back to school. She moved about restlessly, with a dust rag: down the long staircase, wiping off the banisters, with their deep scratches made by buttons and buckles; around the library, with its battered sofa and the faded globe that creaked when you turned it, and the tall bookcases whose glass doors reflected the May sunshine and the green, moving branches of trees. Blindfolded, she could have found any book in those bookcases. Then out into the lving-room, where there were papers and books and toys to pick up, and through to the dining-room with its shelves of old glass and silver and copper luster. She had not known that any one could love a house so much—an empty house.

A little later she sorted over her mother's clothes and all her personal belongings. Some they could use . . . the others . . . when she had emptied the closet and all the drawers and had everything heaped about her on the floor, Margaret came in from school and found her looking helplessly on the havoc she had created.

"Whatever in the world are you doing?"

"Mother's things. What shall we do with the ones we can't use? I can't bear to throw them away—"

"Pack them in her old trunk in the attic."

"But that's just leaving my job for some one else. They'll have to be disposed of some day."

"Why can't they just stay up there, forever and ever, like all the other old things?"

"It's conceivable that you may all grow up and leave . . . and Father would hardly stay in this big house alone." She smiled at Margaret's bewilderment.

"You mean we might *move?* Oh, Derrick, we never should! One of the boys will marry and live here, and his grandchildren will rummage in the attic and will dress up in these old things and come downstairs, and Hunter, or Henry —or whichever one it is—will be dreaming by the fire, and will look up and think it's Mother . . . you know, the way they always do in books." She broke off and picked up a high pile of clothes, digging her firm young chin into the top to hold it steady. "Come on—I'll help you."

They emptied the room, which, in spite of the fact that their parents had shared it, had always been and would always be their "mother's room"—except for the dressing-table, which they did not touch, but left with the faint sweetness of powder and perfume hanging about it.

Derrick did not realize, until she talked to Hunter one night, that she had not made clear to them her intention of staying at home always. Of course, she had been away so long that they hardly regarded her as a permanent member of the family; she had been away since before Henry and Rosanna could remember, and even Hunter was only thirteen when she left for the first time. Perhaps even he did not feel as if he knew her. Queer, when she knew him so well! When he came in late one evening after every one else had gone to bed, and found her reading in the living-room, he greeted her with surprise.

"Good Lord, Derrick! You didn't think you had to sit up for me, did you? No one ever does, in this family—not even for Margaret."

"I didn't sit up for you particularly. I wasn't sleepy, and liked the book. And now I'm hungry. See if there's milk in the ice-chest, won't you? I know there's gingerbread in the bread-box."

He brought a tray and sat down with a glass of milk in one hand and gingerbread in the other, silent, morose. Derrick studied the lean, brown face, the smooth hair, the sullen mouth—he looked tired. Either he was going out too much at night, or was working too hard, or was unhappy . . .

"How old are you, Hunter?" she asked suddenly.

365

"Twenty-one in the fall. Good night! Can't you remember?"

She shook her head. "I'd have to count up. What kind of a job is it you've got at the mill? Are you just killing time, or is it going to get you somewhere?"

His face hardened. He looked at her suspiciously, and his voice was surly. "Why?"

"Because I want to know. Don't look at me like that. I'm not going to nag you. But Mother had more faith in you, once, than in any of the rest of us, and I—" She stopped then. His face was white and set.

"Don't, Derrick! For weeks I've been afraid that it was partly because I'd disappointed her that Mother was sick . . ." He sank back into his chair and stared at her, like a frightened, grief-stricken small boy. She knew at once all that had burdened his mind. The Furies! How quiet he had been! If he had only let her know sooner, she could have said something . . .

"She didn't feel so badly as all that, Hunter. Her only disappointment was in the thought that you had wasted two years doing the wrong thing, and she didn't want you to waste another one. As for her being sick because of you"— she smiled, half-fearfully, not sure how he would take it— "she wrote me once that she thought it would be good for you—would put you in your place."

"It did, Derrick. It certainly did! I was awfully sure that I was an important person. . . . And ever since, I've thought of nothing but how she argued with Father to save me from medical school, and then how I'd failed her."

He had forgotten, then, which of them had done the arguing!—but she let it pass.

"You haven't failed her yet. Don't be silly. She won you your freedom to do what you pleased—now you must be sure to do something. Remember that she counted on you. She said to me once that Billy was sure to be all right— steady, reliable—all that sort of thing—but that you could be something much greater than that—or something infinitely less."

They sat in silence for a moment, then he rose to put his glass on the table.

"It's nice to have you here, Derrick, but what about your job? Will they keep it for you forever?"

She stared in amazement.

"But, Hunter! I'm not going back! Didn't I say so? I told Father, I know."

He shook his head.

"Not to us, and Father hasn't said anything. I know the kids think—they've been wondering. . . . Look here, Derrick! You don't have to, you know. There's no reason why you should stay fussing with us, and doing housework that you hate. Aunt Sue would be glad to come up here."

"No—she's too old for the responsibility. Besides, I want to stay. After all, home is home."

"Well, if you want to. Of course, while Mother was here it was different. Why didn't you come then?" Then he changed the subject abruptly. "I say, Derrick—if you're going to be home, maybe you can do something with Margaret."

"Margaret! What's the matter with her?"

"She used to talk about how fast I was—remember? Well, compared to what she is now!" He whistled through his teeth. "And the funny thing was, Mother didn't seem to notice it, or couldn't manage her, or was too tired to be bothered."

"That was it, I suppose. But she never liked to manage us any more than was necessary. What's the matter with Margaret?"

"Oh—all kinds of hours and parties and clothes, and Kenneth McCampbell—"

"What about him? I haven't seen him since he was in knickers, but he used to be a nice enough little towhead—"

"He's nice enough, I suppose—but she just can't see any

one else. They're like an old married couple, right now, and at her age! She's a mere babe! I don't know how far they've gone, or might go—but I know darned well some of those kids don't care how far they go—"

"Oh, Hunter!" She laughed. "You don't know how funny a brother's solicitude is to a girl. Don't worry about Margaret. I'll keep an eye on her, but I don't think she needs it. She's trying awfully hard to be in style—at seventeen you have to be." She remembered herself at seventeen and smiled a little wryly. "If I were that age this summer—or Rosanna—you might have something to think about. But Margaret! Underneath, she has exactly the same temperament Bill has—she's as steady as a rock, no matter what immoralities are fashionable."

"You may think so." He shook his head sagely as he rose to take the empty plate and glasses back to the kitchen. "But there's no doubt in my mind she'll bear watching. Come on upstairs, and let me turn out the lights. And to-morrow be sure you tell the kids you're going to stay, and relieve their minds."

Derrick had breakfast with her father and Hunter in the morning before the others were down—it was Saturday, and they had taken advantage of the immemorial privilege of American school-children to sleep late. Afterward, when she had gone upstairs to make her bed, she heard Rosanna romping in the hall with Hunter—he had come up again for something he had forgotten, and had met her outside the bathroom. She hung over the banisters until he had slammed the front door behind him, then she came to Derrick's threshold and stood there, a little timidly, bare-armed, bare-kneed, in her short petticoat, a faded gingham dress in her hand.

"Derrick, would this dress be all right for Saturday morning? Just to play in?"

"I should think so. Why not?"

"It's kinda short. Last time I wore it, Marg'ret said I was a disgrace to the fam'ly. My petticoat showed."

"Is there a tuck in the hem? We'll have to let down all your dresses, I expect." She took the dress and examined it. "Bring me the scissors from the dressing-table, and I'll fix it."

She watched the scrawny child as she crossed the room, noted the patched petticoat, the shabby, kicked-out shoes that were placed so lightly on the bare floor with such a quick grace. She felt a sudden pang. Was it possible that they had not paid enough attention to Rosanna? How thin her cheeks were! Nothing of the baby left, and she was only seven . . .

She brought the scissors; then, while Derrick sat on the edge of the bed and ripped the tuck, she returned to the dressing-table, picked up the hair-brush and began to brush down the short, thick black hair.

"Derrick—"

"Yes?"

"Hunter says you're going to stay here."

"Yes. To see that your dresses are let down, and your petticoats don't show."

"Just for that? Stay here always?"

"Not just for that. I'm sick of New York, and glad to be home."

Rosanna caught her eye in the mirror, and smiled a little doubtfully; then her glance fell to a picture on the dresser.

"Tell me—can you remember Mother when she was like that?"

She crossed the room with the photograph and held it out before her. Derrick was startled. It was "like that" that she always thought of her mother—illumined, laughing, light in the eyes, a certain vigor even in the sweep of the pompadour. That pompadour and the high-boned collar and the full sleeves had not made the picture in her eyes in the least old-fashioned.

"When that was taken, I was as old—older than you are now. Of course, I remember." Then she looked at Rosanna, pityingly. . . . Their mother had not been like that for a long while, and neither of the two youngest had known her when she was most herself. Derrick could hardly bear to face the child: it was as if she had unfairly deprived her of something. She put her hands on her shoulders and said, for comfort, "It's funny to think you didn't know her when she was like that, for you're the only one of all of us that's in the least like her when she was young. You have her eyes and hair." Then she shook out the dress and slipped it over the child's head. "Here—it should be pressed, but never mind—it'll never show on a galloping horse, as Mother would have said. Let me button you, and then you must run on down to breakfast. Some day I'll tell you what fun Mother used to be when Billy and Hunter and I were about as old as you are now."

For several weeks after her conversation with Hunter, Derrick watched Margaret engage in her frivolous pursuits, and decided that he must have been right so far as her absorption in Kenneth McCampbell and his in her was concerned. She regarded them with some amusement, but decided to see what she could find out from her sister— whether they took themselves seriously. She asked Margaret to go to market with her one Saturday afternoon; she would not suspect that a conversation carried on casually between inquiries as to the prices of vegetables was premeditated. They passed one of Margaret's friends as they moved from wagon to wagon beneath the elms around the court-house, and that gave Derrick the opportunity she wanted.

"Who-all are in your crowd now, Margaret? I've been away so long I can't remember."

Margaret named them.

"All those boys? I never heard you mention any of them except Ken."

"I never go with any of them except him," she said frankly.

"Why not?"

"They don't ask me. They've all got girls of their own.

Besides, he's the only one of the lot that has any sense."

Derrick stopped to ask the price of a bushel of cherries. Theirs had been frost-bitten that spring, and the overflowing basket at her feet tempted her. But Margaret put a restraining hand on her arm.

"You can get them cheaper if you go out to the fruit farm and bring them yourself. Mother always did.'

"I'd better, I suppose. I'll take a couple of quarts of these" —she turned to the market-man. "Enough for pies for dinner to-morrow." Then she said, as they started away, "You don't imagine you have any lasting feeling for Ken, do you?"

"I don't imagine anything." Which was cryptic, to say the least.

"You're much too young to let yourself get tied up with one person. You'll miss half the fun of your life if you aren't absolutely heart-whole while you are going through school and college."

"Of course. I can see that easily enough. It would be better not to know the only man you could ever marry until after you were through college, but if you do, how can you help it?"

Derrick laughed then with such amusement that Margaret regarded her with not a little displeasure, and she hastened to change the subject. . . . How could anyone argue against such a matter-of-fact attitude as that? Margaret would have to be left to her own devices.

Sunday, Derrick decided, no matter where you spent it, was a depressing day; the hours dragged endlessly along, and there was nothing you could do but sigh and fidget—but Sunday in summer was torture. It had been so hot in church that morning that her thin dress had stuck to the back of the pew, and the harsh stuff of the cushion on the seat had scratched unendurably through all her clothes. She had gone into the row with Aunt Anne's family; the younger Thorntons formed an overflow and had had to sit in front of her. With the recollection of all that had gone through her mind while she as a child had sat where they were sitting, she watched as they put their heads together, engrossed in something in Henry's lap. Tit-tat-toe, probably, she thought. She noted how Rosanna's black hair was cut straight across the back of her head . . . she had a sudden impulse to run her hand up through it . . . she could feel it in her fingers, thick and soft. Henry's hair was the dull brown color of her own; it grew down in a point on the nape of his neck, beneath the stiff Eton collar that he wore, rebelliously, on Sundays . . . and it curled just enough so that it stood up, untidily, from his forehead. It was too long—she must remember to send him to have it cut in the morning. She wished she could see, as easily, what was inside their heads; she was curious and interested . . . they had stopped their game— would they do as she had done, count the lights and the organ pipes, doze, dream great vague dreams of the future? She did not know those two children at all, really . . . she would not ask them to endure church again while the weather was like this . . . next week they would take a picnic dinner and go off somewhere in the car, spend the day on the road. . . .

After dinner, the heavy Sunday-ness of the atmosphere descended upon her even more depressingly. Thunder-heads in the distant sky warned them not to go out for a ride; Hunter and Margaret disappeared upstairs, Rosanna after them; Dr. Thornton went into the library. In desperation, Derrick told Henry that, if he would put up the card-table, she would play rum with him. As she dealt the cards, her father came back into the room with a fat brown volume of Dickens under his arm. He eyed them uneasily.

"Your mother never would let any one play cards in her house on Sunday."

"Oh, dear! I'd forgotten. Would you rather we didn't?"

"No . . . oh, no. It doesn't matter to me, one way or the other."

"I tell you what. If you'll read Dickens aloud to us, we'll stop, won't we, Henry?" Henry agreed docilely.

"I've no objection to reading aloud, I'm sure, but with this storm coming up, I may not be able to make myself heard. It is 'Barnaby Rudge' I brought out—do you think Henry would get anything out of it?"

"Of course. He's no moron. But first—it *is* going to storm —I'll turn up the chairs on the porch—and Henry,—you call to them upstairs to watch the windows."

In a moment, she had returned to one of the big living-room chairs, and Henry had lain down on his stomach, on the rug before the empty black fireplace, his face buried in his arms. As the thunder began to crash and roll, the doctor opened the book.

" 'The evening with which we have to do was . . . . an evening in March when the wind howled dismally . . .' "

"Just like to-day—" Henry lifted his heels in the air, and turned his head to smile at Derrick, contentedly.

The doctor read on, only pausing now and then when the thunder drowned his voice; they were as oblivious to the storm as it is possible to be when there is a wind that shakes the house on its foundations, and lightning that smites you in the eye, and hail that knocks against the windows—until Hunter came in and interrupted them.

"Where's Rosanna?"

"I thought she was with you. If she isn't, she must be with Margaret. Why? What difference does it make?"

"Margaret's in the bathroom, getting ready to go out. It doesn't make any difference, except that she's scared to death of lightning, and has probably crawled into a closet or under a bed somewhere."

"Afraid of lightning? How can she be? Mother never let us be afraid of it. Don't you remember how she used to call us to the window and pretend not to notice how we dodged and trembled while she made us say how lovely it was?"

"Yes—but she never went to all that trouble with the little kids—I don't think she even noticed that Rosanna was frightened—"

"Look here," their father interrupted, "am I reading to you or not?"

"Yes, of course you are." Derrick turned back from Hunter. "Go on, won't you?"

Hunter went upstairs and came back in a little while with Rosanna.

"The nests are sure to be blown out of the trees in this wind," he said, as they entered, "and if we see them in time, maybe we can save the baby birds before they're beaten to death by this hail."

He stationed her in one of the French doors that looked out across the terrace and the side yard, and he himself stood in the other.

"Now, watch!" he commanded, "and don't blink that way at the lightning, or you won't see."

Out of the corner of her eye, Derrick watched, too, and saw Rosanna flinch and quiver, then press her face again to the pane, as the thunder followed each flash. What with its noise and the howling wind and the continuous crash of the great marble-sized hailstones, it was impossible to read aloud; the doctor laid the open book against his chest and stretched out in his chair to doze.

Henry rolled over to tease his dog Jeff, which had retreated cowering beneath Derrick's chair. She kept an eye on Rosanna; she thought she could not endure much more of it, and she was right; the next bolt sent her back from the window, her hands before her face. She turned and found Derrick smiling at her, so came to her chair.

"Do you want to sit in my lap, honey? Hunter can watch for the birds himself." She picked up the trembling child, who for a moment pressed her face against her shoulder.

Henry looked up at her from the floor.

"Why don't you crawl under the chair with Jeff?"

"Don't tease her, Henry——" Derrick began; but Hunter interrupted.

"See here, young man. If you don't mind the lightning, suppose you come stand in this other window."

Rosanna sat up, squared her shoulders, set her jaw.

"No, I'm coming, Hunter, truly—' She slid off Derrick's knee.

Funny child! She would have gone through fire and water at Hunter's command. She had been in the window but a moment when she and Hunter cried out together. They actually had seen a nest fall. . . .

"Upon my soul!" he exclaimed in some surprise. "The redbird's nest out of the tulip-tree! Come on now, help me look for the birds before the hail kills them—" It had almost stopped hailing, as a matter of fact, but he made it seem an affair of life and death. "Put on your raincoat—"

"Oh, Hunter, I can't—"

"Not to save a bird? All right, I'll go alone—"

With a cry she sprang after him across the porch and the terrace, leaving the door open so that the wind swept through the room. In a moment they were back. Hunter held in his hand a drenched fledgling, its eyes half shut and glazed, its wings limp and dragging.

"Maybe his wings are broken, but maybe not," Hunter said. "Get a box to put him in, and fill it with cotton."

Derrick rose and looked at the bird. "I think he's drowned, myself, but we can see. There's an empty candy-box in the buffet, and cotton in the medicine-chest in the bathroom."

Rosanna brought the cotton, and Hunter took bits of it and dried the wet pinfeathers tenderly, until they were restored from a dark sodden mass to a bright-colored down, and the bird looked less redly naked.

"He'll be all right," he encouraged Rosanna. "His wings aren't broken, anyway, nor his legs. We'll leave him in the box of cotton to get really warm and dry, then we'll feed him and let him go. The mother bird's probably just about frantic."

Rosanna went out on the porch again to see. The storm was practically over; the hail had ceased to fall, and it rained only a little, in sudden gusts as the wind shook the trees. She called to him.

"Here's the big bird, Hunter. It's found another one." She dashed out again and returned with another fledgling, which she held out to him with infinite faith. He laughed as he took it.

"I can't warm this one, honey. He's absolutely dead."

Her eyes dilated with horror, and she touched it with a wet forefinger.

"Try, Hunter—please—please—"

"It's no good, I tell you."

Her lower lip trembled.

"If we'd stayed out longer before, we might have found him in time."

"I doubt it. The fall must have killed it."

She shook her head, tears in her eyes, and wrapped the dead bird in cotton. . . . Derrick watched her with sympathy and understanding. The child was facing the thought that if she had not been afraid . . . There was no further need to wonder what went on inside her head—she knew her— a pitiful small Calvinist, taking issue, at seven, with her own particular brand of original sin. Derrick sighed . . .

After they had watched the bird swallow with some enthusiasm the soft breadcrumbs they offered him, they took him outdoors, and put him on the ground where the mother bird had found the dead one, and where she still flew about, distractedly in circles. When they returned to the living-room, their father stirred from his pretended nap and lifted the book from his chest where it had lain, his hands locked together above it.

"Is the hubbub over?" he asked, amused and twinkling— "shall I go on with the book?"

"We'll be good, now, and listen, if you will." Derrick returned to her chair and Hunter took the couch; Rosanna brought a doll and a tea-set and played her own private game at her father's feet. Jeff came out from beneath Derrick's chair, stretched, and lay down on the rug beside Henry, who

threw an arm around his neck and suffered his face to be
licked. And Dr. Thornton read on, without a break, until
supper-time.

Through all those summer months, Derrick alternated
between a keen, almost passionate affection for her brothers
and sisters, with an accompanying profound contentment in
their presence, and a desperate loneliness that assailed her
at odd and unexpected moments. Strange that a house
where six people dwelt could seem so empty! Something in
the very air, at times, in the staring walls, the vacant door-
ways, reminded you constantly: that one had gone whose
presence, once, had been the whole house . . .

With that thought in her mind, one morning, Derrick
climbed the stairs to the attic, determined to be melancholy.
She thought that Henry and Rosanna had gone out to play
somewhere, so that it was with some surprise that she heard,
as she stood outside the door to her mother's "studio," a
long-drawn-out, half-choked sob. She turned the knob and
looked in; Henry, seated at a deal table where there stood
before him the clay model of the head of a child—Rosanna's
perhaps—was gazing at it despairingly and wiping the tears
from his cheeks with the back of his hand. She understood
only too well: there was no room in the house so empty
without their mother as this rough, half-finished one beneath the roof.

"I didn't know you were up here, Henshi." Then, to give
him time, she crossed to one of the long windows under the
eaves. "It wouldn't be quite so hot if you'd open this—" She
flung it wide, and turned back to him. "That's a good head.
I'd know it anywhere."

He shook his head dismally. "Mother showed me how to
do this one, but I can't do it without her."

"Do you want to go on having lessons? Why didn't you
say something long ago? I'd forgotten all about your modeling—but they must have classes for children at the Art
School in Cincinnati. You will have to go back to school

here in a little while now, but if you would be willing to give up your Saturday mornings—"

"Oh, I should, Derrick, I should!"

"I'll speak to Father about it."

She smiled to herself as she went downstairs: she could not believe that at his age Henry really cared about modeling: no doubt he desired the certain *kudos* it must give him among his playmates, to be able to say that he went to Art School—and yet—how old was she when she had begun to write poetry in mottled-covered blank-books?

She spoke of it to her father, as she had promised, and he agreed to take Henry to the city on Saturday mornings. He seemed to feel that this was the sort of thing it was well to work off while you were young—that if he indulged Henry in his fancy now, it would clear the way for more serious purposes later. His attitude disquieted Derrick not a little. Did her father understand Henry at all? A dreamer, who cared nothing for books, little for games, nothing for most people, passionately for a few—his mother—her, Derrick (she did not flatter herself—this was obvious fact), and perhaps Rosanna—most passionately of all for his dog. Quiet, docile, his life a thing apart, of the clouds . . . what would his father have him do?

She spoke to Hunter about it when they happened to be alone together that night.

"I hope you haven't forgotten how Mother argued to save you from having to be a doctor?"

He looked at her in hurt surprise.

"I remember well enough. Don't rub it in."

"I didn't mean to. I only wanted to say that, when it came time for the same argument on Henry's behalf, you must stand by me."

"Henry?" he echoed blankly.

"Yes. It must be obvious to you that Father has always had his heart set on having one of his sons a doctor. Family tradition, you know, and all that sort of thing—and there's only Henry left."

"But he couldn't be a doctor in a thousand years! Henshi and his mud-pies! It would kill him. Besides, don't you suppose Father saw how pleased Mother was when he asked her for lessons, and how she gloated because one of her children, at least, was bound to be an artist?"

"I don't know. I'm crossing a bridge I haven't reached, anyway. He's only—what?—ten? I just wanted to remind you."

If Henry and his father were to reach the city with the morning before them, they must of necessity take the six o'clock train down. Derrick rose at dawn to get their breakfast—Cassie did not come until seven—and when they had eaten she followed them to the front hall to help Henry find his Sunday cap.

"Derrick, keep Jeff shut in the back yard till I get home, will you? If he's left loose, he'll be run over, sure."

"He's impossible to manage when you're not here. He acts like a very demon, but I'll do the best I can."

"Where is he now?"

"Out somewhere. I let him in this morning and he tore upstairs to waken you, then tore down again and out the kitchen door. He can open the back screen himself, unfortunately. When he comes back, I'll fasten him. Run on—you'll miss the train. I'll not let anything happen to him, truly."

When Hunter came down and sat with Derrick at the breakfast-table, the runaway dog dashed onto the porch and jumped up on the screen door of the dining-room.

"There's Jeff now." She rose and put down her napkin. "I told Henry I'd shut him in the back yard."

Then she paused, horror-stricken.

"Hunter! What's the matter with him?"

Where his nose had been against the screen as he stood on his hind legs there was a long streak of foam—

"What can he be eating?" Then she saw it was not that: he had dropped to all fours, with his head hanging, and the foam dripped from his jaw onto the porch floor. He quivered from head to tail, and rolled his eyes beseechingly . . .

Hunter was on his feet in an instant.

"Poisoned! Get me some raw eggs, Derrick, quick!"

When she flew back with the basket of eggs and a saucer, the dog was on his side, rigid, shaken with convulsive twitches. She shut her eyes.

"Hunter! It's too late . . ."

"Maybe not. Give me those and telephone the veterinary."

He broke a couple of eggs into the saucer. "Wait, Derrick. He won't take it. We'll have to feed him—" He seized the dog's jaws and held them apart while she poured the contents of the saucer down his throat.

"Now go. . . . He'll take the rest all right, I think—"

She waited to see Jeff lap up the eggs eagerly, as fast as Hunter could break them, then ran to the telephone. A minute later she returned.

"He wasn't there . . . they say he's at the livery-stable. I'll take the car and go for him. It would kill Henshi to lose that dog."

Hunter shook his head. "He's mighty sick, and I don't know anything to do but keep on giving him eggs. But I'll stay right with him—you run along—*shoot!*"

A short while later she was back with an unflurried young man in tow; they found Hunter still beside the dog, outside the dining-room door. Jeff lay outstretched, breathing in gasps.

"Oh, Hunter! Is he dying?"

"I don't know"—dismally.

"No, he isn't dying." The young doctor stooped and opened his case. "If his heart stands the shock, he'll be all right. The eggs probably saved him. I'll give him a stimulant."

He thrust a hypodermic under his foreleg.

"Now give him these—" He gave Hunter the medicine. "He'll lie like that all day. Don't rouse him, nor excite him."

"I'll stay right here and keep an eye on him." Hunter

threw off his coat, rolled up his shirt-sleeves, and sat down on the edge of the porch beside the panting dog.

By that time, Margaret and Rosanna were at the door; they eyed the veterinary curiously but waited until he had left to ask for an explanation. He looked around the anxious circle with a hint of amusement in his eye.

"I'll be back this evening to see how he is." And he lifted his hat and went out across the terrace and the lawn to the front gate.

"What on earth happened?"

"Jeff was poisoned, but Hunter saved him."

"Hunter!" They looked at him in amazement.

"I did nothing of the kind. You poured the eggs down his throat."

"While you held his jaws! You were the one he might have bitten. Besides, I shouldn't have known enough to give him eggs."

Hunter spent the day, with a book on his knees at the side of the indifferent dog, who regarded him languidly. Jeff's whole being seemed concentrated on the effort to draw his breath, but late in the afternoon he dragged himself to his feet and walked, stiff and trembling, across the terrace to the fence at its edge, where he stretched out again at full length, on his side, in the thick cushion of the vines that grew there.

When Henry and his father came in, just before dinner, Rosanna flew to meet them; Derrick was close on her heels, but too late to silence her. She jumped up and down on her toes in her dreadful excitement.

"Henry, Henry, Henry! Jeff was poisoned!"

Before Derrick could add a word, he was past her.

"Where is he? Oh, Derrick! You promised to tie him! Is he *dead?*"

"No, Henry—listen! He's better now. Hunter knew what to do."

"Hunter gave him raw eggs," Rosanna added. "Did you know, Father, you could save a dog's life with raw eggs?" She clung to his hand, still dancing excitedly.

"Where is he?" Henry demanded.

"Hunter is with him, on the terrace . . . Wait a minute, Henry. He's an awfully sick dog, still, but the veterinary says he will be all right if his heart doesn't go back on him—be careful not to excite him."

Henry tiptoed across the terrace, but the dog knew his step, and struggled to his feet, even wagged his tail feebly.

"Poor ol' Jeff!" Henry rubbed his head gently, then turned to Hunter, beside him.

"Is he better, Hunter, truly?"

"Lots better. It's the first time he's wagged his tail to-day."

Henry threw himself on the ground beside the dog, and Jeff lay down again, very slowly, very carefully. . . . The boys could hardly be persuaded to go into the house for their dinner, and afterward Henry returned immediately to the terrace. Derrick picked up a book, her father and Hunter went out, and the girls went to bed; she forgot both dog and boy until Hunter came in some hours later.

"How's Jeff?"

"I haven't heard anything from him. . . . Upon my word, Hunter, I believe Henry's still out there with him. I didn't see him come in."

She went out, and then called to him in a low voice, laughing.

"Hunter, the blessed child's stretched out here, sound asleep. I hate to waken him."

The older boy followed her, took Henry by the shoulders, and dragged him to his feet.

"Wake up, Henshi! You must come in—it's bedtime."

Henry staggered, buried a tousled brown head in Hunter's waistcoat, then drew back and looked at him out of starry blue eyes.

"Hunter—if I ever have anything in the world you want, I'll give it to you." He turned, stumbled up onto the porch and into the house.

Hardly a week had passed before Jeff was able to swing

on the clothes on the line, as of old—much to the annoyance of Annie, the laundress—but it was not that long, even, before Hunter came to Dr. Thornton with an astonishing proposal. He chose an evening, intentionally, Derrick thought, when she was with her father on the porch. Perhaps he was afraid of what might be said—it was dark, and she could not see his face as he dropped on the step at their feet.

"Father," he began bravely, "I don't know whether you'll think it's too late or not, but I've decided I do want to be a doctor, after all. I know I've been an awful fool, and wasted two years. . . ."

"What has made you change your mind? Why do you think now you would like it?"

Derrick remembered with a sudden fear his old penchant for giving away his greatest treasure when he was penitent. Was he offering his freedom to Henry? . . . At any rate, he answered his father without hesitation.

"Well, it sounds silly—but first that bird we found in the storm, and then Henry's dog—you see, I found out how I liked to cure things."

"Where do you want to go?"

"I've quite a bit of money saved. I thought I'd go down to Cincinnati and combine University and Medical School. I know if I'd had any sense I'd be almost through college now . . ."

"Never mind about that. If you're really serious about this, I'll see that it's arranged. You and Billy could have rooms together somewhere . . ."

How quietly, Derrick thought, were the most momentous decisions made! In spite of all that had gone before, the two men were, seemingly, less excited about this than they had been over Jeff's poisoning . . . yet . . . she heard her father breathe heavily in the dark.

Later, Derrick followed Hunter into the house for a moment's private conversation.

"It wasn't what I said about Henry that made you decide this, was it?"

"What? Oh, no." He spoke awkwardly, uneasily. "It's kind of hard to explain. I guess it was the way Henry looked at me when he knew Jeff wasn't going to die, and thinking how it would feel to be able to do what would please people as much as that."

In September, then, Hunter packed up again and departed. But before he left there occurred an incident that showed Derrick how the family spirit had been restored . . . it was the first time that they had all laughed together . . .

Her father had asked her at noon if she would not like to drive him into the country, rather than have him go off for the afternoon with the car; she could take a book and read while he called on his patients. As she went into the garage, she heard a scuffling and the sound of voices overhead, in what had been the haymow when the garage had been a stable, but was now a kind of storeroom—a place of dust, broken furniture, shadowy corners. . . . Derrick stepped to the ladder and called through the square hole in the floor.

"Henry!"

An unkempt head and dust-streaked face appeared over the edge.

"What is it?"

"What are you doing up there?"

"Nothin'. Just playin'."

"Well—be good, won't you—don't hurt yourselves. I'm going away, and Cassie won't be here until four."

"Look, Derrick—come up here a minute. We want to ask you sumpin'."

Holding herself as far away as she could from the dusty steps of the ladder, so as not to soil the ruffles of her blouse, she climbed up and stepped out on the floor of the loft.

"Well?"

They stood around her, Henry, Rosanna, and another boy and girl.

"Tell us what this is, will you?"

They indicated a cobweb-hung contraption which they had dragged from its corner to the light of the window.

"It's a fruit-press. I'd forgotten we had it."

"What's a fruit-press?"

"You press fruit in it—to make wine. I can remember when Cassie used to make elderberry wine every summer."

"Father was saying just the other day we'd better make some wine," Henry said thoughtfully. "How does it work?"

She humored him. "You put the elderberries, or grapes, or whatever it is, in this bucket thing, with the cracks between the boards; then you turn this crank and the lid comes down and squeezes the grapes, and the juice runs out between the cracks into this groove and down this spout into the kettle."

Henry turned the crank, which squeaked stubbornly.

"It needs oiling," he said, "and washing." He swept his hand around the interior to gather up the cobwebs.

"Yes—I shouldn't do it to-day, if I were you," she responded genially. "Wait till Sunday, when Father will have time—" She lowered herself down the ladder and started off in the car.

The doctor's patient lived in a farmhouse back in the hills; as Derrick stopped to put him out at the gate, she said that she would leave the car there and get out for a walk; when he was ready to go, he could blow the horn for her . . . then she sat for a moment and looked at the house. It was built of warm yellow stone after the old pattern followed by those who had come into the county from Pennsylvania and Maryland; but it was in a sad state of decay: there was no paint on the square pillars of the set-in porch, the chimneys hung dangerously awry, and there were holes in the roof . . . it was the house you would buy if you were an artist or a poet who loved the country, its foundations and traditions, and wanted to live there in the midst of them, apart. You would restore it, and fill it with antiques, and live in it from April to November. What an ideal diversion for old age—restoring old houses!

For an instant she saw herself as an aged philanthropist, a benefactor of the country. But perhaps such houses would prefer the more natural end for which this one seemed destined—would rather fall to pieces untouched, eventually deserted, since all that they had been truly a part of had so come to an end. In pensive mood she alighted from the car, turned back to the road, crawled through a sagging wire fence, and climbed to a low hill she had noticed as they had passed, curious, not as to the nature of the square enclosure on its top, surrounded by a brick wall—the family burying-grounds of the pioneers were common enough to be recognizable—but as to who, and how many were buried there, and why they had died. . . . The wall was lined inside with rows of sickly yellowing hemlock trees . . . why did they plant evergreens, always, above their dead? . . . and in the hollow square thus formed, a score or so of graves, the headstones scaling slabs of slate, broken, obscured by the tangle of long grass. Infant mortality! Once, women had lived here among the sun-blessed hills only to bear children and lose them, and to come at last to sleep beneath the stunted, motheaten evergreens. They let their hogs root in the oak groves . magnificent trees, for one's body to fertilize! . . . but above the dead, once beloved, slim and white, they planted hemlocks. . . . Symbolic? Of what? The little they cared for the flesh and the earth, so sure of heaven? Derrick sat down in the grass and leaned against one of the trees; she watched the clouds and the dim blue horizon. A drowsy day, and how silent. . . . She wished, whimsically, for a cigarette. To startle the dead. Life was so different, now! Or was it, really? Perhaps these women had had their corncob pipes. . . . She laughed at the thought, but, nevertheless, when her father sounded the horn, returned to the road in a profoundly melancholy frame of mind.

This mood she cherished all the way back to town, so that she was startled, almost shocked, as she stopped the automobile engine in the garage, by the sound of the ringing laughter of many voices. Hurriedly she came out into the back yard and looked upon an amazing sight. On the back porch, Cassie, Margaret, Henry, Rosanna, all laughing; on the ground, rolling as though in agony, clutching his ribs, yet still laughing, Hunter; on the step, Jeff, his tail between his legs, drenched, shivering, humiliated. On the porch floor, what looked like the stains of battle: a puddle of red liquid, that had dripped down the steps, that had been spattered on Henry's blouse, on Rosanna's dress—an overturned kettle, and, in the center, the fruit-press.

As she came up the walk, Cassie caught her eye, stopped laughing, and burst into an angry tirade.

"Looky hyah! D'yo' evah see such a mess? Yo' can jes' do yo' own scrubbin'—Ah done got 'nuff to do, cookin' fo' yo'-all. An' all them grapes, Derrick, whut yo' paw paid Ben fo' pickin', done wasted—utte'ly wasted. Henry, yo' dese'ves to be sent to bed—"

Derrick remembered that she had gone away and left on the back porch a bushel of grapes, picked by Ben that morning from the top of the arbor. The grapes and the fruit-press. It had been too much for Henry.

"Explain yourself, Henry."

Hunter sat up to listen, his arms around his knees. Margaret snickered.

"It was Marg'ret's fault. She let Jeff out, after we had shut him in the house."

"My fault!" Margaret wiped her eyes. "How was I to know what mischief you were up to? He wanted to get out, and I let him . . ."

"What had Jeff to do with it?" Derrick tried not to laugh herself as the bedraggled dog looked at her pleadingly.

"He upset the kettle."

"But didn't I tell you to leave the fruit-press until Father had time to do something about it?"

"Well—you didn't sound much as if you meant it. An' the grapes were here, and might 'a' rotted. An' I thought what fun it would be to have the wine all made for Father, to su'prise him."

"And instead of that, you've only made a lot of work for yourself. First of all, you must scrub Cassie's porch, before the police come around to see who's been murdered—then you must bathe Jeff. This is not an unmitigated misfortune, because Jeff's been needing a bath for some days. And, Rosanna, you must help, because you heard me say to leave the fruit-press alone."

Later, Margaret called her to her bedroom window, which overlooked the back yard.

"If you think you are punishing those children . . ."

They leaned out the window above the porch roof. Henry, who had taken charge of the hose, drenched everything in sight by his reckless mismanagement of it: Rosanna, Jeff, himself . . . an angry expletive from the kitchen announced that the water had even been thrown in through the open porch door . . .

At the dinner-table Derrick told her father of the scene he had missed.

"It's too bad you didn't come home with me this afternoon, instead of going back to the office." She no longer made any attempt to conceal her amusement, now that it was over. Henry and Rosanna laughed with them, rather pleased with themselves.

"But a whole bushel of grapes, Henry!" the doctor expostulated. "How much good wine is that wasted? We can't afford to pay Ben to pick grapes for you to throw away. Every remaining grape on that arbor is to be picked when it is ripe by you, young man. Do you understand?"

"Yes, I understand. But y'oughta seen Jeff! He was so su'prised! You know how clumsy he is—all feet. And when he brushed against the kettle an' it went rolling after him and clattered down the step on top of him, an' drowned him in grape juice . . ."

They laughed anew. . . . Derrick thought afterward that the incident, trifling as it was, had somehow cleared the

air . . . it was the first family joke since she had come
home . . . and thenceforth they laughed more easily. Even
the children's friends felt it: they came back into the house
freely, as they had done before, no longer awkward, oppressed by the consciousness that Henry's, or Rosanna's,
mother had died. (Poor Henry! or Poor Rosanna! *They
haven't any mother!* That was what their friends had not
been able to forget all summer long. Derrick remembered
how once Hunter had sent a grubby, detestable little boy in
his class two valentines instead of one, because his mother
had died. It was better for the children to be out from under
the shadow of pity.) And Margaret's friends came, too—
they were Seniors in the High School this year, and very old
and wise—they danced, or made candy, or played red-dog
on the dining-room table, and ate fantastic meals at all hours
of the night, while Derrick sat up and kept a watchful eye
on them, suspecting them of unnameable indecencies, of
which she saw no sign.

Christmas might, Derrick foresaw, be rather difficult—
she dreaded it; but her Aunt Anne appreciated, too, how
hard for them the holiday would be, at home for the first
time without their mother, and so invited them to dinner
down at the old Ferguson house. Derrick was profoundly
grateful. The boys came home, Billy for several days, Hunter
for two weeks, so that the house was full of noise: mysterious
runnings in and out, up and down stairs, whisperings and
conspiracies—and for that she was grateful, too. They were
to go to Aunt Anne's early in the morning, so that Derrick
and Margaret could help with the dinner consequently,
they had their own presents for each other at the breakfast-
table. Derrick saw then how completely they had accepted
her in their mother's place. Each of them had always been
given a certain small amount of money to spend on presents;
as much of it as could be saved was spent for their mother
—every gift that was made by hand meant so much less
spent on those less loved, so much more saved for hers, the
one "boughten" present. And this year they had saved for

Derrick. For each other, calendars, blotters, hemstitched handkerchiefs; for her, books, gloves, a string of beads, a vase. . . . For her the wide-eyed watching, the suspense, the almost tearful joy at her exclamations of pleasure and gratitude. She knew at once that if such were her place in their eyes, then, no matter what happened, she could not leave them, could not go away again.

When all the gifts had been collected in piles—each his own booty—on the chairs and tables in the library, they picked up the basket of knobby, tissue-wrapped packages for Aunt Anne and her family, and scuffed down Main Street hill through the falling snow.

All day long, beneath the babble and excitement, Derrick was conscious of the irony of life, its uncertainty: the old house built in the solemnity of the Covenanters echoing to the celebration of a festival as old as time, that had been ignored while Great-Grandmother Ferguson lived, because it was "Popish": the great-aunts, enjoying life only after her death, when they were already old—too old to revel in such merriment, to giggle like girls. How could they have been so repressed by that feeble little old woman, whom they must have been able to remember as a young woman, their mother, to be wheedled and cajoled? Derrick was glad that her mother had been spared old age. How incomprehensible it all was! A ghastly joke, as she had decided so often before —and the sooner ended the better—except that there were so many people to be fond of, and little enough time for it. . . . Derrick caught Rosanna's eye on her as she toyed with the plum pudding before her, and she fingered the beads around her neck to show the child that she had never once been unconscious of the new glory in which she had been decked. . . .

So far I have given, as I remember it, all that Derrick told me—as I remembered it on the train that September afternoon when I was being carried away from Tecumseh. The impression that the sum of it left on my mind was, I admit-

ted, not unlike the impression left by my childish perusal of
the works of E.P. Roe. Was it possible that Derrick had let
herself sink into sentimentality—that that was the change
in her—if there was a change? Where did one draw the line
between sentimentality and affection? Or was her absorption in the children not quite genuine—a way of escape
from thoughts that might have goaded her? Did she think
of them deliberately, in order that there might be no time
to think of herself? How much of what had gone through
her mind in those first months had she concealed when she
told about them? That after Christmas she had suffered a
violent reaction against the family and against Tecumseh,
she admitted—but she could not have denied it, since at the
time she had confessed it in her letters. Whether or not she
had been unhappy before that, I could not tell.

OF THE FIRST MONTHS after Christmas, Derrick told me little when I was with her; what I knew from her letters, brief though they were, with nothing in them of her old love of description for its own sake. I think that afterward she did not like to be reminded of the mood of rebellion which those letters had expressed, but which she had stifled successfully.

When the excitement of Christmas had come to an end, when Hunter had gone back to the city and the children to school, she remembered with dismay, and with surprise at the dismay, what she had thought on Christmas morning. She had taken her mother's place with the children; she could not leave them now if she wished to. But she had not intended to go away again; she had decided that long ago. Why, then, the strange sinking of her heart? Was it possible that she had been contented for more than six months simply because she had known she could depart at a moment's notice, and leave no one the worse for her absence? How perverse of her! Suddenly her life in Tecumseh seemed insupportable—the never-ending drudgery of housekeeping, the constant claims on time and energy, and, worst of all, the lack of friends.

There were the Stewarts, to be sure, and Mary was not unsatisfactory as a friend, but the farm was a long way from town, and Derrick could not always be sure of finding Mary when she got there; she played as hard at being a farmer's wife as Bill worked at being a farmer. One might meet her

on a summer evening in the road behind a hay wagon, a wide
straw hat over her flushed face; in the threshing season she
kept an army of women in her kitchen to cook for an army
of laborers; she even brought the cows in from pasture.
. . . She had no other interests. No one who saw her at a
bridge party in town would have suspected it, but, even
there, when she talked of her children, she boasted that they
were truly Stewarts—farmers born—that already there was
no pleasure so great in the eyes of the older baby as being
taken by his grandfather to watch them ring the hogs' noses!

Even if Derrick had had no friends at all, there were
always books. . . . No life is quite unbearable while new
novels are printed spring and fall. In a burst of extravagance,
she ordered from Cincinnati all those which she had seen
praised in the reviews, or which we had written her about,
and which she had not expected to read until such time as
they should appear in the Tecumseh library. If only the
children would let her alone to read them when they came,
and not insist upon dragging her into a game of cards or
their everlasting parchesi, or into chaperoning them. . . . She
opened the books with gloating one Friday afternoon,
fingered them all, chose to begin with the latest Swinnerton,
and was half through it by dinner-time. Then, at the table,
the expected happened.

"Want to go to the movies to-night?" It was her father
who asked.

"No, thank you, I don't think I do. I've got some new
books."

"Oh, very well," he said, taken aback. "I just suggested
it for your pleasure. I don't care about it myself . . ."

"You go, and take the children."

"It's Doug Fairbanks," Henry urged. "You know you like
him."

"I don't like him. I detest movies."

"Why! You always go!"

"Never mind, Henry," Margaret said; "Father and I'll
take you, if Derrick has a grouch."

"I haven't a grouch! I should just like a little private life, for a change."

But Rosanna took it up and chanted: "Derrick's got a grou-ouch, Derrick's got a grou-ouch!"

"Hush, Rosanna!" Her father stopped her. "We'll go off and leave her alone with her book, if she insists. Leave her here with her conscience, which will rebuke her for having hurt our feelings by refusing our kind invitation. . . . You know that's exactly what will happen," he added to Derrick, twinkling. She laughed, and of course went with them.

As they stood in a group to wait while the doctor bought the tickets, she caught the words of two women behind them, whom she had not particularly noticed—the words "snob," and "high-and-mighty." She looked up into the mirror on the outside of the ticket booth and saw behind her own reflection those of two acquaintances of her mother's, members of the Ladies' Aid. She would have spoken to them before had she not been preoccupied; she was about to turn when she realized that they were talking about her.

". . . Now she's lived in New York, she'll never be able to speak like a human being to anybody again. I reckon she thinks Tecumseh's mighty small punkins . . ."

So that was what people thought! How preposterous! She shepherded the children before the ticketman at the door. She was amused, but horrified. As if she had ever felt that she belonged in New York! As if she were not as much a part, as irrevocably a part, of Tecumseh, as they were! . . . And all the while that people had been saying these things, she had been feeling sorry for herself, a "solitary"! What a fool! . . . She must win back for herself a place in the community, a part in community life. She detested all that the words connoted, but she must show them. Friendliness—neighborliness—she grimaced, safe in the dark. . . . When the doctor, still intent upon giving them pleasure, took them to the Greeks' for refreshment, she spoke warmly to the swarthy, smooth-haired waiters who had been familiar figures since she had been in High School, and able to eat the indigestible messes with the florid names which the children ordered. . . . She must begin at once and go into this whole-heartedly!

A few days later, her Great-Aunt Ursula telephoned to ask if she would have Cassie bake a crock of beans for the church supper. Derrick said that she would, asked when it was to be, in order that she might be sure to get her family there, and then—rather to her own surprise—offered to help beforehand if they needed her. That, perhaps, would show them!

It was hard work, the church supper—she was not to win clear from the opprobrium cast upon her without some cost. She moved shyly among the elderly women, and sought to keep, for the sake of protection, in the neighborhood of one of her aunts; but after she had explained to a dozen different women in low asides that she had been away so long that she hardly knew any one any more, and that she hadn't heard anything that had happened in the last half-dozen years, she found them friendly and eager to talk—they stopped to whisper to her about each other as they set the long tables that were really only boards on trestles. Particularly, they were anxious to talk about the young married set —most of them new people, they hastened to assure her— probably the crowd she would get in with, when she had been home awhile, but they whispered and shook their heads.

She was properly amused by their austerity, by their grim delight in the wickedness of others; but when, as she helped to serve the clamorous multitudes at the tables, that night, and the various members of "that set" were pointed out to her, she recoiled in horror from the suggestion that here she would find her friends. Hard, cheap, blatant—she could imagine the sort of life they led. Better solitude and books, or, if one must have a part in town life, better an association with the older women who divided their time between gossip and good works. . . . The church . . . she shrugged her shoulders.

But the church as an outlet was denied her. In the morning, as she ascended the stairs from its basement, where she had helped to wash dishes and clean up the confusion left the night before, she encountered the minister, on his way down. She had known him heretofore only as a preacher, but she had been predisposed to like him because the children did. Now he stopped her and shook hands.

He was a white-haired old man, and his face was kind, but his voice was bland, oily. "It is very gratifying to me, Miss Thornton, to see you take a part in the affairs of the church. It is exceedingly beneficial to the young people to have before them the example of one they have looked up to and admired from their babyhood, who has come back from the East, from a Great College, and from *New York* to take her place again in the town, in the work of the church of her fathers. It proves to them the great and enduring strength of a faith inculcated in childhood . . ."

She escaped, finally, and, safe outside in the clear wintry air, exploded "Whoof!"—gustily. Why had he attacked her? Why must he assume that she had any faith at all?— particularly that of her childhood! The man must think she had no mind! At any rate, that was that. She would not go near the church under false pretenses.

She might try the Community Service League. She asked her father at dinner what the name stood for.

"They support a clinic for those who can't afford a doctor, and they have a visiting nurse—and they help the school board support separate schools for the mentally deficient. They look after the poor, generally. They might set you to work collecting and distributing old clothes."

"Which is not a bad thing to do if you can't find something more useful. . . . And no doubt one could hope to be promoted to—to—"

"Bathing babies for the clinic?" Her father laughed at her —but she was quite serious. . . . In the next two or three weeks she saw enough poverty as she distributed old clothes, or whatever she did distribute, to make her write us: "Do you remember the patter of the sociologists that we used to scorn? 'Social conscience? I've developed a social conscience."

"That's always what happens to people who settle down like Derrick," Alice interrupted the letter to say. "They degenerate into moralists."

I did not answer, but continued to read. "Once upon a time, as an artist I should have said, 'Leave them in their picturesque filth and degradation, and I will make them immortal.' Now I want to build them a row of hideous, warm, square little houses and pass legislation to require cleanliness. You would not believe the things I have found. . . ."

But Derrick's social conscience was almost as short-lived as her zeal for church. It was killed by an argument over a boy of sixteen for whom the League found work in a bakery; he was the oldest of nine children, who had been deserted by their mother (the wonder was, Derrick wrote, that any one would want to elope with a woman who had lived always in the direst poverty and had borne nine children) and whose father was dying of tuberculosis. The secretary of the League had rejoiced when she found the job for him: he was to go to school in the daytime and work in the bakery two nights a week. Derrick rejoiced, too, until she encountered him one day in the League office. She had not seen him before. His clothes were rags, his blond hair unkempt, unclean, his face and hands covered with festering boils and ringworms, some plastered over, some uncovered.

"What can that boy do in a bakery?" Derrick demanded, when he had gone. "Of course if he scrubbed the floors . . ."

"He watches the ovens. Puts the bread in and takes it out."

"That filthy creature?"

"He doesn't touch the bread, only the pans. And he wears an apron and a cap."

"An apron, on top of that dirt—" Derrick shuddered. To go within three feet of him was to be offended.

"He can't help being dirty. He hasn't any other clothes. And they need the money."

"But they can't live on what he makes two nights a week."

"No. But it is better for them not to have to live on charity entirely."

"At the cost of spreading disease over the whole town! I must say I don't agree with you." Derrick when she left intended to speak to her father about it, but she met Mr. Devlin on the corner and, as she walked home with him, told him the story. He offered to give the boy a place in the mill if he would leave school.

"Down there his dirt won't matter. They're all dirty. Jack, I suppose, would say it was our fault, but if you put bathtubs in their houses, they keep coal in them." Mr. Devlin had, as a matter of fact, built a street of houses for his workmen after Jack's death.

Derrick thanked him for his kindness. "There's no reason why the boy shouldn't stop school—you can't learn anything if you're starved to death, and he has probably learned as much as he's capable of learning, already. I haven't a doubt that all his teachers will consider him a problem off their hands."

When Derrick wrote to us of the episode, she admitted that her social conscience had died, and that she was off to fields and pastures new. That was in February; she lived through March and April somehow; it was not until the end of May that she succeeded in finding a satisfactory new field. Margaret came home at noon one day to ask her to look in the attic for some kind of frieze their mother had painted with Dutch scenes, one time, for a school bazaar. They planned to have again a "Trip Around the World," with booths to represent different nations, for the benefit of the school for backward children.

"What kind of a painting, and where do you suppose it is?" Margaret had not made herself clear to Derrick.

"Somewhere in one of those closets in the attic. It is just a long strip of cambric. Mother pinned it up around the living-room wall and painted it in about an hour—one scene all the way round, blue and white, like a Delft plate."

They went into the attic together and found the roll, finally, in an old trunk, and held it out. It had been hurriedly painted, but it was still fresh and bright, and very decorative, windmills and canals, barges and dikes on which strolled in pairs full-skirted maidens and full-breeched youths.

"You see," Margaret explained, "we pin this around the top of the booth, and wind the poles in white and blue, and wear costumes to match. And sell blue-and-white things."

"You'll want help with your costume, I suppose?"

"Maybe. I have to make mine and Ken's, too—but I must say I think I'm a better sewer than you are."

"You and Kenneth are to be Dutch together, are you?"

"Yes—he's so blond and I'm so fat. And Kitty Ferris and Ted Wright—and we're all going to do a Dutch dance together after the grand march—you know the one—clump—clump—clump, clump, clump—with your wooden shoes." And Margaret, to illustrate, jumped from one heel to the other and tapped Derrick's cheeks alternately with fingers black with attic grime.

"But, Derrick, if you had time and wanted to help, you might go up to school this afternoon. Some people's mothers will be there. They'll only let us help when we have study periods . . . if your fingers are as dirty as mine must have been, judging from your face, be careful how you handle the what-you-may-call-it."

Derrick tucked the cambric gingerly under her arm and they went down to wash; she admitted that there was no reason why she shouldn't spend the afternoon at the schoolhouse, and so walked back with Margaret. The two vast halls and the wide stairs were scenes of confusion when they entered; only one or two harassed teachers had kept their heads and remained aloof from the delightful excitement. Derrick admired them: they knew what had to be done and did it—they were not aimless doers of good works—all this was to them a part of their job. Theirs was a hard life—Derrick longed suddenly for a hard life; she offered herself to one of them and, under orders, worked like a slave all afternoon, nailing, unnailing, lifting, carrying, arranging and rearranging. She was not so exhausted that she could not return on the next afternoon, and on the next evening when the carnival was in full swing, with her father, genially tolerant, to pay admission fees for her, for himself, for Rosanna as a Japanese and Henry as a Scot in kilts made from an old plaid pleated skirt of Margaret's, cut down.

Several hours they endured, laughingly, of a din composed of shrill voices, shrieks, outcries, and tunes played by the school orchestra in which a saxophone and a drum predominated—of discomfort caused by shoving, trampling, confetti, ticklers . . .

It was only by chance, in the midst of the multitude, that Derrick overheard one of the teachers say to another, "Miss Parker's fiancé is here—have you seen him?" The other replied, "She brought him around and introduced him. They tell me they're going to be married as soon as school is over." Miss Parker was one of the English teachers. Impulsively, Derrick touched the arm of the woman who had spoken last—the mathematics teacher who had led her through the torture of logarithms.

"Do you mean that Miss Parker isn't coming back next year? Have they got any one in her place?"

The woman turned in surprise. "Oh—it's you, Derrick. No, not that I know of, they haven't. Would you like the job?" She laughed. It did not occur to her that any one not driven by the necessity of earning a living would teach school.

"Do you know, I rather think I should—"

The wispy little spinster blinked at her in amazement.

"But, Derrick! You don't have to—"

"No. But I'll go mad without something to do."

"Yes, I suppose so," doubtfully. "But it's such hard work. You don't realize—"

"I've worked hard before. I'll come to see the superintendent the first of the week."

Derrick thought it all over after she was in bed that night, made her plans and explained them to the family at breakfast the next morning.

Her father was troubled. "Haven't I given you enough money, Derrick, to run the house and have some over for yourself? I should think, with charge accounts at all the stores—"

"I've had plenty, really—but it isn't quite the same as having money that is absolutely your own. But it isn't that so much as having something definite to do, on schedule—"

"I should think you had enough to do, with the house—"

"I know." She was half-apologetic. "There's enough to do to keep any one busy, and now that Cassie's getting old, she's awfully slow. But I'd rather hire another servant with my salary than do the work myself. Cassie's niece gets through school this year, and she's looking for a place for her. She could do the cleaning and bedmaking, and Cassie could stick to the kitchen."

"It sounds sensible. There's no reason why you should waste your life making beds. But there's no reason why you should waste it teaching in a third-rate high school, either. Are you sure you aren't ready to leave us and go back to New York?"

"Quite sure, thank you. I want to be where I can keep an eye on you-all."

She called at the superintendent's office on Monday, offered herself and what recommendations she was sure she could get—he smiled upon her, would make no promises until he had seen the recommendations, but was obviously glad to have his problem so easily solved. Before ten days had passed, she had signed the contract.

It was only when she wound up her account of the year that she admitted that she had done any writing since she had been home. That had been January, in those weeks when she had first regretted, because she had first realized all that it meant, that she must henceforth and forever stay at home. There might not be time for long pieces of work, but for poetry . . . and those who had thought she could write at all had thought it should be poetry.

And then, one night, she had a strange dream. She knew, in the dream, that it was the middle of the night, that she lay on her back, asleep; she thought that some one had hold of her arm, was shaking her . . . she knew that she must waken, but it was as if she were buried under a hundred layers of sleep, and to struggle to win her way up, through, and awake, took almost superhuman effort. . . . At last she opened her eyes, breathless, exhausted, and looked into the pitch-black of the room. Her first thought was of her mother, but she remembered at once that those nights were past; she thought of the children, and listened, but heard not a sound. It was nothing: she had dreamed that some one had her by the arm because she had been asleep with it thrown up across her breast, and it was numb from lack of circulation. But she could not go back to sleep, and in an unreasonable midnight state of mind, she interpreted the dream to herself. She had been called to waken before it was too late. Too late for what? To write poetry? And, aghast, she realized suddenly all that she had thrust out of her mind when she had renounced her ambition. For years, almost since she could remember it had been all that she had thought of— or, at least, it had been at the background of every thought. The basis of every idea, the motive of all that she had done —all cast out of her life, without a second's hesitation. It was as if she had cut off an arm without realizing until too late how it had bled. . . . In horror she buried her face in her pillow; she was now, all at once, far too wide awake.

It was not until the next afternoon that she could sit down at her desk. She felt driven, desperate. Anything, anything, to put down rhyme! She had nothing to say, but it did not matter. Words would do, if she could still handle them. . . . The sonnets born of this desperation she sent off to magazines that had previously published her poetry—and at once, when they were gone, regretted her haste, and sank into a gloomy calm. She should have waited until she had something to write about, even although that might not have been until long after all editors had forgotten her. But no matter how she searched her mind, she found it still empty. What had happened to her in less than a year? She was not surprised when the sonnets came back to her with polite but frigid notes; she did not even re-read them to see if they were as bad as she thought, but tossed them into the waste-basket. Having deliberately torn from her what had not for years left her mind, she could not expect to get it back. And that was that. She accepted it fatalistically. Even with relief, she insisted, when she told me about it.

"It was only at that moment," she told me, "that I realized how good it was to be able simply to accept things—as ugly or beautiful, good or bad, without thinking of them as going through my mind, being touched up in the process. So—so peaceful to realize it—if you know what I mean." We laughed: the trite phrase was an old favorite of hers—it had so frequently been obvious that her auditor did not know what she meant.

"Then you are perfectly contented?"

"Perfectly," she mocked. But a strange light flickered in the inscrutable eyes. I should ask her again some day when she was not on her guard.

And yet why shouldn't she be content? . . . We sat at the time in the shade on the porch; above us were the distant tops of the tulip-trees, and in the wide spaces between their rather scantily leaved branches shone the clear sky; before us the fountain played steadily, a rainbow in the sunlight, the spray blown across a vivid streak of the grass. . . .

Derrick noticed my eyes on the fountain.

"Margaret says it must go—that it's a Victorian atrocity.

But I remind her that the day is not far distant when Victorian atrocities will be Antiques. And the sound of running water is so pleasant in hot weather."

The house was open behind us, and we could hear Margaret talking animatedly over the telephone. From the corner of the lawn came the sound of a child's voice, singing, and we caught glimpses, now and then, of the bright plaid of Rosanna's gingham dress, as she moved about at her solitary game under the syringa. The great bush stood in the corner formed by the lattice between back yard and front and the Devlins' side fence, and beneath it Rosanna lived her private life, undisturbed. An impenetrable forest of stems upheld the green roof, and a green curtain of branches came down to touch the grass all around, from lattice to fence, yet left space enough beneath for Rosanna to stand upright if she so chose. She loved her secret little green room, and had shown it to me when I first came, holding the long twigs aside for me to stoop and see. The shaded grass there was fine and delicate; there was thick moss on the ground close to the stems of the syringa, where she had put a flat stone from an old pavement for a seat. On this particular day, she must have gone out there directly after lunch; I had not seen her since.

"What do you suppose Rosanna's doing under the syringa bush?" I queried idly.

"I don't know. Hasn't she taken her dolls out with her? She's probably giving them tea made of sugar and water and crushed roseleaves. Or perhaps she's drawing. She loves to, but is so sensitive about it that she won't do it where there is any one around to criticize."

"That's it, then. . . ." I could see that she lay flat on her stomach, reading or writing.

At that moment Henry became visible to us where we sat, walking without a tremor on the top of the lattice.

"Derrick, that boy will break his neck."

"On the lattice? Nonsense—it's four or five inches wide.

There isn't one of us that couldn't walk a ridge-pole if necessary. Watch him, but pretend not to—he's showing off for us."

Henry had stopped halfway across and taken a sling-shot from his pocket; he fitted a missile the size of an egg into the rubber and took aim at a row of pigeons on a neighboring barn.

"He will fall, Derrick. Besides, you aren't going to let him shoot those pigeons?"

"It's only a mud-ball."

He let the shot go, and the mud splashed on the roof of the barn among the pigeons; they rose with a whir, circled aimlessly a moment, and drifted back. Henry resumed his walk on the lattice to that point where the spreading upper branches of the syringa left him no foothold; he climbed down then and ventured into Rosanna's stronghold. Derrick made some comment on a passing neighbor at that moment, and our attention was turned away from the children until we heard Henry's voice lifted in angry rebuke, and Rosanna's in an answering wail of anguish.

He crawled out finally from under the bush and came across the lawn, shame and contrition in his face.

"I hurt her feelings, Derrick, but I didn't mean to, an' she won't stop crying . . ." He dropped on the porch beside me as Derrick went down the terrace steps.

"She was drawing a picture of a face, an' I laughed at it. I didn't know it was *Mother* she was trying to draw"—horror looked out from his blue eyes—"or I wouldn't 'a' laughed—"

"You mean—she was drawing—from memory?"

He shook his head.

"She had that old picture that Derrick keeps on her dresser—you know? An' a thin paper on top of it, tracing it—that's why I didn't see it was Mother—she had the face covered—and when I saw it, I told her Derrick wouldn't thank her for ruining it, making dents with a hard pencil point. It's the only picture of Mother Derrick's got . . . an' how was I to know she would carry on like that?"

Jeff came up the terrace steps just then and jumped up on Henry, who rolled over with him onto the grass. I went into the house, so that Rosanna need not be deterred by my presence from coming out from under the syringa bush. When she did come out, it was with Derrick's promise that in the morning they would look in the attic for another copy of the old photograph, one which she could have for her own.

"Let's look now," I heard her insisting, as they came up on the porch.

"The attic's too dirty to go up there in the afternoon. You wouldn't have me ruin a white flannel skirt, would you?"

"Then what shall we do this afternoon?"

"First of all, you take this picture back to my dresser where you got it—and then ask Cassie if she won't let you make lemonade for us all."

I saw them from the living-room, through the open door, as they stood in the sunlight on the terrace. Derrick pulled a handkerchief from her sweater pocket and wiped the child's face; she shook her black mane indignantly, and then, relenting, threw her arms around Derrick's neck and swung herself high off the ground in the violence of her embrace. . . . It was easy enough to see that Derrick might say, truthfully, that she was content.

Nevertheless, I returned to the question that night. I had determined to try all my persuasive powers before I went back to New York, and to convince Derrick that she could not spend her whole life as she had spent the last year, that some day she must go back with me.

"Do you really want to teach school, Derrick?"

"Yes. I don't see why I shouldn't do it fairly well, and, after all—"

"There's no reason why you shouldn't go back with me tomorrow."

"The most valid of reasons—a signed contract."

"Can you say honestly, Derrick, that you are as satisfied, inside, as you pretend to be?"

"Do you mean, do I have spasms of temper and revolt? Of course I do."

"That isn't what I mean."

"I know it isn't." She relented, suddenly. "But I don't know how to answer, or explain. Why will you be sophomoric, and insist upon discussing these Great Questions— Mind and Soul—and all that sort of thing? At our time of life it is enough to know that we have fairly serviceable bodies—"

"Now, Derrick!"

"You expect me to be consumed with remorse? It isn't being done now—pacing the floor is not this year's convention. That's a good line, it's easy to go on from there—" She murmured to herself a moment, then laughed and continued:

"But she was not one to pace the floor at midnight,
    Nor did she think of those more dramatic ages
When sinners scourged themselves down crooked streets,
    And left their confessions on gold-illumined pages . . . .

Just to show you that I can still think in iambs. But seriously, Sue: the inside of my mind is all confusion—and I do as many things as I can to keep from looking at it and seeing the confusion, because I can't find any way out. There isn't anything there to get hold of."

"What should you expect to find?"

"I don't know. Whatever it is that older people find in religion, I suppose. Religion means nothing to us. Do you know any one of our contemporaries who believes in God —any God outside of abstractions like Law and Truth?"

"No." I waited for her to go on.

"So you would have to find the connection of yourself with those abstract things—to find that everything actual is one—that the individual life does exist."

"What should you have when you found it?"

"I think you would have a sure knowledge of the continuity of life."

"You mean that you would believe in immortality?"

"That you would know that life is immortal. And knowing is a different thing from believing. Don't you remember how I used to tell you that once in a while I knew? I suppose I can't expect that again—" She laughed, somehow embarrassed. "It is easy enough to be sure of yourself, but impossible to feel that self a part of something else. And it's awfully important." There was a certain challenge in her eye as she faced me. "To find some shadow of the knowledge that all life is one—that it does not matter whether it's your life or mine or our children's children's, but that it does go on, and is always the same. . . . Sue, I'm furious with you for making me say all this. I hate to explain things—it binds them with such hard edges—even more than giving them words in your own mind. But I've told you so much before this that I suppose a little more or less now doesn't matter."

It was hard for me to decide, after all, when, on the train, I had gone so far in the recapitulation of all that I knew of the past year, whether or not Derrick had changed. Not very much, surely. . . . The children were not enough to fill her mind; she was confused and unhappy—she admitted—but there was still, for her consolation, her love of the country. I forced myself to remember it as I looked out at the cornfields, and shuddered.

But truly Derrick's country was more beautiful than this, although so few miles lay between. I saw again in my imagination the road we had taken only the day before when Margaret and I had gone with her to the fruit farm, for peaches for Cassie to preserve.

We had turned away from the pike and circled into the hills on a gravel road whose aim seemed to be to omit no farm in the township from its embrace. The land that at night seemed always to flatten itself down, away from the sky, showed itself in the afternoon sunshine to be one low rise after another, fields, orchard, long stretches of woods; at the foot of every hill a stream crossed the road, bridged back in the woods by loose boards laid on crosswise, that rattled beneath the wheels. Some of the creeks wound through pastures where they were lined with willows and sycamores; some of them through untouched forest where they were hidden by the luxuriant underbrush; some of them, on more prosperous farms, had been "ditched"—made to run in straight lines, as far as the eye could see, with high walls of sloping earth, and here the corn grew to the edges of the banks. The whole history of the county was visible along that road: near the town, prosperous new farmhouses, trim and white, with wide screened porches, concrete barns, silos, and over the barnyards the great electric lights which at night illuminated the whole cluster of buildings as brightly as any city corner; beyond and between these were the older, ornate houses, with the carved wooden decorations of cornice and porch—and the still older and only really beautiful places, of whitewashed stone or brick, with their long straight lines, low roofs, slender pillars. It was not until we had gone well down into the hills that we passed log cabins in the woods Chimneyless, falling to pieces, daylight showing through their walls . . . Derrick took the opportunity to give me a history lesson . . .

"Here, you see, the course of empire northward took its way—up from Cincinnati in the footsteps of Anthony Wayne." The fire of the zealot flashed in her eye. "Mad Anthony! No one has done him justice—some one should! . . . But I am not going to try it myself," she added. "I don't want to spoil the shivers that run down my spine when I think of him."

The orchards and the vineyards of the fruit farm stretched far down both sides of the road before we came to the mailbox and the gate. The apple trees, long rows of them, were heavy with fruit, warm yellow and scarlet, and from the vineyards the fragrance of the grapes blew across the road, and over them the bees hummed back and forth in the warm, drowsy sunlight.

The house itself stood back behind a half-circle of grass shaded by maple and catalpa trees; the barns and sheds, a weather-beaten red, were at one end of the half-circle; we passed them and stopped before the house. The chickens that had been in the road fled, squawking, a dog barked, and a baby in a hammock on the porch wailed breathlessly. A windmill beside the barn screeched as it turned, and from somewhere in the sheds came the steady chuff-chuff of the Delco engine.

"Imagine that windmill making your nights hideous. It sounds like all the ghosts of Christendom, gibbering." Then Derrick caught sight of a child who stared at us stupidly from the shelter of some bushes beside the steps.

"Look here, sonny—is there any one at home?"

"Yes'm. Ma."

"Would you mind asking her if we could have some peaches?"

"Yes'm."

He kicked up his bare feet and scurried away. A moment later a woman came to the door.

"Peaches was it, you wanted? Well, I'll tell you—the men have gone down to the city with their trucks loaded, an' there ain't none picked, in the barns. I can't leave the house an' baby, but if you'll take a basket an' go off into the orchard yourselves, I reckon you could find a bushel left on the trees. They wasn't all ripe when the orchard was picked."

We accepted the basket gladly and followed where she pointed to an orchard across the road. We climbed the fence and struck through the long wet grass, which had gone to seed and caught in our shoelaces and dropped inside our shoes. The trees had evidently been heavily laden, for the props that had supported the branches still lay in the grass beneath them, but now there were only a few peaches left. These were soft, sweet, rose and gold, and so ripe that they

came off in your hand at the slightest touch, and if by
chance you let one drop, it burst on the ground and had to
be left for the bees. We wandered the length of the orchard,
calling to each other now and then, strolling back with an
armful of the fruit to the place where we had left the basket.
It was late in the afternoon when Derrick and I lifted it
between us, and half dragged, half carried it back to the car.
Margaret stopped to break open a peach and bury her nose
in it, leaning over so that the juice would fall on the grass
and not on her blouse, while an envious bee buzzed angrily
about her head.

We lifted the basket into the car. Margaret reminded
Derrick that she had promised to let her drive home.

"And so you may, my cherry." Derrick came in with me
and the peaches. "Let's not go back—let's go on—this road
comes back onto the pike a little beyond here, and we'll
make better time if we take the pike back than if we go
through the hills again. Only remember there's a bad turn
at the foot of the next hill—it's all fresh gravel, you can see
from here, and at the curve there's a stone culvert, so there's
no room to slip, or turn out for any one."

As chance would have it, we met one of the gravel wagons
at the very spot, but the driver saw us in time to stop before
he reached the culvert; he pulled out into the grass to let us
go on. It was while Margaret slowed down to wait for him
to get out of her way that Derrick chose the largest peach
in the basket, wiped its fuzz off with her handkerchief, and
held it under my nose.

"Smell that—and then look around you—how can you
be so blind as not to see that, no matter what might be in
one's mind, one would only have to come out and look at
this—"

The whole prospect of hills and valleys was radiant in a
sunlight still warm and golden, despite the lateness of the
hour. I pointed to a brilliant level field in the distance.

"What are those flowers? 'I know a meadow flat with
gold'—"

Derrick laughed. "It's only a field of soy beans, not 'A million million burning flowers.' Their leaves turn yellow so early—but the field of alfalfa next to it is as green as if it were still April. Have you ever noticed—the nicest thing about this country: wherever you are, unless you're actually at the foot of a hill going up, you seem to be on top of the world? Everything slopes away from you, for miles and miles and miles, so that you can see to the very edge of things. Do have a peach, Sue—and you watch, the rest of the way, and see if it isn't true."

When I remembered all this, I was able to look at the flat country outside the train with a more kindly eye. We were still on the top of the world.

~~~~~~~~~ **III** ~~~~~~~~~

Two years passed before I saw Derrick again. Throughout the first winter our correspondence was voluminous; we persisted successfully in our endeavor to keep it up, in spite of the fact that there was little or nothing to write about. In the summer Derrick went abroad to spend her vacation with Madeleine in London and Paris; then, when she had at hand all the material for a thousand letters, time was too precious to be spent writing them, and she sent me picture postcards, which I regarded with indignation. She departed and returned by way of Montreal, so that I did not see her, but I wrote to Tecumseh reproachfully, expecting instant reform. Reform followed, but it was spasmodic. By the second June our correspondence had dropped off to the most meager, infrequent notes; we took each other for granted, however, and both knew that I should spend August in Tecumseh.

Once more, therefore, I regarded from train windows, as we pulled around "Nigger Curve," the approach to the town. This time I felt no misgiving as to Derrick herself; whatever she did, however much I might hate to see her doing it, she could not have changed any in two years. I was so old now (I must have been twenty-seven or -eight—I have forgotten exactly) that I regarded two years as almost nothing, insignificant. As a consequence it was only natural that I should find Change in everything and be bewildered by it the moment I dropped from the car steps into Derrick's outstretched hands. Henry took my bags and shuffled off with them, swaggering under an assumption of toughness; Derrick explained him: "He's at that age . . ." That Age, one saw at once, was inevitably marked by certain signs: unkempt hair, grimy hands, scuffed shoes, a cap over one eye, growls. . . . And Rosanna—how she had pulled out! Like Tenniel's drawings of an Alice who had eaten unwisely, she left one with an impression of knees, elbows, neck, and collarbone. I should have remembered what two years will do to children;—but when I scanned Derrick, confidentially, I saw that here, too . . . and my heart sank . . . I might have imagined any change that I thought I saw two years before, but not this. It was undeniable. And yet so subtle as to be impossible to describe: I can only insist that the change was there, that it was not simply that we had grown apart, that I cared for her less, that I saw her with clearer eyes. I saw her contented, as satisfied as any one ever is with his own particular lot; I saw her serene, grave, and wise in her management of the house, of the children, and knew that she must be the same in the school-room. Lovable, and therefore I cared no less for her than I had always cared—but beyond that, nothing; and so I felt for her now no least echo of the old awe, the old admiration. She accepted the world and all the people in it as they were, without curiosity, with only tolerance, sometimes amusement, sometimes a mild disgust. She did not notice strangers on the street-corners; she saw only those whom she knew. To be sure, a school-teacher knows almost every one in a small town: girls ducked their heads at her shyly, sheepish boys took off their caps: "Hello, Miss Thornton," or "How-do, Miss Thornton," and said, "Yes, ma'am," and "No, ma'am," when she talked with them.

I saw all this in a day or two, but could say nothing. To what end should I reproach her? . . . But I must try to find out if she was as unrepentant as she seemed . . . if so, I must let her go her own way. My opportunity came one evening when she and Rosanna and I were alone together. The

doctor had accepted for Henry and himself an invitation to
a father-and-son banquet at the Rotary Club; Margaret had
gone off in the car to an all-day picnic at Fort Ancient.
Derrick suggested that we might walk into the country with
a box of sandwiches for supper, and spend the evening by
the roadside.

"Or we can climb Sawyer's Hill," she added, "and watch
the sun set. We'll be so glad to see it go."

The three of us set out late in the afternoon; it was not
an unpleasant walk, in spite of the heat, along the creek-bed,
through woods that shaded the long brown grass. We wandered languidly, picked pennyroyal and mint and watercress,
and nibbled as we walked—sometimes we crossed the creek-
bed on unstable rocks, sometimes crawled through barbed-
wire fences, or chased straying cows from our path. The east
side of Sawyer's Hill is heavily wooded; we sat there on the
twisted roots of trees to eat the sandwiches, and only
climbed to the top of the hill and over the fence between
woods and pastureland at sundown. At the foot of the slope
before us, a few motionless cows stood deep in mire round
a spring where there was a clump of willow trees; beyond
them were a road, a farmhouse with scattered barns, and, in
the distance, a country schoolhouse set in the midst of trees,
between whose branches shone a flaming sun. Tranquillity . . . and that was just the trouble with Derrick—too
much of it. I sat down in the short grass, sighing; she
dropped beside me and sighed even more heavily.

"Look at the sun! Simply fiery! We'll have another day
like this to-morrow."

"Derrick!"

"Isn't that right? It's what I've always heard—"

"But to make solemn old-maid remarks about the
weather! As though it were important!"

"I suppose you think I should rise and address the sun in
rolling hexameters?"

"Exactly." We laughed, and fell silent. I knew well

415

enough how futile was discussion of this point, and yet—

"Derrick—"

"Yes?" Indifferently.

"Remember that biography of you that I planned to write?"

"M'hm."

"When I go back to New York I'm going to start it."

"What?—Oh—you worm! You mean you're going to tell how I didn't, instead of how I did?"

"Good idea, don't you think?"

"Beautiful. Not an inspiration to the young, but a warning. Go to it!"

"You take it calmly. . . . I hoped you would do something to prevent such an ignominious immortality."

"You're modest about this little book you're going to write."

She turned away to say something to Rosanna, and I was left to enjoy in silence the descending twilight. I was soon overcome by the peace and languor of the summer evening, and lay flat on my back to watch the sky change from rose to lavender, and from lavender back again to blue, to watch the gray haze deepen at the land's end. When Derrick was prepared to give me her attention, I pretended to be asleep; to annoy me, she dropped a handful of grass on my face, but I refused to be annoyed; she wandered a little farther afield and brought back a handful of strong-smelling mint and pennyroyal and tossed it down on me.

" 'Strew on her roses, roses
        And never a spray of yew—'

Wake up and tell me the next line."

I opened one eye.

        "Da-dum, da-dum, da-dum-da,
        'Ah, would that I did, too.' "

416

"Philistine! You're no good to me. Go back to sleep."

Unduly amused by her whim, she sent Rosanna down to the spring for a rock, which she placed at my head; she brought from the fence corner a spray of goldenrod, which she laid across my chest, so that the end of it tickled my chin.

"Now, you're a beautiful corpse. Don't stir."

She sat down beside me, and Rosanna came and lay with her head in her lap. We stayed that way, while the sky darkened, while the stars came out. The herbs she had strewn over me wilted, and their fragrance was pungent in my nostrils. . . . After a long while, reluctantly, we rose, descended the hill, walked past the sleeping cows, that might have been low bushes, darker spots in the darkness —and climbed the fence, and started home. Over the town, at the end of the uncurving road, hung the Great Dipper.

When we had taken the empty picnic basket into the kitchen, Derrick sent Rosanna upstairs for her "Oxford Book."

"I must look up that missing line," she said as we went out onto the porch. "Things like that bother you so. . . . When are you going to begin your 'Warning to Young Girls, or, What Every Child Should Know'?"

"As soon as I get back. And you needn't be so jocose—"

"I'm not. I'm interested. You'll have to explain just why I didn't."

"Oh, no. I'll just state the case, and let the reader draw his own conclusion."

"That's no way to write a warning. You should paint white bands on the telegraph poles along the way, and put up signs: 'Avoid this wrong turn.'"

"Just the same, you might come back. They don't need you here."

Rosanna came out, then, with the book.

"What's she saying to you, Derrick?"

417

"She's talking nonsense, honey. Don't pay any attention to her . . ."

She held the book in the light from the window to hunt for the poem she wanted.

"Of course. 'Reposes.' I should have known. 'Roses, reposes.' It couldn't have been anything else." She left the poems on a chair and moved to the edge of the porch, where she dropped to the step. I pulled her shoulders back against my knees.

"I had forgotten to call your attention to the fact that we still have the fountain. Margaret has been won over: she admits now that it is an antique, and she even wishes we had an iron dog on the front lawn."

"Al, with her customary enthusiasm, is now chasing antiques—" I was reminded, and we slipped into a discussion of her affairs and her future. Rosanna after a while went in to bed; Margaret drove into the garage, came out long enough to tell us about her picnic, and then went upstairs. We sat on in silence for a moment. But I had not given up.

"Derrick, doesn't it worry you not to be doing something besides teaching school?"

"Sue," she mocked, "look at the stars. Doesn't a glance at them convince you of the uselessness of our scrambling little attempts?"

"You've become a confirmed sitter."

"I suppose so. But there must be sitters in the world. How dreadful it would be if no one sat. There'd be nowhere for the others to go with their tales of accomplishment, for applause. Interesting thought, but I can't go on with it. It's too peaceful a night to spoil with argument. Good old Vega!" She indicated the star with a sweeping gesture.

The tall trees on the lawn hid from us all the lower sky, but from the edge of the porch we could look up at the blazing splendor of the Milky Way. . . . It was magnificent, but I refused to be diverted.

"Do you remember how the last time I saw you, you admitted the confusion in your mind?"

"Huh?"

"Yes. That you were sure of yourself, but weren't sure that yourself was connected with anything else.'

"How crudely you express it! Yes, I remember."

"Well—did you ever find the connection?"

"Look here, Sue!" She shook a pedagogical forefinger under my nose. "This is to be the last time we discuss this subject, forever—do you hear? I expect never to mention my Soul to any one again as long as I live—" But from that she went on to tell me. I listened with a dreadful feeling of finality. She seemed really to believe that, when she had told this, she would have told all, and would never need to explain herself, past or future, again.

One morning in the spring the whole family had gone out to hunt mushrooms, and because it was the custom of the town to turn out almost to a man to scour the woods in mushroom season, they had determined to start early, and so backed the car out of the garage at exactly four o'clock in the morning. It had rained in the night, and at that hour, before sunrise, the mists were still heavy and the winds cold. It was not a long drive to the woods they had selected as the most likely, so that it was still dark, with only a suggestion of gray penetrating the fog, when they came to the end of the lane; because it was hopeless to begin their search in the half-light, they perched on the snake fence to wait for the sun to come up.

Woods at dawn, wet, pungent—the smell of the mist, of rotting logs, covered with moss, the exciting tang of new buds, new twigs, new green everywhere . . . the sound of the mist dripping from trees, of the wind in the branches, of a wood-pecker somewhere away off in the woods . . . the sleepy notes of other birds. Then, with more light, through the lifting mists the white of dogwood trees in flower, appearing like lines of cloud beneath the boughs of the taller trees. Then daylight, even into the thickest woods. They watched, between the tree-trunks, the rising sun, the light creeping through to the ground beneath their feet: wet brown leaves, a wide green patch of may-apples, all the flowers still un-opened.

They separated to search for ash trees, and under them, the mushrooms, like pointed brown sponges. Finally Derrick could not hear even their voices—could hear nothing but the triumphant chorus of birds. Alone, she dropped to her knees on the edge of a little stream where the violets were thickest; close to the smell of the earth, of the water, she began to pick them. She felt under her knuckles the damp earth, against her hands the leaves of the violets, in her finger-tips their stems, down to the roots. How familiar to her touch were those smooth thin stems! Familiar, remembered by her fingers for twenty years, or a thousand. Suddenly time did not exist. Spring and violets, autumn and drifting leaves. In her mind, or in her fingers—that did not matter—nor whether the fingers were more real than the violets. Memory was enough—of the fragrance, of the flowers, of her fingers, of herself. She did not matter either—but memory—of other moments like these when she had known, for an instant—of more ordinary moments repeated and repeated—digging in brown earth, covering the sweet-pea seeds, raking the leaves and burning them. Memory that had become knowledge—knowledge of the earth, dogwood boughs, mossy tree-trunks, sky and sun—knowledge so intimate, so whole, that you did not know them as things apart, but as one—your being, and theirs. Their being. That was the end, the secret—in you and of you, in them and of them. . . . She remembered lines of poetry, too, and it became a part of the whole. A chorus from the "Bacchæ":

"Will they ever come to me, ever again,
    The long, long dances,
On through the dark till the dim stars wane?
Shall I feel the dew on my throat and the stream
    Of wind in my hair?"

The familiar touch of finger-tips to the stems of flowers . . . to have remembered it twenty years or two thousand . . . to remember Derrick Thornton, to remember a mænad . . . it did not matter.

> ". . . dear lone lands, untroubled of men
> Where no voice sounds . . ."

Those lands were yours, if you could remember. This was serenity, certainty. The inner core of being. Not of the flesh, not of the mind. . . .

Henry came upon her from the other side of the stream, and jumped across.

"Hi—looky here—" he called to Rosanna, who was behind him. "Derrick isn't huntin' mushrooms at all. She's pickin' violets." Disdain in his voice.

"But think how glad you'll be to have them on the table."

"We've got flowers to burn, right in the yard. Come on and help us."

And Derrick left the violets on the sweater she had taken off, and went with them.

"I don't suppose I've made you understand," she said, when she told me. "I never do. It sounds so simple—as if all those months thinking about it would have given me the same assurance."

"I'm afraid I'm a slave to reason. How about it when the feeling is gone? Or can you keep it?"

"And live this life? No—to do that one would have to sit forever at the foot of an ash tree at four o'clock on a May morning. The *vita contemplativa*. But you know it may come back again, sometime. That is all you can ask for, this side of the grave."

"But what of the Calvinist in you, that it doesn't make you *do* something?"

"It does. Something for my country, fellow-man, and God —none of which exists except in the mind of man, I know."

421

And she laughed at me, the sweet familiar mockery in her voice. "And so I teach school. I love teaching, Sue, and as long as I must be Derrick Thornton—I shall keep on doing it."

And she did—until the day of her death. . . . But she had not been untroubled by doubt, despite her alleged certainty. . . . When Rosanna, long before that day, came East for her first year at college, she brought me a paper she had found by chance in Derrick's desk; when she had asked about it, Derrick had laughed and had said, "Give it to Sue. It is my one expression of remorse."

There was nothing to indicate when the paper Rosanna brought had been written, except that it was dated October:

"On the terrace on a Saturday afternoon in October. It is late in the afternoon, but the sunlight that might be pale and thin is intensified, the air is radiant, with the scarlet-and-gold of the trees. The leaves that have fallen Ben rakes into piles; Rosanna will come soon, with her cohorts, shouting for joy, to race through them and scatter them to the four winds. Ben is getting old, he moves slowly; once he looked like a brigand, now he is bent and grizzled.

"My mind is full of sorrowful and lovely poetry, learned a long while ago. 'Remember now thy Creator in the days of thy youth . . . or ever the silver cord be loosed or the golden bowl be broken . . . then shall the dust return to the earth as it was.' How beautiful it is: 'or ever the silver cord be loosed.' And 'I was afraid and went and hid thy talent in the earth' . . . And I remember admonition. 'Do not doubt that you will be held accountable!' Who said that to me, I wonder? Accountable to whom, and when?

"And my mind is full of stories of all the good people— the dull people of this dull old town, who have loved the scarlet-and-gold of October, of the children: barekneed Rosanna, with her troubled eyes, who is so often afraid: of Henry, who cares for so little, but for that little so profoundly; of my own children, whose names would have been the old Dutch names scrawled in faded ink in the hymn-books that came down to my mother from her people: Gerrit and Reneltje and Tunis and Jannetje. Children playing in the sunlight, old folk musing while they watch the leaves come down. . . . Why do I not go and put them down on paper? Only because I cannot make myself sit down at a desk and take up a pencil. But I am tired: we have been making apple butter all day, Cassie and I, and there is no time. . . . No, Derrick Thornton. That is no reason. 'The slothful man saith there is a lion in the way.' Cassie did not need you in the kitchen.

"How the leaves fall! A blue jay screams in the maple tree, and it will rain to-morrow. Once, when Jack and I were marking on the lawn the outlines of a house whose walls were fallen leaves, a blue jay called with that same note, and Jack looked up at me solemnly. 'It will rain to-morrow. Ol' Mr. Blue Jay knows.' And it did rain. . . . The little boys with the Dutch names would have been solemn, like Jack, yellow-haired, blue-eyed.

"How amusing to allow one's self to be thus sentimentally melancholy! I shall forget it when I hear the children's voices in the street . . . but this remains certain: you cannot have your life and live it too—and if I choose to squander in living rather than to hoard for writing, why should I be 'accountable'?

"Perhaps I could have done it if I had been different. If I had cared less for the people I did care for, if I had been able to shut myself off from them. But I was not different. I could have made myself different? Perhaps! But how am I to know that I should not have regretted that even more? Either way, it matters very little. Regret is not hard to live with, when you know beforehand that you would have to live with it: you set aside a space for it in your mind, you accept its existence, you go on as if it were not there. No agony of spirit—only that slight misgiving so easily dismissed to an obscure corner of consciousness. 'I went and hid thy talent in the earth' Yes—but it is with relief that

423

I know that there need be no further struggle to dig it up
—that it is too late. . . . Too late! . . . I say it easily, without
a sigh, while the blue jay screams, and the gold-and-scarlet
leaves drift on the wind and fall into the pool beneath the
fountain."

Helen Hooven Santmyer: A Profile

XENIA, OHIO—With the exception of the tornado ten years ago, the most newsworthy event in Xenia in this century has been the announcement that ". . . *And Ladies of the Club*" by eighty-eight-year-old Xenian Helen Hooven Santmyer was to be reissued by G. P. Putnam's Sons and has been chosen as the August Book-of-the-Month selection.

As soon as it was announced, the media arrived at Hospitality House East, where the author has lived since 1982, with cameras, microphones, tape recorders, and notebooks to fire questions at the writer. As many as forty reporters crowded the reception area of the home in one day.

". . . *And Ladies of the Club*" follows the lives of members of a women's literary club in Waynesboro (read Xenia) from 1863 to 1932. Their lives—marriages, children, grandchildren, deaths—and those of scores of other members over the years, are detailed against the political, religious, medical, legal, and industrial history of those seventy-five years.

"What a prodigious amount of research you did," young interviewers say to the author. "Not at all," she answers. "Except for checking the dates and a few small details, it was all in my life's experience. I wrote what I knew."

Xenia city fathers have commissioned a plaque to be mounted on the Santmyer family home at 133 West Third Street.

Brown-eyed, gray-haired Helen Santmyer is taking the fuss with good grace. She thinks all the bustle is fun, although she is disconcerted because the young reporters want instant information. She likes to take time to consider her responses, but modern media do not stay for the answers.

She has frailties—heart trouble, some arthritis and emphysema—but her lifelong interests in reading, sports, politics, games, and conversation have not diminished.

Helen, born in Cincinnati in 1895, went to Xenia with her parents, Joseph and Bertha Hooven Santmyer, when she was three. She has a younger sister, Jane Anderson, who lives in Xenia, and a brother, Philip, of Houston. Her father was associated with the Kelly Company, makers of rope and twine.

Her first memory of the town is of the courthouse on a summer afternoon, with the hot sun drenching the tiled roof and wilting the elm trees that surrounded the building. The four-sided clock in the courthouse tower has always been an essential part of Xenia lives.

When Helen was growing up, the clock was lighted only until midnight. "There was a queer mixture of impressions on the mind," she wrote in *Ohio Town*, her third book, "when out of doors late at night, a first glance toward it showed the courthouse tower wiped out and a black hollow in the sky in its stead: Blank surprise followed by the scuttling, frightened whisper down old paths in the brain: 'It's late—awfully late,' and then by a sense of exhilaration at one's audacity—all in an instant, before maturity could assert itself against those echoes."

Midnight was the ultimate hour when Xenia girls and boys had to be in after a party. Once, at a farmhouse party, the clock struck midnight and the party broke up in a panic. When their horse clattered into town, Helen and her beau saw with relief and chagrin that the clock was still lighted. The farmer's clock was on sun time; they could have stayed a half hour longer.

In early days, Helen's grandmother attended the Methodist-supported Female Seminary on Church Street, as did two aunts. "When I was a child," Helen says, "they never impressed me as being learned or intellectual." More representative of the seminary was that group of elderly ladies who were distinctly, in an elegant white-glove way, Blue Stockings, and who, through the Women's Club, the D.A.R., and the library board, spoke as the town's authorities in all matters literary, artistic, and historical.

"During my childhood when the Women's Club assembled at a house in the neighborhood, you suspended your rowdy games while carriages stopped at the curb; you watched in awe until they were all indoors; and then you withdrew to a remote back yard lest the rude breath of another world disturb the delicate air they breathed."

It was twelve of these women from the Female Seminary who formed the club in "*. . . And Ladies of the Club.*"

Helen attended the Xenia public schools for twelve years, along with some forty other boys and girls. She was mischievous, yet intelligent. Although she loved school, she never really liked her teachers. In fact, one she hated. Her first-grade teacher, Miss Baker, shook her so hard one day that she bit her tongue. Helen had refused to stand up straight on command. She never forgave her teacher.

Early in her school years, Helen decided to be a writer. The decision came after she read *Little Women.* Years later she wrote of Derrick, the heroine in her first novel, *Herbs and Apples:*

> Derrick sat alone on the terrace steps and stared with unseeing eyes across the dusky lawn at trees and fountain. Her heart thumped in her breast, in her ears, and she breathed heavily; the world rocked beneath her. A revelation had come to her from the last pages of the book she had been reading: *The Life, Letters and Journals of Louisa May Alcott.* The veil had been lifted, she had Known. She would be a Great Writer when she grew up.

The church played an important part in growing up in Xenia. Helen attended the church of her great-grandparents, her grandmother, and her mother, the Presbyterian church on Market Street. "Searching back in my memory," she says, "I find no beginning of my knowledge of that vast auditorium, bare and clean in a cool clarity of light, its amplitude of air shaken by the music of the organ when all the stops were pulled for the doxology."

Dressed in her Sunday clothes and carrying her Bible and quarterly under her arm, Helen walked to Sunday school with her sister and brother. They rehearsed their catechism as they passed through the alley, across Second Street and Main Street, past houses of family friends.

They thought they understood what the Calvinist doctrine meant and considered it superior to that of the Methodists. Many were the school recess-time arguments between the Presbyterians and the Methodists, with the Episcopalians, the German Reformed, and the Baptists listening on the sidelines.

During Helen's high school days, the town held a revival in a tabernacle built for the occasion. Helen attended on Friday nights and was surprised to learn that in the eyes of the Lord, all denominations were equal.

After the revival, the town's young people attended Sunday-evening services at churches other than their own. As a high school girl, Helen disapproved of the Episcopalians, who read their prayers and rattled them off in an unintelligible singsong: she did not like their tiresome bobbing up and down, on and off their knees.

She thought the Methodist hymns were loud and noisy, and the United Presbyterians ungracious because while the Presbyterians sang the psalms in the UP church, the UPs stood mute during the Presbyterian hymns.

High school studies in Xenia were rigid. Everybody took at least three years of math, two of science, four of English, and four of Latin. She often looked out of the school library windows, toward fields and pastures beyond the town. "You looked and longed to be out and away," she said, "whether just to cross those fields to the nearest woods where violets and wild phlox grew or whether to cross the horizon and never come back."

She did cross the horizon in 1914, to spend four years at Wellesley College. Helen graduated from Wellesley in 1918. Her plans were to do graduate work at Oxford University, but her father said that she would have to stay home a year before he would send her abroad to study. As a result, she lived at home for a year and taught English in Xenia High School. She also began writing a novel.

The next year she secured a secretarial position with Charles Scribner's Sons in New York and shared an apartment on Eighty-second Street with a friend she met in New York. She completed the novel *Herbs and Apples* during the New York years.

It is autobiographical. The book is written in the first person, but the storyteller is a minor character. The heroine, Derrick, is in many respects Helen Santmyer.

She put into Derrick's mind her own beliefs that "a woman's life is governed by her desire to win someone's approval—not just a lover's or a husband's, necessarily, but the person she cares most about. Perhaps the approval of a group of persons—but only in rare cases of the multitude."

When *Herbs and Apples* was accepted for publication by Houghton Mifflin, Helen left for England and graduate study at Oxford. She was twenty-eight.

She enrolled as a home student, as did all American women students at the time. She lived in the town. Her tutor was a Rhodes scholar—very pleasant but not much of a tutor. She pursued her studies independently and chose as her thesis subject a kindred soul, an eighteenth-century novelist, Clara Reeve (1729–1807), who wrote three Gothic novels and two based on English life in her own day. Her thesis was accepted and Helen received a degree in literature in 1927.

Herbs and Apples had been published while she was at Oxford. On her return to Xenia, Helen obtained, with the help of her friend, Mildred Sandoe, a position with the

Dayton and Montgomery County Public Library. She lived at home and commuted. In her off hours she wrote a second novel, *Fierce Dispute*, which was published in 1929. It foreshadows "*. . . And Ladies of the Club*" in that it is a story of a small-town girl growing up in a home that had been occupied for years by her ancestors.

Neither of Helen's books was a best-seller. Because she was not a professional librarian, her work at the library was a dead-end job. In 1953, she became head of the English department and dean of women at Cedarville College. She continued to write during her teaching years, setting down in longhand stories from her childhood and descriptions of the Xenia where she grew up. In 1956, a nostalgic essay, "The Cemetery," appeared in the *Antioch Review*. It gave an account of childhood Sunday-afternoon walks in the town burying ground. "We used to follow haphazardly the twists in the road as they opened out," she wrote. "We might pause to note some new clayey mound or cross the grass to see who had lain so long in the earth that the name of his headstone had filled with lichens or even, holding our breaths, to peek through the broken corner of a moss-grown sarcophagus."

Even more interesting than the gravestones were the cemetery records that gave the names of the dead, the date of death, the next of kin, the cause of death, the name of the undertaker, and the location of the grave. "Historians and novelists may turn to the records when they please," she wrote, "and recreate with its help the town of a hundred or eight-five or seventy years ago."

As she wrote, she planned two books, a profile of her home town and a novel about the families whose members lay in the cemetery.

Cedarville College was a United Presbyterian school, founded in 1887. In 1928, when the sponsoring church affiliated with the Presbyterian Church of the U.S.A., the college became independent, giving four-year courses leading to the B.A. and B.S. degrees in education.

In March of 1953 came the announcement that Cedarville would merge with the Baptist Bible College of Cleveland, with the 100-student Baptist school moving to the Cedarville Campus. The General Associations of the Regular Baptists would operate the school.

The new administrator, Dr. James T. Jeremiah, called the faculty together and asked them to sign a statement that each believed every word in the King James version of the Bible as it was printed and would promise never to smoke, drink, or dance.

Helen could not in honesty sign the statement, but even if she could have, she would have refused on philosophical grounds. She resigned. In the end, Jeremiah fired the entire Cedarville faculty.

Helen returned to her job at the Dayton library, until her retirement in 1960. The following year, her profile of Xenia, *Ohio Town,* was published by the Ohio State University Press.

She continued to live in the big house on Third Street after the death of her father and mother. She began her novel, writing in large ledger books.

Mildred Sandoe, who had taken a job in the Cincinnati Public Library as director of personnel, drove back and forth daily from Xenia. Because the trip made her very late every day, Helen said, "Why don't you stop here on your way home, and I'll have your dinner ready."

After a while, Mildred sold her house and moved in permanently with Helen.

Mildred helped Helen every bit of the way through "*. . And Ladies of the Club.*" Weldon Kefauver, editor of the Ohio State University Press, asked for the book as soon as he knew Helen was working on it. After about sixteen years, the manuscript was delivered.

It was much too long. Kefauver asked Helen to cut out seven hundred fifty pages. It was during the editing that Mildred worked hardest. "I would read her a passage and say, 'This could come out.' Helen would say, 'Well, put a check mark in the margin.' The next day she would tell me whether to take it out or leave it in."

"I didn't want to cut any of it," says Helen. "I thought if people wanted to, they could skip part of it."

Late in 1983, Gerald Sindell, a California film producer, visited his mother in Shaker Heights. She had recently read an old library copy of ". . . *And Ladies of the Club*" and told her son it was the best book she had ever read. He read it and saw it might be a bonanza for his business. The result of his promotion efforts was that Putnam decided to reprint the book, the Book-of-the-Month Club picked it up, and talk of TV and film rights proliferated.

The first flurry of interviews and callers had died down, but Helen Hooven Santmyer knows that it is not all over.

The above was excerpted from a feature story by Roz Young which appeared in *The Magazine* of the Dayton (Ohio) *Daily News* on July 1, 1984, shortly before the reissuing of ". . . *And Ladies of the Club*."

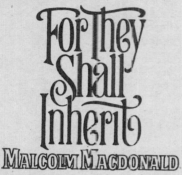